A MATTER OF TRUST

Sandy Loyd

Published by Sandy Loyd
Copyright 2012© Sandy Loyd
Cover by Kelli Ann Morgan at InspireCreativeDesigns
Edited by Pam Berehulke at Bulletproof Editing
ISBN: 978-1-941267-13-4

For more information on the author and her works, please see www.sandyloyd.com or visit her Amazon author page http://www.amazon.com/author/sandyloyd

This book is also available in electronic form from some online retailers.

Dedication

As with all my stories, <u>A Matter Of Trust</u> is dedicated to my husband. Without him behind me I wouldn't have written so much.

Other books by Sandy Loyd

Contemporary Romances

The California Series

Winter Interlude – Book One
Promises, Promises – Book Two
James – Book Three
Dancing With An Angel – Book Four

Second Chances Series

Tropical Spice – Book One

A Christmas Miracle – A short story

Romantic Suspense

D.C. Bad Boys Series

The Sin Factor – Book One
Raising the Stakes – Book Two

Running Series

Running From Love – Book One

Deadly Series

Deadly Misconceptions – Book one

A Matter Of Trust

Kicker's Legacy

Chapter 1

"This is going to be a changing day in your life." The edict circled in Cat's mind, like a hamster running on a wheel, as she guided her four-wheel drive Nissan Xterra into Buchannan Aeronautics' parking lot. Screeching to a stop in one of the dozen empty spaces, she tried to expel the annoying voice from her brain, but it wouldn't budge.

Heck, she didn't even like the guy and rarely watched the TV show, not like her best friend Cheryl, a Dr. Phil groupie who never missed an episode, thanks to TiVo. Annoying or not, the quote had become her mantra.

Out of habit, she scrutinized the few cars in the lot and checked her rearview mirror. Then she snorted and forced her eyes to focus elsewhere. It wasn't as if her ex had somehow tracked her down, not after four years. Last she'd heard he was still in Afghanistan, most likely terrorizing some other gullible woman.

"Remember, Cat, you're taking charge of your life," she said out loud to give the words more emphasis. She was safe. Bozeman, Montana, was thousands of miles from her past.

With her gaze on the airstrip, she switched off the ignition and sat for a moment, gripping the wheel and drawing massive amounts of air into her lungs.

A Piper Warrior landed. She smiled. All that studying had paid off. She actually recognized its make and model. The entire time the small plane wove its way to a hangar on the far side of the airstrip, Cat continued her mental pep talk.

Yep! Life-changing summed it up, all right! She sighed. Learning to fly was going to change her life…change her way of thinking.

Her heartbeat thumped faster. Galloping horses came to mind and no amount of deep breathing would slow them. Rather than wait for her nerves to settle, she shoved open the car door and climbed out. Behind her, another plane taxied on the runway, lining up for takeoff.

She turned to watch until the twin engine was airborne, then straightened.

Head held high and shoulders back, Cat ignored the knot tightening in the pit of her stomach and marched toward the building's plate glass entrance like a soldier ready for battle, or in this case, ready for her life-changing day.

From this moment on, living in fear was no longer an option. She'd escaped her ex and had left the bad memories behind, including those of her parents' deaths. Now was the time to move forward.

Near the door, she caught her reflection in the mirrored windows. The woman staring back revealed only confidence. Nothing about her appearance hinted at her inner turmoil.

A bell tinkled above her head as the door swung open. Joel Smith glanced her way.

"Hey, Smitty. I made it." Cat nodded to the blond, well-built man with chiseled features who sat behind the counter. Flashing a ready smile and gazing into his startling blue eyes, she halted a foot in front of the young Val Kilmer look-a-like. "Is Brad around? I'm here for my lesson."

"Hey yourself, gorgeous. I haven't seen Brad." Smitty returned her grin. A second later his eyebrow quirked. "When're you gonna drop his sorry ass and go out with me?"

"You're already taken," she teased back, laughing. Smitty dated her best friend, Cheryl Green. He also introduced her to Brad. Both men taught flying for a living and were always trying to one-up each other. If Smitty reminded her of Iceman from her favorite classic movie, *Top Gun*, Brad was a dead ringer for Maverick.

It was Smitty's idea for her to take lessons. Without his or Brad's encouragement, Cat would never consider something so crazy, not when she hated flying commercially…a complete understatement. She'd rather have her fingernails yanked out one by one than step onto an Airbus 300. Becoming a pilot was about the most terrifying thing she could think of, and in her mind, if she conquered that one huge fear, she could conquer all of her others.

A man strode out of a corner office to draw her focus across a large reception area that looked much like a doctor's waiting room, flanked with two serviceable sofas, a couple of worn chairs, and a table. He swept past the furniture with a graceful ease for a man of his height.

"Got that schedule for the new guy worked out?" he asked Smitty, stopping a few feet away.

He towered an imposing eight inches above her own five feet seven inches, and Cat couldn't help feeling small and dainty standing next to such broad shoulders. His perfect torso tapered to a lean waist, and long, muscular limbs extended that perfection. The whole effect was topped with jet-black hair. Intimidating dark brown eyes accentuated with blacker than black slashes that doubled as eyebrows only added to his larger-than-life guise.

"Yeah." Smitty cleared his throat and sat up straighter. "I just closed out the file, so you can view the changes online."

"Thanks, Smitty." He then turned in her direction and she had his full attention. "I'm Josh Buchannan," he said in a no-nonsense voice.

Cat smiled. So this was the much-heralded boss who walked on water that Brad and Smitty were always talking about.

As his gaze raked her from head to foot, she clenched a fist and subdued an impulse to check her pale blue silk blouse for stains or to smooth her black slacks.

"I take it you're Candace Tyler—the student scheduled for a four o'clock lesson?" he asked, after completing his silent inspection.

"The one and only." Her voice held more moxie than she actually possessed as their stares locked. For a split second she caught disapproval in those dark eyes, before he hid the look behind a cool smile.

Tightening her jaw, Cat threw her shoulders back. "My friends call me Cat." She forced herself to hold eye contact. "For my initials." Her middle name was Angela, but she swallowed the words. After all, this whole assertive kick was still a little new to her. Before losing any more bravado, she quickly decided to behave her way to success, another Dr. Phil-ism from those same irritating TV ads that once seen, stuck in the memory forever.

As their stare-off continued, she tamped down rising apprehension as her resolve stiffened. So what if everything about the guy was impressive, not to mention a tad scary? After her divorce, she'd vowed no man would intimidate her ever again. "I'm here to see Brad Maxwell."

Despite this guy's looming stance, Cat only had to remember he was a mere human who put on his pants one leg at a time just like every other person on the planet, including her ex. She purposefully relaxed her shoulders and offered a smile that any bee would mistake for honey, except the thoughts behind the act weren't as sweet. Then, imitating his scrutiny, her gaze swept his form and she imagined him dressing. But the tactic backfired when an image of him naked snuck into her brain.

She squelched the vision. Hard.

Okay. The guy was extremely attractive. Yeah, but he probably thinks he's God's gift to women, all wrapped up in a sexy male package.

"Maxwell's still up with a student who came in unannounced. He may be awhile."

Brad wasn't here? Cat's smile faded. "Define *awhile*."

"Half hour. Forty-five minutes at most."

"I can't wait that long." Her shoulders slumped and her puffed-up bubble of confidence burst faster than a popped balloon. There was no way on earth she could hold on to her nerve for another ten minutes, much less thirty. Not after expending most of it on enduring this guy's presence.

Why oh why didn't she watch that damn show so she could at least have a backup plan to her life-changing day? Learning to fly was supposed to be the first step to a new Cat Tyler, and Brad had promised to ease her into it. "How could he be busy? I scheduled him last week online, just like he told me to do."

"Sorry about the mix-up, but it shouldn't be a problem for your first lesson. I'm free to take you up," Josh said, giving a single-shouldered shrug.

"You?" Her eyes grew wider. "No. I don't think so," she said too quickly, turning to go. No way could she go up with *him*. "I'll reschedule with Brad and come back another time."

"You're not really here to learn to fly." His voice, full of challenge, stopped her in midstride. "Are you?"

"Oh?" She spun back around, not sure she'd heard him correctly. "And why do you say that?"

"Because I know your type."

"My type?" Her jaw dropped open. Was he serious? She scanned his face and caught intense disapproval reflected in his granite expression. For the life of her, she couldn't figure out why. She didn't even know the man and here he was judging her.

"This is a lark to you. I mean, you are dating Maxwell. Let me guess, he probably talked you into it. He loves to show off his skill, but quite frankly, I'm tired of him using Buchannan Aeronautics as his own personal amusement ride so he can score. This is a legitimate business."

Cat took a deep breath and counted to ten, working to stop the heat now warming her cheeks, which meant only one thing. She was blushing, a bane of her pale complexion. So much for moxie and behaving her way to success. Bluffing was hard enough to pull off without a red face. "It's amazing you're still in business, if this is how you treat all your new clients."

"When they look like you do and date Maxwell, I treat 'em as I see 'em. I've got news for you, Ms. Tyler. You're one in a long line of many." He shrugged. "All I can say is, it's an expensive way to get a guy's attention."

"Are you always so judgmental?" She fought to keep her tone even, but her voice still cracked with emotion. Brad did have a reputation and a weakness for scoring. But so what! He also had a few redeeming qualities, namely he was lots of fun. Cat liked him. They were just friends. She had no interest in sleeping with him, or anyone for that matter, and he was well aware of the fact. Of course, if they ever did do the dirty deed, she knew darn well she'd enjoy herself, considering his reputation. Unfortunately, she couldn't compartmentalize sex.

No. She was better off remaining celibate. Sex only complicated her life and always led to her over-involvement, and somehow Cat lost her true self. Her experience with her ex had taught her that much. As a result, she wasn't in the market for any kind of relationship other than friend, even a casual sexual one. Not now, not tomorrow, not ever. Period.

Cat inhaled a steadying breath, not about to cower. "You know nothing about me."

"Oh?" His gaze made another thorough scan of her body. "Admit it. You're only here to impress your man of the hour." He snorted. "Women like you don't belong in the cockpit."

"You're wrong." Her hand curled into a fist. Cat released it, resisting an urge to wipe that smug, knowing smirk off his face. "I've spent hours preparing for today and I *am* going to learn to fly." Her chin lifted as she glared at him. "Dating Brad Maxwell has nothing to do with my decision."

"If that's the case, you'd go up now and prove me wrong."

He could have been a matador and she the bull, considering the taunting gleam emanating from those ebony eyes of his. With red cape effectiveness, they bored into hers and delivered more challenge. His eyebrows shot up, waving the cape and goading her further.

She'd be damned if she let him or his words get to her. "Fine." She'd had her fill of chauvinistic, controlling men who thought they knew everything about women. One in a lifetime was lesson enough.

He turned back to Smitty and barked, "Is the spare headset in the cockpit of Seven Sierra Lima?"

Smitty nodded. "I put it there myself." He offered Cat an apologetic half shrug and lifted his eyebrows as if to say, "Sorry. There's nothing I can do."

"All right. What are we waiting for?" Josh held out his hand with a satisfied air and gave a slight nod in the direction of the door. "After you."

Next thing Cat knew, she was buckled in to the plane and was ready to start the engine, wondering how the jerk, sitting too close for comfort in the tiny cockpit, had so deftly maneuvered her here. She should have walked away and let him think what he wanted. Now she was stuck.

"What are the four stages of the working engine?" Josh's voice boomed out of the silence.

She hadn't expected the question and didn't readily respond.

"So, that pretty little brain can't handle how an engine works?" he snapped, swiftly picking up on her confusion.

Her gaze narrowed and his meaning registered, but her reaction still came too late.

"You said you prepared for today. The question's right out of the manual, at the end of the first lesson." He threw out a snort of disgust. "In order to fly safely, you need to know this stuff. It's not like driving a car where you start the engine and forget about it." Everything in his mannerisms—his tone, his contemptuous sneer, and the skepticism pouring out of his eyes—shouted condescension. "You have to understand what's going on."

Her entire body stiffened and heat infused her face. Did he really believe she was clueless?

In a flash, her resolve returned full force. Not caring that her complexion was probably beet red, she pierced his mocking stare with hers and said between clenched teeth, "Listen up, because I'm only going to say this once. Since you know so much about women, I'll try to put it in a way a Neanderthal like you can understand."

When his eyebrows rose and mild surprise flitted over his face, she flashed a syrupy smile. Then, going for more moxie, she dropped her voice to a sultry, almost taunting tone. "Like sex, there are four stages. First is the intake—you know, penetration—and the gas enters the chamber. Next we have compression. That's when the piston thrusts hard down the chamber, causing the pressure to build. This leads to the third stage, combustion. Better referred to as the stage where all hell breaks loose, which ultimately results in the exhaust stage or the end of the event. *You'd* probably smoke a cigarette afterward, or roll over and fall asleep, but an airplane engine keeps firing as long as it has fuel."

"Interesting way of explaining the mechanics of engines," he shot back without missing a beat. "But I guess a girl like you would know all about firing engines."

"Well, Mr. Buchannan, I use what works to get my point across," she answered sweetly. "And you know nothing about a *girl* like me." She glanced at the plane's ceiling and swore under her breath. This could be a long first lesson, but at least her fear had taken a backseat to her determination to prove him wrong.

"No one calls me Mr. Buchannan, Ms. Tyler. Josh or Buc. Take your pick, but not Mr. Buchannan."

Josh or Buc, take your pick, she mentally mimicked. The guy was too much.

"Now that we've finished the preliminaries…" He cleared his throat and his grin stretched. "We can start the engine. Get all that combustion going."

At that, she did roll her eyes.

He droned on, his voice taking on a teacher-like tone while turning the key. "But before you can leave, you gotta call Ground Control. A lot of students are intimidated by the radio at first and choke up or say things wrong." He stopped talking and glanced her way, his look telling her she was one of those students. "It might help if I write out some scripts of common calls so you can refer to them until you're confident that you can handle it. But for now, I'll call them."

"I can handle talking on a radio, Buc-man," Cat said, tossing out her spur-of-the-moment nickname to irritate him in hopes of gaining a bit of mental leverage. When he ignored her little gibe, she added, "Despite your low opinion of me, I have done my homework."

"Really?" One brow slanted up. "Then we have the latest weather information from ATIS, right?"

She nodded. "Information Bravo."

"Okay. Tell them who we are, where we are, where we're going." After a quick demonstration, he ended with, "Got it?" He watched her face closely, then at her nod encouraged, "Go ahead." Yet, his indulgent smile shouted his opinion. She would not succeed on her first try. "Make contact."

"Okay, Buc-man. Watch this." Cat mirrored his smug expression and pressed the mic button. Her confident voice shot through the mouthpiece.

"Gallatin Ground, Cherokee Seven Sierra Lima." A moment later, her earphones came to life.

"Cherokee Seven Sierra Lima, Gallatin Ground, go ahead."

"Gallatin Ground. Cherokee Seven Sierra Lima is departing left to the practice area and we have information Bravo."

"Seven Sierra Lima, taxi runway three zero."

"Taxi runway three zero, Seven Sierra Lima." She turned to Josh and couldn't stop her smile from spreading from ear to ear. "How was that?"

"Actually, that was pretty good." His grin matched hers.

"Thanks," she said unable to keep the "I told you so" tone out of her response.

"But." He tsk-tsked. "You forgot to tell them where you are. Also, you should say you're departing to the west, not to the left."

Her smile faded. "Since I forgot to tell him, why didn't he ask?" She slanted a contrite glance in his direction and wished she hadn't screwed up, not then, when the outcome meant so much. "Doesn't he need to know?"

"This plane flies out of here a lot so he probably recognizes the tail number as a Buchannan Aeronautics plane." Josh offered a nonchalant shrug. "Plus, this is Bozeman, Montana. If you look around, you'll notice that we're the only one out here right now with a prop turning. He can see us from the tower." His earlier patronizing tone had returned, erasing the bit of camaraderie that had sprung up before he spoke. Then he added, switching back to his boring, teacher-like mode, "Still, you always want to follow proper procedures. That's how you stay safe."

She rolled her eyes skyward and prayed for patience, also praying she could be anywhere but here in the cockpit's cramped space.

But her prayers went unanswered and the rest of the lesson went downhill.

Josh Buchannan showed no patience for her beginner status and pointed out her every little error, clearly trying to dissuade her from pursuing her pilot's license.

Yet in the course of the hour-long plane ride, Cat's will strengthened.

If the guy thought a few terse words would rile her, he was in for a huge epiphany. She'd overcome an ex who thought women should be geisha girls with no thoughts of their own, and Buc-man was Mother Teresa compared to him. He was also wrong. Learning to fly wasn't just a passing fancy, and it would take more than this lousy lesson to convince her to quit.

Chapter 2

A flash of movement caught Cat's attention. Her focus moved to Josh's face. How she'd lucked out in having him for her long cross-country flight, she didn't know, but she still found it hard to gauge his thoughts, even after a couple of months. Nothing in his featureless expression alarmed her, but the severity of his tapping finger over a dial sent a trickle of unease down her spine.

His usually relaxed posture radiated tension and added to her apprehension.

"What's wrong?" Cat finally asked.

Rather than answer, Josh said curtly, "Tell me what you'd do in case of a forced landing with no engine."

When her brows furrowed in confusion, he barked, "Do it."

"Trim to glide speed of seventy-three knots," she shot back automatically, too stunned by his vehement command to do anything else. "Then I look for somewhere to put down."

Cat glanced out the window and her heart skipped beats.

The storm system they'd been watching on the western horizon appeared to be traveling faster than predicted. Her focus shifted lower. From an altitude of nine thousand feet, the only color she noted below other than the green tops of coniferous trees was brown...from granite boulders jutting out from the ground. Nothing looked remotely accessible for landing in the rocky, mountainous terrain.

"Next I check out the cockpit." Reining in her fear with a firm hold, she gave a brief rundown of all the little things she'd memorized before finishing with, "And then I send out my Mayday and unlatch the door." Cat had kept her voice even, but inside she seethed.

How dare he try to scare her? Her spine stiffened and her grip on the yoke tightened until the blood left her fingers. She took another deep breath and threw him a frozen smile. "You can shelve the theatrics."

Nothing, it seemed, had changed since that first day she'd stepped into the cockpit with him. How she'd been so lucky to have his company this afternoon, she didn't know. But she did know one thing—she was totally, irrevocably, and completely tired of his game.

She avoided using him as an instructor because he'd always zero in on her mistakes during the lesson to reinforce his original opinion that she shouldn't fly, which only increased her determination. With the memory of that first flight resurfacing, Cat did now what she'd done then—prayed for more patience.

"Emergency procedures were in my last lesson," she said, once she had her emotions back under control. This obvious ploy would not dissuade her from flying any better than his other attempts had. "And I can assure you," she purred, offering a more genuine smile. "Brad was thorough. I don't need a refresher course."

"Carburetor's iced over. Hear that?"

She listened with half an ear. The engine coughed and sputtered, emitting a sound that was nothing new to an experienced pilot.

"Yeah?" She snorted, rolling her eyes. "Then turn on the carb heat, Buc-man."

"It's not working." He flashed his patient-father-dealing-with-errant-child expression that she'd grown to hate. "And you know what that means."

She gritted her teeth and squeezed the yoke harder, quelling the urge to pull her hair out. The effort to stay one step ahead of him when they flew together always tested her restraint. Why should today be any different?

"Look," she said through gritted teeth. "I know you don't think I should fly, but I don't appreciate the scare tactics."

Her annoyed gaze slid across the cockpit. In the next instant, the engine died. Anger stuck in her throat. All blood left her face, its warmth diminishing as fast as water going down a drain when the invisible, spinning propeller abruptly slowed and was now visible just four feet in front of her.

In the now deafening silence, Cat swallowed hard and glanced wide-eyed at her instructor.

Releasing a few soft expletives, Josh took over. "I've got the controls. Try to restart the engine and prepare for a forced landing."

He dialed in the emergency frequency, 121.5, and firmly squeezed the mic button. "Mayday, Mayday, Mayday. Cherokee

Seven Sierra Lima is thirty miles southwest of Bozeman with complete engine failure, going in for a forced landing north of the wilderness area." After several attempts, the engine gave no response.

Cat set the squawk at seven seven zero zero and pushed Ident. The seriousness of the situation slammed into her with the force of an SUV hitting a concrete wall, as he repeated, "Mayday, Mayday, Mayday," and repeated their location once more. "Does anyone copy?" Josh turned to her and nodded at the chart. "Check for obstacles and any private strip suitable for landing."

Dear God, they were going down! Cat's hands shook as she looked at the chart. Fear gripped her so hard she could barely focus. "I don't see any landing strip, but watch for power lines." With control relinquished, her task accomplished, and nothing else to do with her hands, she could only grab her seat with a white-knuckled grip. The whole time she continued inhaling, then exhaling, in a forced effort to relax. Panic would only make things worse.

"Cherokee Seven Sierra Lima, Salt Lake Center copies that you are thirty miles southwest of Bozeman. Report lives on board," a welcome voice said in their headsets a long moment later.

"Salt Lake Center, we're heading two eight zero with two lives on board, Cherokee Seven Sierra Lima," Josh said. The board-like stiffness of his back relaxed somewhat as he expelled a huge breath.

"Seven Sierra Lima, radar contact confirmed. You are twenty-nine miles southwest of Bozeman, descending through eight thousand, five hundred. There's a private airstrip directly west of your position. We've notified local law enforcement and the Civil Air Patrol. Godspeed."

When the transmission died, Cat's focus moved from the chart to the window. "I see the strip on the map, but I haven't spotted it yet." While scanning the rocky terrain more closely, her efforts to remain calm disintegrated into outright terror. In the few minutes she'd been preoccupied with restarting the engine, the topography hadn't changed. In fact, the emerald canopy of trees grew denser and worse, spiked brown rocks still jutted anywhere there was no green. Besides not seeing the landing strip, she didn't see a road or flat piece of land that would work for a forced landing.

"How can this be happening?" she whispered. "This was supposed to be a simple flight."

"Yeah, well, sometimes things don't go as planned," he said, unlatching the door. "Hang on. Make sure your seat belt's fastened snugly. This could get ugly."

Oh God! This had become a changing time in her life, all right. She was going to die. His body language confirmed the idea. His usual air of bland condescension had long evaporated, while an expression holding no emotion whatsoever had replaced it. That, together with his movements, executed with precision and total concentration, had her looking up.

Please, dear Lord! Don't let me die. Not now. Not with him.

She closed her eyes and leaned back in the seat. Surely God couldn't be so cruel as to let her last moments on earth be with Josh Buchannan.

She'd always heard that in times like this her entire life would flash before her eyes, but all she could remember was her life since she first started taking flying lessons. The vivid memory of the day she met the man sitting next to her stuck in her brain, along with Dr. Phil's voice. Both intertwined and played over and over and over.

The only thing worse than dying with Buc-man was doing it with that annoying voice in her head.

❈

"You ready?" Josh all but shouted. "Cat...? Come on, Cat. Stay with me. Now's not the time to freak out."

Josh watched Cat's expression change as the turmoil in her eyes diminished. The irritated glare she gave him told him she was back. "Nice of you to rejoin us."

"God help me," she whispered under her breath, while her attention moved to the window. "I'm going to die with Buc-man as my last human contact."

His chuckle crackled in her ear. "I heard that. Sorry to disappoint you, but we're not going to die—not with Buc at the helm," he said, in an attempt to cut through the tense mood hanging in the cockpit.

"I've looked out the window and I don't see an airstrip or any clearing long enough to land."

"Have you no faith in my abilities?" He snorted at her look of total disbelief. "Leave it to me. I'll get us down and in one piece." His expression hardened as his attention returned to fulfilling his promise to Cat and to staying alive.

By this time, they'd dropped to fifteen hundred feet above the ground, flying over the clearing he'd spotted earlier. He began a slow circle that would hopefully bring him to the end of that patch of land as the last precious space between plane and earth was spent.

A swirl of fall leaves blew sideways across the clearing. He expelled a long breath, working to still his racing heart. The space was smaller than he thought from above.

A short-field, soft-field landing in a strong crosswind without power was no easy feat. Toss in the ground-softening rains of the past few days and conditions couldn't get much worse. Great!

"With full fuel, fire's our biggest worry if things don't go as planned. Be ready to unbuckle and get out as soon as possible."

Looking over at Cat, he could tell her hard outer shell had developed a crack. Cat's personality had chafed his backside worse than a bad case of poison ivy from the moment he'd met her, when he'd pegged her as one of those spoiled princesses who thought the world revolved around her. Regardless of his dislike, she was still his responsibility.

"We're not going to die, Cat. I'm going to pull your pretty little butt through this, so stay with me. You need to be ready."

"I can handle it, Buc-man."

A glimpse of heat flashed in her eyes before they iced over, making it seem as if the temperature had gone down twenty degrees in the cockpit.

Considering her words and cold glare, she was more than ready. Thank God, because he had no more time to worry about her or her fear. They cleared the last of the trees, flying at an altitude of fifty feet with full flaps barely over stall speed. So far, so good.

The wind gusted from the left. He dipped the left wing and threw in right rudder to keep them straight. The stall warning blared. The piercing noise indicated the plane was just above the ground. He had seconds left. Josh prayed silently while pulling hard on the yoke as first the left wheel gently touched, then the right. Though both wheels met the ground, they weren't out of danger yet. The plane still had momentum.

He held the nose off as long as possible, but the approaching mountain of rocks meant short-field technique took precedence over soft-field technique. He lifted the flaps. The nose wheel hit the soft ground. He braked. Hard. It was almost a perfect landing until the nose gear went into a deep depression with enough force to break off.

The plane stopped inches from path-blocking boulders rising toward the heavens.

Both Josh and Cat sat in silence for long seconds, staring at the wall of stone in front of them.

He glanced at Cat, who still had a firm grip on her seat. Then she took a deep breath. "Well, Buc-man, I forgive your cocky pilot overconfidence," she said on the exhale.

"Gee, thanks for all your faith," he replied, going along with her mocking tone. Her snide humor was most likely an attempt to hide her true fear of what could have happened. Hell, he was a little rattled, as well. The forced landing had definitely made an emotional impact. On both of them. Another few feet of momentum and they might not be joking at all. "Come on. Let's get out of here. There could be a fuel leak and we could still have a fire if it hits the hot engine."

"You've got to be kidding. That was a near perfect landing," she said, throwing him a look of disbelief.

Ignoring her, Josh barked, "Move," while giving his door a hefty shove, creating an opening. "We can get back in after I've checked it."

He climbed out. Then, before turning to assist Cat, he instinctively lifted his flight bag from the back.

"Grab your gear. Better safe than sorry," he said, pointing to her bag. He couldn't leave the cockpit empty-handed. Not when too many years spent in a prior career of being prepared had kept him alive.

Once out, he started walking around the plane. "I don't see any leaks, but I'll check more closely under the cowling after we stow our gear over by those trees. That way they're clear if a fire does start."

When she again looked at him as if he'd grown a second head, he sighed.

"It may seem overly cautious, but years of training never die. We may need those flight bags." Okay. Maybe he did sound a little over the top, making him realize right then that, as with so many times in his life, some things never changed.

"Wait! I'll go with you." Cat walked alongside him, carrying her bag. "I need to take a walk in the woods. I don't suppose you have any toilet paper in that bag we so *desperately* need to save?" she asked flippantly when they got to the edge of the tree line.

"What? A glamour girl like you surely must have Kleenex and full makeup with you at all times," he shot back, not mitigating his sarcasm despite the fact that she was still a little shaky and her words were most likely another stab at gaining control by using glib humor.

If he kept their sparring alive, she'd have less time to think about their near miss. But his motives weren't entirely pure. Not when he got intense enjoyment from yanking her emotional chain and watching her light up with annoyance. She never failed to rise to his little taunts. And hell, he didn't have to be Freud to grasp that deriving such pleasure played a major part in why he kept trying.

She ignored his comment and said over her shoulder, while heading into the dense woods, "You look for your fuel leak and keep your distance, Buc-man. I'll be right back."

He chuckled and dropped his bag by a tree as the distinct drone of a fully aspirated, four-cylinder Lycoming engine sounded in the sky above. Rather than run to the plane, Josh reached inside his bag for the handheld radio and tuned to 121.5 in time to hear, "Cherokee Seven Sierra Lima, CAP flight Five One Seven Two Charlie, do you read."

Wow! The Civil Air Patrol was sure responding quickly. "CAP flight, this is Cherokee Seven Sierra Lima. We read you beautifully! We have no injuries—just a broken plane."

"Roger. You're lucky we were in the area. We have your coordinates and will notify local authorities to come get you. You need to stay with the plane. Do you understand?"

"Don't worry, we're not going anywhere. We'll be standing by on 121.5."

He listened to the engine becoming more distant and turned off the radio to conserve the battery before placing it back in his bag. Might as well use up the battery on the useless plane and sit comfortably out of the wind.

Josh headed for the clearing to check for fuel leaks when he heard the Civil Air Patrol flight returning. Since he was still near the trees, he ran back to grab the closer handheld and turned it on. As the plane began a low approach, he waited for the loud engine to pass before calling to see what else they needed.

Hopefully they decided to drop an emergency survival kit. Of course, that could be bad news. Maybe it's bowling night and the talk with local authorities wasn't as promising as he'd hoped.

"Please, Lord," he muttered under his breath. "Don't let me be stuck with Powder Puff all night." He might like taunting her, but he certainly had no desire to be trapped in the Montana wilderness with one of Brad Maxwell's princesses. Even his patience had limits.

He crossed his arms and leaned against a tree as the plane drew near.

Suddenly, he straightened.

Something's not right, he thought.

Josh's heart began hammering. Blood rushed to his head. The hairs on the back of his neck stood on end.

Why's he flying so low and fast?

He shoved away from the tree and eased closer toward the clearing for a better look. At the edge of the tree line he stopped short, darted back behind another pine, and made himself invisible from the air.

In stunned fascination, Josh watched the light plane aim straight for his Cherokee. A wing-mounted cannon fired, hitting the target dead-on, and right before his eyes, his plane burst into a ball of flames. He blinked to make sure he wasn't seeing things.

"Ah, shit." Springing into action, he threw his bag over his shoulder and bolted on the balls of his feet through the dense brush toward Cat. Thick green-needled branches slapped him in the face as he spied her out of his peripheral vision. She'd finished her business and was winding her way back to the plane.

Her concerned expression told him she'd heard the explosion.

"Come on, let's go." He grabbed her and pulled her with him, giving her no choice except to follow. It seemed someone wanted him dead. He wasn't about to hang around for whoever it was to figure out he hadn't succeeded. He'd work on why later. Now, instinct took over. Staying alive became his main concern.

"What?" Confusion was clear in Cat's voice. "What's going on?"

"You wanna stay alive?"

"Stay alive?" She tugged on his hand. "But we are alive."

"Not for long if we don't keep moving," he said insistently, his patience snapping. She'd just have to trust him. He had no time for explanations that eluded him. He intended to be long gone from the plane as quickly as the terrain allowed them to travel. He increased his speed. In an effort to create a trail where none existed, he thrust his way through branches, taking the brunt of the pine slaps as she placed a firm hold on her bag and stumbled behind him.

The foliage grew less dense the higher they went. By then, he was all out moving as fast as he could, and he knew she was barely able to keep up. Still he urged, "We have to move faster."

"What happened? Was there a fuel leak? Is that why the plane blew?"

He strived for patience. It wasn't enough that someone blew up his plane. He had to get stuck with a stubborn powder puff, one who seemed bent on questioning his every move.

"I'm not sure what happened. I never got to check for a fuel leak, but the plane blew up all right," he offered in the order in which she asked, not slowing his pace.

"What?" She dug in her heels, working to slow him, at the same time exerting more effort to yank out of his grasp. "Wait, stop! You're not making sense."

"Move," he barked. "We can't stop. If we stay here, we die."

Chapter 3

The pilot watched the flames from the air, then made another pass, satisfied no one had survived the explosion. While heading back in the direction he'd come, he took off his headset and pulled out a satellite phone, one sending a secure signal that couldn't be intercepted. He hit one of the preset numbers and brought the phone to his ear.

The call was answered after two rings.

"Tell me you have good news."

"Mission accomplished. Both targets are dead. I'm heading back now."

"Good. 'Patience is beautiful.' It's also the key to freedom." There was praise in his tone. "Upon verification, you will be rewarded. Are we clear?"

He smiled. "Yes. I don't expect a long wait. Salt Lake Center had them on radar, so there's a definite trail to follow. Such a bad accident. Buchannan's been hanging out with the wrong element and he should've known better. They don't like to be crossed," he said chuckling, before ending the call and sticking his headset back in place.

ඥ

"Wait," Cat begged, totally out of breath and trying without success to yank her hand out of Josh's steadfast grip. They'd been streaking through the brush for too many minutes. In that time, she'd barely avoided tripping over rocks and roots. Her lungs felt ready to burst. She looked over at him briefly and couldn't help but notice his determined features. There was nothing easy in his manner. She also managed to glance around and focus on her bearings. They were deep in the forest with no trail to speak of, just trees, brush, and rocks to avoid, along with stickers from calf-high weeds that had obviously sprung up due to a wetter than usual fall.

"Why are we moving so fast? And why aren't we waiting near the plane?"

He only grunted. Cat's morale, already at an all-time low considering their forced landing and exploding plane, descended lower. Finally, she hissed, "Why won't you tell me what's going on?"

"I spoke with CAP. Planes are grounded. The weather conditions are deteriorating, so we're hiking for cover."

"Okay." That made sense. "But we have to slow down. My legs aren't as long as yours."

His speed slackened. She let out a huge breath and sucked in another one quickly, doing it over and over, still struggling to keep up. "How far are we hiking?" she was finally able to ask.

When Josh didn't answer, she repeated her question. Again, he just kept going at his steady pace, pulling her along, her words bouncing off his obstinate head like a rubber ball.

She sighed, deciding to conserve her energy and keep up as best she could.

They traveled for another fifteen minutes. Finally she stopped abruptly, causing him to lose his grip on her.

She crossed her arms and glared. "I'm not moving another step." Then she stalked over to a big boulder, sat, and placed her bag in front of her. Clutching her arms to her chest, she crossed her legs and held her head high, daring him to deny her right to rest.

"I guess it is time for a break." He let out an audible sigh and moved to sit beside her.

"You think?" she lashed out, not bothering to hide her irritation.

When he didn't say anything, just kept his constant gaze traveling over the landscape, first right, then left and back again, her patience completely disintegrated. "Exactly what is it we're looking for? Where are we going and why do we have to travel so fast to get there?"

"Why do you think?" Josh's attention still roved over the dense brush as he talked. "Considering the weather, we need to keep moving." He dug into his flight bag and pulled out a map and a handheld GPS. He spent a few minutes going over the map while punching numbers into the device. "I'm familiar with this area. We're headed for a ranger's cabin about five miles in that direction," he added a moment later, pointing.

"Will someone be waiting for us at this cabin?" she asked,

hoping against hope she wouldn't be stuck in some cabin with this crazy man who acted as if the devil was after him. "Can't we call someone to help us?"

"How? Cell phone service is sporadic at best out here." He shook his head. "And even if we got a hold of someone, I doubt our rescue would be able to reach us tonight."

Not what she wanted to hear, she thought, watching him reach into his bag.

He dragged out a bottle of water, opened it, took a long drink, and then handed it to Cat.

"Drink up. We're not stopping again till we make it to the cabin."

"Who died and made you God, Buc-man?"

"Look around." His hand pointed to the bank of threatening dark clouds. "That cold front we were ahead of is fast approaching. Rain is imminent. There's only one thing that'll make this experience worse and that's if the heavens open up on us."

"So? If I get a little wet, I won't melt."

"You won't say that when the temperature drops. In case you haven't figured it out, this is Montana. When night hits and the wind chill factor sets in, it's going to be cold. Trust me. You won't want to be wearing wet clothes."

Damn, the urge to hit him was strong. How could he sit and calmly spout off about rain and Montana nights when they'd just gone through such a harrowing experience? The desire to curl up in a ball and cry overwhelmed her. All she wanted at this moment was to fill a tub with hot water and soak and forget she'd ever decided to learn to fly. She was cold, every muscle in her body hurt, and most of all, she was tired of running. But knowing he'd make some snide comment about being a princess, she placed a stiff smile on her face. "Point taken. But could we please go a little slower?"

Josh turned his attention to her face for a long moment. Those chocolate bedroom eyes of his bored into hers, as if searching for some clue hidden deep beneath the surface of her eyes. Not comfortable with the scrutiny, or the heat that intense stare generated, she lowered her gaze. Then she bent to pick up her bag and rummaged, not really looking for anything, merely using the task to keep from having to peer into those incredible eyes. Somehow he seemed to see things she preferred to keep hidden.

"After you're done searching for whatever it is you're so

determined to find, we should move." His sarcastic tone permeated the cool air and hinted at her motives.

Her hand inside the bag clenched into a fist. Just one shot! If she ever got one good shot at him, she'd try real hard to knock him out.

"You can be such a pig, Buc-man. How you call yourself a member of the human race is beyond me," she said, meeting his amused gaze with eye daggers.

"Is that the best you can do?" He only laughed and stood, pulling her off the rock with him. "Come on, we're burning daylight."

"Jerk," she muttered. Her jaw clenched when she caught another amused chuckle.

She snatched her flight bag while he replaced both his map and GPS in his bag before picking it up and grabbing her hand. Cat gave an audible sigh, reluctantly becoming Josh's shadow once again, only this time, thank God, his pace was much more manageable.

Chapter 4

Though Josh had cut their pace in half, they still made good time.

Almost to their destination, he stopped at a fast-moving stream near a trickling waterfall.

"This is a good place to fill our bottles after we drink up. I'm not sure what's at the cabin. We may need water to boil. I sure as hell don't want to trek back after night falls."

"Fine." Cat dropped her bag and plopped down on a fallen log, while letting out a long, slow breath. "How much further?"

"A half mile, maybe less," he said, glancing at her and noting pure exhaustion creeping into her posture. He hadn't given her any choice but to follow, but he certainly hadn't expected her to follow his commands so readily without complaints. Trained men he'd led in the past weren't as cooperative. Her pluck amazed him, adding to a notion he hadn't dared admit. Until now.

"You surprise me, Cat."

The sound of his voice hung in the air, much like the clouds overhead that seemed ready to dump their moisture at any moment.

A rosy pink color stole up her face. He stifled his smile, hiding it behind the task of guzzling a long drink. If only he could deny his interest. Josh sighed, grasping another uncomfortable truth as he gulped down more water. Ignoring her wasn't an easy task. The woman intrigued him.

Definitely a contradiction and definitely not one of Maxwell's usual powder puffs.

Not once in the handful of times he'd flown as her instructor could he find fault with her preparedness, and it had become a challenge of sorts to catch her off guard. In fact, he'd found he looked forward to taking her up, even spent energy rearranging lessons so he could, despite her best efforts to prevent it. No. He finally had to face facts. Cat Tyler seemed nothing like the self-centered, flighty, pilot-chasing princess he first thought her to be. And the idea didn't bode well. Josh preferred to think the worst of people. That way mental barriers stayed in place and left little chance of forming attachments. Attachments only complicated his life.

Cat bent to take a bottle of water out of her bag. "Why did the plane explode?" She uncapped it, lifted the bottle to her mouth, and swigged a long drink. When done, she wiped her mouth with the back of her hand. "Was there a fuel leak? I just realized you never told me."

Yep! Definitely a quick mind, he thought, as his smile stretched into a wide grin. He'd been evasive on purpose, hoping she wouldn't ask those exact questions.

"I'm not sure," he answered honestly, while watching her movements. They seemed to be more of a distraction than anything else.

"I guess I owe you an apology," she said sincerely, recapping the bottle.

"Oh?" His eyebrows lifted an inquisitive inch. "How do you figure?"

"That was a near perfect landing after the carb heater quit and I know I'm only sitting here because of your skill." Cat shrugged. "I guess I owe you doubly for my life. If you hadn't forced me out of the plane, I'd be toast right now."

Josh grunted and didn't answer, unwilling to alarm her with his uneasy thoughts. Until he unraveled what was going down, she was better off not knowing the full truth of their situation. The news would only scare her, and scaring her would serve no purpose.

The carb heat failure might not have been a freak happenstance. If so, someone had gone to a lot of trouble and why was his biggest concern.

His gaze followed Cat as she stood and walked toward the waterfall with her empty bottle. She knelt to lap water with her hands and sluice it over her face. "You might consider moving," he said. "With all this rain, the bank is slippery. You'll fall in if you keep leaning over like that." Josh threw out a short laugh when she shot him a look that clearly shouted, "Butt out, Buc-man."

Still, she straightened up to move as he brushed past her to a spot further downstream where the ground appeared less slippery. The water appeared to be a little deeper here too. Josh crouched, submersed his bottle, and patiently waited for it to fill.

Suddenly, a loud splash interrupted the quiet behind him and laughter exploded from his chest like a rocket. He didn't have to look to know she'd somehow fallen in, even after his warning. "I told you so."

He glanced over at Cat and his outburst slowed to a soft chuckle as she flailed about, looking much like her namesake, albeit a drenched one after her fast exit out of the cold stream. His laughter almost broke free again, but his smile died when he noticed her fuming stare, daring him to so much as breathe another laugh. "Cold, isn't it?"

"Shut up, Buc-man." Still glaring, she stood rigidly, dripping wet with fists clenched as if she couldn't wait to take a swing.

"Save your energy, Powder Puff. You're going to need it to make it to the cabin." Josh ignored her while picking up his bag. When he caught her expression, sending him daggers with those hot eyes of hers so ice blue in color, he laughed outright. Damn if she didn't amuse him, he thought, shaking his head.

How in the hell she do that? Put off so much heat, surrounded by all that cold?

"Come on." Josh proceeded up the trail, not waiting to see if she followed. "Cabin shouldn't be too much further, but now that you're wet, it won't matter if it rains or not."

෮

Cat snatched her bag, tossed it over her shoulder, and marched after him. Why not just stamp "Stupid" on her forehead? She'd known the ground was slippery and should have had enough sense not to try retrieving a gemstone she'd glimpsed while filling her bottle.

All at once it became too much. Tears of frustration snuck out, despite her best efforts to hold them back. Every now and then, she wiped them off as she trailed a good distance behind Josh, squishing with every step.

There was nothing worse than having to walk in wet jeans and running shoes. Nothing except being beholden to and having to depend upon the one person who'd made her life so miserable, after surviving a plane crash and then having to walk with him after the plane blew up.

This was surely hell. What had she done to bring on such bad karma?

"You coming?" Josh asked a few moments later. He'd stopped a ways ahead and was waiting for her.

"I'm right behind you, Buc-man," Cat sneered, keeping her same slow pace until she stood beside him.

"Look, I'm sorry you fell in, but I tried to warn you."

"Shut up and walk." She moved past him.

Josh easily caught up to her. "Do you know where you're going?"

Cat snorted. "You know I don't." But kept walking.

"Then why are you in the lead?"

She stopped and spun around. "Do you enjoy baiting me?"

"As a matter of fact, I do." He halted in front of her. "I can't help myself. You bring it out."

"Oh, like that's a surprise. I should've known better. You were right. I should never have taken flying lessons." Suddenly, her tears gushed forth and no amount of blinking would hold them back. "There, are you happy?" she asked, wiping at the deluge. "For two months you've been trying your damnedest to make me cry. Well, you've succeeded. So, please stop."

Josh swore under his breath and dropped his bag. Reaching out, he tried to pull her into his arms, saying, "I'm sorry," but she stepped back quickly, avoiding his touch. If she let him touch her now, she would surely shatter into a million tiny pieces. At this point, she didn't think she'd be able to get them back together again.

"Are you okay?" Josh asked, concern etched on his face. "I didn't mean to hurt your feelings."

Could this get any worse, Cat wondered. Now she had his pity as well as his contempt. At that moment, she wished she could fall into a hole, also wishing she didn't feel the heat emanating from his warm body—a body that loomed much too close for her liking.

"Look, forget it, okay? Let's move. I'll keep my mouth shut from here on out." Cat backed up a few steps and attempted to brush the rest of her tears away. "I only want to get somewhere I can get warm."

Nodding, Josh picked up his bag, strode ahead, and said over his shoulder, "It's not far. I'll get a fire going once we get there so you can get warm."

Cat stood rooted to the spot, not moving. For two months, he'd made her life miserable. She certainly didn't want to find him attractive. The man was a jerk. That may be, she thought, eyeing his receding back, but she had to admit; he had a damn fine body.

"Stop it, Cat!" she muttered. "The man is not attractive. Repeat twenty times and don't look at his butt."

When he turned around and gave her a look that said, "Are you coming?" she wiped off the last of her tears, and heaved a resigned sigh. She then grabbed her bag and followed, keeping her pace steady behind him, squishing the entire way.

While walking, she kept her mental monologue going. Imagine him in the water. Better yet, imagine him blowing up with the plane. Yes, that's it. She laughed. Yeah, right! No way Mr. Perfect Landing would ever be killed by something so stupid as a leaky fuel line. If it weren't for him, she'd be dead. Okay—there you go, Cat. You owe him. That's why he's attractive to you. After all, he did save your life so you should be nice to him until we get home.

Within fifteen minutes, the cabin came into view. The air smelled like damp earth and the breeze hitting Cat's cheeks had dropped a few degrees. Her teeth chattered. Though the early October day wasn't cold by Montana's standards, the cloud cover and biting wind chilled her bones. Of course, the wet, harsh denim plastered to her legs only made her colder. She was freezing from the outside in. All she wanted at this point was warmth.

Closer to the cabin, Josh slowed his pace. Cat easily caught up with him.

"Do you have something to change into?" He nodded toward her bag.

"I brought a change of clothes," she said, coming to a stop at his side. "I packed it when I read the part about a pilot always being prepared, in case I might need it sometime."

"Good," he grunted distractedly. "Being prepared is my motto." His attention focused on the cabin. He gave the small wooden structure a complete once-over, then looked around the area before traversing up the stairs.

"What's wrong?" she asked, when he stopped abruptly on the porch.

"I wonder if it's open and if not, what's the penalty for breaking and entering."

"Well, step aside, Buc-man." She rushed up the steps. "I can handle the law, if and when they arrest us for breaking and entering." She was tired, hungry, and cold, and nothing was going to keep her from going inside. "No way can they arrest us for such a paltry crime when we have to rescue ourselves."

"Go for it." Josh offered a half laugh, standing to the left of the cabin's entrance. "God help anyone who gets in your way."

Cat gripped the knob and almost choked on her frustration when she realized it was locked.

"Why would they lock it?" She vented all her fury in the words and kicked the door with as much force as she could muster. "There's no one out here."

"We are."

"Oh yeah. Like we're a real threat."

"Move over." He slung his bag over his shoulder. Then, reaching above the frame and feeling along the edge, he retrieved a key. "You made a good point. There's no way they'll arrest us for breaking and entering when they should've rescued us."

"Now you're making fun of me." She couldn't help smiling.

"Maybe," he agreed, placing the key into the lock. In the next instant, the door opened. Josh straightened, grinning triumphantly. "But admit it. I did get your mind off your misery for just a moment, didn't I?"

Cat pushed past him, ignoring the way his grin tugged at her insides. Don't look at him. He's too confident. Too cocky. "How'd you know that key was there? What were you in your previous life? A spy? Or a cat burglar?"

"I take the Fifth," he teased, following close behind her.

After dropping his bag, he immediately walked over to the fireplace, the main focal point in the large room. Next to it was wood, stacked high.

Her smile only widened as she watched him. What had changed in such a short time? What was it about him that had heat streaking along her spine, churning her insides into tingles, and now made her want to smile more, especially when he'd always been so hard on her?

No. Don't even go there, she mentally warned herself. Pushing her errant thoughts aside, she intentionally moved her gaze around the room, taking in exactly what their haven offered.

The large room, while not extravagantly furnished, had everything they needed to be comfortable. Amend that. There was no sofa or plush chair and only one double-sized bed. Unwilling to think about what that meant, Cat turned her attention back to Josh.

"Do you think we'll be here all night?" She rubbed her arms, wishing his tall, muscular maleness didn't take up so much space.

The man simply exuded raw masculinity, she mused, observing his capable movements.

"Yeah, I do. You got a problem with that?" he shot back, his concentration centered on building a fire.

"No." She prayed her voice didn't reflect her dismay as the reality of being stuck with him loomed in front of her. The room seemed too small for the both of them. "I was hoping we could maybe notify someone and they could come and get us." While he worked so competently, Cat focused on his back, then opened a cupboard. She had to admit he did come in handy.

"No phone service here and the nearest access road is miles away." On his knees, Josh faced the fireplace, adding first kindling, then tinder, and finally a few logs. Once he had it set, he struck a match and lit the kindling in several spots. Within seconds, the small fire came to life, building slowly to a roaring blaze. Warmth immediately spread from the hearth. He sat back on his haunches, poking at his handiwork distractedly. Satisfied, he placed the poker in its spot and rose to his feet. "It's almost dusk. Another half hour, it'll be dark. We'll start out again in the morning."

"Great," she said unenthusiastically, turning to rifle through a couple of shelves.

Josh came up behind her and grabbed the cabinet door as she stepped back. "Look on the bright side, Powder Puff. We're alive and we're safe for the time being, with shelter and heat, and we won't starve, judging by what's in this cupboard."

He turned and captured her gaze with his eyes, holding it way too long for comfort. Her breath caught in her throat. She couldn't move, stood frozen like an animal sensing danger, while goose bumps that had nothing to do with being cold streaked up her arms. Finally, a smile snuck across his face, while his dark brown eyes danced a jig. He knew she was nervous and he knew why.

If she had any doubts, his next words disavowed her of them.

"And you're safe from me. I'm not into pilot groupies. I thought I'd already made that abundantly clear."

"Jerk!" Cat squeezed her eyes shut and prayed the heat she felt going up her face wasn't a blush. But judging from his expression when she opened her eyes, her pale blonde looks had given her away. Her face was probably beet red.

She snatched her bag and marched in brusque, although squishing, movements to the bed, and presented her back. It was going to be a long night, she thought, as his amused chuckle wafted past her ears.

"I'll leave you so you can get out of those wet things," he said on his way to the door. "I'll be back in about thirty minutes." An instant later, he was gone.

Cat heaved a weary sigh and began undressing, peeling off the sodden jeans an inch at a time.

CB

Once outside, Josh moved swiftly, his gaze scouring the area as he hiked to the top of a big hill behind the cabin. The entire time his mind centered on the contradiction he left back at the cabin. He didn't like admitting to himself that for one long moment, his thoughts had mirrored hers. Hell, who would blame him? Cat was put together well, and powder puff or not, when heat flared from those ice blue eyes, he couldn't help but respond.

"Still, it's no excuse," he muttered under his breath. For Christ's sake, he was a professional, and he had his rule about getting too close to a woman, especially one like her. Nor was he about to tread upon someone else's turf. Though Maxwell was a player, Cat seemed into him. She appeared to be too smart not to know his true character, so she obviously was a player too. They deserved each other.

Finally, after climbing the last bit of uneven terrain, he found the perfect spot, a huge boulder. He reached the top. Night encroached, giving him barely enough time to accomplish his task before the last of the light receded. Thank God the rain was holding off. But menacing black clouds swirled above him. It wouldn't be long before the heavens opened up.

Josh reached into his bag and snagged a collapsible, battery-operated satellite dish, hooked his phone to the piece, and turned it on. In seconds, the phone came alive. He flashed a self-satisfied smile, then quickly punched buttons, pressed Send, and brought the small device to his ear.

"Yeah, Murphy here," a voice shot back after several rings.

"Murph, it's me, Buc." Josh released his rigid shoulders as the tension along his back eased a bit.

"Buc? What's up? Considering your last report, I figured it'd be a while before I heard from you again."

"Someone wants me dead."

"You're kidding, right?"

"No, I'm pretty sure they were aiming at me."

"Come on, Buc. Be serious." Murphy's snort burst into his ear. "Like I don't have enough worries eating a hole in my gut, you got to invent some." Josh's smile grew. Some things never changed, he thought, listening to his usual litany of complaints. "I'm popping Tums like candy and my doctor says I gotta stop drinking and eating rich foods and get more exercise."

"I am being serious and he's right," he replied, chuckling. "Have you ever considered following his advice?"

"Yeah, yeah, yeah. Don't start. Now, why do you think someone wants you dead? What's going on?"

"One of my planes went down today." Josh rolled his shoulders, easing some of his pent-up tension. "Things happen, but when someone comes at my plane with a wing-mounted cannon, creating a fireball in the process, I tend to take that a little more seriously."

"Holy shit. Are you okay?"

"Yeah. We're fine. Got a student by the name of Cat Tyler in a cabin I've used before out in the middle of the woods." Josh rubbed the back of his neck and took long, slow breaths. "Of course, my plane's gone. The insurance company isn't going to be too happy with me."

"You're out of the business, so it seems a long shot that someone found out about your past. Not in Montana."

"I agree. I'm sure this is something else entirely. I've caught some inconsistencies in a couple of flights on the books. Looks like one of my pilots is doing something on the side and I'm guessing he's discovered that I'm aware of it."

"Enough to kill you?"

"The guilty son of a bitch has to be someone close enough to realize I'm not about to let anyone use my property for illegal activity," Josh said, thinking of the evidence he'd stumbled upon two days ago. No, he didn't take kindly to anyone putting his planes in jeopardy. He'd damn sure find out who was responsible. And once he did, the asshole involved would wish to hell he'd never messed with Buc Buchannan.

Murphy chuckled. "Sounds like you have things under control. Why call me?"

"Merely precaution and information."

"Ah, yes, that famous caution. What can I do?"

"Put out feelers. See if there's any reason my past might be haunting me, any reason why I might've all of a sudden become a target." He shrugged and glanced around. "Like I said, I'm just being cautious."

"I trust your instinct, Buc, and your caution. I'll ask around and I'll be thorough."

"I'd appreciate it." Josh's gaze continued roaming over the landscape. "Let's keep this conversation just between the two of us for now, okay? I don't want to alert Smitty until I have something more solid than a few discrepancies." Joel Smith owned ten percent of the business, but he was more than just a business partner. He was family. So was Murphy. The earlier hell they'd been through together created a bond stronger than blood. Nothing could break it.

"Sure. You be careful, though. People do desperate things when they're cornered."

"I plan on it. I'll be in touch." Josh pressed the Off button and quickly punched in another preset number, this time to his office, wondering what kind of reaction this call would draw.

"Buchannan Aeronautics," came the voice on the other end almost immediately.

Josh smiled. It was obvious his office manager had been waiting by the phone for his call, even though she was usually gone by this time. "Gloria? It's me, Josh."

"Josh? Oh my God," she proclaimed in a relieved voice. Then her voice changed to concern. "We're all worried here. CAP says your plane went down, but it's too dangerous to attempt a rescue until the weather clears. What happened?"

"A little accident, but I'm fine and Cat Tyler's fine, too."

"A little accident? Are you sure you're both okay?"

"Yeah. Plane lost power and we had to do a forced landing. Then it caught fire, but we were able to get out in time. We're on our way back now. It could take awhile as we're on foot. Would you spread the word, notify the authorities, and let everyone know we're fine? I hate to think people are worrying for nothing."

Josh heard her in the background telling someone, "They're okay. They're safe and sound. Isn't that great?" before she asked him, "Where are you?"

"We've found a creek and have been heading downhill," he said, after giving her fake coordinates, not wanting to give out their exact location. "We've stopped for the night and we'll move on in the morning."

"Okay, sir. I'll spread the good news. Everyone's here, waiting for any word from CAP. Brad's manning the front desk and Jack's around somewhere. Jim's doing paperwork. Smitty's been trying to keep it together, saying we should stick to business as usual and not jump to conclusions until we know all the facts. We canceled all lessons, saying the ceiling dropped too low. So everything's under control."

"Thanks, Gloria. I knew I could depend on you and Smitty."

Josh carefully packed everything inside his flight bag. Then hefting the bag over his shoulder, he headed in the direction of the cabin, wondering if he'd given Cat enough time.

He sighed. It was going to be a long night.

Chapter 5

Gloria Goodman hung up the phone and smiled. "I can't believe they're safe. I gather you caught the gist of the conversation?"

"Yeah. It's great news. Now that we know they're all right, why don't you go home?"

"I will after I make a few calls, letting people know he's okay. Plus Josh asked me to notify the authorities."

"Go on," he insisted, sporting a lopsided smile. "I'll do it. I know you want to get home to your sick husband. You've already put in two hours past your shift."

"You sure you don't mind?"

"Are you kidding? It'll give me something to keep me busy. Now go," he urged, taking her light coat off the rack and handing it to her. "No sense in both of us having to be here."

She reached for her coat. "George does get upset if I'm late." She shrugged on the coat, walked to the door, and turned. "I do appreciate this."

"Sure, Gloria." He nodded, sat back at the counter, and picked up the phone. "See you tomorrow."

As the door closed behind her, she walked briskly. Her high heels beat a staccato rhythm all the way to her car. She pressed the keypad and the headlights of her SUV flashed twice. The inside of the vehicle lit up and she swiftly climbed inside.

"Don't know why I feel on edge," Gloria muttered, gripping the wheel and taking a deep breath. She stuck the key into the ignition and gunned the engine. In easy movements, she backed out of the parking space, keeping her focus on the mirror.

"Calm down. George will be okay," she said under her breath. It wasn't the end of the world if his dinner had to wait. Her husband would just have to deal with it.

Gloria pulled onto the main road and punched the accelerator, picking up speed.

Her attention left the wet pavement momentarily to turn on the radio. She switched to her favorite channel, then glanced back to the road. Her scream halted in her throat. An oncoming car's headlights aimed straight for her. Instinctively, she turned the wheel sharply. Her tires caught the edge of the road, which jerked the car toward an irrigation ditch. She tried to correct her mistake, but it was too much too soon on the rain-slicked road. As if in slow motion, the Ford Expedition flipped and flew into an embankment. Then everything went black.

Chapter 6

Cat had finally been able to breathe normally once Josh left the cabin. Earlier, after shedding her wet jeans, sweater, and shirt, she'd donned her shorts and T-shirt from her bag, then placed her wet clothes to dry on a makeshift hanger in front of the fire. Her wet socks and panties were now drying over the fire screen, with her shoes at the edge of the hearth. She'd also washed her face as best she could with her precious water.

With nothing else to do, she paced, working off nervous energy as dusk set in. She found several lanterns, lit two, and put one on the table. The other she carried toward the fireplace.

Great, she thought, spying the nylon panties displayed so flagrantly in front of her. Praying they'd dry quickly, she set the lantern on the mantel. It wasn't enough that he pitied her and had contempt for her. No, now he would most likely assume she entertained ideas of jumping his bones as well. She certainly didn't want to give him more fuel to think such thoughts with her underwear hanging suggestively about.

She snorted. Like that would ever happen. She might find him attractive, but no way would she act on it. Ever. Even without her vow of celibacy, she wasn't forward enough. That was part of why she was taking flying lessons, to take charge of her life and do something daring.

No, Cat Tyler would never be so bold as to act on her attraction to Josh Buchannan. She was all talk and no action, unless someone made the decision for her. Mark had been the pursuer in their relationship. And she should have known better than to be fooled by his charm. A fact she hadn't grasped until after her parents' deaths.

She fingered the panties and nodded. Good. They were almost dry. She turned them over, placed them back on the screen, and began her nervous pacing once again.

It wasn't too much longer when Josh's stomping on the porch alerted Cat.

She sprang to the hearth, grabbed her undies, and rushed to her bag resting on the floor. Turning swiftly around as he entered, she prayed her features showed nothing of her thoughts.

After shutting the door, he glanced her way. "Why the guilty look?"

"No reason," she said, not meeting his eyes.

"Yeah, right. You have a very expressive face. You should never play poker."

"Thanks for the advice." She moved to the table, pulled out a chair, and said as she sat, "I was just putting away my unmentionables."

Cat lifted her chin, daring him to say anything else.

"This is the twenty-first century." He grunted, nodding at her bag. "I've seen women's underwear without succumbing to lust. I think I can resist the allure." He strode further into the room.

Immediately, the space shrank as he passed her on his way to a cupboard.

"I'm hungry." Ignoring her, he opened a door. "What's for dinner?"

"I found some spaghetti and sauce."

"Sounds good." He pivoted and snared her gaze. His eyebrows slanted upward. "Aren't you gonna to fix it?"

"Me? Why would I?" Her temper flared. She straightened to her full height and met his challenging stare.

"Isn't that what you do?" Josh shrugged. "I consider cooking a pink job."

"Pink job?" she sputtered, as confusion registered. Surely he didn't expect her to cook simply because she was female. He couldn't be that chauvinistic.

Josh didn't answer right away, his attention now absorbed in his task of pulling several items out of the cupboard and placing them on the counter. "Yeah. As opposed to a blue job."

"Blue job?"

"Okay, now say it three times really fast," he shot back, facing her.

Not sure she heard his words correctly, her forehead furrowed deeper and her gaze flew to his, searching. When she noticed the way merriment lingered in his eyes, the meaning finally sank in. Her giggle erupted. All of a sudden, it seemed as if the overwhelming stress of the day hit her and she needed a release because the giggle took off. She couldn't stop laughing.

"Come on," Josh urged once her laughter died. "Help me fix something to eat."

"Thanks, I needed a good laugh." The weight of her troubles had somehow lightened with his teasing. Smiling, Cat rose from her perch and walked over to him, trying hard to ignore the warm, mushy sensation his engaging smile stirred in her belly. "You're good at that, you know?" It was next to impossible to remember right then how much of a jerk he'd been all those times when heat still radiated from his smile.

"Yeah, so I've been told," he murmured, engrossed with the contents of another cupboard. He looked back at her, held her gaze, and said, "You have nothing to fear from me."

She nodded.

Josh pulled out two pans, placed them on the counter, then picked up another big pot and veered toward the cabin's exit. "I noticed a well outside with a hand pump. I'll see about getting some water for the spaghetti, if you start on opening the can of sauce along with some canned vegetables." At the door, he glanced back. "When I get back, I'll light the propane stove." He winked. "That's a blue job."

Cat only shook her head and watched him go, amazed at how totally relaxed she was. Somehow, in the course of a few hours, he'd gone from a jerk to someone she found attractive. And that didn't bode well.

Despite her mental warning, her grin stayed in place the entire time she worked the can opener.

⚃

Josh strode to the pump, wishing he could rid the thought of Cat not wearing any underwear under her shorts.

"Shit," he muttered under his breath as the water trickled once he began pumping.

The woman seemed a little prudish. She'd been totally embarrassed, amusingly so.

Unmentionables? Was she for real? Maxwell would never hook up with someone that naïve and that nervous. It had to be an act.

As he worked, it started drizzling. The soft rain felt cool on his face and eased some of the heat strumming through his veins. Using exertion to dispel the rest of the tension now tightening in his groin, he got the water really flowing to fill the pot, relieved the well wasn't dry as it sometimes was this late in the year.

Since it had taken a few minutes, his self-appointed task, along with the drizzle, had done what he'd intended. Once again, he was under control. But when he headed back inside, one thought stuck in his mind. This was going to be a long, frustrating night.

Josh shoved the door open with his shoulder and stepped into the large room. He used his foot to kick the door shut behind him, while carrying the heavy pot with both hands.

"How we comin'?"

"Fine. How hard is it to open two cans," Cat said.

Walking past her, he ignored how the sound of her soft laughter grabbed at his gut. Without looking her way, his attention stayed on igniting the stove's pilot light. He worked harder still to ignore the warmth emanating from her voice when she spoke.

"I've decided you're right."

"Oh?" he asked, finally succumbing to the urge to sneak a peek at her while she emptied the cans' contents into the pans he'd put out earlier.

"We do have everything we need right here."

Wrong thing to do, he thought, glancing back at the stove. It wasn't enough that her voice and laughter clenched his gut. The sight of her was too much for his system to ignore.

Her disheveled appearance—windblown hair, fresh, clean face, made more innocent because of a lack of makeup, and wearing an oversized T-shirt hanging over shorts showing off shapely legs that ended with sexy bare feet—told him exactly what she'd look like in the morning after waking. The only thing missing was the satisfied expression he knew would be there after a night spent making love with him.

Damn, he thought, shaking the mental picture his mind tenaciously clung to. He had to get his errant thoughts back on track. Having finished his task, he leaned against the stove. Risking another glance toward her, he asked, hoping his words would do the trick, "So, how'd you hook up with Brad Maxwell? You don't seem to be his type."

Cat's smile died as she squared her shoulders. Her movements became clipped and full of irritation as she emptied sauce into a pan, then picked up the can of green beans to open.

Good! This Cat he could handle.

"I'm not a pilot groupie, whatever that is." She glared at him and he bit down hard to keep from smiling. Every muscle in her body was taut and heat flared from her eyes, contrasting with their cool blue color.

"So, you're not dating him because he's a pilot?" Josh asked, still holding on to his smile as it tugged at the edges of his mouth.

When pink infused her face, he did smile. "Never play poker. You'd lose all your money."

"Are you back to being a jerk?"

"Honey, I never left the ballpark. I am a jerk. And the fact that you're dating Brad because he's a pilot makes you a groupie." His attention returned to the stove. He lit a burner and placed the big pot of water over the flames. "There have been quite a few of them parading through the school since he started working at Buchannan Aeronautics last year," he added, leaving out details about the two groupies besides her who Maxwell was also currently impressing. It wouldn't be so bad if one or two of Brad's women actually went past the first few lessons. Josh had mentioned his concerns, not comfortable with what seemed a lack of seriousness considering what flying entailed. Still, Maxwell was a good pilot, if a bit self-absorbed, and the lessons the women did take added to the school's profitability, as Smitty had pointed out when Josh had complained to him.

"Point taken," she said through clenched teeth, grabbing both pans and coming up next to him. She slammed them on the burners, then moved to sit at the table, ignoring him.

"What? You concede so easily, Powder Puff? The least you can do is strive for a halfhearted denial."

"Why bother denying it when you're right. I'm using Brad to learn to fly."

"Why do I believe there's more to this story?" he said, shaking his head and picking up a spoon.

"Don't you think you're getting a little personal?"

"Maybe. But we're sharing a room, so I'm bound to." He stirred each pot on the stove and adjusted the heat under the two smaller pots. After placing lids on them, he pulled out a chair, straddled it, plopped his elbows on the back, and fought another amused smile. When she instinctively scooted her chair away from him, his grin broke free. Unable to stop the words from popping out, he added, "Feel free to get personal back."

"Jerk," she said.

"So we've established." When she didn't say anything further, just sat staring at the floor, he sighed, stood, and went to check on the water. It was beginning to boil. He added spaghetti to the bubbling contents, adjusted the heat, and stirred the pot. "Come on, Cat. Tell me more about you and Brad and learning to fly." He turned around and leaned against the counter. Keeping his gaze on her, he crossed both arms and legs.

"Why? You've made your point."

He gave a half shrug. "We need something to talk about. Otherwise, it's going to be a long, boring night." When she ignored him again, he pushed. "You're a contradiction. On one hand, you're the perfect, spoiled princess, no different than Maxwell's other princesses. But the more I'm around you, I realize that's only an illusion you seem to want to instill. Why is that? What are you hiding?"

She rolled her eyes and glanced at the ceiling, looking as if she was mentally counting to ten.

"I'm not hiding anything," she said, blowing her pale blonde bangs with a slow breath, at the same time drumming her fingers on the table. "My life's hardly worth the effort of your questions."

"How'd you meet Brad?" When the look she gave him clearly said, "What do you care?" his grin was quick. "Call me a nosy jerk."

She snorted.

His eyebrows lifted. "So?"

"It's no big secret. Smitty. He'd been dating my best friend, Cheryl, for a couple of weeks when he introduced us. Smitty told me Brad was a pilot—a flight instructor." She met his gaze. "Brad's a lot of fun and I like him, which is why I went out with him, but I can't deny I was thinking of learning to fly at the time, so I picked his brain to find out more."

"Why'd you want to learn to fly?" he asked distractedly, draining the noodles.

Dinner was almost ready.

"It was Smitty's idea." She moved to set the table, adding over her shoulder while he finished with the spaghetti, "I'd been talking about doing something different for a long time. Something courageous. Something I would never do in a million years."

He glanced at her, giving her his best *no way he believed that* look. She shrugged. "The main reason I went out with Brad in the first place was because he was a pilot and I knew he could help me achieve my goal."

"You make it sound so impersonal," he said, divvying the food onto plates. He picked them up and started for the table. "Aren't you two an item?" Maxwell was good at juggling women, good at making a powder puff think she was "the one," though she was usually one of two or three.

"We date," Cat replied. But the words were cold and the warmth had gone out of her eyes, leaving a closed wall behind.

"You date?"

"You don't have to pretend. I know what he's like."

"What he's like?" he asked, already knowing the answer. That she did too, floored him.

"Come on. It's no secret. He's not the most faithful man."

"Since you know his character so well and seem so disapproving, why are you still dating him?"

"Brad's okay and we have an understanding." She cleared her throat and shoved a lock of hair behind her ear. "If you must know, I'm not into a relationship with him or anyone. At this point, I guess you could say he's a means to an end."

"Really?" Cat Tyler was definitely a contradiction and the more he was in her company, the more he was finding that out.

"Yeah. I do like him, but he's not exactly my idea of a keeper," she said, studying her fingernails. "And he's helping me get my pilot's license, but that's it."

Josh nodded.

For the rest of the meal, both ate in silence, the muted sounds of utensils hitting plates the only noise intruding on the quiet.

Once the dishes were done, he sat and watched Cat test her jeans for moisture and turn them.

Now what?

"They're almost dry." She glanced his way. "What do we do now?" she asked, voicing his thoughts.

"I guess we should try and get some sleep. Tomorrow may be a long day." He looked over at the bed, which seemed to grow in the large room. His gaze traveled back to her. "The cabin isn't insulated. It's getting colder outside and there's only one blanket." When she gave him a rounded, wide-eyed stare, he cleared his throat and swallowed hard. "We're adults here and should be able to be reasonable. Do you think we could share the bed?"

Cat's pacing increased and she wouldn't meet his gaze, too preoccupied with checking her clothes a second time. He could tell his words upset her. Hell, he wasn't exactly thrilled with the idea.

"Look, since you already have a low opinion of me, you should know I'm really not willing to sleep on the floor without the blanket. The planks aren't tight and I can feel the cold air coming up from the ground right now. That'll leave you with no blanket," he said, shocking the hell out of himself because he'd had the guts to voice his thoughts aloud. However, he was on a roll and decided to continue. "It seems the best solution would be to conserve heat. The fire won't stay lit all night and it'll only get colder in here. Besides, we'll be fully clothed. You said it yourself...your jeans are almost dry."

She stopped and looked back at him. Her expression was torn. She chewed on her bottom lip, eyeing him thoughtfully. Though he'd usually been able to read her thoughts before, he had no clue what was going through her mind just then. He only knew that whatever it was, she was waging a fierce mental battle.

"You promise to be a gentleman?"

He bit back a smile. Damn, the woman amused him. "Of course." Josh nodded. "I'd never force myself on anyone who doesn't want me."

Okay, now what, he wondered, as another blush stole up her face.

I need air, that's what, he thought. He jumped out of his chair and grabbed the big pan. "I'm going to get more water and scout around outside. Make sure things are safe."

At the door, he turned back. "What?" he asked, when she stood there staring at him.

"You're sweet." Her eyes glowed with warmth.

"I thought I was a jerk." He opened the door and stepped out into the dark night, while ignoring the way everything about her— her expression, her spirit, her words—twisted his gut into a knot. Nor did he miss her parting shot, which earned another quick grin.

"Of course you are, but you're still sweet."

He sauntered across the porch and stopped at the railing. His smile faded somewhat while he scanned the wet darkness for unseen threats in the brush beyond.

Working slowly, he pumped the water, then made a pit stop. After that, he walked the perimeter several times, delaying the inevitable moment he'd have to return to the cramped room.

The cabin was elevated slightly with high windows that were difficult to reach from the outside. Thick green shrubs on three sides of the structure made the crawl space underneath inaccessible, plus it wouldn't be easy to place a ladder below the windows. Although unnoticeable, the cabin had been built with security in mind. The weakest point was the front entrance with the flammable propane tank next to the porch steps. The open area leading to the porch was all gravel. A good thing, thought Josh. He picked up a handful of the small rocks and spread them along the steps. Any unaware intruder would kick them, making noise.

"Just being cautious." The sound of kicked pebbles would be enough to wake him.

He sighed and trekked up the stairs, wiping his sweaty palms on his pants. "Stop it," he muttered softly, clutching the door handle. "Get a grip, Buc."

She's only a woman. This is Powder Puff you're thinking about. Nothing's changed. Cat's simply an irritating bit of fluff. Okay! She's not fluff, but you can handle her and you can handle a night without losing it.

Josh sucked in a big gulp of air and let it out slowly, then repeated his words to himself a handful of times before opening the door and walking purposefully inside.

Cat, pacing nervously, had changed into dry jeans. He must have made a noise because she spun around as if he'd startled her. Josh ambled further into the room without speaking, eventually setting the big pan on a burner. He lit it. "Once this heats up, we can wash off the dirt of the day."

"Where's the bathroom?"

"There's an outhouse outside, not too far from the porch." He grabbed a flashlight from his bag. "Here, take this so you don't hurt yourself."

"Thanks."

During her lengthy absence, he washed, stoked and added more logs to the fire, and was already lying on the bed with his eyes closed when she re-entered the room.

Josh sat up and watched her turn off the remaining lantern. She appeared much more relaxed while she hurriedly washed in the firelight. Once done, she glanced over and caught him staring.

Warmth radiated from her expression. "I feel better. Thanks for the water."

"Come on," he urged, invitingly patting the spot next to him. "You should try and get some sleep. Morning will be here too soon."

She walked toward him. "For some reason I can't explain, I feel very safe climbing into bed with you."

The deep breath Josh had just inhaled stuck at the back of his throat as he clenched his fists. Then, giving her his back while she got comfortable beside him, he pretended not to notice how her total acceptance affected him. He felt rather than saw her head settle onto the soft pillow. She let out a contented sigh, and judging from her even breathing, was sound asleep within minutes.

Josh left the bed to spread his pebbles. Afterward, he lay awake for lingering moments, trying to ignore the way her soft body curled into his. Finally, he let out a frustrated breath and punched the pillow, moving effectively away from her heat.

୧

Cat woke with a start. Someone's hand covered her mouth. Confusion and fear engulfed her for a brief moment.

Where was she? It was dark. Moonlight filtered into the room, yet nothing seemed familiar among the shadows. She turned on the bed and everything came back to her as Josh released her mouth. He placed a finger to his lips. Silently, she nodded. When he motioned for her to get her bag and put on her shoes, she nodded again.

The bed squeaked softly as she stepped into her shoes, and tied up the laces with trembling fingers. Once done, she glanced at him. Her breath caught. Her lungs wouldn't inflate. Her heart rate sped up and the beating was so loud, she was sure he could hear it. Everything about his body shouted at her, alerting her. Josh's features were taut with tension. His movements were those of a stalking cat preparing for a kill.

When he signaled for her to follow him, she moved quickly with her heart in her throat to an open trapdoor near the corner of the cabin. How did he know about the door?

He motioned for her to go down.

Oh God, she thought, as she climbed into the cramped, dark space. What was going on?

In moments, he was behind her.

Single file, they crawled to the edge of the cabin around wood, stacked high, with just enough space for a body to squeeze through.

"When I give the signal," he whispered. "You run to those trees and keep going. You got that?" He stopped for a moment, listening. And then he added, "I put a compass in your bag. If for some reason we get split up, run due east. Eventually, you'll hit a main road. Okay?"

She nodded again, fighting to keep fear from overwhelming her.

Next thing she knew, he pushed her out, saying softly, "Go. And don't stop."

Following his instructions, she was up and out in a swift movement. She ran as fast as she could. Not knowing why. Only knowing that Josh's fervent commands wouldn't let her slow despite the snow beneath her feet. The thumping of her heartbeat increased with every step and pounded out of control.

Please Lord, she prayed. Don't let us get separated.

Heaven only knew what would happen if they did.

In the next instant, Josh was next to her, grabbing her hand and pulling her faster.

The temperature had dropped dramatically during the night. A few snowflakes floated on the air, dancing their way to the ground. Blood pumped furiously through Cat's system, keeping her warm for the moment because she was keeping up with Josh. How long before the cold seeped into her bones?

They hadn't gone more than a quarter of a mile when all of a sudden the night exploded.

"Oh God, we're going to die," she said, unable to stop the sheer terror from sounding in her tone.

"No, Cat. I won't let you die. But we've got to keep moving," he urged.

His words brought some calm until she looked back through the trees. The orange and yellow flames of the burning cabin spread an eerie light into the darkness.

Panic filled her. She turned to Josh Buchannan. His intent expression, focused on the dark terrain in front of them, told her she probably wouldn't get a response. But she asked anyway.

"Who are you?" she demanded in wide-eyed awe, her voice full of panic.

Chapter 7

"Who are you?" Cat repeated, as a déjà vu feeling swept over her. "What's going on?"

With yesterday's same determined expression plastered on his face, Josh ignored her questions as if she hadn't asked them. Nor did he slow his steady pace, resolutely pulling her behind him. Since it was clear she wouldn't get answers, she kept up.

Flecks of morning light began peeking out from the darkness, making their trek through the woods easier as they could now see the terrain. Eventually, the sun made a full appearance, added some warmth, and melted the freshly fallen snow where it hit. But a muddy trail that impeded their progress was the result when the sunshine slipped back into hiding as dark clouds filled the sky.

When a cramp dug into her side, Cat stopped suddenly and pulled out of Josh's grip. Her patience had dwindled, along with her ability to catch her breath.

She stood glaring at him, breathing heavily, and rubbing her side. "I'm cold, and I'm tired of running." All the frustration that had built since the crash came out in her voice. "And I want an explanation. No, I deserve one." She crossed her arms. "I'm not going another step until I get one."

Josh snorted. "It appears someone doesn't like my methods of instructing." He paused. "You'd be my first suspect, except you're with me."

"This isn't funny." Cat dropped her hands to her side, balling her fingers into fists, as he nonchalantly moved to sit on a fallen log as if he were on a Sunday stroll rather than running for his life from cabins and planes exploding around them. "What's going on? Are you some kind of agent?" She stomped toward him, dying to take a shot. "I don't appreciate you treating me as if I'm an idiot."

"I've never taken you for an idiot." He began rummaging

through his bag, eventually finding his water. He took a big gulp, drinking half the bottle before wiping his mouth with the back of his hand. "A self-absorbed princess maybe, but not a stupid, self-absorbed princess."

"Quit being such a jerk for one minute and answer my questions."

Remaining mute, he viewed her through narrowed eyes, searching, as if those answers were hidden deep beneath the surface of her features. Yet, the entire time he stared, his expression revealed nothing of his thoughts.

"Who are you? Did the plane really explode because of a fuel leak?" Another flare of annoyance burst from within. She ground her teeth and tightened a fist by her side. What was it about this particular man who attracted her one minute, and the next made her so angry that all she wanted to do was get in one good shot? At some point, she knew her patience would snap and she'd clip him. Clenching and unclenching her fingers, she took several deep breaths. Right now, answers were more important than satisfaction. "Why did the cabin blow up?"

"I'm not sure," he finally said. He expelled a slow breath and rubbed the back of his neck. "I have a theory, but nothing concrete. All I know is someone's tried to kill me. Twice. I'm trying to stay alive." Then he glanced back at the landscape with such intense concentration. He was clearly looking for someone or something. Eventually, his eyes refocused on hers and he displayed an apologetic half smile. "Since you're with me and you're caught up in all of this, I'm trying to keep you alive at the same time."

The fact that he was talking deflated her anger somewhat. She sat down next to him. "What happened to the plane?"

"I now doubt the carb heater malfunction was an accident. We were meant to go down, so that the plane I assumed was our rescue could blow it up with us still inside."

Someone tried to kill them! Cat absorbed this piece of news stoically while her tummy did somersaults. Dear God, why had she asked? She swallowed her fear, took a deep breath, and glanced at him. Her gaze narrowed as she studied his face. His blank look was impossible to read.

"If they thought we were dead, then why blow up the cabin?"

He took his time formulating an answer. Finally, he shrugged. "Somehow they found out they didn't finish the job, is my best guess."

"How? Why?"

"Good questions." He sighed and rubbed a hand over his unshaven face, drawing her attention to his rugged features. Rumpled and with bed head suited him. Liam McIntyre came to mind. Appearing every bit the legendary warrior, Josh could easily step off the *Spartacus* set. "I think this involves what I stumbled upon a few days ago. Someone's been using my planes for some kind of drop-offs. Drugs, most likely."

"Drugs?" Not what she expected to hear.

"Yeah," he said, nodding. "Given our proximity to the Canadian border, my interference could likely screw up their operation. Dealers tend to be violent when protecting their turf."

"How'd you know the cabin was going to blow and how'd you know about the trapdoor?" she asked, pushing away thoughts of some crazy drug czar trying to kill them.

"The cabin belongs to a friend. I'm a light sleeper and I woke up to someone setting a little surprise. The space we crawled into is usually full of wood to keep it dry and free of snow."

He swigged another long gulp of water. "Being prepared is my motto. Something I learned early on. Once acquired, it's a hard habit to break." He broke off and stared into the horizon. "Of course, whoever is responsible probably doesn't know we escaped and that fact is keeping us alive for the moment."

"For the moment?" Cat gaped at him. "You really think we're still in danger?"

"Yeah. Until I figure out who's targeting me and can stop it, we're in danger."

Cat didn't want to think about drugs and targets and danger and planes and cabins exploding. She bent to search through her bag, working to contain her fear. Josh Buchannan wouldn't let her die. And she had to admit, she felt safe with him. Sticking with him was her best option. When she fingered her water, she sat upright, yanking it out of the bag.

"What about the authorities?" Cat asked, uncapping the bottle. "Shouldn't we notify them?"

"Be my guest. Do you see any rangers or cops out here? We're not exactly in downtown Manhattan."

"Jerk," she muttered, rolling her eyes.

Josh grunted. "Some things never change." He stood. "We need to keep moving. Cloud cover is dropping and it's turning ugly. With the temperatures slightly above freezing, rain won't make hiking fun. By my calculations, we've got at least twenty miles of national forest to climb through till we can get to the road we want." He reached for her. "Come on."

"Wait," she protested, attempting to pull out of his firm grip. "You never answered my last question. Who are you?"

"You know who I am, Cat." Josh gripped her hand tighter and kept moving.

She shot back a huffy, "No, I don't."

"Yes, you do," he said in an amused voice. "I'm the jerk who's saving your gorgeous butt. Now move!"

"You got that right," she said through clenched teeth, wishing she didn't enjoy the warmth spreading up her arm from the contact of their joined hands.

Chapter 8

"Wait up," Brad Maxwell yelled to Joel Smith as his car door slammed shut.

"Sure." Smitty stopped near the double glass doors of Buchannan Aeronautics. "Have you heard anything more about Cat or Josh?" he asked as Brad caught up to him. "Authorities are hopeful of survivors and have begun searching for the crash site."

"Yeah." Brad sighed. "We should've heard something from them by now, though. I'm praying they didn't die on impact."

Smitty didn't say anything for a long moment as a sad expression flitted over his face. "I know him. Josh would have made contact." He grabbed the door and waited while Brad entered. "It's wishful thinking to believe they made it out alive after this long without any word."

Once inside, both men glanced at the two men standing at the counter talking to Bill Anderson, another pilot who worked with them.

"Are there any other questions?" Bill asked.

Smitty reached the trio. "What's going on?"

"No. We're done. We'll get in touch with you if we need anything further," the shorter, stockier man, said, ignoring Smitty's question to write in his notebook. The man carried at least fifty pounds on his belly. His looks had started to deteriorate, most likely from bad living habits. The other guy was a good six inches taller and much leaner. Laurel and Hardy, the comedy team of late night cable TV, came to mind as Smitty observed them.

The shorter man flashed his badge. "Special Agent Hank McMann and my partner, Special Agent Frank Adams. We're questioning all Buchannan Aeronautics employees. I take it you two work here?" He gave each of them a once-over before flipping a page in his notebook and cocking an eyebrow at Smitty. "And you would be?"

"Joel Smith. We're both flight instructors, but I'm Buc's partner," Smitty answered amicably, moving to the other side of the counter. "What's this about, Special Agent McMann? Have you found Buc?"

"You're referring to Joshua Buchannan?" When Smitty nodded, he said, "Not yet. We're still asking questions."

"Why? I thought we were quite thorough in our report. Flight operations have been suspended for the time being." He picked up the clipboard that held the day's canceled schedule before refocusing on the agent's steely gaze. "We'd like a few answers ourselves."

"We're following up…doing all we can," McMann said in a dismissive manner. He turned to Brad with the same expectant expression and waited until Brad offered his name.

"When will you know something?" Smitty struggled to maintain a pleasant tone of voice.

"Don't know." McMann grunted. "Investigating takes time. You gotta minute?"

"As a matter of fact I do, since we've rescheduled lessons." Smitty put the clipboard back on the counter and gave a careless shrug. "But Brad's only here in the mornings, so I can wait."

"Sure." McMann nodded to Brad. "Let's step over here."

Brad followed the two agents to the chairs and sofa in the lounge area across from the counter.

While they were talking, Smitty's gaze went to the young woman manning the counter. "Hi, Livie. How are you holding up?"

"I'm okay," Olivia Jenson said, giving him a sad smile. Then her smile faded. Tears clouded her eyes. "Did you hear about Gloria? She was traveling too fast, hit a slick spot on the road, and lost control."

"Geez. I didn't know. Is she okay?"

Livie shook her head, losing the battle against crying. "Apparently she died on impact and her car caught fire." A tear broke loose and trickled down the left side of her face.

"Gloria's dead?" His and Buc's office manager was dead? He stared at her open-jawed, completely stunned. "It's unbelievable! Have you talked to her family?"

"No. A friend called in this morning. Senseless accident. Mr. Goodman's not well, so her death can't be good for him."

Smitty reached out and gripped her shoulder, giving it a

comforting squeeze. "I'll stop by later to see what we can do and offer my condolences." He let go. "Such a tragedy."

Livie nodded and glanced at him with hopeful expectation. "Have you heard anything more about Mr. Buchannan?"

"Not since early this morning. According to the last report from the Civil Air Patrol, they've begun searching for the wreckage. I'm sure they'll keep us posted," he said, trying to sound encouraging, but failing miserably. He headed for the coffee machine, busying himself with pouring a cup of coffee, uncomfortable with her sadness, as well as the false hope he caught in her eyes.

"So, you're part owner?" Agent Adams, the quieter of the two men, asked Smitty an hour later. "Tell us what happens when you close up for the night."

Narrowing his gaze, Smitty watched Adams. Amazing! The guy actually had a voice. The tall, slender man—almost gawky in his movements—had carrot red hair and washed-out green eyes. Taking in the agent's sunken cheeks and sullen features, he wondered what his life was like. Obviously, pretty boring.

"What has me being part owner or how we close up have to do with Buc's crash?" he asked, not bothering to hide his irritation. He owned ten percent of the company and he didn't like what they were insinuating. They were fishing for information. Why?

"We're interested in anyone who has access to the planes after hours," Agent McMann interjected calmly.

"There're no set rules. Whoever is here has access and brings the last plane into the hangar."

"So, there's plenty of access after hours?"

Snorting, Smitty shrugged. "Why would anyone want access?"

"You tell me."

"I have no idea." Smitty met McMann's hard gaze. "I'm not sure what you're getting at, but we all have keys to the building. It's a small operation. Buc trusts us and we trust him."

"So, the planes are accessible after hours and anyone with a key to the building can access them. Correct?"

"Yeah. When you put it like that, it sounds like something sinister is going on." Smitty's attention stayed on McMann, scrutinizing his expression before staring at Adams. Unable to read anything in either face, he let out a slow breath. "Do you think Buc's crash might not have been an accident?"

Still wearing a blank expression, McMann lifted one shoulder in a careless shrug. "I don't know. You tell me."

Smitty laughed and shook his head. "You guys can't be for real." His forced laughter died off and he wondered, not for the first time that day, who sent them and why.

Chapter 9

Cat and Josh kept on the move, climbing at a deliberate pace for hours. On the downhill the going was easier, but Cat noticed Josh didn't increase their speed. When they came to a stream, he slowed, leading her to a fallen log.

"This is a good place to rest, drink some water, and eat something." He released her hand and pivoted, thoroughly surveying the landscape. "But we can't stay too long. Those clouds don't look promising."

"I'm not complaining." Cat glanced around and rubbed her arms, shivering. Though frozen from the outside in, her legs were starting to feel like melting, wiggly Jell-O. "How much further? Do you think it's okay to stop? Are we safe?" Fear slipped out in her voice. Great! Just what she needed—Josh Buchannan to see how scared she really was.

Halting his surveillance in midturn, he scanned her face. His muttered, "Shit," along with the concern spilling from his intense, dark gaze, made her realize she hadn't kept a tight enough rein on her emotions.

"Have I failed you yet, Cat? Stick with me and we'll be safe and sound in no time. I promise you."

Warmth filled her. Warmth she needed to ignore. "I could use a break." Cat certainly didn't like the heat building within her system that those bedroom eyes elicited, allowing her to forget for the moment how wretched she felt. "But I do have one question, Bucman."

Cat plopped down on the log, wishing her insides would quit burning from just a look. "What are we going to eat?"

"Check your bag." Josh sat beside her.

She stared at him suspiciously, then opened her bag. Four breakfast bars she hadn't noticed earlier peeked up at her.

"My, my. Imagine that. You're just a regular boy scout," she said, only too happy to have something to focus on beside him. She pulled out one of the bars and concentrated on tearing off the wrapper.

"I told you, being prepared is my motto," he said, watching her eat.

Paying his amused indulgence no heed, she polished off one bar and then opened another, ravenous after hours of hoofing it over hill and dale. She took a bite and started chewing. After swallowing, she asked, "So, who are you, really?"

"An adult boy scout?" The innocent grin transformed his rugged, unshaven face from guarded wariness to boyish charm. He tore open a bar, bit off a chunk, and continued studying her with dark eyes that still held too much warmth.

"Yeah, right," she countered, looking purposefully at the ground as sparks shot through her system. Everything tingled where the sparks hit. A flush of heat washed over her before the sparks, tingles, and flush began anew.

After many calming, deep breaths, she refocused on her breakfast bar, taking slow, easy bites as it whittled away to nothing.

She stood, brushed her jeans, and picked up her water bottle. "So, you're not going to tell me who you really are?"

"Joshua Harrison Buchannan III, same name that's on my passport."

"Where have I heard that name before?" she said, wondering why he said passport and not driver's license. When she shot him a questioning glance, he stiffened and remained silent. Hmmm, even more interesting. With raised eyebrows, she waited.

Finally he relaxed, lifting his shoulders in a slight shrug. "My flight school's in the local news occasionally. Reporters are always using my full name, trying to connect me with my dad. But there is *no* connection, outside of him being a junior with the same name."

She cringed inwardly at the terse way he spoke of his namesake. Definitely something going on there. But who was she to cast stones when she had her own parental issues? And considering her parents were dead, hers would never be resolved.

"That's not it," she said, noting his now closed features. She downed half her water. "Somehow I sense you're hiding something."

"What about you? I could say the same."

"Me? I'm an open book. You said so yourself. I can't even play poker without giving myself away." Cat stopped talking and then laughed. "You're so good at that, you know?"

"Good at what?" The grin taking over his face could win over babies and old ladies alike, but not her.

"Moving the topic of conversation from you to me, which in my book is evasion, Buc-man. Now, what're you evading?"

"I've already given you my answer." He stood and set off for the spring, then crouched on his haunches to fill his water bottle.

"Really? You'll have to tell me again because I don't remember hearing an answer."

"I'm taking the Fifth."

"Oh, I get it. If you told me anything important, you'd have to kill me?" Cat teased, shaking her head. The man certainly had his evasion technique down.

"Something like that." Josh stayed crouched, letting the water gush into his bottle before he turned to watch her.

Ignoring the heat of his gaze, she came up next to him and followed his movements, being very cautious of the water this time. Suddenly it dawned on Cat that knowing next to nothing about him didn't bother her. She was alive and safe. Strange combination. She stole a quick look at Josh. What was it about him that made her feel those two things? Maybe that was the attraction.

When both bottles were filled, he stood. "Come on. We've rested enough. We should get moving."

"You're not going to tell me?" She threw out a disbelieving snort. "You expect me to follow you blindly through these woods without giving me any clue as to why?"

"I already told you why."

"But you're not telling me everything."

"I don't know everything."

"I don't believe you."

"That's your prerogative." Josh started off down the trail, leaving her no choice but to follow.

But Cat didn't follow. Instead, she stood rooted in place, watching him.

"Come on, we shouldn't linger. It looks as if it could start raining at any moment." When he turned back to her, finally noticing her hesitation, he cocked a brow. "Well? What are you waiting for?"

She sighed and rushed after him. How she'd love to read his

mind. Given that resolute expression, he wasn't about to divulge more, so she kept silent. Annoying or not, at least his pace was manageable, and despite having survived a harrowing experience and wondering why drug dealers would be after him, she had to admit she felt totally safe while with him.

They hiked for less than an hour before the drizzle started. The temperature dropped dramatically, causing them to increase their speed.

☙

Smitty looked up from the counter, spying Laurel and Hardy emerge from a dark government-issue Ford. Seconds later, the bell above the door tinkled when Agents McMann and Adams stepped inside.

"Anything more I can help you with?" He eyed the two suspiciously.

"We're still investigating. You told us this morning we could go through Buchannan's office. Then we'd like to talk with Brad Maxwell again."

"Maxwell's gone for the day, but I can give you his home address," Smitty offered. He nodded behind him, indicating a closed door. "Buc's office is right through there. Have at it." He went back to his computer screen. "If you need anything else, just shout."

McMann grunted his thanks and the two disappeared into the hallway.

Smitty waited until the two men closeted themselves in Buc's office before reaching for his cell phone. "Murph, it's me, Smitty. I'm following up on our earlier conversation. I think we have problems."

"Yeah? Whatcha got?"

"Those two Feds are nosing around again. They're not with the FAA or NTSB and I'm worried."

"No need to worry," Murphy said in a calm voice. "Like I told you this morning, it's under control."

"Why are they here and what are they looking for?"

"From what I can tell, Buc's call to his friend in Helena brought in those two. He suspects someone's been using the flight school's planes for illegal drug activity."

"Buc never mentioned it." Smitty glanced at the hallway. "I don't like it."

"Neither do I, but it's out of my jurisdiction. I told you, Buc thinks his accident was a result of his discovery, so we need to wait and see what the Feds come up with."

"Laurel and Hardy don't seem too competent. This has all the earmarks of a witch hunt. Something's not right. Their nosing around could blow my cover." Unlike Buc, who only fed information, Smitty was an agent working closely with Murphy, investigating more thoroughly anything Josh found suspicious, using his job as a flight instructor as a cover.

"We have no choice. I've got my orders. This has nothing to do with our current assignment." Murphy was head of a division for Homeland Security, whose main task entailed monitoring all flight schools in the country that came under closer scrutiny after 9/11. "I'm still waiting for Buc to check in," Murphy added. "I'll keep you posted. In the meantime, you keep your eye on those two agents. Make sure they don't screw anything up."

"Will do."

ଓ

McMann typed furiously at the keyboard attached to Buchannan's computer. After a few moments of digging through files, he sat back wearing a smug smile. "Well...well...well. Bank statements are telling me all we need to know. Josh Buchannan isn't as lily white as we thought."

Adams positioned himself behind McMann. "Hmm. Interesting. Those hefty deposits aren't accounted for. And his withdrawals match Maxwell's deposits. Fuckin' obvious. Guess he never thought anyone would bother looking."

"His past is a little murky. I'd say he's gotten his hands dirty in all that murky water. It's always the ones you don't suspect." McMann grabbed a thumb drive from a pile on the desk and copied the information. When done, he pocketed the drive and stood. "I think this gives us enough to dig deeper and clear up some of those questions. Grab the hard drive, Frank."

Nodding, Adams swiftly disconnected the computer, then picked it up.

As McMann headed out the door with Adams on his heels, he said, "Call Helena and have them send in a team, I want anything else that's on his computer. Buchannan's going down and I'm going to be the one to fell the bastard."

ଓ

It was late when Josh and Cat came upon another cabin, much larger and nicer than the quaint cabin the two had been forced to vacate. They'd hiked for most of the day in the cold, sporadic rain.

Josh stopped, and gave his usual thorough perusal of the area.

"Looks like a weekend getaway. What do you think?" Cat's voice held fatigue. Josh heard it as clearly as he heard her soft, weary sigh when she dropped her bag as if it weighed a hundred pounds. Her shoulders slumped. "I'm frozen and tired of walking. Do we have to keep going? You said it yourself. Whoever's after you thinks we're dead. They can't be following us."

Josh eyed Cat critically. Exhaustion lined her face. She was shivering and her lips were turning blue. Remorse shot through him at how hard he'd pushed her to keep moving. Admiration had long replaced disdain. She'd kept up and had done it without complaint.

"We have no choice but to stop. The place looks deserted." He bent to pick up her bag, threw it over a shoulder, and grabbed her hand. "Come on. Let's check it out. At this point, I'm ready to risk a B and E charge."

"B and E?" He smiled at the concern evident in her voice. "Oh my God, you're right. If no one's home, we really will be breaking and entering, won't we?"

His steps slowed. He glanced at her, meeting that cool blue gaze so full of fatigue, and flashed a toothy grin. "Yeah. But don't worry, it carries a lighter sentence for first-time offenders."

"Great! We're breaking into someone's house, and all you can do is joke."

He stopped, all humor vanishing instantly. "Would you rather keep going?" He really didn't see how she could go much further, especially given the nasty weather, but if she felt she could, so could he.

"No. I don't think I can."

"Then we have no choice but to use what's in front of us for survival," he said softly, while tugging on her hand to get her moving.

"The way our luck's been holding, we'll get arrested, and I'll have prison to worry about if I ever get out of this alive," she grumbled under her breath.

"Cat, you worry too much. We've come this far. We'll make it. See that?" he said, pointing to a dirt road.

Her eyes narrowed. "So?"

"It's a road, which leads to a main road and civilization." Suddenly, liquid bullets dropped haphazardly from the sky, slowly increasing in intensity. "But our journey to civilization will be delayed, due to the weather. Come on, we've come too far to get dumped on now."

He pulled her with him, his speed picking up as he broke into a run. They dashed to the covered front porch. Hitting the last step, Josh couldn't contain his triumphant laugh.

"See? Our luck's holding. We made it just as the heavens opened up. That's got to be a good omen."

Cat yanked out of his grip and rushed to the front door, turning the knob. She took a step back, then looked at Josh expectantly. "Well?"

Dropping his bags, he walked past her, reached above the door frame, and felt…nothing.

"Darn it," she expelled through shivering lips. "What are we going to do now? I'm so cold. All I want to do is get warm." She looked so pitiful and sounded so disappointed, his heart practically melted. "I'm freezing and all you can do is laugh?" Her chin went up, and she glared at him. "Answer my damn question. What do we do now?"

"I guess we break in," he teased, in an attempt to distract her from her misery.

When he noticed her back stiffen and her hand clench like she wanted to hit him, he grinned at how easy it had been.

"Well, hurry up and get it over with," Cat said impatiently, still glowering at him.

"You want me to do it?"

"Stop messing with me and open the damn door." She flexed her wet fingers, opening and closing them, before rubbing them together and blowing on them. "I'm sure you know how."

"No patience," Josh muttered, checking several places and coming up empty. He surveyed the porch. Next to the front door sat a large, dirt-filled clay pot. He looked underneath and voila! A key. After opening the door, he bowed. "Your castle awaits, my princess."

"See? I was right." She hurried past him, rubbing her arms in an exaggerated manner, but the delight in her voice told him she was as happy as he to have someplace in which to take a break and get warm.

Josh surveyed their new digs as she asked, "So, what are you? A spy, a drug dealer, or a cat burglar?"

A smile snuck out. "I can't divulge my secrets," he said distractedly. His grin widened at Cat's, "I know! If you did you'll have to kill me. Yeah…yeah…yeah."

Nice house, he thought, still sporting a smile as he walked through the big, open rooms with wall-to-wall windows that brought the outside in. With all the glass, it probably cost a fortune to heat. Obviously the person who owned this home had money. Though off the beaten path, the house had all the amenities, electricity and running water being the two most notable.

Okay, so we must be closer to civilization than I thought, he mused. That was good. He'd take out his GPS and get a direct reading later, once they both had a chance to clean up a bit.

A worried expression formed on Cat's face as she strode over to the windows, scanning the horizon. "Do you think we'll be safe here? Maybe we should keep going once the rain stops?"

"It doesn't look too promising." Silently, he came up behind her and ignored the fact that the sound of his voice made her jump. His gaze took in the windy, raging storm outside. "Once it gets dark, it'll probably turn to snow. We're better off staying put for the time being. No one knows we made it out alive. I'm sure that fact will keep us safe."

"We've certainly picked a nice place to stop." She swept around in a three-sixty, giving a low whistle. "Pretty cool digs for a cabin in the woods, wouldn't you say?"

Josh nodded, keeping his focus on the storm, searching the vast forest beyond.

"These people really rough it." She ambled over to the plush sofa and plopped down. "I hope they don't mind that we're using it."

"I ask myself if it were mine and someone was in the same situation we're in, would I mind?" Josh spoke while turning away from the window. He quickly began an inspection of the house, walking through the kitchen, rummaging around, opening cabinets as well as doors as he went.

"I like the way your brain works, Buc-man. Right now, I'm just too cold and tired to feel guilty for using someone else's house."

"I'll write a brief note before we head out in the morning and leave some cash for the convenience and anything we use. As long as we leave it like we found it, that should work," he called to her from the other room. His voice broke off until he returned to the living room. "Water's on now. I found the power box and there's a switch for the water heater. Hopefully, we'll have hot water in no time. Thermostat for heat's set at fifty. I turned it up to sixty-eight."

"Sounds good," Cat murmured before moving her attention to the coffee table. She picked up the remote, waving it. "Look...TV." She hit the On button.

"How nice! That'll come in handy," Josh replied, coming to stand next to her.

"All the comforts of home." Cat flipped through the channels. "I think this has more stations than I get. Of course, I don't have satellite."

"You wanna check out the rest of the house with me? Stake out your territory, so to speak?" Josh lifted both his and Cat's bags and said over his shoulder, as she turned off the TV and stood to follow him, "You should get out of your damp things. Water for a shower should be hot in about fifteen minutes."

Chapter 10

"At least we picked a house with two bedrooms for our foray into crime," Josh said to Cat, after checking out the second bedroom on their quick tour.

"Having hot, running water is worth a prison stint. I don't think I'll ever get warm."

He left her to change out of her wet clothes, then waited until he heard the shower running before heading for the front door. Once outside, he pulled the satellite phone from his bag. His eyes scanned the scenery, slowly moving over the trees in front of him. Then his attention centered on his phone and he punched in a preset number.

"Murph here. That you, Buc?"

"Yeah. Had another incident. Someone's trying awfully hard to send me to a fiery death."

"Christ. I thought you said you had it under control?"

"I do." Josh grunted. He leaned against the wooden post and let out a long, slow breath, listening to the soft drumming of rain pounding on the metal roof above him. "I'm alive, aren't I? And so is my student. We've found another haven for the night. We'll make it out of here tomorrow. I want whoever is responsible to relax and think he's succeeded for the time being."

"All you have to do is say the word and my men are there."

"Yeah, I know, but this has become personal." Josh rubbed the back of his neck and searched the horizon. "I don't take kindly to someone trying to kill me."

"Now I remember why they call you Buc. Always bucking the system. You know, we've always frowned upon agents taking undue risk."

Josh ignored the comment and asked, "Do you have anything to report?"

"A couple of things," Murphy answered. "First, two Feds are

nosing around due to your earlier call to your friend. From what I gather, their investigation has generated enough probable cause to interest DEA. Meth labs have been popping up all over rural America, which in itself is enough to cause Washington a few headaches, but the problem's spread out of control and now the labs' funding has become a concern. Rednecks in trailers aren't the only ones burning this shit. Intelligence suggests dozens of recently closed labs in pockets across the US were set up using outside money. Big money. My guess is they're trying to make some connection to your flight school."

"A few flights over the border? That's their connection?" Josh rolled his eyes. "Sounds like something a higher-up in the alphabet soup would concoct to justify his position. I damn sure don't need two gung-ho Feds or DEA chasing after nonexistent evidence to prove weak theories, and scaring my quarry away before I figure out what's what."

Murphy's chuckle shot through his ear. "They're federal agents, not incompetents, on the same side, you know. Working for the same goal. You and Smitty take this rivalry shit too seriously."

Josh only grunted.

"Anyway, I doubt they'll alert your quarry while they chase their tails. Plane crash aids in their cover. Different agencies, different initials, but same look."

"Good." He walked the length of the porch, then turned and resumed walking.

"Smitty's as worried as you about those two Feds. Calls them witch hunters and doesn't like them digging through your files. To be honest, I don't like it either."

"You're the one who believes they're competent, which means they'd be thorough."

"Yeah, maybe."

"What else?" Josh asked, brushing off his concern. He had nothing to hide.

"Did a little digging on some of the names you sent in your last report."

"Find anything?"

"I'm not sure. Brad Maxwell has been making large deposits to his bank account. He's definitely my candidate for involvement in any kind of drug operation. But here's something you might find even more interesting. About your student, Candace Angela Tyler."

"Cat? What about her?"

"She's divorced now, using her maiden name."

"Really?" Cat seemed too prudish to have an ex. The woman definitely had inconsistencies.

"She's the daughter of Vivian and Preston York Tyler. Both now deceased. Her wealthy, nutty parents were missionaries, who tried to save the world. They were killed by friendly fire four years ago in Afghanistan while helping refugees."

"Missionaries? Cat's parents were missionaries?" And now he had his answer to her inconsistencies. So, which woman is the real Cat? The naïve, almost Victorian prude, or the vixen who put him in his place during her first flight.

"You might remember them as Brother and Sister Tyler. The girl's formerly known as Candace Zinger. Ring any bells?"

"Christ." Stunned, he stopped in midstep. "She's that Candace Zinger, related to those Tylers?"

"Yeah. You were in charge of the unit responsible for the friendly fire, Buc. Your last mission."

Of course. Why hadn't he immediately made the connection? Too much coincidence to be merely chance that brought her to his flight school. "Do you think she knows?"

"Your guess is as good as mine. Lives with an elderly aunt. Her parents' trust fund left her well off and she has connections, so she has the means to find out."

"Shit." A sense of dread threaded through his stomach and formed a knot.

"Could she be involved in the recent happenings?" Murphy's question was already roaming around in his brain.

"I don't know. It's unlikely, since she's the student I went down with." Was she so open about Maxwell not being a keeper, hoping to divert his attention? "What a nightmare." Josh rubbed his temple, thinking and remembering, though the incident had been something he'd spent too long trying to forget. "Maybe she thinks I was responsible for her parents' deaths as so many in the group of missionaries did." Was Cat working with Maxwell to exact revenge for her parents' deaths?

Thoughts of that day four years ago raced through his mind. Hell, he'd tried to keep them alive, but when Sister Tyler, bent on playing hero, stepped in front of a woman wired with explosives right as a sniper took his shot, the fanatic who'd been spared the sniper's bullet self-detonated. The Tylers had taken the brunt of the explosion before the crazy woman—all in the name of Allah—could reach her main target, a school full of children run by American missionaries.

What a tragic, horrible day. All those deaths, including Cat's parents, were ultimately his responsibility.

"Maybe you should give me your coordinates. I'll send someone to pick you up," Murphy said.

Josh shook his head. "No, I'm safe for now."

"That answer worries me." Murphy's voice was full of concern. "I've done more checking and your student's affiliated with several sympathetic, questionable groups. Gives generously to their causes."

"Don't worry." He couldn't stop, not now when things were heating up. "I'm going with instinct. This is related to my discovery, which has to be tied into some kind of drug operation. Not to the FBI's extent, but I'm betting whoever's responsible thinks I'm dead. I plan on letting them think they succeeded." Josh shrugged. "Now that you've warned me, I'll be more cautious."

"Go!" Murphy practically yelled. "Do it your way for the time being. But keep me posted. Check back with me later tonight. Since the girl's a lead, I'm still digging for more information."

Josh nodded. "Good. It pays to be careful."

"So I've been told. Take care, Buc."

"I plan on it." Josh cut the connection. While storing his equipment, his mind spun. Was Cat involved? He had no clue, but he sure as hell didn't believe in coincidences, so he had to take the connection seriously. Damn, this definitely wasn't racking up to being one of his better weeks.

He turned when the door behind him opened.

"Shower's free. What're you doing out here?" Cat demanded teasingly. Offering a small smile, she stepped onto the porch.

"Just checking." Josh ignored the tightening of his gut her smile generated.

"I'm hungry. How 'bout you? I'm not a whiz in the kitchen, but I noticed eggs in the fridge and bread in the freezer. I think I can manage that while you shower."

"Sure," he said, moving quickly past her.

"Josh?"

"What?" He stopped and spun around, not making eye contact. Now that he knew about her parents, somehow he couldn't meet her gaze without revealing his guilt.

Shit. This was un-fricking-believable.

"You okay? Did something happen?"

Josh sighed at the confusion in her voice. "Everything's fine," he said softly. He turned to go back inside and added over his shoulder, "I'm going to shower. I'll be out in a bit."

❧

Cat watched Josh's receding back, wondering what was going through his mind. It bothered her that he wouldn't look her in the eye. Even harder was admitting to missing the warmth so readily present in his expression during much of the day when he looked at her.

Did Josh know she found him attractive? Was that his concern? She leaned against the railing. He obviously found her amusing, but she couldn't stomach the thought of his amusement changing to indulgent pity.

Staring at the torrential rain hitting the ground, she shook her head. No, all day long, she'd kept her attraction hidden, so it had to be something else.

Maybe they weren't as safe as he'd led her to believe. Maybe there was something he wasn't telling her, like maybe someone was after them again. Oh God! Her mind raced in overtime on maybes—imagining all sorts of things—unknown assailants coming out of the woodwork the most prevalent.

"Stop it," Cat mentally chastised. You've always been too afraid of life. You want to change and stop feeling afraid. Look at this as an adventure. You're secluded in the wilderness with a hunky specimen. And though he's got a jerky side, he also makes you feel alive and safe. This is a perfect opportunity to set your words into action. Put your money where your mouth is and quit playing lip service to the thought.

"Buck up and enjoy it. No pun intended," she murmured under her breath, intent on obeying her mental prodding. "Quit worrying about what-ifs."

❧

The long, hot shower did wonders for Josh's psyche, refreshing him and washing away his worries as well as his guilt. These few minutes alone had given him time to put everything into perspective. Hell, he thought, turning off the water. He'd dealt with it before and he'd deal with it again. He only had to remember too many variables had a hand in the Tylers' deaths—the fanatical killer with the death wish contributing to ninety percent of them.

While drying off, he also pushed away the threat of Cat's involvement. After donning a pair of running shorts and a T-shirt he'd retrieved from his bag, he shaved.

She couldn't be involved, he decided, looking at his clean-shaven face in the mirror. He would stay cautious, but he was convinced whoever wanted him dead thought he'd died in the fire. It had to be related to the drug operation he'd stumbled upon. Even the Feds thought so, and if the DEA was investigating, this would all be over soon. A logical assumption. And he agreed with Murphy. Brad Maxwell was the strongest suspect. Although Cat dated the guy, she wasn't one of his usual conquests. If Maxwell was involved, he'd be dealt with in due time.

Carrying his towel, wet jeans, sweatshirt, and polo shirt, he walked barefoot into the open room, feeling much like his old self. He spied Cat with an apron tied around her waist.

"Smells good. I guess I am a little hungry," he said, realizing at that moment he was ravenous.

"I have my clothes ready to go, if you want to add yours and turn it on." She nodded to the pile in his hands.

Once in the laundry room off the kitchen, he followed her instructions, then walked back into the room. "All done."

"I found a bottle of inexpensive red wine that we could easily pay for when we write our note. Would you like a glass?" She held up a bottle.

"Just make yourself right at home, why don't you?" he teased. She appeared too young and innocent to be plotting plane crashes or blowing up cabins. Her damp blonde hair was tied back and her face, though devoid of makeup, was animated, her complexion rosy. She wore the same shorts and T-shirt from last night, and his eyes were drawn to her legs, made sexier with bare feet sporting pink nail polish. Too damn sexy, he thought, wishing he didn't find her quite so hot.

"I have," Cat replied, tugging his attention from *her* to her words. "Hey, if I'm going to get busted for B and E, I might as well make it worth my while."

"My sentiments exactly." He took the bottle from her and

poured wine into a glass she'd set on the counter.

"Should be ready as soon as the toast is done. Sit, and I'll serve you."

"I like the sound of that." He picked up his glass and sipped as he proceeded to sit at the center island in the kitchen without taking his eyes off her. Her movements were graceful and a pleasure to watch as he drank his wine and enjoyed the way her body moved while she worked.

The wine tasted good and went down fast. He reached for the bottle and poured a second. "Would you like another glass?"

"Yes, as a matter of fact, I would." Her quick smile grabbed his insides.

Ignoring the tug, he refilled her glass. Then, deliberately looking around the room, he sipped.

Seconds later, Cat snatched the two plates she'd prepared and walked toward him, a pleased expression on her face. "It's not much, but it'll stop the hunger," she said, placing one full plate of eggs and toast in front of him before sitting next to him with her plate.

Depends on what the hunger is for. The thought ripped through him lightning fast. He sucked in a deep breath. Damn, he chided himself. Don't even go there.

"Well? What are you waiting for?"

Her voice drew his gaze. Her questioning eyes were too expressive. He looked away to take another deep breath, then picked up his fork and dug in, focusing on the food in front of him and shoving out all other thoughts of hunger.

"This is good. And exactly what I needed," he said, when her manner indicated she was waiting for some word about how it tasted.

"So, are you from Bozeman?" Cat asked, interrupting the quiet of the room.

"Hmm?" Josh's gaze flew to her face, having been lost in his thoughts.

"I asked a personal question." She waited a heartbeat, then asked, "Is that too personal?"

"What?" Caught off guard, he couldn't answer for a moment.

"We need to talk about something and I figured since I was so open last night, it's your turn." Cat eyed him expectantly. When Josh only stared at her, she let out an exaggerated breath. "Not ready to divulge personal information? I guess I should go first...*again.* Maybe that will loosen your tongue."

Watching her, he couldn't help smiling. "You go ahead. I need another glass of wine before I'll be ready to loosen up."

"Okay, but I expect you to reciprocate." She flashed him a no-nonsense look, then downed another hefty sip of wine and a few more bites of food before she spoke. "I'm not from Bozeman originally. It's the closest place I have to permanence, so I consider it home. My aunt lives there and I used to stay with her for long periods when my parents were out of the country, saving the world." Cat stopped talking, using the break to eat. When she continued, her tone was more subdued. "I only wish they'd have thought more along the lines of saving their little girl from loneliness, rather than saving everyone else." She broke off abruptly, appearing embarrassed, as if she'd given away too much information.

"Why would you say that?" he asked, not comfortable with the hurt he heard in her voice.

She tossed out a loud snort. "Oh no, you don't. That question will only be answered if you tell me something personal about yourself. I can't allow the balance to be disrupted."

"Balance?"

"Yeah. You're much too confident, Buc-man. So I can't let you in on any more of my deepest secrets without hearing some of yours. Otherwise our balance will get out of whack and I'll lose my edge in dealing with you."

"You have an edge?" Was she for real? He leaned back and searched her face, trying hard to figure out why she made him smile. Damn. He was in deep shit. Not only was he sexually attracted to her, but he also liked her. Too much. And that didn't bode well.

They'd both be better off if he kept his distance. Her more so than him.

"Yeah, I do." Her chin lifted an inch and her icy eyes flashed heat. "And you have to admit, you've been trying to rattle me since the very beginning. I'm not about to let the events of the last two days interfere in my efforts to thwart your attempts."

He laughed. She was simply too amusing and he was having too good a time not to want to continue. He took another sip of wine, eyeing her while his mind spun.

"One personal thing for another? Is that it? And you think the bit about staying with your aunt was personal?" It was all he could come up with.

"Yeah, it was, so it's your turn. You'd better hurry up because I'm getting a little toasted with all this wine."

"Your secret'll be safe with me. I won't tell anyone we're illegally sitting in someone's kitchen, drinking stolen wine, eating stolen food, getting toasted in the process." The sound of her soft laughter went straight to his groin, but at this point he was too toasted himself to care about the dangerous game he was playing with her.

"Why don't you go first?" Josh encouraged, ignoring the warning his brain was shouting, and completely forgetting that he usually avoided such sweetness because hanging around someone like him could only sour her. "That way, I'll have time to think of something to tell you."

"I've already thought of something we can share. Biggest regrets."

When she didn't add to her words, his eyebrows shot up. "Well? I'm waiting."

Fanning herself, she laughed again. Cat took a few minutes to compose herself before finally clearing her throat. "Nice try. But it won't work."

"Sounds a lot like truth or dare," he whispered, brushing an errant lock of hair that had come loose from its clip, behind her ear. "You show me yours and I'll show you mine."

"No," she denied breathlessly, pulling away from his touch. "We're just killing time here. I know what you're doing. You're trying to rattle me and it won't work. You need to go first or the game's over."

"Ah, you're on to me," Josh admitted, leaning back and chuckling to get his mind off what he was really thinking of doing. He'd been so close to losing his head and yielding to those luscious lips. His hand still twitched from wanting to wrap around her gorgeous, slim neck.

He took a deep breath and eyed his wine, thankful to have the moment interrupted, but wishing he wasn't so disappointed by the fact.

"Biggest regrets. Hmm. Let me see." It took some time to clear his mind—to come up with something he could use to get her talking. He decided on the truth.

"My biggest regret is being on a job out of the country when my grandmother got sick with Alzheimer's," he said, once he felt calm enough to speak. "By the time I was back in the States and discovered how ill she was, she didn't know me any longer."

"I'm so sorry," Cat said softly, placing her hand on his arm.

He hadn't planned to add any more, but her heartfelt sympathy yanked on his gut. When he met her gaze, one that held understanding, he couldn't stop himself from lancing the wound further, letting out more pain. Pain he never knew he was holding in.

"My mom died when I was a kid. Grandmother took over her role and raised me, so I owed her. I should've been there for her when she needed me, but I wasn't. And by the time I made it home, she no longer remembered me. She supposedly had lucid moments. Only I was never there when she was coherent, though I made it a point to see her almost every day until she died, which was a blessing. Alzheimer's patients can last years and not know anyone. The mind is gone, but the body is fit as a fiddle," he explained, sighing at the memory of the empty shell that had once been a vibrant, caring woman. A woman he'd viewed as a mother and loved just as much.

Josh took a big, steadying breath, as well as a gulp of wine before continuing, unable to keep the grief from slipping out in his voice. "My biggest regret, and one I'll have 'til my dying day, is I didn't get to tell her how much I loved her during one of her lucid moments. You think you have all the time in the world and suddenly you realize you don't."

"What about your father?"

Cat's question filled his ears as anger engulfed him. "My father?" Just mentioning the man sent his blood pressure soaring. The man he shared a name with was a lousy father who acted more like a dictator. And after what he'd done to his own mother, the elder Buchannan sank even lower in Josh's estimation.

"You mean the man who provided sperm?" After noting her shocked expression, he added, in an effort to explain, "He never loved me, never treated me like a son after my mom died. Grandmother made excuses and took over his role, and what'd she get for her troubles? He stuck her in an institution and never visited. Not once in four years." His fist hit the counter. "And how did I repay her for saving me from a life of hell with a hard man? I was off saving the goddamned world instead of being there when she needed me most." His words abruptly died when he realized he'd gone into raving-lunatic mode. Shit! Why had he divulged so much information?

Despite already indulging more than enough, he gripped his wineglass like a lifeline and gulped, happy to have the diversion to rein in his emotions. He knocked back one more swallow before he risked looking into her searching stare again. The moment their eyes connected, he knew why. She understood. He could see the same regret and grief mirrored in those ice blue eyes. Though cold in color, genuine concern shone in their heated depths.

This was too much. He closed his eyes to break the contact. He didn't want to feel a connection with her, but somehow he felt he had no choice. Everything about her drew him. Get a grip, Buc, he commanded mentally. Nothing has changed. He took a steadying breath and then another. Countless seconds ticked by before he felt in control enough to open his eyes, and many more before he could meet her sympathetic gaze, drawn by the soft sound of her voice.

"You can't blame yourself for your father's actions. You're not responsible. I know what it's like to regret unfinished business with parents. But I believe once they're dead, they know all. I forgave my parents for doing what they had to do, and no doubt your grandmother's looking down from heaven with complete and total understanding of your absence. She had to know how you felt about her. I feel it now, so how could she have not?"

"You think?" he asked, somewhat cheered by her words.

"Yeah, I do." Her hand settled on his arm again. Immediately, heat seeped at the spot, burning him. Her warm smile only added to the heat of her touch.

In a nanosecond, desire streaked through him—desire so strong it almost knocked him off the barstool.

"Okay, I told you my biggest regret. Now tell me yours," he said too quickly, using the words as a distraction, pushing away the want her gentle, expressive eyes elicited from his soul.

He refocused on his wineglass, then consumed another sip, hoping to numb his need in the effects of more alcohol. He knew without a doubt if she had any idea of the thoughts roaming around his head, she'd be running from him, not sitting here consoling him. It took another moment and many more gulps of wine before he felt he could control the impulse to drown his sorrows in her eyes. Still, he didn't dare look at her.

Cat remained silent for the longest time. When Josh was about to prod, thinking she wouldn't respond, her soft voice filled the air around them.

"I had a bad marriage."

Though Murphy had mentioned a divorce, her admission astounded him, drawing his attention. He certainly wasn't expecting it.

At his raised eyebrows, she offered a rueful smile. "I know, I know. Most people have a hard time believing it. But I am twenty-eight and I do have a past." Then her smile became genuine as she teased, "Though I'm sure my past is nothing compared to yours."

"No fair. We're talking about you now." His eyebrows shot up and down suggestively. "I showed you mine, now it's your turn to show me yours."

A laugh bubbled out of her. The sound tickled his foundation, sent more signals to his groin.

Josh reached for the wine bottle and refilled both glasses, concentrating on what she said rather than on covering the sweet noise of her laughter with kisses.

"Go on," he encouraged, when he could finally speak coherently.

"Okay, okay. But it's not a pretty story." She hesitated and what joy remained on her face faded into a mask of solemnity. "I regret wasting so much time and energy on an abusive man who didn't love me. What's worse, I didn't love him.

"My parents saw through Mark, though. I realized too late their disapproval played a huge part in why I married him. When they were alive, they were never around. I think my anger at them led me to rebel, and what better way to rebel than marry a man they hated?" She stopped talking and sighed. Offering him a half shrug, she said, looking at her hands, "That's so stupid, isn't it?"

"What's stupid?" he asked gently, hoping to ease the pain laced in her words.

"When I married Mark I at least had their attention, even if I didn't have their love. Yet all it did was make me miserable. Once they died, I knew I had to correct my mistake, divorce him and move on."

Her voice trailed off. She raised her wineglass to her lips and sipped. She turned to him, finally meeting his searching gaze. The torment spilling out hit him squarely in the gut with a force so hard he sucked in major air and glanced away.

Swearing under his breath, he quickly downed more wine, eyeing his glass as she continued.

"Mark was an abusive monster who thought he was the perfect man for me. He certainly tried to control me. I was able to escape his clutches and moved back to Bozeman to get clear of him. To this day, I still pray he has no idea where I am. If I'm lucky, he'll have found some other poor soul who's too afraid of life to torture."

"Why do you say that?" Josh asked, once he found his voice and could risk another glance in her direction. "I don't think you're afraid of life."

"I'm a fraud." Cat snorted, going back to her food. "So afraid of life that I let a man use me."

"No, you're not. You don't strike me as being afraid of anything."

"That's because I'm changing. Flying was the first step." She flashed another sad smile that twisted his insides into a tighter knot.

"Then the changes must be for the better," Josh whispered, unable to stop himself from reaching for the side of her face to gently brush a strand of hair behind her ear. He kept his hand on her neck this time, rubbing his thumb over her cheekbone. He tilted her head toward him and observed her expression closely, seeking the truth in her words.

She met his gaze, nervously running her tongue over her bottom lip. The innocent action was like a punch to his gut. Desire engulfed him once more. Get a grip, Buc, his mind screamed. For an instant, the thought of pulling her into his arms and forgetting everything but the same need he saw mirrored in those icy blue pools was overwhelming. More than anything, he wanted to believe her, but doubts suddenly sprang into his mind.

Using the doubt as a shield, he quickly grasped on to it. He sighed, dropped his hand to his side, and resumed eating his dinner as Murphy's words came hurtling back.

Cat's parents had been killed by friendly fire—friendly fire he'd been responsible for. She had a motive. Plus, he'd seen the handheld radio in her bag, so she had the means. Did she have enough time to make a quick call on the radio, knowing he would be going back to check on the plane? Was she somehow involved with Maxwell in an elaborate plot for revenge? He didn't want to believe it, but he couldn't ignore the possibility. Someone wanted him dead. Of course, whoever blew up the cabin would have taken her out too. Maybe she'd become a liability. He didn't know what to believe anymore.

❦

"What were you thinking just then?" Cat asked, clearing the dishes away when they got up from the island.

"Shit," Josh muttered under his breath, reaching for his wineglass. "Why do you ask?"

Standing by the sink, Cat eyed him intently, but he wouldn't meet her gaze, his attention absorbed with taking a sip.

"Did I do something wrong?"

"Something wrong?" Josh eyed his wine and cleared his throat. "That's a silly question."

"Call me silly, but your expression changed all of a sudden." For one fleeting moment he'd had this ravenous, intense look about him, like he could eat her alive and then, in a flash, the look turned cold and unyielding. Now he was being weird. Wouldn't meet her eyes again. Was acting awfully suspicious, as if he was hiding something.

Damn, she thought. She'd done or said something stupid. She just knew it. Up until a few minutes ago she'd begun to think he was as attracted to her as she was to him. But that obviously wasn't the case, so she had to make things right again. "Look, I'm sorry if I said or did something to upset you."

Her apology got his attention and he finally looked at her, searching her face for what seemed like forever.

Then he flashed his sexy, disarming grin before erupting into uncontrollable laughter.

Great! Now he was laughing at her.

Cat turned and stormed out of the room, only she didn't get very far. He'd followed on her heels and now gripped her arm, stopping her.

"What? Am I amusing you?" she yelled, fighting to keep from crying. She would not cry. Not in front of him.

"As a matter of fact, you are."

"Jerk," she cried. "You've made your point, so let go of me."

"Oh, no. I haven't begun to make my point." He pulled her closer. The next second his lips were consuming hers, kissing her as if he couldn't get enough. His tongue invaded her mouth while he inhaled her, not letting her back off, demanding a response. And then she felt his hands roaming over her body, gripping her, making her come alive with want and need. His lips broke from hers, and he trailed kisses across her face, causing even more sensations to course through her.

"You feel that, Cat?"

He licked her ear and nibbled on her lobe, eliciting a moan she couldn't contain. It felt so decadent. So wonderful.

"That's called an adrenaline rush. That's what I'm fighting. Have been fighting since yesterday when my plane blew up."

When he moved into her, pressing against her so she could feel the heat from his full arousal, Cat almost erupted into flames as hot lava flooded her system with more pleasure.

"The attraction's an illusion. It's not uncommon for someone in our situation. We've been riding on the edge of fear and I'm dying to have you," he whispered urgently in her ear, exacting another moan. "I want you so damn bad I can barely hang on. Do you understand what I'm saying?" He hesitated a heartbeat. "Your attraction is caused by a surge of hormones designed to keep you alive in times of crisis. It's not real."

Once the words were out, his mouth covered hers. Only this time, his lips and hands gentled while he kissed her for what seemed like forever. All of her senses came alive and she succumbed to his mouth's demands. She could taste the wine on his tongue, could smell the faint scents of deodorant and soap.

His soft lips were still thorough, still invading, still not letting her back away.

When she moaned into his mouth, totally absorbed in his kiss, he finally pulled away, breathing heavily as if he'd run a five-minute mile. "You'd better stop now. This is all I can take without finishing. You want this. Fine. You don't. Fine. The choice is yours. But make the decision now and make it knowing where the emotions are coming from."

This can't be happening, she thought, searching his earnest gaze. His eyes were like liquid fire, causing her to flinch from their intensity. Oh God. He was leaving the choice up to her and at the same time, he was telling her it meant nothing. If it was nothing more than elevated adrenaline, then why did she feel as if she would die if she backed away? Giving in to the tears that had threatened earlier, she couldn't stop their trek as they slid down the sides of her face.

"Why is it so hard to back off?" she asked softly, voicing her thoughts.

"Shush, don't cry." He kissed her tears, which only made them flow faster.

He wrapped his arms around her, holding her tightly while his comforting hands stroked her back slowly, soothing her. She smiled into his chest when she heard his next words.

"Think about how before yesterday's crash I was nothing more than a jerk riding your butt. I'm still that jerk. But I'm not a big enough jerk to take advantage of this situation. If we make love, I don't want your regrets in the morning."

"Why do you care?" she asked, sniffling to stop her tears. Leaning back and capturing his gaze, she tried to read his expression, find some meaning in the handsome, chiseled features of his face now etched with concern.

"Because I like you and because you don't seem to be the type for a one-night stand or short-term affair. You're a keeper, Cat. But I'm not a person who keeps. Understand?"

She nodded then, averted her eyes to his chest, unable to hold his intense gaze —one that seemed to see into her soul. How did he know her so well? Did she have an invisible sign reading "Nice Girl" or something similar on her back? Did he know she'd only had two lovers in her entire life, and neither one had excited her as she'd been merely minutes ago?

No! He couldn't know that. He'd never know that.

"Now what do we do?" she whispered, suddenly embarrassed as the warmth of a blush flowed up her face. "Don't tell me I'm red again." Sighing, she pulled away from him.

"Okay, I won't." He chuckled, and let her go. "But you're adorable when you blush so easily, I can't help myself," he explained when she glared at him.

Josh kept his gaze on her. Finally, she jutted out her chin. "Well?"

"Oh yeah. What do we do now?" He shrugged. "I have no clue." He broke eye contact and moved over to the windows, looking out into the dark, rain-soaked night.

Glancing past him, she couldn't see what he was searching for, but he seemed intent in his purpose. "You don't think we're safe?"

she asked, voicing her worst fear.

"Safe enough. Don't mind me. It's only nervous energy. You know?"

Oh yeah, she thought, repeating his phrase in her mind. She definitely knew about nervous energy now. Feeling his gaze on her face, she couldn't believe another blush was making an appearance.

He only grunted. "Boy, did I ever have you pegged wrong." He shook his head slowly and refocused on the storm outside. "I'm usually a better judge of character."

"I don't know if that's a compliment or an insult."

"You know it's a compliment."

"I guess I should count myself lucky," she said on her way to the laundry room. "I'm going to check on the clothes."

He nodded, continuing to stare out the window. He hadn't moved when she came back into the room. His gaze stayed fixed for several more minutes before he seemed satisfied.

Then he glanced at her with slanted eyebrows. "Maybe there's something good on TV?"

"Maybe," she offered, advancing toward the sofa, thankful to have something to get her mind off how attractive she found him. Knowing what she was up against, why make things worse by wishing for something that would never happen?

Still, as Cat plopped on the sofa and leaned against the cushions, she couldn't stop the overwhelming pang of regret. She'd wonder from this day forward what would have happened if she'd had the guts to take him up on his offer. Throw caution to the wind.

No. She wasn't that brave or that stupid.

Chapter 11

"What about you? Are you from Bozeman?"

Josh bit back a smile when he heard Cat's question. The woman never failed to amuse him. He'd followed her, joined her on the sofa, making sure to keep a reasonable distance. He was strong, but not that strong.

"I can't tell you." He grabbed the remote, clicking the button. The TV sprang to life.

"Why?" Her eyes clouded in confusion. He could tell the moment his teasing dawned on her because in a split second her face came alive with amusement. "Oh, I get it. If you told me, you'd have to kill me."

"Something like that," he murmured, settling back against the cushions, hauling his feet onto the table, and working hard to ignore the tightening in his gut. He aimed his attention on the TV in front of him and wrapped one arm around his head, getting more comfortable.

They'd been watching for an hour when a newscast flashed, showing his business and a shot of the burned plane. Cat and Josh both sat up and took notice at the same time. Josh flicked the remote, increasing the volume as the story about their fiery deaths blared.

"Wow," Cat said softly, voicing his exact thought. "They really think we're toast."

"I guess the weather's hampered search and rescue, so they have no way of knowing there're no remains in the plane."

"How eerie." She was quiet for a moment and then blurted out, "Oh my God. I have to call my aunt. She'll be beside herself with grief. I can't let her think I'm dead."

"We'll call her in the morning, once we hit the main road and can get to a phone. I promise."

This assurance mollified her and she nodded, relaxing into the cushions. "You think the person who is after us thinks we're dead?"

"I hope so. But I'm a cautious man, Cat, and I won't rest easy until we're home and I've put the bastard who did this behind bars."

"Want anything else to drink?" Cat asked, as she got up from the sofa and started for the kitchen.

"No. I've had enough."

Amid sounds of her rummaging around in the kitchen, he kept his attention on the TV. He sat up straighter, turning up the volume another notch when the next news story hit. The screen came alive with Gloria Goodman's face, followed by a picture and a full reporting of the fiery car accident before moving on to another story.

Gloria dead? The news stunned him. He couldn't believe it.

"Shit," he muttered under his breath, pushing out sadness as it sank in why the newscaster reported their assumed deaths. Gloria probably told Brad Maxwell about his phone call because he was working the desk last night. Did she notify anyone else before she left the office? Most likely not. She'd be in a rush to get home. Just one more offense to add to his guilt. If she hadn't been waiting for news of him, she wouldn't have been driving too fast on rain-slick roads.

Was that why the cabin blew? Maxwell knew about the cabin. He'd been there, along with all the other male instructors last summer over Fourth of July for a fishing weekend. The more he thought about it, the more convinced he became of Maxwell's involvement. Josh was positive he hadn't known about the trapdoor, though. But why would Maxwell want him dead?

"Something wrong?"

Cat's voice cut through his thoughts. He glanced up and offered his warmest smile. "No. Why do you ask?"

"Sometimes your face gives you away," she replied, coming up to the sofa and plopping down.

"Really?" Josh's attention moved to her expressive eyes now flashing humor.

"Yeah, except when you do that."

"When I do what?" His eyes narrowed and he bent his head at an angle.

"Compose your features so your face goes completely blank. But before it does, I see things."

"What do you see?" Josh's eyes were drawn to her lips still

holding a hint of a smile and he subdued more than a twinge of regret. Don't go there!

"I can't tell you." An impish grin took control of her face.

"Why?"

"'Cause then I'd have to kill you."

Laughter shot so readily from his chest, it took him a moment before he could respond. Damn if she didn't make him want to keep smiling. "You really are something."

They would never make love. He wouldn't—no, couldn't—get that close to her. But for the moment, he decided not to dwell on the events of the last thirty-six hours, the sadness of Gloria's death, of Maxwell and his suspicions, or on someone trying to kill him. He would enjoy the rest of the evening instead.

ႠႽ

"I think I'll clean up." Cat jumped up from the sofa an hour later. "I want to leave everything as we found it. Our clothes should be dry by now," she explained, when Josh's inquisitive gaze met hers.

Josh watched her flit about the house, wiping off things, ridding the place of their presence. Her movements seemed soothing and natural, as if they shared this same routine every night. Yeah. Right, Buc. Quit dreaming, he told himself. He definitely wasn't the kind of guy for someone like her—a happily-ever-after kind of girl. Hell, he'd spent his life fighting what he'd decided was a losing battle and had run from that fact, unable to deal with the horrible truth. His choice had kept him from being there when his grandmother needed him most. What made him think he could be there for Cat? He didn't bother responding to his mental question because his answer wouldn't change anything.

"Your clothes are on the dryer, Josh."

"Thanks." Swallowing another gulp of regret, he stood and headed toward the laundry room to retrieve his clothes, noticing how clean everything was.

"Cat obviously has the same nervous energy strumming through her veins," he murmured, pushing away the memory perched at the edge of his consciousness—one too reluctant to budge. Too many times in the last hour, the urge to yank her into his arms and smother her with kisses had been all but overwhelming. He had no idea how he'd been able to calmly sit next to her for so long without so much as a sign of what was really going through his mind.

Josh could still taste her, and his arms ached to hold her again.

He was in deeper shit than he realized, he thought, detouring to the wall of windows, where he stayed rooted, just staring and searching the forest beyond for some clue as to how to handle his attraction.

The house's floodlights allowed him to see quite a distance. The rain had diminished, and while a few snow flurries gusted about, not sticking, the worst of the storm had obviously blown over. He turned and headed in the direction of the laundry room without any real solution other than avoidance.

He grabbed his clothes off the dryer and headed for the bedroom he'd staked out, saying as he went, "I'm beat. I'll do a quick check outside, then I'm turning in."

Once there, he changed into clean clothes. Minutes later, he was scouting the lighted perimeter of the property. The wide-open, well-lit area surrounding the house at the edge of the encroaching woods would hinder anyone's attempt to catch him unaware. After satisfying himself that he'd done all he could, he meandered back to the porch, then retrieved the satellite phone from his bag perched by the door.

"Murphy here." The voice came through loud and clear in Josh's ear.

"Murph, it's me, Buc."

"Thank God! Buc, tell me where you are. We've got problems."

"I know, I caught the evening news. My office manager died. Everyone thinks we're dead."

"You may wish you were dead after this conversation. I didn't know you had a couple of Feds for enemies."

"What are you talking about?"

"McMann and Adams have dug up more than dirt. They're convinced you're involved with Maxwell with drugs and DEA is all over it."

"What?" Josh asked, stunned. Christ, this was all he needed to make the day a total bust.

"That's not all. Top brass in Langley believes there's a leak. Agents, linked directly to your last operation in Afghanistan, the same one we were discussing earlier involving the girl's parents, are dropping like flies."

"How's that possible?" he whispered, his question coming out after a full minute of silence between them.

"I don't know how, but I can't keep you safe without bringing you in. From either side. Understand?"

"I can't come in. Not yet."

"That's not the right answer."

"Tell me what's happening and let me try to figure it out."

"Reynolds was killed..." Josh missed Murphy's next words when a voice behind him said, "What're you doing out here?"

"Shit," Josh muttered under his breath. How had he allowed her to sneak up on him? "I gotta go. I'll check in with you later."

"Buc, don't hang up. Tell me your coordinates." Murphy's voice became more frantic. "Don't do this. Buc. You—"

Josh closed the phone, effectively breaking the connection in one flick of his wrist while he turned to face the woman behind him. A cat with her claws unsheathed.

"You're talking on the phone," she accused, her expression flush with anger as awareness settled over her features. "You've had a working phone this entire time?"

"Cat, I can explain," he said, trying to get her to see reason when reason seemed out of reach, based on those icy eyes flashing pure molten fire and all the heat directed solely at him.

"Bullshit. You had me running through the frozen forest all day, made me break into someone else's house, and you had the means to end it?"

"It's not that simple," he explained, realizing she was beyond livid. Volcanic was a better word. There was nothing of the fearful woman she claimed to be earlier. Everything in her stance told him she wasn't afraid of him. In fact, looking at her now, he was a little afraid of her...or of what she'd do next.

"Oh? It's very simple, Buc-man," Cat sneered. Her hand shot out. "Give me the phone so I can call my aunt."

"I can't do that." He dropped the phone inside his bag.

"Wrong answer. Either you let me call my aunt or I'm out of here right now."

"There are things you don't understand."

"Fine, make me understand."

"I can't," he sighed, rubbing the back of his neck in agitation.

Cat turned and stormed back into the house, snatching her bag and stuffing her things into it. She'd changed out of her shorts and was wearing jeans and a sweatshirt.

Ignoring Josh, who'd followed and was now eyeing her warily, she shoved past him.

"Where do you think you're going?" he asked as she neared the door.

"Home."

"You can't leave here," he said, unable to contain his incredulous tone. Was she serious?

"Watch me." She reached for the handle and yanked the door open with force.

"Cat, please." Josh rushed across the room, placing himself in front of her to keep her from leaving. "Think about what you're doing! It's barely above freezing out there."

"I'll take my chances. I'd rather freeze than be lied to," she said calmly. She took a step back and crossed her arms, glaring at him.

"Come on, Cat. Calm down and be reasonable," he pleaded, placing his hand on her arm.

"Go to hell, Buc-man." She jerked out of his hold and slipped around him.

When she was halfway down the porch steps, he yelled, "Okay, okay. Call your aunt. But don't tell her where we are."

"How can I? I don't know where we are," she shot back, her voice rising at the end.

"By my calculations, we're a couple of miles from a highway going into Butte. But I'd keep the information to yourself, if I were you," he said, sighing and handing her the phone. "Call your aunt. I trust you."

ೞ

John Murphy hung up his phone and swore softly. "Goddamned loner. Never could play by the rules." He punched another number into the keypad. His face contorted with pain as he pushed in on his stomach and popped another antacid into his mouth. "I don't need this shit right now," he muttered as a voice blared from the receiver. "Yeah?"

"Smitty? It's Murphy. Our problem's getting bigger."

"Have you talked to him? Is he coming in?"

"Yeah, I talked to him, and no, he's not cooperating."

Smitty's chuckle crackled in Murphy's ear before he said, "Sounds like nothing's changed."

"Like that's fricking news?" he hissed into the phone, pushing against his stomach again. He took a deep breath and added, "And according to the phone calls I'm getting, every agency in the alphabet is on alert. Talk to me. Tell me about McMann and Adams. Are they trolling or do they have a real bite?"

"I'm working on it."

"Well, work faster because those two are doing more than ruffling feathers in Langley. They're yanking them out of the goose."

"You can't believe what Laurel and Hardy are saying? The way I see it, they've both got their heads up their butt looking to smear Buc, while making a name for themselves in the process."

"Of course I don't believe a goddamn word," Murphy ground out impatiently. "Buc's one of the best operatives I've ever worked with, outside of you, that is," he expounded, popping another antacid into his mouth. "Fucking loners, both of you." He touched his fingers to his forehead, rubbing it for a couple of minutes, thinking. When he spoke again, he was a little more composed. "They've got to have something because there's too much activity going on. Plus, Reynolds and Jenkins were killed. Execution style. Gunshots to the head. Higher-up intel points to your mission in Afghanistan—that there's a leak somehow and Buc's responsible. We need to find him. Bring him in."

"I'll do what I can."

"Keep me posted," Murphy said before hanging up.

∞

Cat stopped her descent from the porch stairs and turned around, looking closely at Josh's desperate expression, not quite sure she'd heard him correctly. Josh trusted her? What a laugh. What was trust? Nothing!

"Please, Cat. Don't go off. It's not a smart thing to do."

"I just want to go home," she admitted softly, praying the tears lurking wouldn't fall. This couldn't be happening to her. All she'd wanted from flying was to do something different, something that would keep her from being afraid of life, and right now fear was all she felt. "I'm not in the habit of having to run for my life while things explode around me."

"And you think I am?"

"Yeah." Cat nodded. "I do."

At this point she was torn. Indecision engulfed her. Her shoulders sank in the defeat of no longer having the unwavering resolve to continue walking into the cold, dark forest.

Dear Lord, why couldn't she be stronger and simply walk away?

"Cat?" His tender tone got her attention. She looked up. Met his sincere gaze.

"Call your aunt," he urged, stepping closer. "Tell her you're safe but ask her not to say anything to anyone."

"Why? Why can't I call the authorities too?" she whispered. Her question hung in the air.

Because if you do whoever's trying to kill me may succeed.

She could see that answer clearly in his eyes, but he never actually voiced it, saying instead, "I can't tell you. All I can do is ask you to trust me. Please?"

"I'm not very good at trusting, Josh." Mainly because she didn't trust herself to make the right choice.

"Then we're even. But somehow I trust you."

Seconds ticked off and still she eyed him, hating that she had to make a decision.

Finally, she nodded. "Okay. I'll trust you." She reached for the phone he still held out and quickly punched in her aunt's number.

In seconds, her aunt's familiar voice shot through the device.

"Aunt Marge? It's me, Candace." She brushed tears away.

"Candace?" There was silence on the other end for several loud seconds. Then her aunt asked question after question in rapid fire, not waiting for answers. "My God, you are alive just as Smitty said. How? I don't see how. They told me you'd died. Where are you? Why didn't you contact me sooner?"

"I'm sorry, but we've been hiking through the mountains. I can't talk long. I only wanted you to know we're safe."

"We're? Are you still with that pilot? Joshua Buchannan?"

"Yes." She slanted a glance at Josh and stiffened when she noticed his scrutinizing expression, watching her every move.

"Your friend Brad has been by. He's worried." Cat concentrated on maintaining a neutral expression as her aunt's concerned warning shot into her ear. "Apparently, there've been agents asking all kinds of questions about Mr. Buchannan. Candace, they say he's involved in something. Drugs or worse. He sounds dangerous."

"Don't worry and don't believe everything you hear. I'm fine," she said firmly, working even harder at remaining calm when doubt suddenly filled her. "Look, Aunt Marge, I've got to go. Please don't say anything to anyone that you heard from me."

"Why? Your friends have been calling all day asking about you."

"I can't explain right now. I should be home tomorrow and this will all be over."

"I don't understand..."

"Please? Can you wait until morning before you call anyone?"

"I guess so."

"Good," Cat said on a relieved sigh. "I love you, Aunt Marge. I'll see you tomorrow."

"Okay, dear. Please be careful. Don't trust that man," was the last thing Cat heard before she snapped the phone closed and handed it to Josh. "Thank you."

"You're welcome." He stuck the phone away, then slung his bag over his shoulder and held out his hand. "Come on. Let's get inside. The temperature's near freezing."

Cat placed her fingers in his, wondering why she trusted him when everything inside was screaming for her to run as far away as she could from him. But like she'd done at least one other time in her life after deciding to marry her ex, she ignored those mental warnings and walked hand in hand into the house with him.

"Good night." Standing with him a few moments later outside her room, Cat studied her hands. She cleared her throat, suddenly tongue-tied. For some reason, it seemed as if he was dropping her home after an evening out. A first date—the awkward moment when neither knew the other well enough to take the risk, so both remained exceedingly polite, complete with an uncomfortable, cloying silence between them. The whole ordeal brought a rueful turn to Cat's lips. She let out a soft sigh before starting into her room.

"Cat?"

The gentle question floated in the air, danced around her ears, and captured her attention. The one word sounded so full of longing. For a moment, Cat wasn't quite sure if it was wishful thinking or if the sound was genuine. She stopped her advance and met his gaze. Josh's features yielded nothing and caused her to ask, "What?"

"I'm glad you decided to stay." His lips, feather light, brushed hers in a kiss that was over before it began. "I won't let you down." Then he gently urged her inside. "See you in the morning," he added, moving swiftly away from her.

She spun around and watched him disappear, wishing for the second time that night she had the guts to take him up on his offer.

If she ever did throw caution to the wind, she knew without a doubt, it would be the exact second in time she'd no longer live in fear.

"Dream on, Cat. You aren't that brave," she told herself. Grabbing a blanket, she fell onto the bed fully clothed, not bothering to get under the spread.

ଔ

"Cat?" Smitty asked, with eyebrows quirked, after Marge Tyler replaced the handset. He'd just hung up from Murphy and was on his way to rejoining the group when he'd caught the gist of her phone call. When she nodded, he added, already knowing the answer, "I take it from your conversation that she's safe?"

"You've heard from Cat?" Brad Maxwell asked, coming up behind them.

Smitty nodded. He, Brad, and Cheryl had spent the evening with Cat's aunt, offering their support. The phone call had done what none of his assurances could. Settle her deepest fears.

"Yes, she's safe." Marge Tyler gave Brad an unyielding look. "You two didn't argue, did you?"

"No. Why do you ask?"

"She doesn't want anyone to know she called. It seems such an odd request."

"I'd worry more over the idea of her being with Buchannan. He'll more than likely get her killed."

"Buc'll keep her safe," Smitty said in a firm voice. "I've worked with Buc for years. He's one of the best."

"So you say." Brad snorted. "Those cops don't think so and they're lumping me with him. And I know nothing about him before he came to Bozeman." He turned to Smitty, his gaze accusing. "Matter of fact, I know nothing about you."

Smitty smiled. "The Arabs have a saying, 'Change is as good as a rest.'"

"You and your fricking sayings. What the hell does that mean?"

He laughed. "Don't judge Buc or me because our pasts are unknown. He has his reasons for coming to Bozeman, just as I had mine. We both needed change."

"McMann thinks he's turned against his country, that he's become worse than the terrorists he used to fight, and you're speaking in riddles as usual. I say you live long enough among the animals, it's only a matter of time before you become one yourself."

"Careful, you're revealing your ignorance. You know nothing about him or the terrorists we've gone up against. All people have their causes. Some are more willing to die for them than others." Smitty threw him a disdainful look and snorted. "I'd venture to say even you have one if you dug deep enough."

"Right now all Ms. Tyler or I care about is Cat's safety."

"Cat said she was safe," Marge broke in, eyeing Brad intently. "I'm still confused as to why she'd insist on keeping the news from you, if you two are such good friends."

"Who knows?"

"Well, I kept my word and didn't call you, but you'd better not let on that I told you."

"You didn't tell me. I overheard." Brad smiled at her raised eyebrows. "Your secret's safe with me." He then grabbed his coat. "I'll call you in the morning, so you can tell me then. Wouldn't want to make a liar out of you. I'll let myself out."

"Don't mind him," Smitty said when she stiffened. "He's pissed because he spent the afternoon being questioned."

"Hmmm." Marge kept her attention on him as he sauntered out the door. She turned to Cheryl Green, who'd come into the room after retrieving her purse, and said, "What does Candace see in him besides his obvious good looks?"

Cheryl laughed. "Don't worry, Aunt Marge. They're only friends."

"Thank God. That one smiles too much, yet he doesn't seem sincere. I always thought her more discriminating, not easily fooled by smiles. Well, if you discount her ex-husband," she grumbled under her breath. "But that relationship I lay at Vivian and Preston's feet." She sighed and returned Cheryl's smile. "Candace isn't a pushover, but anyone can be caught off guard by a pretty face."

Smitty waited while the two women hugged. "Good night, Ms. Tyler."

"Good night," she said, then added in a louder voice, before they could completely escape, "You remember that, young lady. Pretty faces hide a lot and can be deceptive."

"I'll remember." Cheryl laughed and grabbed Smitty's hand. Together they walked to his car.

"So, you really think she's safe despite all the rumors flying around?" she asked, once he'd climbed in beside her and started the engine.

"Couldn't be in safer hands."

"You've known him a long time, right?"

"Yeah." He nodded. "Buc and I go way back. I can't talk about what we did, but I can tell you there's no better person to have beside you on a mission."

Cheryl nodded and, much to his relief, remained silent during the rest of the ride.

After ensuring she'd made it safely inside her apartment, Smitty pulled out his cell phone.

He backed out of the driveway as Murphy's, "Yeah, what have you got?" blasted in his ear.

"Cat's made contact with her aunt. Thought you should know. She'll probably do so again, so Marge Tyler's calls should be monitored."

"Someone's already on it."

"Have you got a location yet?"

"Not yet. How about you? Have you learned anything useful?"

"No. Only that they're safe and she expects to be home tomorrow."

"It's not a lot to go on." Murphy sighed audibly. "You're both in danger. You should disappear until we figure it out."

"I could." Smitty grinned. "And maybe I should." With his ear for languages—he spoke many including the several Arabic dialects he favored—he was good at disappearing. A handy skill to possess for undercover work, especially after spending years in a country where being a blue-eyed blond was a detriment. He'd learned a thing or two about blending into his surroundings. But he had a job to do and until he completed the job, disappearing wasn't an option. "I'm fine. We need to find Buc and fast."

Chapter 12

Josh left Cat outside her room and headed straight for his.

Unfortunately, sleep was elusive. Lying on top of the bed with one arm behind his head, the day's events ran through his mind like a video, playing and replaying, all the while he mentally searched for something he'd missed. He purposefully kept his thoughts off the woman down the hall for the express reason that if he thought about her, he wasn't sure he could stop from doing something stupid. Like forgetting his resolve of leaving the choice up to her, push past her defenses, and make the choice for her. He had no doubts he could do it, he simply didn't want to live with regrets. Both hers and his.

It was a long while before he was able to drift off to sleep and when he did, his rest was fitful. Around two, he finally left his bed for an inspection.

Josh stopped at the threshold of Cat's room and glanced inside when he noticed the open door. Her sleeping form was shadowed in moonlight.

Sighing wistfully, he continued down the hallway to check the grounds. While he walked, he thought about regrets.

Abruptly, Josh halted and blinked. "Grandmother?"

She stood in the shadows, only her eyes visible. Lucid eyes. Not the eyes he remembered from their last time together. Sadness had replaced the emptiness.

"Why weren't you there for me? Why didn't you save me?"

"I...um...I..." What could he say? He had no excuse.

"I'm sorry," he whispered as her eyes became more accusing. Then they morphed into another's eyes. Tormenting eyes, the only feature he could see of the woman wearing a burka through the binoculars' lenses. Suddenly he was back on that knoll, back giving the signal to his sniper to take his best shot because she was also wired with explosives. When he peered through the lens one last time, Sister Tyler, who'd come out of nowhere, stepped in her path, arguing, right as a shot rang out. In the split second before the blast that blew the two to bits, both turned in unison. As Cat's mother dropped, the fanatic glanced directly at him.

He'd never forget the look of fear over the realization that she faced death.

As he continued staring at the horror he'd caused, three pairs of eyes, all of them knowing and all of them accusing, blended into one. His grandmother's, the woman wearing the burka, and Sister Tyler's, all of them begging him to…what?

"No. I tried," he yelled, looking away, ashamed that he couldn't help any of them. He wasn't there for his grandmother, when she'd saved him from a lonely life, stood up to his father, and bore her son's scorn to do what she thought was right. He couldn't save the bomb-toting terrorist, not when her distorted beliefs threatened children's lives. Nor could he save Cat's parents.

"I tried to save them." When he glanced back, he was found himself staring into Cat's cool blue gaze. "No. Don't look at me like that. Please," he begged. "I tried."

Josh dragged himself from the nightmare's depths and sat up, taking quick shallow breaths, his heart pumping rapidly. Now awake, he could still see those haunting stares. All of them.

He forced himself to relax, to focus on a shadow on the wall, to forget. When a sound infiltrated his thoughts, he froze.

Something's wrong, his brain screamed. He lay perfectly still, staring into the dim room.

There it was again.

One crunch…then another. In the next instant, a shadow flitted past the shade.

Thank God for the floodlights outside.

He stealthily rose. Fully dressed, he grabbed the 9mm Glock from inside his bag, then moved swiftly and silently through the house to the front door.

Cautiously, he stole across the porch, sticking close to the house while avoiding the light. He sank back into the shadows. Noiselessly shifted into position. Waited.

In moments, Josh was rewarded with a glimpse of movement.

A deadly smile crossed his face.

His opponent was clearly impatient while Josh, using the patience and the cunning of a hunting tiger, had perfected stalking to an art form.

Stupid fool didn't know enough to take his time. Rushing would be his undoing.

Now that he knew where his quarry hid, he kept his unwavering attention glued to the spot, stealing closer. The lone assailant was at one of the windows, searching for some access to the house. Josh lurked, an unnoticed specter, biding his time for the exact moment to strike. When that instant came, he didn't hesitate. The unconscious invader sank to the ground, most likely having no idea what had felled him.

Tucking his gun in his back waistband, Josh knelt beside the inert body. Once he had the culprit lying flat, he quickly frisked him, going over every inch, pulling various items, including a wallet and gun, out of his pockets. He opened the wallet and noted the name on a Washington, DC, driver's license. Anthony Rodriquez. The guy was clearly working for the US government. Compliments of Murphy, no doubt.

"Oh my God."

Josh froze. Though whispered, her voice rocketed through his ears like the loudest shout. Pivoting on his knees, Josh spotted Cat standing beneath the floodlight, her eyes as big as saucers.

"Shit," he said. Could things get any worse, he wondered as he took in her accusing expression, so like the one in his nightmare.

"Who are you?"

"What are you doing out here? Why aren't you asleep?" Josh asked, maintaining eye contact and holding on to his patience by a single thread. It wasn't lost on him that she'd snuck up on him again and that thought unnerved him.

"Who's that?" She looked at him with those icy eyes of hers, daring him to deny her right to be there.

Josh exhaled another deep breath and glanced down at the heap of flesh in front of him. "I don't know," he lied. "But whoever he is, he's not here to help us."

"Do you think he's the one who's responsible for all our problems?"

"Maybe, but he's working on someone's orders."

"You mean someone paid him to kill us?"

"Not us, me," he corrected, going back to his pockets, not adding that they were supposedly working on the same side and that Murphy had most likely sent him to bring him in.

When he pulled a small receiver out of the jacket, the blood drained from his face. He turned back to Cat and commanded in a cutting voice, "We've got to get out of here. Go inside and prepare to leave." When Cat only looked at him as if he'd grown another head, he barked, "Do it now."

"Why?"

"See this?" he asked, holding up the receiver he found. "It's a tracking device. We can't stay here."

Her eyes narrowed. "But what about him?" she asked, nodding to the prone figure. "Is he okay? What did you do to him? Who is he?"

Ignoring her questions, he jumped up and grabbed her hand. "Let's go," he urged.

She resisted. "You can't just leave him there!"

"He'll be fine. Just wake up with a nasty headache. But we won't be fine if we're still here when he does wake up. Come on." He pulled her with him, almost running back to the house. "I don't know how much time we have, so we've got to move."

Once inside, Josh left her to pack while he tore through the drawers looking for rope. When he found some, he rushed back to Rodriquez and hurriedly bound the man's hands and legs together. After giving the rope a final tug, he stood, satisfied with his handiwork. It would be quite a while before he would be able to set himself free. His stalker would wake up with a headache and in a very uncomfortable position. With that task done, Josh headed for the house at a fast jog.

Cat had turned on several lights, making it easier to see in the early morning darkness. He spied her rushing toward him with her bag.

"Bring it here," he ordered, not stopping his trek to his room.

Running to keep up, she followed.

"What's going on?" she asked, halting behind him. "Who was that man?"

Josh didn't answer her, just nodded in the direction of the bed. "Put your bag there."

She did as he requested, placing it next to his. When he dumped the contents on the bed and rifled through them, confusion clouded Cat's eyes.

"What're you doing?" she yelled. "You're nuts. You know that? Certifiable." Ignoring her outburst, Josh continued searching. He had no time to placate her.

"Why aren't you answering me?" she ground out a few minutes later.

He paid her question no heed until she placed her hand on his arm, effectively stopping his movements. Josh's attention flew to her questioning stare and he let out a slow breath.

"Trust me. I don't have time to explain."

"If you expect me to trust you, I need more information, Bucman."

"Please, Cat. We've already had this conversation."

When he was satisfied that her bag was clean, he started on his own. In a matter of minutes he found what he was looking for, sewn into the black lining of his flight bag.

"Goddamn it all," he muttered, lifting the small transmitter out of his bag and pocketing it.

"What?"

"They've known where we were the entire time," he said, repacking everything. Once done, he handed Cat her bag and picked up his own. "I've been set up. We've got to get out of here and fast."

"Who knew? Set up?" Cat stared at him, clearly trying to comprehend all that was happening. She then sat on the bed. Her shoulders drooped in defeat. "You go ahead without me. I'm tired of running, Josh. Especially since I have no clue as to why."

"I can't leave you." Shit! Things were going from bad to worse. "You know you're better off with me than without," he added more fervently, trying to make her understand. He wouldn't give her a choice. She had to come with him. He could not be responsible for another death.

Josh had no idea what Rodriquez was planning, but innocent bystanders too often got mowed down in the hunt. "Please?" he begged, finally letting her see the worry he'd worked so hard to keep from her.

He held his breath, waiting. It was obvious from her facial expressions that she was waging a mental battle. When she said, "Right now I have no choice," he exhaled heavily, relieved he wouldn't have to carry her kicking and screaming down the road.

Cat stood. "But the minute we get to a road and a phone, I'm calling Cheryl and asking her to pick me up."

"Fair enough," he agreed, grabbing her hand and leading her out of the room. "Come on, we've got to hurry."

"You can't just leave here and not turn everything off," Cat said, as they neared the front door.

"Do you think I care? It won't matter if we're dead."

"But I care." She stopped abruptly, tugged out of his grip, and crossed her arms. "I'm not going another step until you make sure everything's exactly as we found it."

Looking into her stubborn face, he sighed. God, the woman was irritating, he thought, as he went to do her bidding. Apparently she didn't realize that a busted frozen pipe wasn't the same as a bullet to the head or dying from an explosion. Still, he hurriedly shut off the water to the outside, flipped the switch to the water heater, and reset the thermostat to fifty degrees, leaving the house exactly as they'd found it.

"There. Are you satisfied?"

"Not yet. Write your note and leave some money," she demanded.

"Shit," he muttered under his breath, pulling out two twenty-dollar bills and writing quickly. "Just my luck to get stuck with my conscience," he added, thrusting the note and the money under a dish. "Now let's get outta here."

He didn't give her time to answer, just grabbed her hand.

଼

The first thing Cat noticed as they started down the dirt road was the cold. Josh's pace, one that made yesterday's seem as if they'd been on a Sunday stroll, kept her warm, making her forget her discomfort for the moment.

Dawn was breaking as they reached the main road. At least Cat assumed it was a main road, considering the blacktop. Also, she figured it must be garbage day because every now and then they passed oversized plastic cans with wheels, next to dirt roads that led back into the forest. This was confirmed when Cat spied a gigantic truck up ahead, stopping every now and then to empty one of the cans along its route. The noisy truck was the only sound of civilization; all others were of the forest now waking up around them. Croaking frogs, tweeting birds and buzzing insects.

Josh let go of her hand and headed for one of the cans. In stunned fascination, she watched him lift the lid and toss the little piece he'd taken out of his bag back at the house into it.

"What're you doing?" she asked, when he closed the can.

"Giving us a little time," he answered, offering a negligent lift of his shoulders and resuming his journey with a determined stance, telling her he had some purpose. As to what the purpose was, Cat had no clue. What had she gotten herself into?

He stopped and turned around, capturing her gaze with an intent look.

She shook her head and sighed. "The man is nuts. Certifiable," she muttered to herself, hurrying to catch up with him, thankful he'd at least slowed his pace. He expected her to trust him. To follow him blindly.

For some reason, Cat couldn't stop herself from doing both, sensing that he'd keep her safe and alive. "Yep—there are those two words again. Safe and alive," she added under her breath, wondering what it was about him that instilled those feelings.

After another hour of walking, they both heard the pickup truck at the same time. Josh stepped into its path and put out his hand, effectively slowing the vehicle. When it came to a complete stop, he walked over to the driver's side as a man rolled down his window.

"Seems a little cold to be out for a mornin' walk. Bet you guys could use some help."

"Actually, we were hoping for a ride into Butte," Josh said with a smile.

"Sure. That's where I'm goin'. Hop in," the driver replied. Cat and Josh quickly climbed inside without further invitation, while the driver added, "Name's Bill Meyers."

Seated in between the two men, Cat glanced over at the thin, grizzled man wearing a cowboy hat, looking much like so many of the Montana ranchers she'd met since coming home. He appeared to be at least seventy. His weathered skin that had seen its fair share of the outdoors aided in the perception. But his sharp blue eyes belied his chronological age, letting her see that while the outside might seem a little worn, the inside still had lots of life.

She offered her warmest smile as well as her hand. "Nice to meet you, Mr. Meyers. I'm Candace Tyler and this is Josh Buchannan."

Meyers turned and spit a mouthful of tobacco juice out the window. "Nasty habit," he muttered, almost to himself, before looking back at her and grinning, showing a mouthful of brown-stained teeth.

At Cat's raised eyebrows, he explained, "Didn't know fifty years ago chewin' this shit would be so deadly or so hard ta quit." Then he took her outstretched hand. "Call me Bill." He nodded to Josh, before energetically cranking the handle on his window, closing it.

Josh returned the nod, saying, as his gaze swept the horizon, "We really appreciate this, Bill."

"No problem," Bill said. He put the truck in gear and started driving. Holding his attention on the road, he asked, "So, what brings you two out on a mornin' like this?"

Cat felt Josh stiffen next to her. When he placed his hand on her knee, squeezing gently, she met his gaze, giving a slight nod of understanding.

She had a hard time keeping a straight face as Josh said, "Our car broke down last night before it really started pouring." The guy was definitely an adept liar.

"You're lucky the storm blew over quickly. It can be nasty an' unexpectedly brutal this time a year."

"Yeah, tell me about it. Not one of my better nights." Josh grunted. "We waited it out till this morning and have been walking for miles."

The ten-mile ride took only a fraction of an hour. Much less than the two hours or so Cat figured it would have taken if he hadn't come along. In that time, Bill and Cat did most of the talking. Josh studied the passing landscape, staying silent.

When Meyers stopped his pickup in front of a garage Josh had indicated on the outskirts of town, she said, following Josh out of the vehicle, "Can we pay you?"

Since Bill had been friendly and chatty on the drive, not to mention a lifesaver, she felt she owed him more than a warm thank-you.

"No, little lady. Kindness doesn't require payment. Just pass it along."

"How about letting us buy you breakfast?" Cat asked, meeting his animated eyes.

"Nope. No rest fer the wicked," he joked, winking at her, flustering her when she realized he was flirting with her. If she'd had doubts, the leer he sent her plus his next words confirmed her suspicions. "Ain't got time. Gotta git to work. But if I did, I'd have you fer breakfast."

Heat flushed her face. "Well, thank you for the lift," she was finally able to get out, relieved she didn't have to add any more because Josh's voice boomed beside her.

"Yeah, the little lady and I really appreciate it. And we will pass it along."

"Good. Take care." Meyers nodded as Josh slammed the passenger door.

"Come on, little lady." Josh dragged her with him along the cement walkway leading to the garage's entrance. "No wonder I mistook you for a Powder Puff. You even flirt with old men."

"I do not." She stiffened. "I was merely being nice to him. He did give us a ride."

"Yeah, right. You bat those icy blue eyes too much. A man can't help but wonder if there's heat behind all that frost."

Hmmm? She secretly observed his face while they walked and saw the lines of irritation etched into the ruggedly handsome features. Why would he mention it if he didn't wonder?

"Jealous, Buc-man?" she taunted. The thought of him being jealous over a crotchety old man tickled her insides. Not a good thing. Neither was the trickle of pleasure rolling over her at the thought of him being one of those who wondered. Don't even think about it, she mentally warned. Still, she couldn't stop the waves of sensation cascading over her because he really did appear to be jealous.

"Come on, let's get inside." He opened the door and waited until she went ahead of him before following.

"He's old enough to be my grandfather, for heaven's sake." Nearing the counter, Cat slowed and took in the grimy room that smelled like rubber and sweat.

"Maybe, but he's also a man and the look he sent you wasn't grandfatherly."

"Which only goes to show how your gender is so easily led by your—" she stopped short when she realized what she was about to say. Looking at him, she clenched her fist, and almost took a swing.

"I thought we'd already established that fact."

One shot was all it would take. "Jerk." She promptly gave him her back.

"That's two for two, Cat. I'm impressed."

"Oh, shut up, Buc-man," she snapped, irritated because she could feel the heat rushing up her face and knew that it was probably maraschino red.

His soft chuckle confirmed this, but her retort stuck in the back of her throat when the glass door, leading to the garage with four bays, swung open and a big, barrel-chested man strutted in.

"Buc," he boomed, striding over to Josh, his ruddy features alive with pleasure. He pulled a rag out of his back pocket and wiped both hands on it before holding one out in greeting. "I wasn't expectin' you."

"Hey, Gus." Josh shook his outstretched hand. "I need a favor."

"Anything, old buddy. Just say the word." Then Gus's interested, green-eyed stare turned to Cat and his eyebrows shot up. "And who do we have here?" Starting at the top of her head, his gaze took a journey over her body, traveling slowly along the curves before turning around and coming back to rest on her face. "I gotta hand it to ya. You always did know how to pick 'em," he said, with approval gushing out of both his eyes and his voice.

"I rest my case," Josh whispered in Cat's ear.

She caught his amused expression and stiffened. Then flashing him a look that he couldn't mistake, she muttered, "Jerk," under her breath.

"You're being redundant," he murmured, before turning his full attention on Gus and adding in a louder voice, "I need transportation that can't be traced to me and I need it fast."

"You know me. I'm always prepared," Gus boasted.

"That's what I like about you, Gus," Josh said, winking and flashing another grin at Cat, who only rolled her eyes.

Together, Josh and Gus veered in the direction of the glass door that led to the garage where several men were busy. One car without tires was up in the air while another was in the process of being driven into an empty bay.

"Got two cars in the usual spot, both with papers. They can't be traced. Yer welcome to 'em. Fer the usual fee, that is."

"Of course. I'll transfer the money as soon as I can get to a computer," Josh agreed, as they stopped at the door.

"No problem. I trust ya."

"I appreciate that. I wish I could say the same."

"Ya always were a smart man," Gus chortled, slapping Josh on the back. "Need a lift to the car?" he asked a moment later.

At Josh's nod, Gus turned to open the door. "Jerry's just leavin' to pick up a stranded motorist. He'll give ya a ride."

"Thanks."

"Thanks aren't necessary when yer payin' the prices yer payin'."

"Maybe. But I'm still thankful."

Gus nodded, moved through the open door, and yelled, "Jerry," amid sounds of clanking and drilling going on in the garage, but she missed the rest of their conversation because the door closed, effectively shutting out all noise from the bays.

"So, you're getting a car?" Cat asked, her low voice breaking into the silence.

"Yeah." Josh sighed, wiping his hand over his face before rubbing his neck in agitation. Or impatience. She wasn't quite sure which.

"Then you can take me home?" Cat couldn't miss the hope in her voice.

"No. I'm not going back to Bozeman."

His words crushed her hopes, paralyzing her with fear. She didn't want to think about how afraid she felt at the thought of going home alone. The sensation was so different from what she felt even an hour ago. At this point, she was terrified of leaving him and even more terrified of staying with him.

Shadows of the past, always lurking in the deep recesses of her mind, emerged. Mental images of a stalking man flashed. She took one deep breath, then another, doing it again and again until she gained a modicum of control.

"Why?" she challenged, pushing through her fear and allowing her anger to erupt in its place. After all, her ex was in the past and this was the present. And most of all, she was so tired of being afraid. "We need to go to the authorities."

"I can't." He walked to the plate glass wall of windows next to the entrance and looked out.

"I don't understand. Someone's out to kill us and you're not doing anything about it?"

After a moment of scanning the horizon, Josh spun around. "Yeah, I plan on staying alive."

"I want to go home," she begged. Her shoulders slumped in defeat. She let her gaze meet his and she couldn't stop her eyes from begging as well. "You promised."

"I promised you could call your friend," Josh said, his expression unyielding. "You should be safe enough once you're away from me. That's the best I can do."

Cat's retort was cut off because Gus came charging through the door, saying, "Jerry's headin' out now. You can meet 'im 'round back."

"Thanks, Gus. I'll be in touch."

"I know. You be careful, ya hear?"

Josh nodded and grabbed Cat's hand, giving her no choice but to follow him out the door.

The next thing Cat knew, she was being hoisted up into an oversized tow truck. Jerry, another large, barrel-chested man, wore grungy overalls and looked like he hadn't showered in a week. Smelled like it too.

Cat tried not to breathe as she sat next to him, also trying to avoid actual contact.

How could Josh just leave her?

Stop it, she mentally scolded. Wasn't that what she wanted?

She took a deep, calming breath. Only it wasn't as calming as it could have been given the smell, she realized, turning her head away and glancing at Josh.

Catching his amused expression, she clenched her fist again. Oh, how she'd love to take a swing and wipe that smug, knowing smirk off his face.

Chapter 13

Rodriquez woke, and after looking around, he figured he'd been out an hour at most. He spent another hour rubbing the sturdy rope against a rough brick until it was thin enough to give way so he could free himself from the hog-tying Buchannan gave him.

By this point, after realizing the man had gone through his pockets and had taken everything, including his cell phone, his endurance was shot.

The bastard was history, Rodriquez fumed, undoing the bindings around his feet.

No one made a fool out of him and got away with it.

After he was completely free, he hightailed it back to his car, hidden in the brush two miles away. Once inside, he activated his spare cell phone and punched in a number, thankful he'd planned that far ahead.

"He got away."

There was a long pause on the phone line before it crackled to life. "Which means you've squandered a third attempt?" The voice halted for a moment and then Rodriquez heard an audible sigh. "I can appreciate the first incident as bad luck and the second as happenstance. But three? Surprise in taking out Buchannan was our strongest weapon, and now we've lost that element. My patience is waning."

"I understand."

"Do you? You were chosen for this holy cause. One that spans generations. Decades of planning. Decades of training. The timing of Buchannan's death is crucial to ultimate success. And our success is in peril because you have failed. Not once...but three times. Another failure is not an option. Are we clear?"

"I won't fail. He found the receiver I was carrying, but he's not as wily as he thinks he is. The transmitter's still sending a signal, so I doubt he realizes I have a spare."

"You still have his signal?"

"Yes. I'm following his trail right now on the GPS. He's not invincible after all."

"Good, but he's eluded you three times and you must use these lessons wisely. 'Arrogance diminishes wisdom.' Overconfidence can only lead to another failure. And more importantly, the clock is ticking. Success hinges on flawless timing. Don't contact me again until you've completed your mission."

The line went dead and Rodriquez swore heatedly while hitting the steering wheel in frustration. He'd hated making the call. Was shamed by failure, yet relieved to know he had another chance. Few were ever given as much within his organization. He felt honored to have so much responsibility, but at the same time, he knew he couldn't fail. One more failure would mean certain death.

⚃

The gal behind the counter nodded to a few empty booths in the noisy diner. "Take any free spot. Menus're on the table. Be with ya in a sec."

Cat followed Josh to an empty booth. Sliding in opposite him, she was relieved they were taking time to eat before calling Cheryl to come and get her. She inhaled scents of coffee, bacon, and butter as her stomach growled. She was starving.

"I guess I should call my friend before I order."

Josh's nose had been in the menu and her statement got his attention, causing him to glance sharply at her.

"You know you don't have to leave. I'll keep you safe," he said, not letting her look away.

"I don't think that'd be wise," she replied honestly. She was too tempted to give in and stay with him. He'd keep her safe. Of that, she had no doubt. But somehow, she didn't think staying with him would be in her best interest.

No! Cat would be safer without him. Her fears over her ex had faded. There was no way he could have found her. Now her fear of making a fool of herself over Josh Buchannan was a bigger threat, giving her a new resolve. Get away from him as quickly as possible. She only wanted to go home and forget she ever met the man now eyeing her as if she meant something to him. She let out the breath she'd been holding in, and lifted her chin. "Besides, you promised."

"So I did," Josh admitted a moment later. "You're really going to leave me?"

Cat fought to ignore the disappointment laced in the words. Don't let him get to you, she chided mentally. He told you himself this attraction isn't real. If you stay with him, you'll eventually do something stupid, something you'll regret for the rest of your life. So, get out while you can. "I'm afraid so." She was amazed her voice sounded so steady. "Not that it hasn't been a pleasure. I always enjoy waking to cabins blowing up and men coming to kill me."

"Really? Somehow I got the impression it annoyed you," Josh teased.

"Yeah? Well, looks can be deceiving."

"Humph. Don't I know it." He then nodded toward the back of the diner. "The pay phone's straight back by the restroom. Do you need change?"

"Why can't I use your phone?"

"Because when I use it now, calls can be traced and triangulated. I prefer to remain hidden for the time being. You should be safe, though."

"You think I could still be in danger?" The fear she'd worked so hard to contain broke through the surface of her consciousness.

"You could be, but I'm the main target. Once they realize we've parted ways, they should lose interest in you, especially if you go to the authorities."

"That makes me feel real safe," she said, not bothering to keep the sarcasm out of her voice.

"If you want to be totally safe, you should stay with me." He went back to his menu.

"I'll pass. I've had my fill of running." She shook her head, glancing at him. While his concentration focused on what to order, she continued scrutinizing. "Are you ever going to tell me who you really are?"

He looked up and his expressive eyes bestowed such warmth when he grinned. She couldn't stop from mirroring him.

"I know...if you told me you'd have to kill me," Cat said, laughing and rolling her eyes. Besides being a jerk, the man could certainly make her laugh. As she bent to reach into her bag and pull out a wallet full of change, regret washed over her. She shoved it back, storing it with her fear, and slid out of the booth. "Someday, Buc-man, I'm going to find out your secrets."

"Maybe. But not today." His teasing voice grabbed at her

insides, making it that much harder to walk calmly away. So did the heat of his gaze landing on her back as she walked between the booths and the counter, heading in the direction of the pay phone.

It took two rings before Cheryl Green answered her work number.

"Cher?" Cat asked, relieved to finally hear her voice.

"Cat? Is that you? Smitty told me you were still alive, but with all the stuff in the news I was afraid to believe it."

"Yeah. I'm not dead yet, though it's not for want of trying on someone's part," Cat joked, blowing an errant strand of hair out of her eyes.

"Jeez, Cat. What's going on?"

"It's too complicated to explain over the phone."

"Are you still with Josh Buchannan?"

The question had her smile growing and she couldn't keep the smile out of her voice. "Yeah. I kind of wouldn't be here if it wasn't for him," Cat said, remembering how he wouldn't let her stay inside the plane. It all seemed as if it occurred so long ago because so much had happened since.

"I'm worried about you being with him. There're a lot of rumors floating around in the press. I don't know what to believe."

"I'm safe enough with Josh." Somehow, deep in her heart, she knew that was the truth.

"Well, you should know Brad's been telling anyone who'll listen that Josh Buchannan's responsible for everything," Cheryl's concerned voice shot back. "But Smitty says not to listen to gossip. He's worked with Buchannan for years and thinks he's in some kind of trouble and needs help."

"Yeah, if you count someone trying to kill him as trouble, I'd say Smitty's dead-on." Cat turned around and caught Josh's penetrating scrutiny. His intent expression had the heat rushing up her face again, causing her to give him her back and plead into the phone. "Look, Cheryl. Do you think you could come and get me?"

"Where are you?"

"I'm in some diner in Butte. Hold on, I'll get the exact address." Cat held the phone to her chest and asked the same waitress who'd been behind the counter and was now heading past her, "Excuse me? Where are we?"

"Honey, if you don't know that, you're in trouble."

"No." Cat chuckled. "I mean what's the address here and how

would I get here from Bozeman."

"Oh. Let me think." She broke off for a moment, then rattled off the name of the diner and instructions, ending with, "We're right off the interstate. Take the first exit into town and we're right there."

Cat repeated the instructions to Cheryl. "When do you think you can get here? I know you're working."

"Screw work," came her friend's declaration, drawing another smile from Cat. "I'll take an early lunch and sneak out right now. I can work late today if I have to."

"Are you sure you don't mind?"

"Of course not. What're friends for if you can't depend on them?"

"Thanks, Cher. You're a lifesaver."

"Yeah, well I have ulterior motives. I have to meet this Josh Buchannan. The way Smitty tells it, the man walks on water. The paragon's still with you, right?"

"Yes." Cat laughed. "Ulterior motives or not, I really appreciate this."

☙

Once Cheryl hung up, she looked up to see Brad Maxwell heading her way. "Well, well, well. Look what the cat dragged in."

He ignored her and nodded to the phone. "Speaking of cats, have you heard from her? I've been hoping for a call, but my cell phone battery's dead and I misplaced my charger."

"Good excuse."

"It's not an excuse. I *am* worried about her. I thought maybe she'd call you."

"She's fine. I'm going to pick her up right now." She stood and pulled an oversized bag out of her drawer and set it on her desk. "Funny though, she didn't ask about you."

"She's safe, right?"

"Yeah, Brad. She's safe."

"I'll go with you, just to make sure."

"She called me, not you, so save the concerned boyfriend act for your next conquest."

"Hey, I care about her," he said with a belligerent tilt to his head. "We're friends."

"Really? Then act like one." Grabbing her bag, she tossed it over her shoulder. "I gotta go. I'm sure she'll call you later."

As she was leaving, her phone rang. Cheryl stopped her retreat and picked up the ringing phone with a minimum of movement. "Green here," she snapped, ignoring Brad who was watching her.

Her stance softened and she grinned into the phone. "Good morning." She listened for a moment, then her attention moved to Brad. She nodded. "Yeah. Brad's right here. And you were right! Cat just called and I'm on my way out the door now. I'm meeting her at a diner on the outskirts of Butte off the interstate." Cheryl then handed the phone to Brad, her eyebrows slanting upward. "It's Smitty. Seems you've got problems and you're late. Agents McMann and Adams are waiting for you at Buchannan Aeronautics."

When he took the phone from her, she hoisted her bag over her shoulder again, saying as she went, "I wonder what you did to piss 'em off."

"They're looking for a scapegoat, lumping me with Buchannan. If you ask me, he knows they're on to him and that's why we haven't heard from him."

"Yeah, right," she snorted, heading out the door.

ℭ

Smitty hung up the phone after giving Brad a piece of his mind. The asshole had a student scheduled in fifteen minutes and should've been in the office rather than out looking for information about Cat.

He sighed and moved his attention to the two morons standing in front of him.

"He's on his way. Maybe I can help?" he offered.

"No. We'll wait." McMann moved to sit on the sofa, while his partner went over to the machine behind the counter and got a cup of coffee before joining him.

"I'll be outside if you need me, fueling a plane for my next student," Smitty said, shoving away from the counter. "Don't worry about the phone. Just let the machine get it, if it rings."

"Do we look like secretaries?"

"No." He opened the glass door and said under his breath, "Fuckin' idiots…that's what you look like to me."

At the plane, Smitty took out his cell phone. Hit the On button. The small device beeped to life. "Yeah. Murph," he said, seconds later. "It's me, Smitty. I got a line on where he might be."

"Where?"

"A diner in Butte. I couldn't get the exact location because

McMann and Adams were standing right in front of me and I didn't want to say too much."

"And you can't leave?"

"Not without raising eyebrows."

Smitty heard Murphy's audible sigh. "I'll see what I can do. I'm keeping this between you and me."

❧

Cat hung up and detoured to the restroom. Peering into the mirror as she washed her hands, the bedraggled reflection staring back shocked her. She dipped her face in water pooled in her fingers, hoping to put some color into her cheeks.

"I can't imagine what Josh's talking about," she muttered, giving her face more scrutiny after patting it dry with paper towels.

Cat saw nothing remotely sexy in the image she glimpsed. Pale and dazed—definitely in need of makeup. She gave a negligent shrug and headed out the door. She couldn't do much about it now. Besides, it wasn't as if she was trying to entice anyone. Just the opposite.

"I ordered a cup of coffee for you," Josh said, as she sat down at the booth.

"Thanks. I could use a cup about now."

She picked up her menu, looking it over as Josh asked, "Do you know what you're having?"

"Still deciding," she replied. After much debate, she decided on the works—eggs, sausage, and hash browns—and was ready to order by the time their waitress walked up with two cups of coffee.

She set one in front of Cat and the other in front of Josh, then reached into her oversized pocket and pulled out a pen and small order pad. "What can I get for you?"

When she breezed away with their order, Josh's eyebrows lifted. "So, is everything set?"

"Yeah. Cher's leaving right now. Should be here in an hour or so."

"Good, that'll give us time to eat."

"How can you remain so calm and collected, knowing someone wants to harm you?"

"I have to eat and so do you. I'd prefer to do it without thinking about all the shit that's been happening, if you don't mind."

"So, you block it out?"

111

"Yeah, when it comes to survival, I do. Eating when you get the chance can sometimes mean the difference between living and dying."

"You're some kind of agent, aren't you?"

"Am I?"

"Yeah, you are," Cat said firmly, totally convinced she was right. Then she bit her bottom lip, noting how quickly his expression snapped shut. He was so good at that. Closing his features so nothing of his inner thoughts showed. "Now I know you are," she teased while he took a sip of coffee, avoiding her gaze. She sighed. He wasn't going to give anything more away. "You know you're just as bad at the flirting. I saw how she looked at you."

Her comment got his attention.

"The waitress," Cat said. "Her gaze was X-rated."

Josh snorted. "She's old enough to be my mother, for Christ's sake."

"Just because she's old doesn't mean she doesn't recognize a hunk."

"A hunk? You think I'm a hunk?"

"I most certainly do not. But she does." Cat nodded at the waitress who was now taking an order at another booth.

"No. Sell me something else, because I'm not buying that." Josh directed his attention to where she indicated for a moment before refocusing those soulful brown eyes on hers, his grin slowly spreading. "Admit it. You think I'm a hunk."

Cat grinned. She couldn't help it because his words along with his earnest demeanor tickled her insides, making her forget for the moment her misery. "You know, Buc-man, you could use a little humility."

"What would be the fun of that?"

She shook her head and said softly, "You really are something," not bothering to hide the warmth she felt.

"So are you, Powder Puff."

Neither had any chance to respond because in the next instant their waitress plopped two plates, both overflowing with food, in front of them.

Thankful for the interruption, Cat concentrated on her breakfast.

Both ate in silence.

"So, what're you going to do?" she asked, after eating most of her meal and feeling uncomfortable because the atmosphere had somehow turned solemn. In an effort to dispel the mood, she added a teasing smile. "That is, if you can tell me without killing me."

Josh appeared to debate his answer. Finally, he sighed. "I need to find out why someone's trying to kill me, and I intend to go to the source who'll give me my answers."

"I thought you said this was related to a drug operation you discovered?"

"So I did. But because of our morning visitor and the tracking device I found on him, I now realize I may be mistaken. Actually, I don't know what to think anymore."

"Why would anyone else want you dead?" Then she stopped and quickly added, "I know, I know. You don't have to answer, but I can't help being curious."

He flashed a self-deprecating smile. "That's a really good question and one to which I can't seem to find a ready answer." His demeanor sobered. "I'm sure I have enemies, but most of them know me as someone else. And Bozeman, Montana, is a far cry from where those enemies are."

"So, I'm right. You're an agent."

"No. I'm not a field op. Not anymore. I used to work undercover a lifetime ago, in foreign countries a world away." This time when he met her gaze, his eyes weren't smiling. Next thing Cat knew, he placed his warm hand on hers, squeezing it in a comforting manner. "I work for myself now. I simply fly and feed information on my own terms. I quit everything else back when my grandmother was dying." He sighed and slowly shook his head. "That man this morning is an agent. An undercover field operative like I used to be. I recognized his tools. But here's the kicker. CIA field ops don't work in the US. Since Montana is out of his jurisdiction, I have to figure out why he's after me."

"Wow!" She couldn't stop the confusion she felt from showing on her face. "What about the drug stuff," she whispered.

He shrugged. "This whole thing is a puzzle I mean to solve."

"I don't understand."

"Neither do I. Something's going on and until I find out what, I can't go back to Bozeman or to the authorities."

"No, I mean why'd you decide to tell me?" she asked, watching his face closely. "You didn't have to, you know." She held her breath, not daring to believe what it meant, yet wanting to with all her heart.

"I know and I may come to regret it. But I don't think so." He went back to his breakfast. "I trust you with the information. I hope I'm not wrong."

A flush of pleasure shot through her. She sensed that he didn't say those words very often.

After that, neither spoke.

The waitress was clearing the table of empty dishes when Cat happened to look outside the plate glass entrance and spotted Cheryl getting out of her car.

"Looks like my ride's here." Mere seconds later, the door of the diner burst open as the bundle of energy named Cheryl bustled inside and over to their table, sticking out her hand. "I bet you're Josh Buchannan."

"You'd win that bet," Josh answered, taking her hand and offering a warm smile.

"I'm glad I finally met you. Smitty's been singing your praises, telling me I need to meet you for too long now."

"Any friend of Smitty's is a friend of mine," he said.

"I made it in record time. Fifty-seven miles in forty minutes," Cheryl boasted. She looked at Cat. "You ready? We gotta get goin'. Old man Benson's on my ass because I dared leave."

"You drive that fast all the time?" Josh asked in an amused voice.

"Pretty much," she replied. "I can't believe he had the balls to tell me I needed to be back in an hour. Like I'm his slave or something," she added without missing a beat.

Josh laughed and met Cat's eyes, his gaze clearly saying, "Is she for real?"

Cat only nodded while Cheryl finished, holding up her hand, showing thumb and forefinger an inch apart, "I was this close to being out of the office without him seeing me."

"I guess time's up." Cat grabbed her flight bag and scooted out of the booth. She turned to Josh as he was climbing out of the booth and added, working to sound upbeat, "I appreciate all you've done for me. I hope everything works out."

Josh opened his arms. Cat needed no further invitation, giving in to the desire to have them around her once more, hoping to extract some last bit of courage from him to make good her escape.

"Stay safe, Cat," he whispered, hugging her. Then he kissed the side of her face and let go of her. "I'll see you when I have my answers."

Cat pretended not to hear the regret in his voice. It was only an illusion caused by all that had happened in the past forty-eight hours. What she felt for him wasn't real.

She nodded and turned quickly, praying her tears wouldn't betray her until she was safe and sound inside Cheryl's bright yellow Volkswagen bug.

Cheryl aided the process. She followed, telling Josh in her bubbly voice over her shoulder, "Nice meeting you. Maybe we can get together sometime under better circumstances."

"Yeah, sounds like a plan."

Cat didn't look back, but the heat from Josh's gaze penetrated her shoulders, so she knew he was watching. She opened the Volkswagen's passenger door and glanced down. Her shoe was untied. Ignoring the warmth of Josh's eyes, she bent over abruptly, blocking his view.

Something whizzed past her head, drawing her attention. In an instant, she saw through both open car doors her best friend's smiling form slump to the ground. Blood now covered her right shoulder.

"Oh my God!" she screamed. "Cheryl? Cheryl!" No. Her mind rebelled. This can't be real. One minute they were laughing and the next, Cheryl lay in a pool of blood on the pavement.

Suddenly, Josh crouched beside her and was shoving her into the car. In a flash, he'd somehow maneuvered himself into the driver's seat and was backing out of the parking space at full speed, yelling, "Stay down."

When the car reached as fast as it would go in reverse, Josh slammed in the clutch and turned the wheel hard to the left. As the bug spun, he shifted into second gear, turning the wheel hard back to the right, at the same time releasing the clutch and slamming down the gas just as the back window shattered.

Thank God he was here, taking charge, as it dawned on her what was happening.

"Someone's shooting at us," she whispered disbelievingly.

"I know," came Josh's quick reply. "So, stay down."

"Cheryl? We've got to go back." She looked up at him from her crouched position on the floor of the front seat. "Josh, she's been shot. We have to go back."

"We can't, Cat. I'm sorry. If we go back, we'll be killed."

"How can this be happening?" She couldn't think. Numbness set in, replacing shock. "Why would they hurt Cheryl?"

Josh pulled out his cell phone and handed it to her. "I don't know, but call 911."

She took the phone with shaking hands, punched in the three buttons, and gave the same information the waitress had told her to the voice on the other end.

"Thanks for the call, an emergency team is already on the way, ma'am."

"They already know," Cat said softly, pushing the Disconnect button. She dropped the phone on the seat. "You don't think my call gave away your position?"

"It's too late for that. Someone's already figured it out."

"Why, Josh? Why?"

"I don't know, but I'm damn sure going to find out."

His earnest words, spoken as if he was making a solemn vow, wafted past her ears and she could no longer hold on to her tears.

Chapter 14

Once Josh decided he wasn't being followed, he drove to a bank with a drive-through window. He pulled up to the open teller window and stopped. When the automatic drawer opened and a voice asked, "May I help you?" he said, glancing at the face behind the glass, "I need to make a large cash withdrawal."

She gave him a strange look. "Yeah? Well, as long as you have the proper ID."

"I do."

"Then I see no problem."

He wrote out a check quickly, withdrawing several thousand dollars from his account, added his driver's license, and placed both in the drawer.

The woman behind the glass drew it inside. After retrieving the check and license, she eyed him for a moment before shifting her gaze to his driver's license then to his face and back again a couple of times. Her voice blared from the intercom. "Did you know your back windshield is gone?"

Josh turned around. "So it is," he said, acting surprised. Then offering his most charming grin, he added, "Thanks for pointing it out."

The teller seemed satisfied with his answer and quickly began punching buttons on her computer. In a matter of minutes, the drawer slid open with his money and she gushed in a perky voice, "Have a nice day, Mr. Buchannan."

"Thanks." As soon as he pocketed his cash, his foot hit the gas pedal. Hard.

Next, he drove to the mall parking lot, the same lot where he'd gotten the car from Gus, driving around to the other side of the stores from where the remaining car sat in a space. He parked and shut off the engine.

Looking over at Cat and seeing her sitting, immobile, staring out the window with tears streaming down her face, his heart skipped beats and remorse filled him. Somehow this entire fiasco was his fault. If she hadn't been flying with him, she wouldn't now be grieving over what had happened to her friend.

"I know you're upset, but we need to move," he said, shoving his door open. "We can't stay in this car. They'll find us within minutes if we do. It's a miracle we've gone undetected this long."

When she still didn't move, he halted his retreat. The seconds ticked by. Ten…twenty…thirty. And still he waited, unsure of what to do. He wasn't even sure she'd heard him until her soft plea filled the silent space around them, permeating the air. "We need to go to the police."

He shook his head. "We can't."

"Why not?" She sniffled, wiped her tears as if visibly trying to compose herself. "We need to tell them what we know. Someone shot Cheryl."

"Right now I can't trust anyone, even the police, and they already know what's happened to Cheryl. He waited a heartbeat, then added, "We're targets."

"You're a target. Not me. Take me to the police."

"I can't, Cat." He didn't want to add fear on top of her grief, so he didn't let on that she was the target this time. The shooter was aiming for her, not him. "Please? Just trust me. You'll be safe enough with me. I won't let anything happen to you. And I'll go to the authorities after I get my answers, I promise."

"What about Cheryl?"

"There's nothing you can do for her, but try to stay alive."

"I can't think. I don't know what to do," she whispered. Her tears flowed faster. "Oh God! Why would someone try to kill her?"

"I don't know."

"You don't think the police will help?"

"No." He shook his head and met her tear-filled gaze. The torment he spied pierced his resolve. Though he wanted nothing more than to keep her safe, the decision was still hers. "If you don't want to stay with me, I'll drop you off at mall security, but I need to go now." He closed his eyes and held his breath, praying she'd stay with him.

"You can't leave me." Desperation now accompanied sorrow as she added, "Promise you won't leave me? I don't want to be alone."

Josh swallowed hard, ignoring the grapefruit-sized lump

forming in his throat. He hated seeing her so upset, but he had no qualms about using her fear for his own means, if it kept her safe. "I promise. But we have to hurry." His hand grabbed for the door handle again. "Can you trust me and hang on until we get to the other car?"

Cat nodded, sniffling, but her tears hadn't stopped.

He sighed. Placing his thumb and forefinger on her chin, he lifted it so he could see into her eyes, eyes that were clouded with pure anguish.

"I'm sorry, Cat," he whispered, his voice full of emotion. "I know this is tough, but you need to get a hold of yourself. We can't attract any attention or it could be our undoing. If we're a couple going shopping, we're invisible. If you're in tears, we'll be noticed. If they find out what we're driving, we're screwed. You understand?"

She took a deep breath and wiped her tears. "I'll be fine. Give me a minute."

"That's just it. We don't have much time. I can go and get the car by myself, if you'd rather."

"No," she said almost too quickly, clutching his arms and holding tight. "I don't want to be alone." Her voice was so panicky and her mien so frantic. There was no way she'd let him abandon her.

"Okay. Here let me help wipe your tears." He took a Kleenex and dabbed it with water from his water bottle. Trying to charm a smile out of her, he teased, "You're a complete mess."

When she looked at him with such woeful eyes, he couldn't help but put his lips to her tears. "Christ, Cat. I'm so sorry."

"You didn't shoot her." She wiped her tears and before his eyes transformed her face, hiding her grief behind her sad smile, doing what she needed to do. "I'm ready."

He heaved a heavy sigh and nodded. "Then let's go. We still need to shop, but I'd rather do it somewhere else away from here."

They climbed out of the car and headed inside a JC Penney's store, going through the mall and using the stores as cover. Josh tried to keep his pace slow enough so Cat could stay with him, but several times he caught himself going too fast and slowing to wait for her.

"We've got to move faster," he urged a moment later. That was all the appeal he needed to make because from then on, she was right with him.

In a matter of minutes, they were seated in Gus's other car.

"You don't think Gus will mind that we're taking his second car?" she asked, placing her seat belt around her and clasping it into place.

"He might, but he won't mind the money I'll wire him."

Josh started the car and wound his way out to the highway again. Soon after, he pulled into a Kmart parking lot.

"We need to shop." He turned off the engine. "Pick up a few things and prepare for the worst."

"The worst? You mean it could get worse?"

He swore under his breath at the panic back in her voice, wishing he didn't have to scare her. But at this point, he felt she deserved the truth. It might keep her alive.

"They seem persistent." He snared her gaze so she could see the seriousness of the situation in his. "I can keep us alive, but you have to follow my lead. Understand?"

He wiped his face with his hand, before rubbing the back of his neck and letting out a long sigh when he saw her eyes growing bigger with fear. She appeared so fragile, as if she was about to come apart at the seams.

"I'm a cautious man, Cat," Josh said gently, purposefully softening his stance a bit. "I won't let anything happen to you. I can go shop by myself if you can't keep it together. But I've got to go now. We don't have much time. Ten—fifteen minutes at the most. Then I want to be gone."

She shook her head and whispered, "I don't want to stay here by myself."

"Okay." He nodded. "We both need to buy a few clothes. Something to tide us over for a few days. Also, I want you to get a couple of wigs. A red one and a black one. We may need a quick getaway. This is only a precaution, understand?"

Her body slackened somewhat and she offered him one of her smiles, nodding.

"Good." He placed his hand over hers and squeezed. "You're doing good. Just hold on."

"I'm fine."

"Okay, come on." He opened his door, climbed out, and rushed around to help her exit the car. He wrapped her in his embrace, kissed her forehead, and keeping his arm around her shoulders for support, spirited her toward the double glass doors.

They spent twenty minutes picking out necessities...toiletries, clothes, and foodstuffs. Josh bought several cell phones that couldn't be traced and made sure he had plenty of minutes with each one. Within another five, they were headed south on I-15. For several hours he drove, keeping his speed to five miles over the speed limit. Traffic was light and they made good time.

Almost to the Utah border, he finally slowed and took the next exit.

"Why're we stopping?" she asked, offering the first sound since they started driving.

"Gas." He scrutinized her face and sighed. Worry and pain were etched like deep scratches in glass, marring her beauty. "How about I call the hospitals in Butte, see what I can find out?"

In an instant, both emotions faded as elation brightened her face. "Would you?"

"Yeah. Let me just fill up the tank and get some change for the phone over there." He nodded toward the phone booth he'd spotted earlier.

"Why not use the cell phones you bought?"

"I don't want to waste the precious minutes. I might need them. I feel safe enough making an anonymous call to the hospital." He climbed out of the car.

When done with the gas and transactions, he exchanged several dollars for quarters, then went to place his call. Luck was with him as the first hospital he tried put him through to intensive care, where Cheryl Green was listed in critical condition.

Josh got back into the car. "She's in critical condition, but still alive. She's in surgery and will be for several hours. I'll call later for an update."

She nodded, flashed him a sad smile, then refocused on the passing scenery.

They drove in silence for fifty miles before he pulled off the highway and into an inexpensive motel parking lot. Cat seemed done in and he didn't want to push her any more than he already had. They'd get a good night's sleep, he reasoned. Tomorrow would be a long day.

Josh left her in the car while he went to register.

After checking in, he drove around to the back side of the motel, saying to Cat, "It's not the Ritz, but it's a place where paying for the night with cash won't raise eyebrows."

"Looks fine," Cat murmured.

He rushed around to help her. Once she was out, he hurried to the motel's door, put the key into the lock, and pushed inside the room.

"The room looks clean and hopefully the bed's comfortable," he explained, when she came up behind him. Spying the king-sized bed, he cleared his throat. "Sorry. I didn't want to attract attention asking for two double beds."

"It's okay," Cat said softly. She walked slowly to the edge of the bed and sat. She stayed put while Josh ran back to the car and gathered all their things, the newly purchased items as well as both their flight bags.

Returning with arms full, he kicked the door closed behind him, glanced at the bed, and noticed her sitting, staring off into space just as she'd done in the car before he'd forced her into action. Noting her hunched shoulders, regret washed over him. He spent a few minutes unpacking and making a pit stop, giving her more time to come to terms with her grief.

When he had nothing left to do but face her, he finally did. She looked so pitiful, his heart ached.

He sat beside her on the bed, reached to pull her into his arms, situating her on his lap. He kissed the side of her face. "Are you hungry?"

She nodded. "I guess I should eat."

"I saw a McDonald's about a mile back. I'll get us some food, okay?"

Though she nodded, her actions weren't enthusiastic.

"Will you be okay alone?"

"I'll be fine."

He released her and stood. "Are you sure?" When she nodded, he went over to the window overlooking the motel parking lot, and gave it his usual scrutiny. Satisfied with what he saw, he said, "You can come with me," as he closed the drapes, shutting out the last remnants of fading light from the room.

"Go, Josh. I'll be fine."

He turned to go, but glanced back at Cat and paused for a moment with his hand on the doorknob, totally unsure he should leave her.

Her chin came up and her defiant gaze locked on his, showing she meant what she said.

"Okay," he said with a sigh. "I'll be back as soon as I can."

He left her sitting on the bed.

ભ

"Murphy here," he said, picking up the phone on the second ring after recognizing Smitty's number. "Tell me you have good news."

"No," Smitty sighed. "Those two morons have convinced everyone involved that Buc's up to his ears in some cartel-like drug ring, and he's double-crossed some high-level drug lord, pissing him off, and that's why the attempts on his life."

"Shit. Just what I need," Murphy said. Pinching the bridge of his nose, he took several deep breaths before he spoke again. "Have you heard from him?"

"No. I was hoping you had."

"Not since last night. How have things disintegrated so quickly?"

"Yeah, well you haven't heard the worst." Smitty sighed into the phone. "They've asked for an indictment with enough evidence to nail Buc for drug trafficking. Now that an innocent bystander was killed, they'll probably get their warrant."

"I thought the girl was still alive."

"I wasn't talking about Cheryl Green." His voice cracked with emotion as he added, "She's out of surgery and getting stronger by the second, thank God." Smitty hesitated a moment, then cleared his throat, and was all business once again. "I was talking about Gloria Goodman. Her death may not have been an accident. The car shouldn't have burst into flames like it did, so they're investigating."

"Gloria Goodman? She's Buc's office manager, right?"

"Yeah. Or she was," Smitty explained, giving a brief overview.

"It doesn't make sense." Murphy's voice held all of the confusion he felt.

"DEA's working on the angle that Buc had her knocked off to hide his involvement. His motive looks good on paper. She had access to all his books and knew the business inside out."

"How long before they get their warrant?" Murphy asked, looking out the window of his office and seeing nothing but pouring rain. Such dreary news matched the dreary day.

"Not sure," Smitty answered. "They've got enough for probable cause on his bank records alone. And they're steadily uncovering more dirt."

"Shit." Murphy rubbed the back of his neck while taking a deep breath. He sank in his chair and swiveled around. He reached for the bottle of antacids and shook out two, before popping them into his mouth. "I don't need this now. What else?"

"Their most damning evidence is Buc's name on a lease for several trailers, one a known meth lab and the others are now suspected to be and are being staked out. The Feds are now tracing money to pockets of closed labs around the country, looking for a connection. Either he has us both snowed or someone's gone to a lot of trouble to frame him. Right now he's only wanted for questioning, but it's not looking good."

The line went silent while Murphy took in this bit of news.

"What about Candace Tyler?" he asked after a long moment.

"What about her?"

"Could she be involved?"

"I doubt it," Smitty replied, almost too quickly. "It's obvious Buc's the main target. She's an innocent bystander."

"Yeah, but what if she's not?"

"I still don't buy it." There was a long pause before Smitty asked, "Why?"

"Two reasons." Murphy leaned back, spinning his chair to face the window. A drop of rain making its way down the windowpane caught and held his attention as he answered. "First, she's dating the other prime suspect. That's a coincidence right there. Then, she's with Buc. I've been doing some checking, digging into her past."

"And?"

"She has an interesting ex-husband. Seems he's an Israeli whose name appeared on several watch lists due to his affiliation with Candace Tyler's parents, before he disappeared completely off Homeland Security's radar not long after she divorced him," Murphy stated, swiveling back around and opening the file he had sitting on his desk.

"So?" Smitty snorted. "There are hordes of people on those lists. I remember hearing about an accountant named Bob Smith, born and raised in Detroit, who is on one."

Murphy didn't say anything while thumbing through the papers. When he spoke his voice held speculation.

"Yeah, but she met her ex-husband while visiting her parents, Sister and Brother Tyler. They were killed in Afghanistan. You remember the operation? You were part of it."

Smitty blew a low whistle. "You think there's a connection?"

"I can't find anything solid, but something about it bothers me."

"Seems like a stretch to think all that's going on now could be part of that operation."

"Maybe," Murphy grunted. Smitty understood the Arab mind better than any field op he'd ever worked with. But he wasn't totally convinced terrorism wasn't involved. His desk job with Homeland Security, complete with a cushy San Francisco office, held none of the risks of his earlier position in the CIA and was a far cry from some hostile hellhole of a country too many miles away. But this entire mess had his instincts on full alert, reminding him of why he took his position seriously. The US wasn't as safe or as impenetrable as everyone believed. Terrorists worked overtime, utilizing America's freedoms to their advantage.

"Whoever's behind this is organized, using sophisticated methods. From what I've read, he could fit the bill." Murphy closed the file, shook out a couple more antacids, and popped them into his mouth. Pulling a hand through his hair, he let out a long sigh and when he continued speaking, his voice held none of his frustration over not having any answers. "He's a nasty fellow. Divorce records indicate stalking and abuse. Maybe he's found her. And there's the connection with Buc to the past. Maybe she's involved to get revenge. I know I'm grabbing at straws here, but there's too much coincidence for my liking."

"Still doesn't add up," Smitty shot back. "Buc's past is too well hidden."

"I don't believe in coincidences any more than Buc does, so something's there. And it fits with what's happening in Langley. The powers that be are convinced their leak is tied to this. Reynolds' and the other agent's death has them spooked."

"Would she have her best friend killed?"

"Who knows about fanatics? Maybe she's no different than her parents, who were almost radical in their bringing Jesus to Muslims, or her husband, who swung in another direction. Weird combination, if you ask me."

Smitty's audible, resigned sigh seeped into his ear. "I'll see what more I can learn."

"You do that and I'll keep digging. Between the two of us, maybe we'll hit more than dirt."

"Okay. But you're wrong about Cat. From what I know of the lady, I can't swallow it any more than I swallow the idea of Buc being behind it all," Smitty said.

"It's a puzzle, that's for sure. You watch your back. Don't discount anything. The last thing I need is your death on my hands, like Reynolds and Jenkins. Unfortunately, both were into some deep shit, which may or may not have been a factor. We may never know why they died."

"I'll take care. I'm just as cautious as Buc."

"Yeah, I know. Keep me posted," Murphy said before cutting the connection.

෮

Brad Maxwell, manning the counter at Buchannan Aeronautics, looked up to see McMann and Adams saunter inside. Both carried large cups of coffee.

"Well, if it isn't our fine federal officers at work, wasting the taxpayers' money," Brad taunted when the two stopped right in front of him.

"Stuff it, Maxwell." McMann grunted. "We've got a few more questions to ask you."

"Fire away. I have nothing to hide." Grinning smugly, Brad leaned back in his chair. "I already told you assholes everything I know."

"You may want to see about hiring an attorney."

"Do I need one?"

"You tell me," McMann said, giving him a look of disgust.

"No wonder our country's going down the toilet. You can't get a straight answer out of anyone anymore."

"I've heard it all before, so save your breath." McMann took a long drink of his coffee, observing Brad the entire time. He then placed his cup on the counter and rummaged through his briefcase. He pulled out several sheets of paper. "Explain these figures for us."

Brad took the sheets and glanced at them for an extended moment, then handed them back. "Not my account. Never seen this before and I know nothing about it."

"That's interesting. Because there's a lady at the bank who ID'd your photo. Apparently you like to flirt."

"This is all you got? Some deposits into a bogus account?"

"Yeah, and the fact that you're working for Joshua Buchannan.

Those deposits happen to match his withdrawals. Same amounts and same days. Quite a coincidence, wouldn't you say?" McMann asked, sporting his own smug smile.

"You're fishing." Brad shook his head. But his smile lost some of its confidence as the special agent handed him additional pages.

"No. As you can see, we've got more. Seems there's been some interesting activity going on in the past six months with students who should've been pilots by now, given all the time they're showing up on the books taking lessons. And you happened to be the instructor."

"That's nothing new," Brad said, taking the pages. "There's no set number of hours for any one student. There's an average, of course."

"Yeah? Well, some of these students say they weren't in the cockpit on half of those dates, so someone's doctoring them."

"What's this got to do with me?" Brad asked belligerently, shoving the papers back at McMann after glancing briefly at them.

"Since your name's on the paperwork, I'm inclined to think it has a lot to do with you. We're not sure exactly what, but we'll find out, eventually. You could save yourself some grief and cut a deal by telling us what you know about Buchannan."

"I don't know shit about Buchannan. If he's in this, he's in it alone and he's framing me."

"Yeah. That's what they all say. When they're caught."

"You got anything else to say to me, say it to my lawyer."

"Figured you'd wise up." McMann picked up his cup and took another sip, eyeing him.

Brad swallowed hard, working at not squirming under his silent scrutiny.

Finally, he turned to his partner and Brad could breathe again. "Come on, Frank. Let's get outta here." Both men started for the door. McMann, who was about to push it open, added over his shoulder, "Don't go anywhere."

He waited a few minutes to make sure they were gone, then picked up the phone and punched in numbers.

When someone answered, Brad shouted into the receiver, "What the hell is going on? Those agents are all over me and this wasn't part of our agreement."

"They have nothing but supposition." The man's voice was almost too calm.

"Maybe. But when I took this job, you assured me there was no risk."

"There's always risk."

"They're linking me with Buchannan, and somehow I'm thinking it's a double cross."

"And why would we? We have an agreement. You hold up your end of the bargain and we'll take care of the rest. All you have to do is keep quiet. Buchannan will be the one to take the major heat."

"No. You listen to me." He pounded his fist on the counter in front of him. "I'm not going down alone."

"Are you threatening me?"

"If you want to take it that way, then I guess I am," Brad shot back, ignoring his menacing tone. "I only agreed to enter a few things in Buc's computer and to take on a few easily hidden flights for some extra bucks. Now there's a whole case against me. I wonder what would happen if those agents knew about you?" Brad slammed the handset into the cradle.

Chapter 15

Josh hustled through the door thirty minutes later. The first thing he noticed was that Cat hadn't moved a muscle and still sat in the same spot he'd left her, staring blankly at the floor.

He dropped the bags of food, along with the room key, on the table by the draped window and turned back to observe her.

"Are you okay?" he finally asked softly. She didn't answer. He wasn't even sure she heard him or knew he was back. "Cat?"

Still, she didn't seem to hear him.

"Shit, Cat. I'm so sorry." He rushed to stand next to her, not knowing what else to say or do.

"Why? It all seems so senseless," she murmured a moment later, glancing at him with those beautiful eyes of hers. Though cold in color, they were now blurred with tears and full of hopelessness. "It reminds me of when my parents were killed."

Josh remained silent, unable to speak. Hell, what could he say? Yeah, I understand fully, I was there? No. It was better if Cat didn't know of his part in her parents' deaths. Not now.

"Why do people have to do such heinous things to each other?"

"I don't know," he whispered. He slid beside her and wrapped his arms around her. More than anything, he wanted to ease her pain, because he felt by doing so, it would ease the ache in his stomach.

"Things like that aren't supposed to happen in Montana. New York, LA, or halfway around the world in places like Afghanistan, maybe, but not here."

"I don't know," he repeated, not having any other answer that would soothe her hurt.

"Why would someone try to kill me and kill my friend?"

"She's not dead," Josh volunteered, offering her hope. "The nurse sounded optimistic."

"What do you think her chances are?"

He eyed her critically for a moment before giving her an honest reply. "It's a toss-up. Her condition's critical and gunshots can go either way."

His answer seemed to be the force causing her leaky dam of tears to break. The giant drops streaked down her face as her grief consumed her.

"Why?" she demanded. Her hands curled into fists, pounded his chest, all the while Josh let her pummel to get her grief out. "Why?"

When she collapsed into a new round of tears, he wrapped his arms more solidly around her, pulling her onto his lap. He held her close and rocked her as he would a baby, kissing the side of her face, trying to console her.

"It's okay. Go ahead and cry. Let it out," he whispered, keeping her close, still kissing her beautiful, tear-streaked face. She complied with his request, sobbing uncontrollably, with him doing nothing more than holding her, every once in awhile adding another kiss to her temple.

Josh didn't know how long he held her while she cried, blocking out everything but the feel of her in his arms. When it seemed as if her storm blew over and she laid her head on his shoulder, relaxing, he simply held her for a while longer, running his hands soothingly over her arms in an effort to comfort her further. He thought she'd fallen asleep until he felt a trail of kisses along his collarbone, heading toward his neck.

When she nipped at his earlobe, his eyes flew open in shock. He responded to the soft touch of her mouth. His blood thickened and his pulse raced, spurred on by lurking adrenaline now pumping at an accelerated rate through his system.

"This isn't a good idea, Cat," he choked out, trying to extricate himself from the situation.

"Why? Don't you want me?"

"Shit," he said out loud, ignoring the hurt in her voice while leaning further away. Only she wouldn't let him, moving closer, rubbing against him suggestively.

Was she crazy? Of course he wanted her. The woman had to have an idea of what her kisses were doing to him. He was dying for want of her. Couldn't she feel the evidence? Yet he couldn't give in to need. If he did, she would hate both him and herself in the morning. And worse. He would hate himself.

"I'm tired of being afraid," she murmured, positioning her

mouth above his. Her head lowered. The soft kisses she bestowed did nothing to slow his desire.

Slipping for an instant, he eased her back on the bed. Kiss after hot kiss slowly devoured his willpower, and he melted, unable to stop from accepting the tongue she slipped into his mouth.

Disappointment as well as relief surged through him when she tore her lips away. Both emotions dissolved in an instant and he couldn't hold back an agonized groan as she whispered, "My best friend could die and I'm alive. But I don't feel it. Make me feel alive, Josh." Then her lips were back, branding him, removing his resolve, and weakening him further.

"Please, you don't know what you're doing," he pleaded, breaking contact after digging deep down and touching the surface of reason. No way this could continue. It wasn't real. Grief and fear had her emotions going haywire. He couldn't take advantage of her. Not like that. If he didn't get out now, while he could, he would be a goner for sure. He tried to pull away. But she held on, clearly having none of it, showing him she had other ideas. "This is crazy."

"No, it's not." She flashed a secret smile before biting his lip and sucking on it, shooting hot craving through his center and out his extremities. "I'm taking charge of my life and Cher would be the first person to tell me to go for it." Her lips nipped across his face, roaming to his ears, laving and sucking the entire way.

"Nothing's changed," he moaned, breathing hard. He closed his eyes and fought the molten streaks of pleasure now surging everywhere. Finally, he was able to add, "Since last night, Cat." But he was losing the battle. Fast. He took a deep breath, blocking out the sensations her tongue and teeth on his ear generated, while also blocking out the feel of her body nestled perfectly over him. "Please," he begged, trying one last time to get her to see reason. "It's emotion talking. You'll regret it in the morning."

"Then I'll regret it in the morning, but not tonight. Tonight, I'm going to live."

Her voice sounded as hot as her breath in his ear and was almost his undoing, as more resolve leaked out of his soul. If he didn't do something quickly, it would only be a matter of time before she wore him down and he'd be pumping into her. He rolled, effectively placing her underneath him, while raining the same wet kisses over her she'd been giving him.

Her low moan sent more sensations of need through Josh. He

smiled inwardly at how quickly she responded to his touch.

Damn! He was so much closer to the edge of reason than he thought. He now had to fight not only his desire, but hers as well.

He removed her shoes and socks, rubbing her bare feet, and slowly moving his hands up her legs to the bottom of her sweater. In seconds flat, he had her bra open. One hand found a perfect breast, kneading and squeezing, while the other fought to unsnap her jeans. When they were open and the zipper undone, he pushed the denim impediment lower. Then his hand followed, lowering panties and finding her core. He stroked. Watched her writhe beneath his touch.

"God, you're so beautiful. Look at how you respond to me," he whispered, gently nibbling on her lobe. Another low moan sent more hot pleasure shooting through him. She was so enticing. So tempting. So hard to resist.

Struggling against her heady allure, he continued with renewed purpose to offer some relief to the driving need he knew pulsed through her. The same need pulsing through him.

He shoved jeans and underwear lower, ignoring shapely hips and thighs, all the while fighting thoughts of her wrapping those limbs around him from taking over his mind.

Doubling his efforts to give her pleasure, he reconnected with her lips, grinding into them while both hands moved over her body, one stroking her breasts, the other found her heat.

Her low moans floated above him. The sound had him increasing his lower strokes. His lips meandered across her face, splaying butterfly kisses all over.

"Let go, Cat," he demanded, right before his mouth moved over hers. "Just let go."

The next moment she erupted and violent spasms overtook her. He waited for her tremors to subside before heaving a sigh of relief and collapsing beside her. Keeping her close while her body floated down from the high of her release, Josh closed his eyes, still fighting for control.

Need pounded through his veins. Desire clouded his judgment and want wouldn't let him relax. Too late, he realized his mistake. He should never have touched her because now he wasn't certain he had the will to continue with his resolve.

He dropped his hands to his side, praying for that last little bit of restraint.

Josh knew the exact moment reality settled over her, when she finally realized he wasn't doing anything more, because he felt her stiffen.

"Why are you stopping?"

He groaned inwardly as her soft voice wafted past his ears, grabbing at his insides and yanking on the thread of his limits.

‮ဆ‬

Confused, Cat sat up straight. "Why are you stopping?" she asked again, in case he hadn't heard her question.

"Josh?" After whispering his name, she searched his face, hoping to find some clue as to why he stopped. But his expression, yielding either pain or disgust, made her feel foolish, sitting there next to him with her body half exposed after having what she knew was her first orgasm. Though the experience had been wonderful, his actions stripped part of her joy.

"Yeah?" he finally replied, his face still taut with emotion. Her stomach clenched tighter as he opened his eyes and rubbed them with his finger and thumb.

Why wouldn't he meet her questioning gaze? Oh, great. He must think her a charity case now.

"I'm sorry," she said too quickly, trying not to cry.

"It's okay, Cat." The words came out in a sigh. "You have nothing to be sorry for."

Her tears broke free. He told her how he felt. How it was only emotion talking and that he didn't want regrets. But what did she do when he told her all this? She totally ignored him. How could she throw herself at him after he'd consoled her? And then what does he do, she thought. He lets me down easy. Says inane things like it's okay. How could it be okay? It was definitely not okay.

"I shouldn't have done that," she said. He probably thought she was some sex-crazed moron going after him. Her tears rushed faster and her face flamed. Had that really been her begging him to make her feel alive? Yeah, he was right about regrets. She had them now.

He put his hand on his face and rubbed it for a moment, his strained voice asking, "Give me a minute, will you?"

The annoyance she caught in his tone stung. She pulled up her underwear, but didn't bother with her jeans as they fell off her legs when she moved to the edge of the bed. Sticking her feet on the floor, she presented her back, not bothering to hide the fact that she was crying, her hunched, shaking shoulders and her wretched sobs a dead giveaway.

When he muttered "Shit," under his breath, her tears increased. Next thing she knew, he sat beside her, consoling her again, his arm sliding around her.

Oh great! More pity.

Shaking her head in agony, she pulled away. "No. Please, just leave me alone. Let me be miserable in peace."

He ignored her pleas and tightened his grip. "Why are you crying?" His gentle tone only made her cry harder. "Please tell me. I hate it when you cry."

"I can't believe you're asking me such a stupid question," she was able to get out in between sobs. Now she really wanted to climb into a hole and die. "Why are you being so nice? I liked you better as a jerk."

"Jerk? I'm trying to do the right thing here and you liked me better as a jerk?"

"Yeah! Why start changing now?"

"I can't believe we're having this conversation." An incredulous expression crossed his face. "You must really think I'm scum."

"Of course I don't think you're scum. I wanted to make love with you and you didn't. I understand."

He rolled his eyes and seemed to be holding on to his patience by a thread.

"That's emotion talking," he said on a long sigh. Though he spoke in a gentler voice, there was no mistaking his frustration. "You're grieving and in shock. We've been running for our lives and you think I should've been a complete asshole to use your emotional upheaval for my own sexual gratification?"

"Forget it." If she heard one more word about how emotionally distraught she was, she'd scream. She knew exactly what she was doing when she'd started kissing him, and nothing in her being would allow her to think she'd feel differently tomorrow or next week.

Of course, it didn't escape her notice that the events of the past few days had aided in her courage, as if they somehow granted permission to actually act on her feelings. "I've already made a complete fool of myself."

"Oh no. I can't forget it. You started this, you can't simply brush it off. Finish it."

"Then why'd you stop?" she asked softly, risking a look at his face. But as usual, his features gave nothing away. She glanced back at her hands, embarrassed that she cared so much about why.

"Come on. You can't believe I'd be such a jerk to take advantage of this situation?"

His statement drew her eyes again, causing her to ask honestly, "How would it be taking advantage if it was what I wanted?"

He eyed her carefully, maintaining his neutral expression. "This seems to be one of those situations where I'm damned if I do and I'm damned if I don't." He flashed a regretful smile and offered a half snort, clearly sad and amused at the same time. "In this case you're damning me because I didn't. Think, Cat. You'd be damning me in the morning if I had let things continue. I can't live with your regret."

The sincerity of his last sentence, spoken with such quiet intensity, left her with the impression that maybe she'd made a slight misjudgment as to why he stopped.

"You're so sure it would be my regret?" she asked, meeting his gaze and letting him see the truth in her eyes as well. "Or are you thinking it'd be yours."

"Christ," he groaned. His hand moved over his face, raking through his hair before resting on the back of his neck. Rubbing, he exhaled a steady breath. "I *am* damned for trying to do the right thing."

"You've made your point, so you can stop worrying." She attempted to scoot away from him. But his arm tightened its hold, locking her in place.

"Why would I worry?" he asked, his expression taking on a teasing quality.

"I understand you're not interested," she said huffily, making another futile effort to slide out of his reach. "I won't be jumping your bones again."

"You're something else, lady. You know that?" Josh said. He pulled her onto his lap and nuzzled her neck. "I want you to sit right there." He paused. "Now, you tell me if I'm interested or not. Feel that, Cat?" he whispered, biting her lobe, his tongue licking the outside of her ear, sending chills along Cat's spine. The heat of her blush stole up her face at his erection so flagrantly close to her center. The heat increased when his voice as hot as burning embers hit her ears. "That's my point. And it's dying to be made inside of you."

She closed her eyes, struggling with embarrassment over both his blatant arousal as well as her own fascination. Maybe her senses were on overload, but she'd never felt so alive and she wasn't about to lose this opportunity to feel more so.

"Does that feel like I'm not interested?" His mouth trailed wet kisses across her face. "I told you last night I've been fighting this and if you think it's been easy with you all but throwing yourself at me, you're crazy," Josh added, before finally meeting her lips, inhaling them for a long, heated kiss.

Then his mouth gentled. And now it seemed his lips were drawing excitement out of her a little at a time, so much so she thought she might shatter into a million pieces, it felt that good. She couldn't stop the moan that erupted from her. At this point, she was ready to explode, was dying to explode, and disappointment spread through her when she felt him pull away from her lips, sending her temperature plummeting.

No. She wasn't about to let him stop this time. Then she stifled a laugh when she heard his strained voice saying, "Nothing's changed since last night." The guy couldn't be repeating himself again, she thought as his lips hovered, barely an inch over hers.

Eye to eye, they stared, his face so close to hers, his breathing labored. Cat could see it in his eyes. He was leaving the choice up to her.

"You know where I stand. Can you walk away in the morning, once the emotion is spent?"

But his expression was too forceful and Cat had to close her eyes. Block out the intensity of his gaze that seemed to be searching her soul for the answer to his question. Self-doubt flooded her, muddying the waters of her decision—waters that had been so clear only a moment ago.

As if sensing her uncertainty, he slowly released his hold, lifting his head and disentangling himself from her.

"No," she shouted. Her vehemence surprised her, but didn't stop her from pulling him back, holding on to him as if she'd never let him go. "That's not my answer." Her frantic voice sounded so desperate. Yet, she was desperate to use this experience to push past fear, tired of being too afraid of life. "Please, Josh. That's not my answer."

Indecision clouded his eyes, making her braver.

"You make me feel alive. I want to feel you inside me. I don't think I could ever regret that. In fact, I'd regret not doing this. Please," she pleaded, letting him see the desire now seeping out of her gaze. Bending her head, she broke eye contact, and added as she placed her lips on his neck, "Don't make me beg any more than I already have."

"God help me, I want you so badly, but I can't," he whispered, just before his lips found hers, brushing them quickly. An instant later, he was separating from her, pulling away. "As much as I want to, I can't do it." Though he was breathing heavily, the words were spoken with a quiet finality.

"Why?" she asked, trying to keep from splintering at the gentle quality present in both his voice as well as his actions. She knew then he wasn't going to continue, making her feel even worse, if the feat was possible. How could he seem so unaffected when everything inside her wanted him?

"The flash of doubt I saw in your eyes won't let me. I can't explain why. All I know is, it doesn't feel right." He stood, bent to pick up her jeans, and handed them to her without meeting her gaze. When she took them, he started for the table, pulled out a chair, and sat. Opening the bag of food, he nodded at it and grunted. "You should eat something."

Watching him, she realized his shuttered look was back. Well! she thought. I guess that's that! She pushed his rejection to the back of her mind. If he could act as if nothing happened, so could she. Only it wasn't as easy as it seemed. Putting on her jeans, she doubled her efforts to keep from crying, asking instead, "What did you get for dinner?"

"Cheeseburger and fries. Only now they're cold." He took out the napkins, made two place settings, and added the burgers and fries. "I hope you're not a vegetarian," he teased, taking two drinks out of the cardboard holder and placing them next to the food.

"No," she said, joining him at the table. Maybe he was right. She was a mental mess. If only she could hate him for making her feel worse, but she found she couldn't because he was only doing what he thought was right. Why did it have to be so complicated? She bit into the cold burger and began chewing, not tasting anything.

"What do we do now?" she asked after several minutes.

He shrugged while taking a big bite, then chewed the mouthful thoroughly before swallowing. "We stay alive until we figure out what's going on."

"Who were you talking to last night? Maybe he can help," she offered, as she stirred a couple of fries in ketchup and popped them into her mouth.

"A contact. Someone I thought I trusted, but now I'm not so sure. I don't know if I can trust anyone anymore."

"That's not good." With eyebrows slanted, she studied his face.

He snorted. "Tell me about it." He paused a moment. "I can't determine why they'd go after you, though."

"They were aiming for you." She shook her head, unwilling to even consider his statement.

"No. From my vantage point, it looked like the sniper knew exactly who he was taking out. If not for your shoelace, you'd be lying on the pavement with Cheryl."

"That doesn't make sense."

"Nothing about this makes sense to us, but I'm sure it does to someone."

She watched Josh take a few more bites of his burger, washing it down with the soft drink. All she could think about was how she wished this whole nightmare would end. Maybe that was it, she mused. Maybe she was living a bad dream and in minutes she'd wake up, safe and sound in her own bed. But knowing this wasn't the case, she asked the question uppermost on her mind since he'd voiced the idea that whoever shot Cheryl didn't do it randomly.

"Why me?"

"I don't know. You tell me. Why you?"

"But I'm a nobody," she declared as the feeling of dread, beginning as a seed a few minutes ago, grew stronger, increasing her fear. Oh God, could her ex-husband have found her? She was so sure Mark never knew that her aunt lived in Bozeman. She'd really begun to believe she could live in peace without having to look over her shoulder. And now Josh was telling her someone wanted her dead.

"Somebody obviously doesn't think so. Otherwise why go to the trouble?"

His question hung in the air and his intent gaze bored into hers, putting her a little on the defensive. He held the contact, not letting her look away.

"What are you hiding, Cat?"

The question, though whispered, pounded through her ears. She closed her eyes and sat back, shaking her head. When she opened them, her attention wandered to her fingers, which were now rolling a napkin into a tube before unrolling it and flattening it out.

Josh placed his warm hand over hers, effectively stilling her nervous gesture.

"Cat?"

Her gaze reluctantly moved to his, revealing the torment she couldn't hide. She took a deep breath and let it out slowly.

"I told you I was married before."

"Yes. I remember you telling me you had an ex-husband from your shady past," Josh teased, squeezing her hand affectionately.

Cat ignored the flush of warmth now spreading through her system caused by his gentle teasing and plunged forth, telling Josh something she'd never told another human being. "What you don't know is the last time I saw him, he told me if I ever left him, he'd kill me. For almost four years I've been living in fear that he'd find me and make good on his threat." She moved her gaze to her hand, which was still covered with his and added, "That's the real reason I took flying lessons. I thought it would help me push past the fear I've been living with for so long."

"Tell me about him," Josh insisted, letting go of her hands and grabbing a few fries. He then leaned back.

"What do you want to know?"

"Whatever you want to tell me. The more the better. If he's behind this, maybe we can sort it out."

"Mark Zinger. That's his name. He's very charismatic. I met him during a dinner party my parents hosted on one of their rare visits to the States," Cat said, eliciting the memory of the worst years of her life. "Most of their time was spent in the Middle East. I was so excited they were including me in their life, but then it didn't last. Mark was going overseas to join their group and asked me to go with him as his wife. I barely knew him. My parents disapproved of him and were very vocal about me not marrying him. I let that cloud my judgment. I was married to him for almost two years before I left him, but I only lived with him for a total of six months. Most of the time, he was overseas. He didn't seem to mind that I had no interest in joining him, which only relieved me. I mean, why would I want to live in a country that treated women as second-class citizens?"

She stopped talking, having mentally gone back to the most

horrible time in her life. A wistful smile crossed her face as she realized right then, while sitting and conversing with Josh, how much she'd changed in the last few years. Most of those changes took place since the day she walked into Buchannan Aeronautics, and the man next to her taunted her into taking charge of her life. The same man who now urged her to talk about her worst fears.

"Go on," he encouraged, prodding a bigger, more natural smile.

"Mark was the one who informed me of my parents' deaths," she said softly, meeting Josh's warm gaze. "You remember I told you my parents were killed?" Not waiting for his answer, she added, "It was a senseless crime. Like this one, only then I knew why. Some crazy fanatic killed them, thinking she had a good cause. But how do you justify killing? How does anyone, whether they're Christian, Jew, or Muslim, justify killing another person in cold blood?" She broke eye contact and moved her attention back to the napkin, nervously fiddling with it once again. She took a moment to compose herself and then continued speaking.

"But back to Mark. When he returned from Afghanistan, he was a totally different person from the one I thought I'd married. He became very abusive and controlling. He also felt he should take charge of the substantial amount of money my parents left me. When the abuse escalated, I ran to a women's shelter. They helped me align my life, putting me in touch with the right resources. Counselors and lawyers. I can't forget our last day in court when he threatened me, though. The look on his face was pure hatred. I didn't know him at all. Made me realize I couldn't have loved him, nor could he have loved me."

After several deep breaths, she grabbed her drink, sucked a large, calming sip, until the fear racing through her receded somewhat.

She risked another glance at Josh, who was eyeing her with his usual shuttered expression, and she laughed as a natural gush of pleasure burst forth as it dawned on her that she did feel better. And her fear, while still real, didn't seem as cumbersome.

"You're so good at that, you know?"

"Good at what?" He met her grin with one of his own.

"Getting me to talk. Taking my mind off how bad things are and making me feel better."

"I didn't do it. You did."

"No. Somehow I feel better and it's all because of you."

"Sometimes voicing your fears is all it takes to make you see how easy it is to face them."

"Maybe," she conceded and took another sip. She sighed. "Anyway, that's all I can tell you about my ex. I've always thought him a little overzealous, but not enough to kill complete strangers."

"Humph. People do crazy things, and sometimes they don't make sense to anyone but the person doing them."

"I can see him wanting me dead. But my death could easily be arranged. An accident of some sort. Why go to so much trouble to kill others? I find it hard to believe he'd actually go to such extremes."

"I don't know," Josh said, shaking his head.

During the next few minutes, they ate in silence. The entire time, Cat's mind swirled with thoughts of what might happen if Mark had found her. Would he kill her innocent friend? Would he rig a plane to go down? It all seemed so implausible.

When done, she tendered Josh a wan smile. "Do you mind if I take a shower and go to bed? I'm done in."

"Go ahead. Just grab what you need from the stuff we bought." He nodded at the packages on the dresser. "You've been through a lot today. We can talk about this tomorrow."

Cat nodded and started for the bathroom, after stopping to rummage through bags on the dresser and pulling out items. She could feel Josh's gaze on her back as she walked away.

Chapter 16

Cat closed the bathroom door and Josh swallowed the regret choking him. She seemed to need him and he hadn't been able to meet her need without hurting her further.

"Shit." He wiped his face, not wanting to think about the real reason he backed down from making love with her. Be honest with yourself, Buc. You aren't protecting her from hurt. It's you. You're protecting yourself, he chided himself. Need for her clutched on to his soul and it was proving almost impossible to shake free.

"Get a grip," he muttered under his breath, finding the packages on the dresser and poking through them. He had more urgent things to worry about than a delectable powder puff who needed more than he could ever provide. She deserved much more than a brief affair with some emotionally bankrupt degenerate who'd never be there for her any more than her parents had been. He was responsible for her parents' deaths, for Christ's sake.

Once he heard the water running, Josh picked up one of the cell phones he'd purchased and punched in the digits that blocked caller ID before punching in John Murphy's number.

Murphy answered on the first ring.

"Murph?"

"Buc? Christ, where have you been?" he asked, his excited tone rushing through the connection. "Things are exploding. We got major problems. You need to come in, buddy. Tell me where you are."

"No can do. This goes beyond problems. I'm only trying to stay alive long enough to figure out what's happening," Josh stated coolly, holding on to his anger. He took a deep, calming breath before asking a little more heatedly than he wanted to, "Did you send Rodriquez?"

"What?"

The one word spoken with pure outrage eased some of Josh's

fury, causing his voice and stance to soften. "I'm asking you. Did you send Rodriquez? Anthony Rodriquez."

"Who's Rodriquez?"

"He had CIA written all over him. Were you tailing me?"

"Shit, Buc, you're not making any sense. I'm Homeland Security now, not CIA. If this guy is CIA, I wouldn't know. I don't follow you? Why do you want to know about this Rodriquez?"

"Someone sent him to kill me. I'm hoping it's not you."

"I'm trying to save your ass and you accuse me of sending someone to kill you? Christ! I don't believe this shit."

"You were my last contact. And he was using CIA transmitters and receivers. What would you expect me to think?"

The line went quiet for several minutes.

"Okay, okay. Calm down. Let's start from the top. Tell me what happened."

The rigid line of Josh's shoulders curved and a slight smile tugged at the edges of his lips. He didn't have to see his mentor and longtime friend to know his mind was working in overtime, even though his words came out in restrained succession. That was Murphy's way. Very controlled and very logical.

Josh spent a few minutes going over the events playing out since Anthony Rodriquez's attempt to break into the same house he and Cat had been occupying.

"I don't know what's going on. My best recommendation would be to come in while I try to find out more about this guy," Murphy advised after another long pause. "Tell me where you are. I can have Smitty or anyone else pick you up, offer protective custody."

"I can't," Josh stated firmly. "Not yet. Not until I figure out this mess. At first, I thought it was related to the drug operation I stumbled upon. Now I don't know what to think. Rodriquez shows up and someone tries to kill two innocent women who had nothing to do with me. Nothing makes sense."

"Buc, there's a lot more going on. DEA and those two special agents are convinced you're involved in a drug ring. I don't know if I can hold them off. Smitty told me they've got your name on leases to trailers around the country used to make the shit, and there are records of big deposits into your account and some withdrawals. Your withdrawals match deposits into Maxwell's account down to the dates and dollar amounts."

"How can that be?" Josh rubbed the back of his neck and began pacing, working to understand.

"I don't know. Someone's gone to a lot of trouble to frame you. If you come in, we can find out together."

"No. I'm sorry, Murph. My cautious nature won't let me."

"Ordinarily, I'd agree and let it go, but there's more. There are bogus hours charged to your planes. Students supposedly used your planes for training. But the training never happened and McMann and Adams are tying it to the drug operation."

"Yeah, I caught that. It prompted my call to a friend in Helena."

"Which brought in Laurel and Hardy, who now think Gloria Goodman's accident wasn't so accidental…was also your doing. You had her killed to cover your tracks."

"Shit." Bile rose up the back of Josh's throat. "What else can happen?" He stopped his pacing, sat down on the edge of the bed, and rubbed his forehead. "This keeps getting worse and worse."

"No shit. I don't know how long before they'll have their indictment. Then you'll be on some Most Wanted list. Buc, this is serious."

This information left him dazed and his gaze dropped to the floor. He studied the designs in the carpet as Murphy's voice pounded in his ear.

"What about the girl? Could she be involved?"

A trickle of unease shot through him. "I don't know," Josh said honestly. "My gut tells me no."

"Could she use Maxwell to frame you?"

Murphy's question hung in the air and doubt wrapped around Josh's soul.

"That's reaching," he ground out.

"Could be. I'm only throwing out possibilities," Murphy admitted. The connection remained silent before his booming voice continued. "I don't know if this is related or not, but Candace Tyler has a very nasty ex-husband."

"Yeah, she mentioned something about him," Josh said, thinking of the man Cat described.

"He had strong ties to Candace Tyler's dead parents and their organization. I may be going out on a limb here, but I think somehow all of this is related to him and maybe her. Maybe the two of them are setting you up, using Maxwell."

"Shit, Murph, that's really going way out. I can believe Maxwell's into drugs, but why would he do all the other? I don't see a connection to Cat's ex and I have a hard time believing Cat's involved." No, he amended mentally. *You don't want to believe Cat's involved.*

"I tried to tell you last night. Reynolds was taken out two days ago. You remember Doug? The communications specialist on your last mission in Afghanistan? At first, it seemed random. Agents die all the time for a multitude of reasons. Until a couple of other agents were killed in the last forty-eight hours, execution style. And today, three others who were involved with you in Afghanistan have been hit. Besides Anderson, who's now deeply hidden, you and Smitty are the only two left."

"Where's the connection to Cat?" Josh asked, taking several deep breaths and rubbing the bridge of his nose with his thumb and forefinger.

"The girl's dead parents are the connection. Think, Buc," Murphy demanded, his voice rising slightly. "You're the one who always told me there are no coincidences. Somehow, this is related to that operation—that past is now mixing with the present, hurling toward us."

"What the hell is happening?"

"I wish I knew. I'm stumped. Yet I'm inclined to agree with the CIA guys in Langley and say there's an insider. But our opinions differ on who it is. You're their number one suspect. They believe that along with drug dealing, you've turned against your country for profit."

How had his life spiraled so completely out of control? Nothing made sense. "It's Rodriquez. It has to be."

"Did he actually try to kill you?"

"I never gave him a chance to get close enough."

"How would he know about the operation in Afghanistan? Or know about the others? That's classified. Could be he's working on orders to bring you in. But the timing doesn't make sense and it's illegal for the CIA to operate in the US. Besides, no one's informed me." The line went quiet for a moment before Murphy asked, "What've you done to piss off the CIA to the point of becoming their target?"

"Nothing. You've been my only contact since I quit. I'm hardly worth anyone's notice."

"So, that leads us back to Maxwell and the girl. And if you add the ex-husband into the mix, it takes another shape."

"Shit," Josh expelled softly, wishing doubts about Cat would quit growing inside his mind, as Murphy's "Please Buc. Tell me where you are," sounded in his ear.

"Let me think about it tonight," Josh replied, shaking his head. He immediately stood and began pacing again, and let out another sigh. "Give me tonight to try and figure it out. I'll call you in the morning."

Josh hung up, turned the phone off and set it on the dresser before going over to the window. He opened the drapes enough to stare out into the now dark, almost empty parking lot. Only a smattering of cars remained. He'd parked on the other side of the motel, well away from the room to be cautious.

What the hell was going on? Who was out to get him and why? If someone wanted him dead, why go to the trouble of framing him? It simply didn't make sense. Were the two incidents separate? Had Maxwell caught wind that Josh was on to him and was he smart enough to divert attention away from himself by implicating Josh? Could Cat be working with Maxwell? Had she told him all that about Maxwell the first night to throw him off?

Damn, he hated the doubts now swirling out of control. Would the two of them try to kill him? But that left out Rodriquez and all the other shit going on. Murphy was right. The only common denominator Josh could find was Cat and her parents' deaths.

The bathroom door opened and Cat padded out. He kept his back to her while she rustled around the room. She brushed her teeth and got a drink of water. When done, he heard her start toward the bed.

Josh closed the drapes and turned around to see Cat pull back the bedspread and covers before climbing into the bed. She grabbed the remote from the nightstand next to her and clicked on the TV.

"You don't mind if I watch a little television before I turn in, do you?"

"No." The word cracked through the air like a snapped whip.

He blocked out the thought of how innocent she looked, fresh from her shower. She'd donned a large T-shirt that hung to her knees, causing Josh to wonder for one brief moment what was underneath.

"I'm going to grab a shower." He stopped at the dresser, ignoring dual urges—one to confront her, and the other to pull her to him, never to let her go. With his concentration on his task, he picked through the bags. "I'll be out in a minute."

After grabbing the things he needed, he headed for the bathroom without glancing back.

☙

Cat eyed the closed bathroom door, wondering why Josh seemed so cold and remote all of a sudden. It was the same feeling she'd gotten the night before when he'd been out on the porch. The man totally confused her.

Oh well. She didn't think she would ever understand him. Spying Josh's cell phone on the dresser, she moved to grab it, then stopped. Josh said he might need the minutes. She would be as brief as possible, but she had to know how Cheryl was doing. After quickly turning it on, she punched in her aunt's cell phone number, pushing thoughts of Josh Buchannan and his weird behavior out of her brain.

"Aunt Marge?" she asked, as soon as the line came alive with her voice.

"Candace? My heavens, I've been worried sick about you. Are you all right? I heard you were with Cheryl when she was shot."

"Yes. I can't think about Cheryl's condition right now. Josh said he'd call the hospital later."

"Honey, I'm in the waiting room, down the hall from her room right now. She's in intensive care. She made it through surgery, and they think she's over the worst."

"Thank God." Tears streamed down her face. Cat wiped them away. "I don't have much time. I knew you'd worry, so I wanted to let you know we're okay." She spent a moment telling her where to find Cheryl's VW and asking her aunt to have the busted out window repaired. Cat didn't want Cheryl worrying about her car on top of everything else.

"Where are you?" Aunt Marge asked after agreeing to take care of it.

"I can't tell you. All I can tell you is I'm safe. Okay?"

"I wish I could see that for myself."

"I know. Hopefully this'll all be over soon."

"Candace, have you seen the news? Josh Buchannan's wanted for questioning in his assistant's death, and now they're pretty sure he's using his flight school as a front for distributing drugs."

"I don't believe that and neither should you." Cat stared at her hand as she wound the telephone cord around it before untangling it and repeating the move. The burden of the world sat on her shoulders. But unlike Atlas, she couldn't hold the weight. The heavy load crashed in around her, overwhelmed her. She couldn't listen to any more. "Look, I've got to go. Don't tell anyone you heard from me. Please?"

"I wish you'd come home. Promise me you'll be careful." Cat smiled at the concern in her aunt's voice. Aunt Marge had always been more of a parent than her own parents, which had prompted Candace's call. She couldn't let her worry needlessly.

"I will. I love you. I'll try calling later," Cat promised, before disconnecting and placing the phone back on the dresser where she'd found it. Then she climbed back under the blankets and picked up the remote. Finding a news program, she turned up the volume.

ᴄꙇ

"Thank God she's okay," Marge Tyler said as she hung up the phone. "Too bad Smitty just left. I know he was worried about her."

"Did she say where she was?" Brad Maxwell asked, his eyes on her.

"No, but she sounded good."

"She's still with Buchannan?"

"Yes."

"Do you mind if I use your phone to call Smitty? My cell phone's dead and I promised him I'd let him know if I heard any news."

"Sure, go ahead, but hurry. All of a sudden I'm tired and ready for this day to be over," Marge said, wearily handing him the phone. "Ask Smitty not to say anything about hearing from her."

Brad took it, moved far enough away from her so she couldn't overhear, and pushed the Call History button. He memorized the number, then made a call on his own cell phone.

"Yeah. You wanted to know if she contacted her aunt again?" he asked, when the phone was picked up on the other end. "Well, she did. What's more I have a number, only you'll have to meet my price."

"Don't be greedy, Maxwell."

"I'm not. Merely being smart."

"Oh?"

"Yeah. Since I'm now being investigated on drug charges, I'll need something extra to help me live a comfortable life well away from Montana's cold winters. The price is five hundred grand or this little number where she was calling from stays right here. You got that?"

A deep chuckle burst from the other end, mocking him. "What's to stop me from promising the money, then taking the number without paying?"

"I'm not stupid, asshole. You want the number and you want me to keep my mouth shut. Both will cost you."

Dead silence. Finally a voice broke through. "Okay. Let's meet tomorrow morning in the usual spot and I'll bring the money."

"Somehow this seems too easy." The rigid line of Brad's shoulders relaxed. He smiled into the phone and shook his head. "You should know I have insurance. If something happens to me, the trail will lead to you. Understand?"

"You'll be paid tomorrow. Now give me the number before I change my mind."

Brad rattled it off and ended with, "Don't double-cross me or you'll be sorry."

"Be there tomorrow and you'll be paid." The line went dead.

Maxwell hung up and walked back to Mrs. Tyler. "Thanks. The call made his night. Since he's stopping by later, I'm leaving now. I'll give you a ride home, if you'd like."

Twenty minutes later, he watched Mrs. Tyler walk up her front path.

After putting the car in gear, Brad turned on the radio and hummed as music filled the air.

While driving, his smile turned smug. He'd be out of the country before any formal charges could be filed. And he already knew which small islands in the Caribbean didn't have US extradition.

Chapter 17

Josh emerged from the bathroom minutes later wearing boxer shorts and an unbuttoned shirt, exposing his chest.

Ignoring Cat's obvious interest, he picked up a razor.

"Look's like the shower did you some good," she said, after watching him for some time.

"I don't know what is it about hot showers that seem to wash the worst of the day away, but it works," he agreed, shaking off thoughts of her sitting half naked on the bed.

The events of the last few days had taken a physical toll. He was beat, ready to close his eyes and sleep. Even sexual thoughts moved to the backseat at this point.

Her attention returned to the TV screen and his returned to shaving.

While running the blade along his face, his gaze secretly roamed to Cat's reflection in the mirror every now and then. Was she in league with Maxwell? Her demeanor seemed so innocent, almost schoolgirl-ish. He sighed and concentrated on his face.

Josh barely finished brushing his teeth when her soft voice filled his ears. "You might want to see this."

He nodded and spit out the last of his toothpaste before rinsing his mouth. He strode to the edge of the bed and sat, his focus shifting to the TV.

The screen flashed a picture of both Josh and Cat while the commentator droned on about how he was wanted for questioning in the investigations of one death and drug trafficking. The wordy picture the newscaster painted of Josh Buchannan wasn't a pretty one, making him out to be public enemy number one. The story also alluded to the fact that one Candace Angela Tyler might be with him against her will.

"Shit," Josh said, rubbing his face with a hand that settled on his neck. He closed his eyes. "What else can go wrong?"

"Why are they saying all that stuff about you?" Cat asked, turning off the set and moving to sit next to him on the edge of the bed.

He picked up on the doubt in her voice and smiled grimly. At this point, there was plenty of doubt spinning around in the room.

"I don't know." His honest reply hung in the air. Opening his eyes, Josh stared at the floor, as if the green diamonds in the carpet held answers. "Do you believe it?" he asked a moment later, his voice whisper-soft. His attention focused on her gaze, searching intently in those ice blue eyes for the truth.

"No," she said quietly, holding his questioning stare without flinching so Josh could see the sincerity residing there.

As fast as a lightning strike, the room shrank. His heartbeat quickened, running at a full gallop in seconds flat. Gone was the fatigue he'd felt only a moment ago, replaced with pure lust, fed with the adrenaline now racing through his system.

The warmth spilling from her gaze, one so cold in color, drew him.

Now I know exactly how a black widow spider's mate feels, he thought. Watching her closely, his resolve slipped, sliding into some hidden recess of his mind while insanity overtook him. He simply couldn't fight his desire anymore. It didn't matter that the woman sitting next to him might be setting him up or that he shouldn't be thinking of kissing her. All that mattered was the message his body received from those eyes...from the look on her face.

"I can't resist those icy eyes flashing so much heat," he whispered, just before his lips found hers, letting her know with his mouth how much he meant his words.

Immediately her arms wound around him and her fingers plowed into his hair, pulling him closer. Utter yearning exploded inside of Josh when Cat's aggressive mouth matched his, inhaling his tongue, offering him a loud moan.

From that moment on, there was nothing gentle about their contact as pleasure slammed at him from all sides. She'd opened up a dam of emotions with her actions and a flood of sensation rushed out through his lips, tongue, and hands. All three were working in conjunction and he had this driving need to force Cat to the brink of desire because he'd flown well past that point.

In one fell swoop, he had her T-shirt pushed up and her panties pulled down and off her legs. The next moment he'd shrugged out of his boxers and was sliding into her heat. Heat that made him feel as if he'd come inside to a warm fire after a cold storm, yanking even more emotion from him.

He couldn't stop his feral actions as he began to grind into her, pumping furiously. Though he knew he should slow down, take his time and give her pleasure, his mind shut off the reasoning side of his brain. It didn't help that Cat met him thrust for thrust, adding more fuel to the flashing burn of his insides. In seconds the heat erupted into one big flame, a fiery inferno, sucking every bit of feeling out of his pores, taking all of his energy with it, leaving him in a pile of spent ashes.

ༀ

After being so completely caught up on the brink of an orgasm that never occurred, Cat took a few minutes to fall back to earth before she realized it was all over. Even though disappointment at what hadn't happened swamped her, she'd never felt so alive the moment Josh lost control. Imagine! Someone losing control over her. It was a heady feeling and something she'd never experienced before.

Cat smiled warmly when she felt him come back to life.

Josh pushed up, meeting her gaze with apologetic eyes. "I'm sorry. I never intended for that to happen."

"You're sorry we made love?" Cat worked to keep the panic out of her voice at the thought of him regretting their lovemaking. She could never regret it and she didn't want the feeling to be one-sided.

"No. I'm sorry I couldn't keep it together long enough to make it good for you."

"It was good," she said, with relief washing over her.

"It could be better," he grunted, withdrawing. "Don't you agree?"

He fluffed the pillows, situated himself on the bed, and pulled her into the crook of his arm. He kissed the top of her forehead. "Give me a minute and I'll make good on my promise." His head fell back against the pillows.

Cat's smile reached all the way to her toes. She felt so safe, especially when his hand slowly began roaming soothingly over her arms. It seemed nothing could intrude on the feeling of well-being spreading through her.

After a while, he sat up and grabbed her T-shirt and pulled it over her head, saying, "I think we can dispense with this," before tossing it on the floor.

"You are so beautiful," he whispered, adding lips to his hands that were still making the journey up and down her arms. In seconds, warm fingers moved lower to include her legs.

Embarrassment inundated Cat and she tried to cover her nakedness with her hands.

"Don't!" Her hands halted at the whispered command and she chanced a glance at him, feeling her face flame. He leaned back against the pillows and snared her gaze, not letting her look away, compelling her to see the truth in his eyes. "Don't cover yourself from me, Cat. I want to look at you."

She forced herself to breathe, to relax while she stared back, taking courage from the appreciation she spied in his expression. Where had the old Candace Tyler gone, the one who was always looking over her shoulder because of a crazy, abusive ex-husband? The old Cat certainly resembled nothing of the bold woman now lying naked on the bed after making love, while Josh's warm gaze raked up and down her body.

He bent to kiss her. But before their lips met, he murmured, "It's too late to change course now. There's nowhere to hide."

"I don't want to hide, but I do feel self-conscious being the only one completely naked here," she said brazenly once he lifted his head, allowing her to think clearer. It was as if she did this kind of thing all the time. What was it about this man that made her brave? Made her forget to be afraid?

He gave a half chuckle and took off his shirt with a minimum of movement.

She blew out a huge breath, totally unprepared for the sight of Josh Buchannan without a shirt. His well-developed chest and arms simply stole her air. But she had no time to dwell on his physique, not when muscular arms went around her and his sensual mouth moved closer, almost touching hers.

"Now, where were we?" he whispered, his head halting an inch away. "Oh yeah. I remember." He grazed her mouth with almost kisses, before taking her bottom lip between his teeth and sucking.

A hot streak of heat shot straight to her core. She moaned, opening her mouth wider, meeting his tongue's thrust and parrying with it. Wave after wave of intense pleasure coursed through her as his lips moved over her, trailing wet kisses in their wake, following his magic fingers. He was so good at using his mouth and hands to bring her body alive with need. She fought desire and tried to reciprocate, doing her best to meet him head-to-head, matching his enticing movements. If his hands slid up and down her legs, she let her hands wander the same way over his. She loved touching his glorious body. Loved seeing him respond.

When he flinched and sucked in his breath, she smiled smugly, reveling in his reactions. Her strokes became bolder. Her hands roamed over his sinewy muscles, and watching them flex, she felt fragile and diminutive, surrounded by such power.

Soon her lips, mouth, and tongue joined in. His breathing quickly became labored, adding to her triumphant, giddy feeling, as well as the excitement building inside her.

He touched her in that private spot and she couldn't hold back a low moan. The sensual quality of the sound shocked her. Excited her further. That couldn't be her making such a feral noise? Could it?

Yet his exquisite fingers didn't give her a chance to contemplate for long. Waves of balmy sensation rolled over her like warm Caribbean waters washing over white sands. While the pleasure lapped toward her core, continually building, her hands found his thick arousal. Touching him…stroking him…watching him grow bigger and spring more to life, as her hand surrounded his warmth, gave her a sense of power.

She smiled wickedly when he sucked in a big breath.

"Christ, Cat. Stop!" His hand quickly covered hers, halting her in midstroke. "Too much too fast. I can't slow down if you do that," he whispered into her ear, seductively nibbling on her lobe.

"But you need to catch up with me," she answered breathlessly.

"I'm ready to explode again and I'd rather you be ahead of me." He groaned, making an effort to still her other hand. "You don't understand. I'm over the edge here."

Cat ignored him, smiling inwardly at the agony in his voice.

"This is not a one-sided affair. You got that, Buc-man? I'll touch you just as you touch me." Then she boldly stroked him again, loving the idea of driving him wild until, in a deft move, she was suddenly flat on her back and he was driving into her. From that moment on, all rational thought fled as he furiously began pumping. She had no choice but to meet him thrust for thrust, as the power of the sensations coursed through her…swept her away.

She climbed the precipice, ready to jump, when she felt him do exactly what he'd threatened earlier. Explode inside her as a strong orgasm held him in its grips and he shuddered uncontrollably. After several long seconds, he collapsed on top of her, a dead weight for several more.

A surge of dissatisfaction hit Cat once reality settled in and she became aware of her surroundings again. With her eyes closed, she lay under Josh, wishing it wasn't quite over yet.

လ

Josh's chuckle interrupted the quiet of the room. "I tried to warn you," he said, lifting up on his forearms. Looking down into her eyes, her flash of annoyance tickled his insides. "But you have a habit of ignoring my warnings. Seems to me you defeated your purpose."

"And my purpose would be?" she asked through clenched teeth, her eyes shooting daggers.

"That was definitely one-sided…again." His gaze raked over her, and he chuckled once more when his eyes rested on her right fist, which was opening and closing. "Go ahead," he taunted. "I can see you're dying to do it. You've been holding on to that punch for months now."

"Shut up, Buc-man," she hissed, slugging him. When he laughed harder, she pushed against him, saying angrily, "Get off me."

"Oh, no. We're not done yet."

"Yes, we are," she choked out, pushing with more force.

"No. We've barely begun now that I've totally caught up with you," he said, as he started moving inside her again.

Within moments, Cat's anger visibly dissolved. This time around Cat flew off the precipice first, but not before grabbing on to Josh and taking him with her.

Chapter 18

Cat's eyes flew open. Totally disoriented, she immediately noticed the hand over her mouth, and a feeling of déjà vu streaked through her. When Josh removed his hand and put his finger to his lips, she nodded. He signaled for her to get into the bathroom. She climbed out of bed. Had no time to grab anything to cover her nakedness as he hurriedly arranged the pillows under the blankets to look as if someone lay beneath them, complete with the wigs he'd bought.

Stark naked, he grabbed his gun and followed her. Cat sat on the toilet with her heart racing, pounding furiously inside her chest, so loud it penetrated the silence.

Another sound pierced the quiet…one that must have awakened Josh.

Her gaze went to the space between the jamb and the bathroom door. Her breath caught in her throat. Metal scraped on the lock at their door. In the next second, it clicked. The knob turned.

Her attention flew to Josh, who stood with his weapon at the ready. She refocused on the space. The intruder pushed the door slightly ajar. Light from the parking lot spilled into the room. A gun with a silencer came into view. An arm straightened, aimed from the door.

Cat couldn't see his target, the lumpy shadows on the bed that was supposed to be them. Her eyes scrunched closed as she covered her ears, blocking out fear, while eight muted shots ripped into the bedding.

Light from a car pulling into the parking lot shone directly onto the man. She couldn't make him out, but considering Josh's sharp intake of breath, he could.

Time passed slowly while Josh stood sentinel at the bathroom door, not moving a muscle, his arm bent, holding his gun. Sitting naked on her perch, Cat rubbed her arms to ward off the cold. The freezing tile under her feet only added to the chill. Irritation engulfed her. She'd definitely had her fill of being yanked out of sleep with threats of dying.

"Why is someone trying to kill us?" she snapped, losing all patience. "Tell me why?"

Josh ignored her outburst and nodded toward the bedroom. "I think he's gone. He's not very thorough, which is lucky for us." He opened the door and gripped her hand, pulling her off the toilet. "Let's move. I don't know how they found us, but we've got to get out of here."

"Josh, I'm tired of running," she said firmly, pulling out of his grasp and sitting on the edge of the bed. Spying her T-shirt in a ball on the floor, she scooped it up, quickly pulling it over her head to cover her nakedness.

"We have no choice." Josh jerked on his boxers, then reached for his shirt lying at the foot of the bed. "And we've had this conversation before."

"Why do I have to run with you?"

The question hung in the air between them. Josh's back stiffened. He drove a hand through his hair and swore under his breath before he returned to rifling through the bags, pulling out clothing.

"Come on, Cat. Get dressed." He tossed items at her, paying no heed to her question. "We need to disguise ourselves too."

"But why do I have to run?" she asked again. When it was obvious he wasn't going to respond, anger erupted. "Answer my question," she demanded, raising her voice.

"Because somehow you're connected to this," Josh yelled back. "I'm not letting you out of my sight until I'm satisfied you'll be safe. You got that?" He snatched the wigs off the bed, flinging one at her. "I'd appreciate a little cooperation. Now get moving and put that on."

His tone of voice stopped her short and she glanced closely at his face. Rage spilled from his eyes. Cat had never seen him this angry, and all of a sudden it dawned on her. Part of his anger was directed at her.

"Did I do something?"

With sharp movements, he pulled on his jeans, zipping them up and doing the button. "Did you?" he asked, capturing her gaze and holding it for several minutes, letting Cat see what he couldn't hide. Doubt and accusation.

Somehow he thought she was responsible.

"You think I have something to do with this?"

His gaze left hers and he didn't say anything more while he finished dressing, purposefully not meeting her questioning gaze again.

His attitude hurt. Why did he believe the worst of her? Josh thought she let him down, and for the life of her, she didn't know what she'd done or how she could fix it. The feeling reminded her too much of how she used to feel with her parents, as if somehow she'd let them down, and just as now, she'd had no idea of how to fix it then either. Screw it. She didn't need him and his damn arrogance. He was the reason she was here, being shot at.

"You make me so mad, Buc-man," she spit out, venting. "Don't try to pin this on me. I'm not the one who's wanted for murder and dealing with meth labs. You are." She finished dressing, pulling on jeans and an oversized sweater. Seeing that it was too big, she became even angrier. "You expect me to wear this damn sweater? It's gigantic on me."

"There's a reason for that, Powder Puff. I'm trying to save your sweet ass," he said, practically growling and slamming his shaving gear, toothbrush, and toothpaste into his flight bag. "Although I don't know why I bother, because there's also a reason why I'm wanted for murder and dealing drugs. Your goddamn boyfriend set me up. And somehow I'm thinking you're in on it."

"You really believe that?" Cat sat on the bed, his horrid outburst knocking all the wind out of her anger. "How could you?"

"I don't know what to think, Cat," Josh finally admitted. "Nothing makes sense any longer."

The honesty in his voice got to her. He really thought the worst of her. Had no faith in her. And it hurt. She blinked back tears, but they'd already made an appearance and were streaking down her face. Brushing them aside, she clenched her fist and jutted out her chin.

She would get through this. "Tell me what I need to do, so I can get the hell away from you as soon as possible." She'd had it with giving in to those people she loved. They never gave back what she needed, no matter what she did. Thank God she didn't love him. And then her tears increased, because though she might be able to hide it from him, she couldn't hide it from herself.

No!

She wiped away her tears with two fierce sweeps of her hand.

This isn't real. You don't really love him. You're riding on emotion because of the events of the past few days, and once you get away from him, you'll be fine.

"Look, Cat." Josh sighed. "I'm sorry." He moved to pull her into his embrace, but she stepped back, avoiding his hands.

There was no way she could let him touch her. If she did, she'd surely fall apart. "Let's get going. Tell me what I need to do."

"Shit."

The expletive exploded behind her. A sad smile crept over her face. It struck her as funny all of a sudden that he used that one word so often. Yes, she thought, as she pulled the wig Josh had handed her earlier over her head, hiding her pale blonde hair…she'd get through this. And maybe—just maybe—when all this was over, she'd never be afraid again.

Several minutes later, Josh came up beside her and she glimpsed his reflection, doing a double take because the Josh Buchannan she'd come to know was gone. The man next to her looked like some kind of scruffy blue collar worker, complete with a belly hanging over his middle, covering up his firm, washboard abs and trim waist.

When he caught her staring at him in the mirror, she offered him a partial smile. "You've obviously done this before."

"Come on, admit it. You think I'm a hunk," he teased, clearly attempting to make her laugh and ease the tension between them. If she hadn't been so hurt by his earlier actions, it might have done the trick.

Instead, her smile faded. "Do I need padding too? I take it I'm supposed to match you."

"Yeah. Here, you need to add these to your eyes," he said, handing her a box of colored contact lenses. "That color's too noticeable."

They spent a few minutes working on her disguise. When Cat looked in the mirror, she was shocked to see a totally different woman staring back.

"I think I could get used to being a spy," she commented, while grabbing her flight bag and stuffing all her personal items back inside.

Josh only grunted as he stalked around the room, picking things up and placing them inside the plastic K-Mart bags.

"Come on," he urged from the door once he was done. "I want to make it to my destination as quickly as possible. We have a long drive ahead of us."

෨

Grandfather clapped him on the shoulder and squeezed as his other hand pointed southeast.

"Remember, my child, we are all chosen, but you are special…your role essential." He lowered his head and whispered in his ear, "This is *our* Jihad. Yours and mine. To rid the world of the immoral and the unholy."

Grandfather broke off and straightened, then said in a louder voice, "Our war requires much patience. Much planning and much waiting. Soon, we will be in position to begin attacking from within, using our enemies' own greed and weaknesses against them. Then, when the time is right, once our holy warriors are in place and we've infiltrated their organizations, their immoral world. We strike and strike fast. Western Civilization will slowly crumble, to be reassembled into a better Muslim world. Only then will our Jihad be complete."

With the memory of that ten-year-old's visit with his grandfather fresh in his mind, he reached for his cell phone.

"It's done."

"You're sure?"

"Yes." He hung his head. Shame for misjudging, miscalculating, filled him. Failure would not only be catastrophic, it was unacceptable. He already carried the shame of his mother's failure and had done his part to atone, yet the Jihad required more of him. Now he must atone for his father's sins—those against Islam and for turning his wife against her people. Punishment for his mother's defection had been his father's death. Yet, that punishment hadn't fazed her. She'd still refused her destiny, had sided with the infidels, and had failed Allah…had failed them all.

Killing her had been his first test as the chosen one. And because so much was at stake, he couldn't fail. Not now, when Buchannan and Cat Tyler had finally been taken out.

"Four slugs to each torso. In a motel room off I-15. There's no way anyone on the bed survived the spray of bullets." Buchannan had made a fatal error letting her call her aunt and leaving a definite trail. The sleeping night clerk had simplified the search. Records indicated only one room had been paid for with cash. He smiled into the phone. "With all the other going on, it'll be assumed their deaths are related to the drug operation we let them uncover."

"Good. Then our Jihad proceeds as planned.

"Yes." Or it would once the loose end named Brad Maxwell was taken care of, he thought, cutting the connection.

◌

When they left the motel room, it was barely three a.m. Josh led her to the car, keeping them both in the shadows. He opened Cat's door for her, threw the bags in the backseat, and waited until she was inside before closing it and moving around to the other side.

Within minutes, he pulled out onto the road. After reaching the interstate, he glanced over at Cat. She looked completely done in.

Josh knew somehow his outburst had hurt her. The woman had the most expressive face and for too many minutes he'd viewed pure torment on it, making him feel pretty low for blaming her. It seemed she'd needed him to believe in her and he'd let her down with his suspicion. Yet, what else could he think? There was no way anyone could have traced him to the motel without some kind of help. The cell phone he'd turned off after making his call had been left on somehow and he'd had to toss it in the trash back in the hotel room. Either that or risk being followed. It had to be her doing. He didn't like thinking she'd set him up, only he couldn't see any other scenario.

Still, his mind wouldn't let go of the fact that once again he'd disappointed someone he cared about. He couldn't give her what she needed most—his trust.

"Why don't you try and get some sleep," Josh pressed, offering her an encouraging smile.

She didn't seem to hear him, instead kept her hand on her chin while her gaze searched the dark night outside the passenger window.

He sighed at her obvious attempt to ignore him.

Some things never changed.

A few miles down the road, he was relieved to notice she'd followed his advice and was now asleep with her head against the window. Too many times, his gaze kept returning to her sleeping form, as if looking at her would provide some clues. Even with the wig and overstuffed clothing, she was gorgeous to look at—her pale complexion perfect. In sleep, she appeared so innocent. Nothing like the viper he'd accused her of being.

With his attention back on the road, his thoughts reverted to what had taken place in the motel room. What the hell was going on and why? How did Rodriquez play into this and why was he stalking him—trying to kill him? Was he on some CIA hit list? Were Murphy and Smitty part of it? Were they attempting to discredit him using Cat and Maxwell? Questions were all he had. Answers were all he wanted.

Josh pulled out one of the cell phones he hadn't used yet and punched Murphy's home phone number after blocking caller ID.

"Murphy here," the man answered a little groggily.

"I didn't wake you, did I?" Josh said, keeping his attention on the road ahead as he drove westbound on I-80. Darkness was prevalent. The sun wouldn't make an appearance for another hour or so.

"Course not. I'm always up at three in the morning," Murphy replied. "That you, Buc?"

"Yeah, it's me. I thought I'd check in while I was still alive."

"You're a piece of work, you know that? Shit's exploding everywhere and you've got to crack a joke."

"Yeah," Josh grunted. "It's better than killing someone, which is really what I feel like doing. I'm getting tired of being a target."

"Something else happen?"

"You might say that. Rodriquez tried to kill me. And this time, eight bullets tells me he's serious."

"Shit," Murphy said.

Josh smiled, envisioning him rubbing a hand over his face and dragging it through his thick head of auburn hair as he asked, "Where are you?"

"Oh no. I'm not revealing that just yet. I'd prefer to remain hidden for a bit longer."

"Okay. I understand. I stumbled over some interesting shit. Are you sitting down?"

"Yeah, go ahead. I'm listening."

"Rodriquez is definitely CIA. But even worse, I think he's Candace Tyler's ex-husband."

"What?" Josh sat up straighter and glanced at Cat, who was still soundly sleeping. "Shit. How?"

"I don't know how and it scares the hell out of me. I've got a hundred men working overtime trying to figure that out. I'm keeping the fact that he's someone else under wraps. God forbid the news should leak out. At this point, he's being investigated as a rogue agent."

"What have you got so far?"

"Speculation. I only found out by accident because of what you said about Rodriquez's involvement. I called in a favor to get his file and I already had Mark Zinger's file on my computer. At one time both pictures were on the screen and I noticed similarities in their facial features, so I combined them," Murphy said. "Wait a minute, let me get my robe." After a long pause, he added, "A lot of points matched. He's had a few hair plugs and surgically changed some things to keep it from matching exactly, but I think it's the same man. He knew exactly what to change without making it obvious. Hang on till I get to my desk."

Through the connection, Josh heard him moving through his room, probably stepping into his slippers before sitting at his desk and turning on his hard drive. Eventually, the familiar tune of a computer booting up sounded, then seconds later keys clicked before Murphy said, "There's only one way this could've happened, and the timing had to be spot-on. Zinger most likely disposed of the real Anthony Rodriquez shortly after he applied to the CIA and then took his place. The kid was an intellectual loner, which was why he seemed perfect for our purposes." Another pause, then Murphy added, "Anthony Rodriquez's parents were deceased—died in a car accident less than six months before he applied—and he had no other next of kin. There's nothing in his security check to indicate anything out of the ordinary. Hell, Zinger probably arranged for the parents' demise, as it seems Rodriquez wasn't a random choice. Zinger's the spitting image of the kid. Only five years older."

"Shit," Josh sighed, absorbing Murphy's news. Though he still had a lot of questions, somehow this answered his main one. How did Cat fit in? His thoughts churned as Murphy's words filled his ears—words now sending more dread through his system.

"We assumed he was of Latin decent, given Rodriquez's background. But because the imposter's of Mediterrancan descent, it was easy to make the assumption, seeing only the similarities. No one ever looked past the surface. Hell, we're in the business of knowing this shit and we didn't catch him. He's some kind of mole."

"It's unbelievable," Josh whispered. He glanced at Cat's still sleeping form, trying to understand. How could this be happening?

"Believe it. This was well planned and executed, Buc. Has to have been in the works for years, and the only connection I see is Candace Angela Tyler and the Afghanistan operation."

"But why? It was a failed mission." Josh rubbed the back of his neck, easing some of the tension he'd been feeling since he woke up to Rodriquez breaking into the room. "What about Smitty?"

"Due to this new information, those two Feds have been given the added assignment of protecting him and have become his shadow. He's not crazy about it. But I'm not giving him any choice, since he won't go undercover. He's determined to find out what's going on."

"Smitty's not crazy about working with anyone."

"No one but you, that is. These two guys irritate the hell out of him. He calls them Laurel and Hardy. I'm sure you can guess why."

"Yeah. I get the picture." Josh's grin was quick. Hell, it felt good to flex his lips. It felt doubly good to find something to smile about in all of this.

"Definitely not a match made in heaven," Murphy agreed, chuckling. "But it'll keep the bastard safe. Of course, they're still convinced you're guilty as sin, even with this latest development."

"Figures. So, let's see what we have," Josh said. "Rodriquez is using Maxwell to get to me. I'm still not sure why, but it seems plausible. And maybe the fact that he's not too happy Cat got away from him, she's a bonus."

"Could be. Or she could be involved somehow," Murphy warned.

"You still think so?"

"I'm not overlooking the possibility. Not anymore. Rodriquez is extremely adept at pretending to be one thing while he's totally someone different. He breached the CIA, for Christ's sake. This Tyler woman could be doing the same thing. Don't underestimate her, Buc."

"I won't. Haven't I gotten this far without being killed? I'm not about to let anyone succeed, including her."

Murphy sighed. "I know I shouldn't worry, but it's habit. Seems strange, all this shit happening to you when you're completely out of the business. I always told you it was a mistake to leave. Welcome back."

"Don't go throwing any parties yet because I haven't come back. I'm merely trying to stay alive."

"Relax. It's only wishful thinking. Keep me posted."

"I'll be in touch." Josh closed the phone, breaking the connection.

He looked over at Cat, who was still out cold. For the next several hundred miles, his thoughts stayed on the information Murphy had shared. Every so often, his gaze returned to Cat's sleeping form. Was she involved?

Chapter 19

"Why're we stopping?" Cat asked sleepily, coming awake and stretching. She glanced around. Josh had pulled into a service station, a truck stop boasting a restaurant.

"We need gas. This is also a good place to eat something."

"I'm not hungry."

"It may be awhile before we can stop again, so I suggest taking advantage of it," Josh answered, getting out of the car.

Cat stayed where she was. When he returned from prepaying, she watched his capable movements as he positioned the gas nozzle into place so it could pump while he went about cleaning the bugs off the windows. He finished the windows as the pump clicked off. Josh returned the nozzle in its spot and got back inside.

He started the car and drove to a parking spot at the entrance to the café part of the truck stop.

"Come on. Let's go," he said, exiting again, then went around to her side, opened her door, and waited.

"I'm only doing this because it makes sense," Cat said, irritated that he was so competent and she wasn't.

"Yeah, I know. God forbid you should do anything because I tell you to."

Having no choice, Cat grabbed her bag, but his "Just get out of the damn car" had her balling her fist. She blinked back tears at the sharpness in his tone.

"Why do you have to be such a jerk?" she asked, once out.

"You're the one who pegged me." He slammed the door so hard the car rocked. "I'm not about to change. Why should I?"

Cat sucked in a breath, totally wishing she could snap her fingers and he'd be gone. How could a man who'd given her so much pleasure the night before be such an asshole this morning?

She followed Josh inside and stood discreetly behind him while he got his change for the gas. When done, he led her into the restaurant. It hadn't escaped her notice this scene was very similar to the one they'd played out yesterday. Except their stage, this restaurant, doubled as a casino with slot machines positioned throughout.

Sliding inside a booth facing the door, Cat's thoughts were on all that had happened in the past twenty-four hours. Her mind spun while she kept her gaze on the outside without really seeing the strangers pump gas. It seemed as if a month had gone by, given the amount of emotion she'd endured in the short time. Add in the two extra days she'd been with Josh, the interlude made her feel as if a lifetime had passed, and quite frankly she was tired of the roller coaster ride.

"Coffee?" asked the waitress, whose arrival at their table interrupted her thoughts.

When they both nodded, the woman turned over two of the four cups sitting on saucers, filling them with coffee. Then she picked up the other empty dishes and place settings, saying over her shoulder, "I'll be right back with menus."

Cat warmed her hand on the hot cup, bringing it to her lips a moment later. The rich brew tasted good and hit the spot. She watched the waitress come striding back to their table, menus in hand.

"I want you to do me a favor," Josh said, once the waitress left after handing out menus and telling them she'd be back in a jiffy to take their orders.

"What?" Cat sighed, looking at her hand on the coffee cup. She couldn't meet his gaze.

Didn't want to see the disappointment in his now expressive brown eyes.

"Call your aunt from the phone over there," he answered, nodding to a booth in a corner of the parking lot through the plate glass window.

His odd request overcame her reluctance, and her attention moved to his face, searching. "Why?" she asked, as a feeling of trepidation erupted and the knot in her stomach tightened.

"I want to see what happens."

"What happens?"

"Yeah. I call it 'baiting the line.'" Josh leaned against the booth, took a sip of coffee, maintaining eye contact. "Doing something to cause a reaction and sitting back to evaluate what transpires. See who takes the bait."

Unable to withstand his penetrating stare, Cat focused on her cup. "So, you think calling my aunt will cause some kind of reaction?" Cat asked, holding her breath, afraid of what the answer would be.

"Yeah. I do."

Cat still felt his gaze on her. She ignored it. Forced herself to breathe, pushing the breath she'd been holding slowly out, as reality struck her head-on. Maybe she held the majority of the burden for what had happened back at the motel. She swallowed hard and tried to pretend it didn't matter. Please God, she prayed; don't let her actions be responsible for the two of them almost getting killed.

"Sure, I guess I can do it," she finally agreed once she could talk. She took another deep breath and shoved her guilt aside, because she didn't see how an innocent call to her aunt's cell phone could bring the man wielding the gun. After all, she'd done nothing illegal. Josh Buchannan was to blame. She'd simply been in the wrong place at the wrong time and definitely with the wrong man. Cat wasn't going to let him twist this around so that it was her fault. "You want me to go now?"

"Yeah. I think this is escalating and they're getting desperate." He dug into his pocket, pulling out a handful of coins. "Here's some change. Make sure you stay on the line for at least five minutes."

Taking the money from him, she ignored his warm hand when it made contact with hers. She didn't want to remember how those hands had been all over her last night, but the memory was all too vivid. In one swift turn, she headed toward the phone in the parking lot.

"Aunt Marge?" Cat asked, as soon as her aunt answered.

"Candace? I wasn't expecting you this early."

"Oh...yeah...well...I got the chance so I thought I'd call and give you an update." A half smile crossed her face at what she was saying. There was no way she could tell her aunt the truth. How did one tell a sixty-year-old woman that the call she received last night might have sent some crazy man to kill her and Josh? Instead, she asked, "Did you tell anyone about my call last night?"

"Why do you ask, dear?"

Cat rolled her eyes, working hard to keep tears from forming at the slight guilt in her aunt's voice.

"No reason." Cat cleared her throat. "I was only wondering if

Brad called," she lied, hoping the fib would get her aunt to admit to talking to him. "I haven't heard from him."

"He was here when you called. He used my phone to call Smitty. I know you asked me not to say anything, but they've both been beside themselves with worry."

"Really?" Cat fought to keep the question nonchalant, even as tears broke free. Now she knew without a doubt that somehow her innocent phone call had almost gotten them killed. Josh had been right. Brad Maxwell had set it up and he'd used her innocent action to do it.

"Candace? I didn't do anything wrong, did I?"

"No, Aunt Marge. I didn't realize Brad cared so much."

"He does. He's been here off and on since you've been gone, hoping for a word from you. Seems his cell phone is on the blink and he says he doesn't know if you've tried to contact him."

Cat smiled ruefully into the phone, adding another fib. "He's right. I have been trying to get a hold of him. I appreciate your letting him know."

"I've never thought much of him and I'm still not sure I like him, but he's been so diligent, I feel I may have been hasty in my judgment."

Cat's smile softened. Her aunt had never mentioned not liking Brad before. Leave it to her to see something she hadn't seen right away. "Yeah, well sometimes first impressions are right and sometimes they're wrong," she cajoled, attempting to sound as upbeat as she could. No sense worrying her aunt. She looked at her watch, noting she'd been on the phone for over five minutes. "Look, Aunt Marge. I've got to go. I'll call you as soon as I get another chance. Can you let Brad know you heard from me?"

"Sure thing, sweetheart. I'll let him know you asked about him. I'm sure the news will make him happy," Marge said.

"You do that." Cat replaced the handset and rested her head against the booth while her shoulders slumped.

She remained immobile for an endless moment, working to compose herself and reaching for courage before she went back inside the restaurant to face Josh. How could she tell him he'd been right all along? She couldn't do it. Somehow she was sure her actions would bring even more disappointment from him. She was so tired of feeling this way.

Okay, Cat! Pull yourself together and cope, she thought. What's done is done. You screwed up, but you didn't do it on purpose. You'll get through this.

Brad Maxwell stepped into the warehouse. Then looked over his shoulder, feeling a bit on edge. He scanned the empty parking lot and heaved a sigh of relief. Nothing looked out of the ordinary. No reason to be jittery, old buddy. You've thought of everything, he told himself. There was no way this could go wrong.

The door slammed behind him as he moved further into the room. He held all the right cards. In less than twelve hours, he'd be sitting pretty on a warm beach.

Double-checking, he patted his pocket and flashed an inward smile. His ticket to freedom, he thought, glancing at his watch. Since he was a few minutes early, he began pacing, trying to get rid of his excess energy.

Minutes passed.

He turned at the sound of the door opening. A grin spread across his face.

Rodriquez walked toward him, carrying a large metal briefcase. When he got to within five feet of him, he offered him the case.

After taking it, Brad strolled over to a table with chairs pushed against the wall. He set the briefcase on the table. Without opening it, he turned to Rodriquez, who'd followed him.

"It's all there," he said. "You've done your part. Now we're doing ours."

Brad nodded. "You don't mind if I make sure? Not that I don't trust you."

"Of course. I expected as much." He offered a sinister smile. "Be my guest."

Brad worked the latch, but it wouldn't open. Noticing the case had a combination lock, he glanced at Rodriquez. "What's the combination?"

"All zeros," Rodriquez answered. He stepped back. Then turned away from him.

When Brad set the numbers to zero, the latches clicked open. He raised the lid. A fine mist sprayed into his face, catching him off guard. He rubbed his eyes and nose. At once, he knew Rodriquez had drugged him.

"Son of a bitch!" he yelled. But his slurred words did no good.

Already the drugs were taking effect, weakening his muscles and causing a general state of delirium.

Rodriquez's smile became more menacing. "Sorry to disappoint you, Maxwell. But you brought this on yourself. The combination of atropine and lorazepam absorbs quickly into the tear ducts and nasal membranes. Won't do you any good to fight the effects."

Fighting the drug, Brad watched Rodriquez swiftly close the case before turning to him and lowering him into a chair. His rubbery legs gave way and made resisting impossible as another man came into the room.

"Hurry. I don't have a lot of time," Rodriquez said. "I've got other more pressing business requiring my attention."

"Don't worry. The muscle weakness will last for quite awhile but he'll be lucid in a moment," the other man said, inserting an IV into his arms. "Then, once this shit hits him, he'll be singing like a baby."

Brad shook off the haze floating in his brain, glanced down at the IV hooked into his arm, and looked up at the two men. A feeling of dread washed over him, as warmth spread throughout his body.

"Good of you to join us again, Maxwell," said the new man.

"Feels good, doesn't it?" Rodriquez asked, offering a half grin. He shook his head and added, "And now, Maxwell, we need to know about your insurance policy. We don't take kindly to threats."

"Oh yeah?" Brad slurred. "I don't take kindly to being screwed over by scumbags."

"He's fighting it," the other man said, monitoring Brad's movements. "His efforts are useless, but it'll take more time."

"Maxwell, look at me." Brad obeyed and his eyes were glazed over, but he was too doped up to hide the definite spark behind the glaze. Rodriquez sighed. "The drugs he injected are effective, so quit fighting. Simply tell us what we want to know and you'll be free to go. And you can take the money with you. We only want to be assured you won't double-cross us."

Brad rolled his head, and moaned.

"See. It does no good to fight. You feel compelled to tell us, so do it," Rodriquez's partner said. "Unburden yourself and this will all be over."

"I should never have crawled into bed with you," Brad whispered, gritting his teeth as euphoria rose up. The need to unburden himself *was* overwhelming.

"That may be, but you've already had the great sex. Now it's time to pay for it. Tell us."

Rodriquez pulled out a chair and sat down on it backward, using the back as an armrest. He kept his attention on Brad.

"I'm asking again, what do you have and where can we find it," his partner asked more urgently a few minutes later.

Another all-encompassing wave of exhilaration swamped him, erasing the rest of his resistance. Brad's head rolled back as he succumbed fully to the drug. Giving in to the urge to confess, his words were slurred. "'sts in my c'mputr. A copy's 'n Buc's desk."

"Good. Very good. Now you can relax," he said as Brad's head fell forward.

Rodriquez got up and made a phone call. Then waited.

His cell phone rang. "Did you get it?" he asked. "Good."

"Take care of him." He closed the metal case and gripping the handle, he carried it across the room toward the door, saying over his shoulder, "Make sure it looks like an overdose. That should connect this loose end to Buchannan rather nicely."

"No problem."

"I'll be in touch."

The man sat on the chair Rodriquez had vacated and watched him leave. Then his attention went back to Brad, who eventually stirred.

"Ah, good. You're awake," he said, grabbing one of the syringes from the table. "I was so hoping to see your face when you realized what was in store for you."

"What do you mean?" Brad whispered. "You said you'd let me go."

"See this?" He held up the syringe. "There's enough meth in here to kill ten people. An overdose. So sad. Whoever finds you will think your suppliers set up a surprise." He scrunched up his nose and lowered his voice. "Methamphetamines will be America's downfall. It takes so little to form an addiction, only you won't get the chance. You shouldn't have been so greedy," he said, as he inserted the needle of the syringe into the IV.

Brad took in his sinister smile. Realization set in. He had seconds to retaliate, if that. Hatred filled his soul as one thought consumed him. No way he'd let this scumbag best him and screw him over.

"You'll feel the rush soon. I love watching Americans die from this shit. That's my rush." He chuckled, clearly amused at his actions. "You'll be dead in a moment, but what a way to go, huh?"

Seeing another full syringe on the counter, Brad only groaned, trying to hold on to his sanity for extra time to achieve his goal. Willing his muscles to work, he jerkily yanked his arm out of the scumbag's reach, stopping him from injecting more. Although it was probably too late to save himself, he grabbed the syringe. In the next moment, he shoved the needle into the bastard's arm, pushing whatever was in the syringe into his assailant's bloodstream and praying it was lethal. "Such a rush, I recommend it," he said as he slowly sank to the ground, smiling at the look of horror on the scumbag's face.

In the next instant, he lost consciousness.

∞

Watching Cat amble in the direction of the entrance after making her call, Josh sighed and gulped more coffee. He'd wondered all morning if she'd been the source, and his answer was written in capital letters all over her face. The woman should never play poker with him because he now knew exactly how Rodriquez had found him. She'd called her aunt the night before. He should've known she would. Why hadn't he checked the phone after his shower?

Then he wondered if she'd ever tell him the truth.

Oh well. It was probably for the better this way.

Josh still wasn't sure he could trust her, but regret washed through him nonetheless. For a while last night, he'd imagined himself as the type to believe in happily-ever-after with her. And this incident highlighted one aspect. He definitely wasn't the type she needed. Wasn't able to give her what she so obviously craved. He would eventually do something to hurt her again and he couldn't live with himself if that happened.

No! Happily-ever-after wasn't in his cards. Never had been. If she wasn't part of this, nothing would change the fact that he was a selfish bastard who didn't deserve what she had to offer. Josh kept his smile in place as she wandered up to the table and sat down, retrieving her menu at the same time.

"Do you know what you're having," she asked, looking expectantly at him with a smile on her face. Only Josh could see it didn't reach her eyes and he felt somewhat responsible for the hidden unhappiness he spotted.

"Yeah," he said, going back to his menu. "I think I'll have breakfast number three. It has lots of protein with the ham and potato casserole." In an attempt to bring a little levity to the table, he added in a teasing voice, "Don't know when we'll be doing this again."

"Oh, that's right. You're the one who can push everything out to survive," she said sarcastically in a harsh tone.

"When I have to," Josh shot back just as harshly. He set the menu aside and reached for his coffee. "You know, Cat. I'm not happy about the turn of events any more than you are, so let's get through them without all the shit, okay?"

"Fine. Order me the number three also. I'm going to the restroom." She got up and left the table without looking back.

Keeping his gaze on her departing form, Josh shook his head and took another sip of coffee. Feisty thing before she's had her breakfast. Not wanting to be amused at her actions, he wondered why she'd always been able to do that—amuse the hell out of him when he was already so pissed off all he wanted to do was hit something.

ଔ

"She's made contact."

"You get a trace?" Murphy leaned back in his chair and swiveled around to face the window.

"Yeah," McMann said. "My guy says she called from a truck stop off I-80 outside Winnemucca, Nevada."

"Good. Means I'm right and he's probably on his way here," he said, watching the sun peek out from behind a cloud, brightening the sky. Even better, he thought, moving his attention back to his phone call. Maybe it wouldn't rain today. "Anyone else listen in?"

A chuckle preceded McMann's answer. "As a matter of fact, you were right. Then he made two calls. The numbers were traced to Rodriquez's cell and to another number in Nevada."

"Someone will show up. Buchannan knows what he's doing. I'm sure he set it up to see what would happen."

"We'll see. I don't have your faith in the bastard. I plan on having him followed."

"He won't take kindly to you using him as bait," Murphy warned, not adding any of his true thoughts. Smitty's ability with languages and Buc's with disguises meant they were too good at knowing how to disappear when undercover in the Arab world. Here in the States it would be easier. McMann was wasting his time. Buc would never give anyone the chance to use him in such a way. Murphy rubbed his eyes with his thumb and forefinger, wondering at the intense dislike he held for the man on the other end of the phone when he'd never met him. Simply talking to him, he felt his blood pressure rising and his stomach burning. Smitty was right. The guy was a moron.

"Maybe," McMann said. "But nothing's convinced me he's as lily white as you think he is. Besides, I have no choice. And neither do you. You've got your orders. Keep your mouth shut until this is over. Do you hear me?"

"Loud and clear. But I'm not rolling over. I've already warned him about Rodriquez. Now I'm warning you, and I'd listen if I were you, butthead. He's done more to uncover this operation by staying alive than you'll ever do in your entire career. You and your idiot partner screw this up and I'll make sure you're both assigned somewhere so far off you'll never see the light of day."

"Can your threats, Murphy." McMann snickered. "We don't work for you."

"Maybe not, but we're on the same team. And I've got a few friends in high places who owe me favors. So my best advice to you would be to heed my words," he said heatedly before slamming the handset into the cradle and popping a few antacids into his mouth. Goddamn Feds. He hated FBI agents, especially those two. Somehow they all thought their shit didn't stink, when in reality it stank more because most of them had the diet of pigs. The fact that he had the same bad eating habits didn't bother him. He knew what he was and didn't need to prove himself to anyone.

❧

Josh had his gaze plastered in the direction of the restrooms, not sure why he was relieved when Cat emerged and strolled in his direction. He didn't want to admit that he'd been concerned she would try to ditch him. Sighing, he lifted his mug to his mouth. The woman had definitely gotten under his skin, and he had to figure out a way to keep her from digging deeper.

"Feeling better?" he asked as she sat down.

"Yeah, Buc-man. As a matter of fact I am."

"Good. I held off ordering and told her to come back when you returned from the restroom."

"I thought you were in a hurry."

"We were, but I've changed my mind. Now we wait."

"Well, let's not wait all day. I'm starving," she said curtly.

"Hey, easy. I'm still reeling from the guilt of forcing you out of the car."

"Jerk."

He grunted as the waitress came up right then, asking, "You guys ready to order?"

Josh nodded to Cat. "Go ahead."

She opened her menu, spent a moment looking for the right entry, and then glanced at the waitress, flashing a warm smile. "I'd like breakfast number three."

"How'd ya want your eggs?"

"Scrambled."

The waitress took Cat's menu, then turned to Josh with eyebrows raised. "How 'bout you? What'll it be?" Josh ordered the same thing and handed her his menu as she said, "Be back in a jiff with more coffee. Food'll take a few minutes."

"No problem. We're in no hurry," he said, his gaze remaining on her back as she rushed about putting in their order and grabbing a full pot of coffee. He waited until she topped off their cups and hurried out of earshot before glancing at Cat again. "Like I said, we're in no hurry and now we wait."

Cat squirmed under his scrutiny. He sipped hot coffee and the edges of his lips curled into a fraction of a smile.

She glared at him. "What're we waiting for?"

"You'll see," he replied evasively, while reining in his chuckle at her haughty tone. Cat Tyler in a snit never failed to make him smile.

"You really think the call to my aunt will do something?"

"Umm-hmm." Yeah! He chuckled softly as he read every thought now written in bold print across her expression. The woman simply entertained him.

"Is my aunt safe?"

"I think so. Especially since part of our wait just walked in." He nodded toward the door where two men wearing suits stood ready to be seated. "No. Don't turn around. There's no way they'll recognize us, but we want to remain unobtrusive. Otherwise, you'll draw their interest. They'll pass by in a moment." His hand went to his weapon, hidden in his jacket. Just in case.

"I feel unobtrusive." Cat looked down at her sweater and shook her head, saying in a disgruntled tone, "You picked out some ugly clothes."

"They're plain and serve a function."

"I can't see what function they serve except to make me look ugly."

"You needed something to tone down your looks." Chuckling, he took another sip, then added, "Otherwise you're too noticeable," while eyeing the two who were now being led to a table. His attention moved back to Cat and he grunted. "Now you can give them a cursory glance. They've already given the place a thorough scan and passed right by us."

"You think I'm noticeable?"

Josh sucked in a big breath when she ignored the two men and looked at him expectantly. Her question sounded so full of hope and he couldn't miss the longing pouring out of her eyes.

"You know I do. I've always noticed you, even when I didn't want to," he stated truthfully. "I only wish I'd never acted on it. I doubt it'll do either of us any good."

Their gazes locked, and in that extended moment before she cast her eyes down, Josh could tell Cat waged a mental battle. Her next words unsettled him, causing hope and want to burst inside his gut, creating his own mental battle.

"Josh, there's something you should know." She eyed her cup intently. She bit her bottom lip, then took a deep breath. "I called my aunt last night," she admitted softly, still not looking at him. "From your cell phone." She concentrated on sipping, hiding her features behind her cup before finally meeting his stare. "I'm so sorry."

The simple apology hung in the air, though her voice was barely audible in the noisy room.

He inhaled another gulp of air and tamped down the desire to respond to the sincerity he saw in her expressive eyes.

The waitress walked up just then and began unloading a full tray of food. Josh blew out his favorite expletive, relieved at the interruption, and focused on eating.

What more could he say without making the situation worse? He needed to let it go. Forget the attraction. This whole mess would be over soon. Whatever was going on would come to a head even if he had to give it a little shove in the process. Then they both could get back to their lives. Such a shame the emotions surrounding them were heightened by circumstances. It wouldn't be fair to expect anything permanent to evolve from them.

"I think I see what you're talking about with those two guys."

Her comment pulled him out of his thoughts and his gaze flew to her face.

She nodded, grinning. "They seem out of place here."

"They do, don't they?" Josh snorted. His nod indicated her plate. "Take your time eating. We're still waiting. It may be awhile."

He took a piece of paper out of his pocket, along with a pen, and began writing. Then got up and said, "I'm going to the restroom. I'll be right back."

Josh headed toward the back of the restaurant, walking by the two men, and tripping on something right as he got to their table. They both moved to help him and he nodded, placing a note he'd written in the bigger guy's jacket pocket. He sauntered toward the men's room, smiling inwardly at the fact that neither noticed his surreptitious movement.

Chapter 20

"So, what're we waiting for?" Cat asked an hour later. They'd stretched breakfast out, and the two men who'd come in earlier were paying their bill. "They're leaving."

"They're not going anywhere. See that car out there? They'll wait there for several hours."

"Why?"

"To see who comes in and who goes out. And you're right. We've lingered long enough." He started sliding out.

"Does this have anything to do with the guy who just came in and sat down?" she asked. When she noticed Josh's lips twitch, clearly holding on to his smile, she prodded, "What? It does, doesn't it?"

"Good eyes, Powder Puff. He's probably showing the waitress our picture to see if we've been here. Now try and remain inconspicuous while we walk out to our car, so we don't attract his notice."

She snorted. "How can I be anything else in this getup?" She followed Josh outside while the man they were talking about gave them no more than a cursory glance, before moving his attention back to the others in the restaurant.

"So, who was he?" Cat's question bounced around the car like a ping-pong ball as she buckled her seat belt. While Josh backed out of the space, she added, "He looked out of place too, only not for the same reason."

Josh ignored her, keeping his attention on driving, eventually pulling onto the interstate, heading west. Cat sighed and shook her head. He obviously wasn't going to say anything else. She glanced out the window, watching the passing barren landscape and tried to pretend it didn't matter, but her resolve lasted about five minutes.

"So, what's going on?" she finally asked, unable to control her curiosity. She was tired of being left in the dark. Josh Buchannan knew more than he was letting on, and she would be damned if she was going to sit here and go along with everything without a better explanation. "I think I have a right to know."

"I'm still figuring that out," he explained, holding his gaze on the road ahead.

"Wrong answer, Buc-man." Did he really think her such an airhead not to have some idea of what he'd been doing? "Since you're not being forthcoming, how about I speculate." When he turned toward her with his eyebrows raised, she rolled her eyes. "Come on. I know FBI agents when I see them."

He didn't say anything. Instead, he shrugged, and his focus wandered back to the road.

Cat continued, not dissuaded by his unyielding attitude. "And the guy who came in as we were leaving? Everything about him shouted Middle Eastern Muslim, definitely not your typical Nevada rancher." She glanced at Josh and noticed the shutters over his thoughts slam into place.

Annoyed, she muttered under her breath, "Damn it all."

The man infuriated her when his features closed so effectively, cutting off any clue as to his thoughts. Wanting to wipe the look off his ruggedly handsome face, she threw out the fleeting notion she'd had while passing the man as they were going out the door. "I'm thinking his arrival is related to us somehow. Maybe he's some kind of terrorist."

That comment got Josh's attention and she snorted at the surprise spilling from his expression when he ventured another glance in her direction.

She almost laughed out loud when he asked, "Why do you say that?"

"Get real. Contrary to general consensus, just because I'm blonde, doesn't mean I'm dumb."

"I don't think you're dumb," he snapped.

"Then why would you ask such an insipid question?" Cat crossed her arms and glared at him.

"It's a valid question. I was curious and wanted to know the answer."

Cat shrugged. "He did seem to be looking for us. And he hasn't been Americanized."

When Josh held her gaze with eyebrows lifted for several seconds, clearly waiting for her to continue, she shook her head in disgust and her eyes went back to the brown scenery passing by.

"Well?" he asked a moment later.

"Well what?" she shot back, totally annoyed.

"Finish your statement."

"Oh, so you can be closed and I can't?" she murmured, leaning her head against the rest. "Is that it?"

"Cat?"

His question held a hint of warning, but she ignored it, remaining silent, giving him a taste of how she felt when he closed up like he did.

"I'm waiting. Tell me."

She let out a long, slow breath and met his searching stare. Why couldn't she be as good as he was at the game? Why did she have this need to explain? "I was surrounded with the culture for years when I was younger." Shrugging, she shifted her focus outside the window. "His superior attitude while he showed the waitress our picture gave him away. Plus, it wasn't hard to recognize the way he didn't even notice me. Not because I'm unobtrusive, but because to him, I'm a second-class citizen and not worthy of the bother. American men see women more equally. It's all in the projected attitude." She snorted. "Believe me. Your male chauvinistic ways are nothing compared to some of the men I met when I happened to venture into my parents' world. My ex-husband could give lessons."

"So, you still think I'm a chauvinist?" he asked.

Cat didn't bite. "Don't think I don't know what you're doing." She fought the urge to smile. "You're very good at that, you know."

"I know," he said, drawing her gaze and offering her a half shrug. "It was worth a shot."

She waited a heartbeat. "Well? Am I right? Is that man somehow connected to us?"

"Shit." He expelled the word in a sigh. "Why can't you be more docile? Why do you have to push?"

"Because, Buc-man. I've decided to change," she said. "The old Candace Tyler would accept your answers and say, 'Thank you very much.' But the new Cat isn't letting you get away with anything. I want answers. Don't you think I deserve them? After all I've been through?"

With his concentration on the road ahead, he rested his elbow against the door and rubbed his forehead with his second finger and thumb, clearly in thought. Watching him, Cat pushed further.

"Come on, Josh. I've been running for three days, while someone's obviously attempting to kill me, and all I'm doing is trying to stay alive. I trust you. Why can't you trust me?"

&

Smitty burst into the warehouse, and spying the prone bodies in the center, he swore under his breath. He ran to check Maxwell's pulse, ignoring the two men who'd followed him inside. Next, he checked the other man. Both were dead. Still ignoring McMann and Adams, he reached for his cell phone and punched in Murphy's number.

"Maxwell's dead. And so is some other guy. He's got no ID, but it looks like he was in on the drug operation along with Maxwell. A disagreement of some kind. Dishonor among thieves, I'd say."

"Well, that lead's gone."

"Any news on Buc?" Smitty asked, his gaze moving to the two Feds who were now checking out the two dead bodies, as well as what killed them. McMann then pulled out his own cell phone. Smitty gave them his back, blocking out McMann's voice as he caught Murphy's, "Yeah, and the girl made contact with her aunt again."

"She did? When?"

"Over an hour ago. Buc checked in a few hours before that. He says Rodriquez tried to kill him. He's heading this way, leaving a trail. I'm expecting Rodriquez to make another go at it, once he learns he didn't succeed."

"Rodriquez was here. He's obviously involved in the drug operation with Maxwell," Smitty said. Out of the corner of his eye, he noticed Adams paying careful attention to him, so he lowered his voice and moved further away from the two agents. "I saw him leave. I should've gotten here earlier, would have if not for Laurel and Hardy. I could've prevented this and picked him up or at least followed him."

"That's hindsight talking. Don't worry about Rodriquez. He's after Buc and Buc's making his way here, so we'll get him then." Murphy sighed audibly. Finally, he said, "What has me stumped now is this whole drug business and Rodriquez's involvement. Doesn't make sense."

"It's got to be revenge." Smitty began to pace the room.

McMann was now off the phone and watching him closely.

"I can understand him going after Buc for revenge if he's

Zinger, but why get involved in drugs, and why try to discredit Buc?" Murphy asked. "Is it because of the girl, or something else?"

Smitty grimaced, then noticed McMann still eying him with interest, and immediately his frown turned around, morphing into a smirk.

Stupid moron, he thought, giving the man his back to gain a bit more privacy.

"Since only Rodriquez can tell us," he said. "I'm going after him."

"Stay where you are. I've got enough to worry about with Buc. I shouldn't have to worry about you too."

"I can't stay here and do nothing." Smitty glanced over at the two agents, whose attention was glued to him. He flashed them another quick grin, and said before disconnecting, "Besides, I have protection. Laurel and Hardy'll keep me safe."

℈

"I trust you. Why can't you trust me?"

Cat's voice wafted past Josh's ears, gripping his insides and piercing his resolve.

Trust. Such an interesting word. Murphy's warning flashed into his head and indecision engulfed him. *Don't underestimate her.* Seeing the need for him to trust her pour out of her gaze tore at him, and the idea of giving in to it twisted his gut into a tighter knot.

He'd lost the ability to trust somewhere along the way, and Josh suddenly realized the incident in which Cat's parents were killed played a big part in hastening his loss. Would she still believe in him if she knew of his role in her parents' deaths?

Intently, he studied the road ahead, reliving the past. By the time of the Tylers' deaths, he'd also lost confidence in his mission. He'd spent the majority of his adult life fighting terrorism for his country as a CIA operative, a seemingly futile task. The system wasn't working. No matter how hard he fought, the battle was never won—only escalated. Then when he discovered how ill his grandmother had been, he resented all the time and energy he'd expended on a lost cause while the one person he'd loved had mentally slipped away.

"What do you want to know?" he asked softly, after deciding to heed her request in an attempt to find all that he'd lost so long ago.

"You're really going to talk to me?"

Cat's question lingered in the air around them.

Smiling wistfully, he nodded. "Yeah. Ask away." Josh was so tired of living his life without having faith in other human beings.

"Who was the guy in the restaurant?"

"I have no idea. He did look as if he could be on a terrorist watch list, though. This keeps getting more interesting."

"So, I was right," she chortled smugly, glancing out the window. Cat remained silent before turning back to him and asking in a worried voice, "You can't think this is tied to terrorism?"

"I don't know. It doesn't play out, and I need more information before I can make that determination."

"It can't be terrorism. It started in Bozeman, Montana."

Doubt shrouded Cat's words. Though he didn't see how this particular incident could be tied to terrorism, her comments made him smile. Why was it so easy for people to believe themselves safe from foreign enemies simply because they weren't living in a big city along the coast?

"What better way to weaken the heart of America than to attack where people feel the safest? To strike where it's least expected and invoke as much fear as possible—to incapacitate? That's the true definition of terrorism," he said, voicing his thoughts.

"Okay. I'll buy your definition, but why? How?"

"Good questions," he murmured.

"So, how're you going to get your answers?"

"I have my ways," Josh answered distractedly, wondering how best to broach the subject of Rodriquez and what he knew. Since he could find no simpler way than just blurting it out, he did. "I don't know how to tell you this, but your ex-husband was the guy at the motel."

"Mark?" Cat gave a disbelieving snort. "No way." She met his gaze, but stopped short once she caught the sincerity he wasn't able to hide. "Oh my God. This is all my fault," she whispered, looking away. She stared straight ahead and right before his eyes, the exuberant pink blush drained from her face while pasty white replaced all color.

Relief swept over him. Josh let out a breath he didn't know he was holding at her reaction. Her expressive face now held pure horror and the fear rushing out of her was genuine.

No! She wasn't part of it. No one was that good an actress.

"It gets worse," he cautioned, wishing he could erase her all-consuming panic. Right then, the desire to stop the bastard and save Cat from any more grief became more than a pressing thought, transforming into a driving need.

"How can it get any worse? The man's a monster and he found me." Cat closed her eyes and leaned her head against the rest. "I should've known it'd only be a matter of time."

"You're not the only target."

"Of course I'm the target!" she cried. "He threatened me and I know he means to kill me."

"He's after me too."

"You?" Her expression held pure skepticism. "Why would he want to kill you?"

"I don't know—yet, but I definitely plan to find out." He broke off. As he drove, he watched the passing barren scenery while his mind churned. After miles of wondering, he slanted a glance in her direction. "Could your ex be involved in terrorism?"

"This isn't about terrorism," Cat said softly, shaking her head slowly and peering out the window. "Well, it is, but not in the CIA sense of the word."

"Cat, he's some kind of double agent. He's the one who sent the guy at the restaurant."

"Mark? A double agent? Now I know you're crazy."

They rode in silence for the next five miles before Cat spoke again. "My call to my aunt. You knew I made the call, didn't you? I mean, before I told you."

"I suspected. You have a very expressive face," he teased. When he noticed her clenched fist, he put his hand over it and squeezed. "I didn't know if you'd done it on purpose."

"I know you didn't trust me." She relaxed her fist and offered him a wan smile. "I could see it in your eyes. What made you change your mind?"

"Sometimes a man has to trust his instinct." He ignored the flush of pleasure that surged through him when he caught her warm smile now spreading over her face, and indicated with his hand over his shoulder. "Hand me one of those phones, will you? It's time to make a call. Find out more information."

"Who are you calling?" She stretched, reaching behind her to rummage through the packages, then pulled out one of the phones and handed it to him.

"Listen and learn." He chuckled at her inquisitive grin. "Some things never change. This is how I always used to ease boredom on long assignments."

He slowed the car to sixty, then punched in Murphy's preset number and waited. The road ahead was long and straight with no other car in sight on either side of the interstate.

"Murphy here. Whattaya got?" came the greeting after two rings.

"A couple of things."

"That you, Buc?" he asked, throwing out an audible sigh.

"Yeah, it's me." Josh flashed Cat a brief smile and winked. She laughed.

"Listen, call those Feds who're on duty back at the truck stop and tell the big guy to look in his pocket. I left him a message."

"Dammit all, Buc," Murphy's irritated voice blasted back. "No wonder these guys're pissed off at you when you pull shit like that."

"Smitty's right. They're idiots. Couldn't find their ass from a hole in the ground."

"So, you actually got close enough to put a note in his pocket?" Murphy asked, not bothering to keep the amusement out of his words.

"The guy should've been looking for me."

"That's damn near impossible when you disguise yourself and you know it."

"It's no excuse," Josh shot back, chuckling.

"Yeah it is." Murphy grunted. "Hell, I still remember the time you bet me to see if I could pick you out of a lineup. Lost forty bucks and never got my pride back. I knew you were there and I couldn't spot you."

"Their problem is they're too lax. Hey, do me another favor, will you?"

"What?" Murphy asked, snorting. "Shit's exploding all over the place, I'm poppin' Tums like crazy, and you gotta be a prankster."

"Tell 'em if they want to blend in, to buy some jeans and a pair of tennis shoes. They had Feds written all over them."

"I'm not tellin' 'em squat. I got more things to worry about than trying to smooth ruffled feathers on some asshole Feds because you insult them."

"Oh? Did something else happen?"

"Yeah," Murphy sighed, his manner sobering over the line. "And it's not good. Maxwell's dead, along with one of Rodriquez's accomplices. Got a match on his prints. Zayed Bin Ali Al Kashid. A known terrorist and someone who's not supposed to be in this country."

"Shit!" Josh blew out. "What's he doing with Maxwell?"

"Good question. I'm keeping this under wraps for now. Smitty and the two agents who've been assigned to protect him are the only ones who know about this latest development until I figure out what they're doing."

"What about the guy in the restaurant? You get a line on him yet?"

"Yeah. Hamad Bin Saleh Al Saud, a well-known leader of at least three terrorist cells. He's not someone we expected to see in the US either, much less Winnemucca, Nevada. Bin Saleh's a particularly nasty fellow. Now that we're aware of his presence, we'll keep an eye on him. None of the watch groups had him on their radar. Lord knows how long he's been in this country illegally without anyone knowing it. Makes you wonder how many others there are floating around. Think of all the damage they could do."

"They're coming out of the woodwork," Josh ground out. "What the hell are they planning?"

"I wish I knew. This freaking mess has another hole worming its way into my gut."

"What happened to diet and exercise?"

"Nothing. I'm working on it. Look, can you get to a computer?"

"Not easily. I'm on the run, remember."

"Well, do," Murphy said. "I've been reviewing the files I pulled from your last mission in Afghanistan, when the girl's parents were killed. I want to send you some stuff. Look at it again and see if it makes any sense."

"Shit, Murph. Don't do this." Josh's grip tightened on the steering wheel and his smile quickly faded, turning into a grimace. "I quit. I'm out of the business. You know that."

"Yeah. And this was your last operation before you quit."

"I got tired of watching innocents get blown up for no more reason than differing beliefs and not being able to do a damn thing about it but keep watching."

"I understand your motives. But everything's tied to this. I can feel it, and no one has eyes as good as yours. You see things others don't—connections others miss. There's something big happening and you're dead set in the middle of it. You and the girl. So, you might as well give in and help."

"I'll be there in less than eight hours. We can look at it together."

"No. This can't wait."

Josh sighed, keeping his eyes on the road ahead while he thought about Murphy's implication. Murphy had picked up on the clues Josh had given him. He knew damn well Josh was making his way there, so this request was his way of asking him to delay his arrival without really asking him. Why? He had to trust his instinct. Trust. Funny how the word kept popping into his mind. "Shit," he muttered under his breath, wishing he could just ignore the request. But he couldn't. Up until all this started, Murphy was the only man besides Smitty that Josh trusted completely.

"What's going on?" Josh asked, lowering his voice, trying to hold on to his patience. "You're not telling me everything."

"I'm asking you as a friend to do this. I need your help, Buc. Please?"

Josh glanced over at Cat for a moment, thinking. His interest caught her attention and she threw him a quick smile. He gave her a half nod before she resumed looking out the window and he centered his attention on the road ahead.

"Okay. I'll do it. I could use a night without someone trying to kill me."

"Just don't make any calls that can be traced."

"That wasn't me."

"My point exactly."

Josh chanced another glance at Cat, who still looked out the window, appearing to be absorbed in her thoughts. He sucked in a huge breath, letting it out slowly with the words, "Don't worry, Murph. No one's killed me yet. I'll be in touch as soon as I can."

Chapter 21

A ringing cell phone interrupted Mark Zinger, AKA Anthony Rodriquez, in the middle of packing an overnight bag.

"Yes?" He held the phone up to his ear while he continued moving about the room.

"Why are Joshua Buchannan and Candace Tyler still alive?"

Rodriquez's back stiffened and he felt the blood drain from his face.

"There was no way they could've survived," he explained, wiping one sweaty palm on his pants before switching the phone to the other hand and wiping the free one. He'd been so positive he'd achieved his goal. He had no idea how they survived. Not with four bullets ripping into each sleeping body. Neither had moved afterward.

"But you didn't stop to verify the fact and the mistake cost you dearly...cost our cause dearly."

"I couldn't do it without taking more risks," he hissed. He paced while raking a hand through his hair.

"Dreams are dissolving with the acid of your incompetence. We've spent decades disguised as friends among our enemies, pretending to be like them, waiting for the day our final battle could begin. You were chosen for your skill and your devotion. You knew the timing of his death was crucial in our holy war, so you should've taken the risk."

"I realize that now." Rodriquez sighed.

"You were careless and quick to make assumptions. He isn't. That's why he's eluding you," the caller on the other end admonished softly. "Just like with Candace Tyler in the restaurant. You should've known they'd still be together. You could've waited, then followed and had the perfect opportunity at a later time. Instead, you rushed."

Rodriquez hated having to admit that his mistakes could be the ruination of their Jihad. He *had* been careless…several times. Josh Buchannan needed to be discredited, but only killing him and making it look as if it was drug related would fully accomplish their goal. Elders had spent years orchestrating such an intricate plan in absolute secrecy and wouldn't tolerate failure easily. He'd disgraced himself with his negligence. "I thought he was moving south, alone. The transmitter was moving south."

"It's exactly what he wanted you to think. I warned you about overconfidence," the voice said with audibly restrained fury. He stopped talking for long seconds before adding in a more controlled tone, "In order for us to succeed, we have to be better than our enemy. It is the will of Allah. You were chosen as were others, and like them have trained for years to prepare for this one week, but your role is more vital. Up until this mission started to dissolve into nothing, I believed you were up to the task."

"He's had some good luck."

"Cease with your excuses. Luck has no bearing."

"I'm telling you the man won't die!" Rodriquez said heatedly into the phone.

"All men die when it's their turn. It comes down to skill and wits. So far, Buchannan has proven he's a better adversary. We can't win if we fall back on luck. I thought you understood."

"I'm working on rectifying the situation."

"It's too late. Plans have now changed. We have to abort our original mission and exploit other options. The chase is leading to San Francisco with two federal agents in tow. I'm adding the two agents to your hit list. You're to take advantage of their arrival. Make sure you get them all together. It's the only way we can salvage what's left of our original mission."

"I see." Though his caller spoke calmly and politely, he knew his failures were the reason for the changes. Rodriquez was completely shamed, only too thankful to be given a way to save face. No one would learn of his ineptitude unless he failed again, at which point his family would bear the brunt. He had to succeed.

"No, I don't think you do. Decades! Decades of planning and waiting have evaporated into nothing. This assignment was your destiny and you failed."

"Yes, I know, and I'll do what needs to be done. I'll kill them."

"Killing them now will never make up for our loss—not totally. Timing was everything. You've failed, and because of your overconfident haste, we've lost much ground. The entire operation is in jeopardy."

"I understand," Rodriquez said, nodding and staring at the blank wall. He'd pay for his mistakes with the ultimate sacrifice. But first he needed to rectify the situation before his death could bring him eternal life in God's garden as a martyr of the holy war.

"Once your targets arrive in San Francisco, they'll most likely meet John Murphy. Remember, he is to remain untouched."

"I understand."

"Since you're now wanted, I booked you a flight using your other identity. There's an electronic ticket waiting at the airport. Don't fail me. If you do, I won't be able to keep it a secret. You'll disgrace not only yourself but me as well."

"I won't fail."

❧

Josh hung up the cell phone and tossed it in the backseat. He drove for countless minutes not saying anything.

When he pushed on the accelerator and the car shot ahead to a cruising speed of ten miles over the limit, Cat glanced over.

"What're you doing?" His movements seemed so competent. He clearly had a purpose. "I thought we weren't in a hurry."

"We are now," Josh answered distractedly. "We need to make it to a place to stop for the night. Then we'll start up again in the morning."

"What happened?" Josh gave her a cursory shrug and she expanded her question. "On the phone? You sounded upset. Something else happened." She scanned his face, noting his determined expression.

"Maxwell's dead."

"Really? Brad's dead?"

"You don't seem surprised," he said, meeting her gaze with slanted eyebrows.

"After surviving a plane crash, almost being blown up, and then shot at, how can anything surprise me?" she replied, offering a half smile and leaning her head back against the rest. "I figured he was involved somehow, since he's the one person my aunt told about my phone call."

"Good point," he grunted. "He was found with an accomplice. Murphy thinks this is tied to terrorism."

"Brad? And terrorism? No way. He might have been a self-centered man who loved to have the world revolve around him...but not a terrorist."

"Humph," was all Josh said. With his focus straight ahead and his expression closed again, he ignored her for the next few miles.

"What's going on?" she finally asked, after enduring the silent treatment for too long.

"I'm not sure." His voice trailed off as he continued in deep thought for more miles. Finally, he asked, "How well did you know your ex?"

"Obviously not as well as I thought." She snorted. "If he's behind all of this."

"I was wondering. You said earlier you didn't think he seemed the type to be involved in terrorism. But evidence points in that direction."

"I don't know. My parents converted him to Christianity, and I was under the impression he had a Jewish background, not Muslim." Cat shrugged. "If I were to guess, I'd have to say no, given the way he was with my parents and given his background. Of course, he had me snowed at first. Maybe it was part of an act."

"He's definitely proven he's a good actor. He'd also have to be a pathological liar. I've never heard of anyone getting through the CIA's rigorous, ongoing security checks. According to Murph, he most likely murdered the real Rodriquez and did away with his body in order to have a full identification. Murph believes the precision of implementation probably means he's been planning this a long time and has plenty of help."

"He's certainly charismatic and charming, and now thinking about his behavior toward the end, I'd say he's a darn good actor to convince me to marry him, so it makes sense he'd be a very good liar as well. I definitely thought he was crazy after I really got to know him."

"But?"

"How'd you know there's a but?"

"I can hear it in your voice," he said, glancing over and snaring her gaze, offering a quick grin.

"You think you're so smart," she replied, grinning back. He didn't answer her, simply held his eyebrows up and waited. She burst out laughing. "Okay, okay. But...he's always struck me as being a follower. Somehow I don't see him as a master ringleader."

"Hmmm. Interesting."

"What's interesting?"

"If he's not the leader, then someone else is."

"That's not interesting. That's scary."

"Yeah, it is. But they messed with the wrong two people." He placed his hand on her knee and gave it a gentle squeeze. "We'll figure it out."

"Not we. You," Cat said breathlessly, ignoring both the warmth of his hand as well as the warmth in his voice. Memories of the night before, of where those hands had been working magic, engulfed her. Oh, how she wished for more between them.

Remember, Cat! It's all an illusion.

She'd overcome her attraction to him somehow. Once this episode was over, she'd go back to her life and he'd go back to his. As painful as the thought was, she had to face the truth. A wistful smile flitted across her face as she realized her fear had changed over the last few days. Now that her ex had actually found her, the idea didn't seem as fearful as how she'd survive when Josh Buchannan was no longer a part of her life. How crazy was that, she wondered. In three days' time her life had completely turned upside down with craziness.

"What?" he asked, drawing her attention away from her thoughts. When she glanced at him, she noticed the questioning look in his eyes before they returned to the road.

"What'd you mean, what?" Cat swallowed the bit of regret now lodged in her throat.

"What're you thinking?"

"Thinking?" she asked, feeling caught and also feeling the heat rising up her face.

"Come on. You're turning red again," he teased, chuckling. "That alone means something. Plus, you were a million miles away and your smile seemed so sad."

"Oh no, you don't. You already hold too much advantage in this whole deal."

"I do not," he muttered, snaring her gaze, holding it for a moment too long. "Tell me what you were thinking just then," he dared, in a voice Cat recognized as the same one he used on the first day she met him.

He was really good, she mused. Good at challenging her and putting her off balance. No way she was going to give him what he wanted.

"You mean I have to tell you," she shot back, letting a gurgle of laugher erupt. "I thought you could read everything on my face—like some kind of psychic face-reader."

She expelled a heavy sigh when he chuckled and released her gaze, his going back to the road ahead while she concentrated on the dreary, brown desert scenery passing outside her window.

"You don't have to tell me. I know you think I'm a hunk," Josh said in a teasing voice.

"Sure, Buc-man. You go with the thought," Cat added distractedly without taking her eyes off the landscape. She took another deep breath and let it out slowly, totally relieved when he didn't add any more to the conversation.

☙

"I've got things to do for a few hours, then I'm off to San Francisco," Smitty said in a deceptively cheerful voice to McMann in an attempt to pretend this whole scene with Maxwell didn't disturb him.

"You can't go without us," McMann countered, after hanging up with whomever he was talking to and now walking toward Smitty with a cocky smirk on his face. "We're waiting on the forensic team to finish. It may be awhile."

"If you two want to tag along, be at Buchannan Aeronautics no later than one p.m., gentlemen, otherwise you can find your own ride," Smitty shot back, not intimidated in the least by the asshole. "I've got better things to do than wait around for two Feds who have no idea it's time to duck when shit's exploding because they're looking in the wrong direction."

"We're assigned to protect you. What're you going to tell your boss when he finds out you left us?"

"Nothing. I think I'd rather let you explain to yours why you let me go without doing your job," Smitty taunted. He turned and stormed in the direction of the main door, saying over his shoulder, "One o'clock, boys. If you're late, I'm leaving without you."

Smitty didn't catch McMann's reply as he left the agents to deal with the bodies. He kept on walking, not really caring what the moron had to say. If the two weren't there when he was ready to go, he'd take off without them. He had a job to complete. But first, he had to attend to more pressing business. As part owner in the flight

194

school, Smitty had a vested interest in making sure everything ran smoothly while Buc made his way to San Francisco. He wasn't about to let Laurel and Hardy impede the process.

He drove back to Buchannan Aeronautics in record time. Throughout all this tragedy, he had to stay focused and keep things together until the worst was over.

With Buc gone and Maxwell's tragic overdose, the school had only three flight instructors left. And if he took the Beechcraft to San Francisco, they'd be down to three planes. Once inside and seated at his desk, he got busy rescheduling, bringing everything up-to-date.

Smitty rubbed the back of his neck, working out the kinks, and stretched. He glanced at the clock after finishing the last of the paperwork. Satisfied with his progress, he stood and walked toward the reception area.

"You think you'll be okay here for a couple of days by yourself?" he asked, his gaze going to Olivia, who manned the front desk.

"Not a problem." She offered a semblance of a smile.

"I've rescheduled all the lessons for next week. There are only three students I can't get a hold of." Smitty handed her the book. "I'd appreciate it if you'd keep trying. I've already spoken to the instructors. They're all happy with the extra hours."

"So, you expect Mr. Buchannan to be back soon?" Her smile died and a shadow of sadness floated across her face. "Mr. Goodman called and told me the funeral for Gloria will be the day after tomorrow. It's hard to believe she's gone."

"I know." Smitty sighed. "Hopefully we'll get all this stuff with the FBI cleared up soon."

"Do they still think he's guilty of those things?"

Just as he was about to answer, the bell over the door tinkled and McMann and Adams stepped into the room.

"I don't know," Smitty grunted, nodding at the two men. "Ask them."

"I'll wait." Olivia scrunched up her nose. "I don't like those two."

"Neither do I." He turned around and faced Laurel and Hardy, who were almost at the counter. "I see you two made it. We'll leave in about ten minutes. I have to check the weather and grab my gear." He did a one-eighty and headed back toward his office, wishing the assholes hadn't been so prompt and he could have flown to San Francisco by himself.

Chapter 22

Josh wound his way into the parking lot of a Hampton Inn advertising a casino, wondering if the place also had Internet connections. If not, he'd have to find someplace in town. He swung into a spot, turned off the motor, and looked at Cat.

"This is a little nicer than last night, but it's still an inexpensive motel," he said, nodding at the building off the interstate outside of Reno, Nevada. "Is this okay?"

"I'm sure it'll be fine. I mean, look. We have everything anyone could need at this exit. Casino, wedding chapel, and fast food, all in one stop."

Grinning, Josh shook his head. "You want to stay here in the car while I get us a couple of rooms?"

"Two?"

He grabbed the door to get out, but stopped and turned back to her when her reply registered.

"Yeah," he sighed, then leaned a shoulder into the seat, and met her gaze. "I figured you'd want some privacy."

"We can't share a room?"

"I don't think it'd be a good idea, do you?" he asked softly, holding eye contact, praying the stark yearning he felt didn't show.

"Probably not," she admitted, as a wild look of terror flitted over her expression. "But I don't want to be alone."

Her panic-stricken manner twisted his insides. Hell, everything about her twisted his insides, and the thought of sharing a room with her had the coil tightening, wrapping around his middle in a vice-like grip. He rubbed the back of his neck while he sucked in long, deep breaths of air and let them out slowly. Finally, he moved his attention to a lamppost in the parking lot and kept it there.

"Please stay with me. We can get a room with two beds. Please? I'll sleep in my jeans and keep away from you, but don't leave me alone. I just want to feel safe and for some reason I feel safe when

I'm with you."

Her pleas came at the same moment she placed her hand on his arm.

"Shit," he muttered under his breath, wishing he could ignore both. The heat of her touch as well as her soft voice only added to the pressure of the vice in his stomach.

When she released his arm and turned to look out the window, acting as if she'd done something wrong, he swore under his breath again. He scrubbed his face with his hand and drew it through his hair.

"I've got to be honest here," he said in a firm, low voice. When she didn't respond, he gently placed his hand under her chin, forcing her to look at him. Though the cool pools of her blue eyes hid behind contacts, her gaze still generated too much heat.

He took another deep breath and ventured forward.

"It's not a good idea. Sex is a common side effect, given what we've been through. Nothing's changed since last night except now I know what it's like to make love with you." Her gaze never faltered, simply met his imploringly, but she nervously chewed on her bottom lip, clearly considering his words and causing him to add, "We've crossed the line, Cat, which makes it all the harder to resist. I don't want to hurt you any more than I already have."

"You haven't hurt me," she said too quickly, as if trying to convince him, gripping his arm again.

"Maybe I haven't…yet." He covered her hand with his and gently squeezed. "But if this goes any further, I don't see either of us coming out unscathed. I don't have a good track record in the relationship department."

"What makes you think I'm looking for something long term?" Amusement readily replaced the troubled look on her face.

"Aren't you?"

"That's so presumptuous," she scoffed, patting his cheek. "And I really appreciate your concern. But you don't need to worry about me."

"Now I am worried." Noting the gleam in her eyes, he groaned inwardly. In fact, those hidden ice blue eyes were now dancing with laughter.

"Come on, Josh. I'm hardly the type to inspire lust."

"You're joking, right?"

"No! Look at me. I'm as frumpy as a cow."

"That's a disguise." He turned her hand over and kissed her palm, moving his moist lips up to her wrist, hoping the action would unnerve her into changing her mind. "I know what's underneath." He chuckled softly at her sharp intake of breath.

"Well, I'll keep it all on," she said firmly, pulling her hand out of his grasp. "That should solve the problem."

Though her face was slightly red, she offered him a warm smile and opened her door. Once she hopped out, she bent back into the car, and added in a teasing voice, "How 'bout if I promise not to jump your bones tonight?"

He sighed. Great! His plan backfired. Now what? For one brief moment, the idea of wiping the grin off her face and showing her just how frumpy he really found her floated across his consciousness. Instead, he tried to reason with her one more time.

"Cat, I don't think—"

"I see no reason why we can't share a room. I can control myself if you can." She straightened, then slammed the door, and proceeded up the walkway leading to a glass entrance.

He let out another expletive in a resigned sigh and watched her go. He got out of the car and followed. Damn! What a dilemma. Problem was he really didn't want separate rooms, but he also knew he was setting himself up for a night of torture.

He hurried to catch up with her, saying halfheartedly, "Cat, be reasonable."

"I am. Plus, it'll be cheaper. We'll be Mr. and Mrs. Smith."

"That's original," he said, rolling his eyes as they reached the double glass doors.

"Well, what do you propose?" She waited while he opened one, and added before going inside, "We can't be Mr. and Mrs. Josh Buchannan."

"No, you're right," he agreed, wondering why the thought unsettled him. They'd be pretending, after all. It wasn't as if he wanted marriage. Hell, he'd never considered it before. His previous job as a field op kept him from forming lasting attachments, and after his grandmother died, he purposefully chose not to form them. So why did the thought that they couldn't pretend to be Mr. and Mrs. Josh Buchannan bother him?

"Shit," he muttered. He needed a drink. The woman was driving him nuts. Instead of arguing further, he meekly followed her into the hotel lobby and up to the registration desk.

"My husband and I would like a room for the night. Is it too early to check in?"

"Check-in's not for a couple hours, but let me see if I have a clean room available." The reservation clerk began typing into his computer. Then nodding, he looked at Cat and smiled. "You're in luck. I have a king room available right now."

Josh put an arm around Cat's shoulder and squeezed. "The little lady and I will take it. How much, Henry?" he asked, seeing the name over his pocket and grinning at the look on Cat's face as he reached for his wallet.

"A hundred and nineteen dollars, and eighty-nine cents with tax."

The clerk cleared his throat when Josh pulled out two one hundred dollar bills and handed them to him.

"If you're paying in cash I'll need an extra deposit of at least fifty dollars, Mr. –"

"Smith," Josh nodded. "That'll be fine. Take the entire amount. I'll pick up the balance in the morning when I check out."

"Certainly, Mr. Smith," he said, handing him a form and a pen. "If I could get you to fill this out."

Josh quickly finished checking in and Henry handed him two card keys. "We have complimentary drinks in our casino. Enjoy your stay in the biggest little city in the world, Mr. and Mrs. Smith."

"Thanks, Henry. We will." He turned to Cat and added, bending his elbow for her to take, "Come on, Mrs. Smith. It's time to start the honeymoon." He smiled inwardly when he caught her fuming expression complete with icy eyes flashing heat he'd come to associate only with Cat.

He reached over and whispered, "What's the matter, sweetheart? I thought this is what you wanted," adding a little louder, "Honey, control yourself. You should wait until we make it to the room before you start trying to undress me," earning a jarring jab in the ribs for his efforts. Yep, he thought as he led her body, stiff with indignation, through the hotel lobby toward the elevator. The woman could certainly entertain him.

"Why did you say that?" she hissed once the doors closed and there was no one to overhear.

"What was I supposed to say? He thinks we're married. It was your idea."

"It wasn't my idea to give him suggestions."

"I was playing the part."

"No, you weren't."

"Sure I was. And so were you. That's how we'd act if we were married." He nuzzled her neck. "Want a demonstration? I could get used to this married shit."

"Argh!" she ground out. "Cut it out." She pushed him away and stared at the door, blowing the bangs of her wig in exasperation. "This is not what we agreed to when I told you we could share a room."

"Oh? Don't you think I'm holding up my end of the bargain pretty well? I'll have you know, I make a fairly decent Mr. Smith." His eyebrows shot up and down suggestively, earning her stifled laugh. "Come on, Mrs. Smith. Admit it, you think I'm a hunk."

"Will you stop?" Her words didn't hold much conviction, considering she was grinning from ear to ear when she said them. She rolled her eyes. "What have I gotten myself into?"

"You're stuck with me for the night, Mrs. Smith."

"Yeah, but I remember telling you I wasn't about to jump your bones."

"Maybe not. But as I recall, I don't remember promising the same thing."

He caught the wild expression she flashed, revealing confused consternation. He sighed, blowing out his favorite expletive at the hurt he saw flicker in those eyes for the briefest moment.

"I was kidding, Cat." He drew her closer and kissed the top of her head. That his teasing was the cause made him feel pretty low right then. "I figured you knew. It's how I relieve stress on the job when things get weird."

"Don't joke about that," she demanded, jerking out of his reach, her attention zeroing in on the elevator doors. "It's not funny." She stared straight ahead, ramrod stiff, not moving a muscle.

He puffed out another expletive. "I'm sorry."

The doors opened, saving both from further embarrassment.

"Come on, let's get into the room, then you can relax." He grabbed her hand and started out, pulling her with him.

Silently, they walked to room 527, the number written on the paper key holder. Cat waited patiently without speaking while he opened the door. When they were both inside, he stalked to the window and made a perusal of the view, eyeing the parking lot from five stories up.

"I'm sorry, Cat," he said quietly, not facing her. "I never meant to hurt your feelings with my teasing."

"And what about last night? Was last night only a stress-buster as well?" The hurt present in her voice tore at his insides, ripping them further when she continued with, "Maybe it meant nothing to you, but last night meant something to me, even if nothing comes from it. I don't make love lightly, Josh."

He focused his attention below, not really noticing the several cars coming in and going out in those few minutes.

"I wasn't making light of what happened last night." He looked back at her as she moved to sit on the sofa, purposefully not meeting his gaze. "And it certainly wasn't about relieving stress. You know damn well it wasn't."

She didn't speak for several minutes. When she finally did, he could tell she worked to keep her tone modulated. "It's okay. Please, let's pretend it never happened."

"I can't pretend. I tried to tell you this would be hard," he defended, irritated now because she seemed so upset over something he'd wanted to avoid. "Why is it you never listen to me?"

"Forget it," she snapped, smoothing her clothes with her hands and keeping her attention focused at her feet. "I don't know why I'm so sensitive."

"Forget it? Now you want me to forget it?" His gaze moved back to the window. "Shit," he muttered under his breath, as incredulity moved over his face. She wants me to forget it and pretend it never happened, he thought. Is she for real? "I can't forget it. Not when last night was the best sex I've ever had and I'm dying here for a repeat," he said honestly. He was totally annoyed at this point, which caused him to vent further. "That just makes me out to be an even bigger jerk for giving in last night. And now I'm stuck with you, still wanting. Christ, I'm nothing but a perverted bastard. I never should have listened to you. We should be in two rooms," he raved, his voice rising at the end. He shoved his hair back with an impatient hand and ground out, "This is unfricking-believable. It's last night all over again. I'm damned if I do and damned if I don't."

He started pacing, holding on to emotions that were ready to explode. Hell, if he hung around he'd only say something that would hurt her more. He stalked to the table by the window and took out his wallet, dropping several twenties on it, along with one key. "I've got to go out. I'll be back later. If you leave the room, make sure you're wearing your disguise."

ও

Cat watched his hurried retreat, feeling both relieved and saddened at the same time. Could this whole mess get any worse, she wondered. She sat on the sofa for a long time simply staring at the door, and wishing. Wishing for what? Wishing she could be different? Wishing she could be someone who could handle a night of great sex without going wacko? Wishing did squat. She hadn't wanted to be alone and now she felt very alone.

Why had she forced the issue of sharing a room? Was she wishing things would turn out differently? That Josh would somehow change and be what she needed? Why oh why had she done the unforgivable and fallen in love with him? No, Cat. This isn't real. Josh told you everything's heightened by circumstances. The feelings aren't real.

Except she couldn't help thinking if these feelings weren't real, then why did it hurt so much?

ও

By the time Josh made it to the car, he had his emotions back under control and was now wondering why the lady upstairs in room 527 got to him so easily. He hadn't liked seeing her so torn up.

"Why did I let things get out of hand last night?" he muttered out loud. "I knew better. And why did I let her talk me into sharing a room tonight? I know why! I'm a glutton for punishment. That's why!" He quickly unlocked the car and slid inside, starting the engine in one fluid motion. While backing up, he continued his mental diatribe. Shit. I didn't ask for this. I never wanted to find the woman attractive. Hell, she's Victorian in her thinking. No wonder you hurt her feelings, asshole.

Though he berated himself, he couldn't quite admit to being sorry for the way things turned out. No. How could he be sorry for the best night of his life even though it ended with him almost getting killed? Shit, he thought. How stupid was that? And then he had to go and make it worse. Leave himself open to want and need again. He was so worried about making a bigger fool of himself and doing something even more stupid like making love with her again. Yeah! No one could be that big of a jerk, not even you.

Get a grip, Buc. Nothing's changed. You've got a job to do, so do it. Don't think of the distractions now. Once you find out who is behind all the shit flying around, you'll go back to your life and she'll go back to hers.

And there before him lay the answer to why he was so upset. Could he go back to his life as if nothing had ever happened?

"Damn it all," he blew out, hitting the steering wheel and punching the accelerator while driving toward downtown Reno, Nevada. At that moment, he realized he'd never be the same again. Nothing would ever be the same again because something had happened. Somehow, someway, Cat Tyler had gotten under his skin.

Chapter 23

Driving along the main road from the hotel toward Reno, Josh spotted a shopping center with a computer store on one end. He made a quick U-turn and within minutes was inside talking to a computer geek, ready to buy an inexpensive laptop that would give him all he needed.

"So, this is Internet ready?" Josh asked.

"Yes, sir," the kid said. "It's wireless ready, and you get ninety days' free service to try it out."

"Good, good. I think this should do it, then."

He picked up a thumb drive and a few other things he might need before heading to the checkout.

After paying for his purchases, he strode to his car with one thought. He wasn't ready to return to the hotel yet. He certainly wasn't ready to be trapped in the room with nothing to think about but what he'd be missing, so he searched out someplace to eat and found a café serving soup and sandwiches, as well as a wireless connection for his laptop.

First thing Josh did, once he got the computer up and running, was divert funds from a hidden account to Gus, paying him for services rendered to keep the man happy. Being a cautious man, he never knew when such services might come in handy again. Then he spent the next two hours working, downloading the information Murphy wanted him to have and finally reading a section of it while he ate a bowl of soup. The files included all the findings of his failed mission. Every detail was listed, including complete background information on all involved. One thing about Murphy, Josh thought while reading—he was a very thorough man.

When he checked his watch, he was shocked that he'd been gone from Cat for over four hours. He looked around and noticed dusk was descending, as the sun hung low on the horizon. Great! He'd left Cat alone all afternoon and she hadn't wanted to be alone.

Shaking his head at how ridiculous the situation had gotten, he gathered his things and stood.

He then went to the counter and ordered two take-out orders of soup and sandwiches. Twenty minutes later, he let himself into the hotel room. With his hands full of his computer, as well as their dinner, he kicked the door closed behind him. Walking further into the space, which seemed to shrink in size the further into it he got, he spotted Cat sitting barefoot and Indian-style on the same sofa he'd left her. She'd showered and had taken off her disguise, and now wore shorts and a T-shirt.

"Hi," he said, in an effort to act nonchalant at the delighted expression that flitted over her face when she looked up. In the next instant she was right beside him, relieving him of the take-out bag. "Careful with that," he warned. "That's our dinner."

"Oh, you sweet, sweet man," she gushed, moving to place the bag on the table near the window. She began taking the contents out of the bag and putting them in front of her. "How'd you know I'd be starved?"

He couldn't miss the pleasure in her voice. Nor could he miss the sight she presented, looking so fresh and clean, like the first breath of spring air after a long, cold winter.

Both sent signals directly to his groin.

Ignoring them, he followed. "I got tired of being a jerk and figured you wouldn't go out on your own." He sat next to her and teased, "I'm beginning to know you. If you're not careful, I'll learn all your secrets."

"I'm an open book," she shot back, grinning. "You already know most of them."

"I see you got tired of being disguised."

"Yeah." She sighed. "I hope you don't mind. That's part of the reason I didn't go out. I couldn't bring myself to put it back on."

By this point, she had all of the food out on the table, complete with napkins and plastic utensils. She opened the Styrofoam bowl in front of her and took a deep breath. "Hmmm. Smells heavenly." She licked first her thumb and then her forefinger, flashing him another warm smile.

With his eyes on her lips, desire shot through him in a wild jolt. Josh sucked in a huge breath and prayed his body would quit reacting to her innocent actions. He pushed away the main thought bouncing around his brain just then, imagining her licking him rather than her fingers.

He sighed.

Muttering his favorite expletive under his breath, he shook his head to clear it, working hard to shut off his mind from homing in on more of her innocent signals.

He took several deep breaths, toying with the food in front of him, while she focused on unwrapping a plastic spoon and started in on the soup.

"This is really good." He barely heard her comment, but he heard the pleasure in her voice. "What's the matter? You're not eating. You're not still mad at me, are you?"

Her questions pulled him out of his lustful thoughts. He glanced over and noticed she'd stopped with her spoon resting in the half-eaten bowl of soup. When his glance roamed to her face, he could see the worry imprinted there. He offered a rueful smile.

"I was never angry with you. I'm angry at the situation and myself. I'm responsible for what happened. I should've kept things from escalating."

"Why? It's not your fault. You're not responsible for all that's happened to us."

"Maybe...but I could've done more to avoid disaster between us."

"Is that how you view it?" Her earnest gaze met his without flinching or blinking. "A disaster?"

"No," he replied, unable to lie. He felt too compelled to tell her the truth. "I don't know what it is. All I know is I'm to blame."

"I disagree." Concentrating on eating again, she took more bites of food. After a few more, she stopped and aimed her spoon at him, as if the plastic piece would help make her point. "You know, Bucman, contrary to what you believe, you can't control everything. And you're not responsible for me. I am."

"Maybe," he conceded. Suddenly, he felt the room closing in again. "Look. I'm not really hungry right now," he said as he stood up. He aimed for the bathroom, saying over his shoulder, "I'm going to take a shower. Get out of these clothes."

"You go ahead. You'll feel better," Josh heard as he closed the door. No. Only one thing would make him feel better, and there was no way he was going there tonight.

He sighed and turned the shower on cold, hoping it would help take his mind out of the gutter.

CR

Morgan Jenkins, AKA Anthony Rodriquez, walked off Delta's flight 229, which landed on time in San Francisco from Salt Lake City at 5:10. He strolled outside the main terminal near baggage claim. Minutes later a car pulled up. Recognizing the individual driving as his contact, he quickly climbed inside.

"Your flight was on time, I see?"

"Yeah, even with the new enforced security."

"Like that's going to keep them safe." His driver snorted, waiting until Rodriquez closed the door before he pulled away from the curb. "Americans are so naïve. With our help, they'll succumb to their own greed and bad habits."

"They believe they are invincible." A menacing smile crossed Rodriquez's face. "Their idea of freedom and equality weakens them."

"You have your orders?"

"Yes," he grunted. "I'll need a car."

"Of course. I've been instructed to provide assistance."

"Why risk exposing your position? This is better done alone, less chance of detection." Rodriquez ignored the smugness in his driver's voice, and his thoughts drifted to the job at hand. If only he'd killed his ex before she'd divorced him, then part of his destiny would have already been fulfilled. They'd have the money her missionary parents used to distort the minds of young Arabs, as well as the life insurance he'd paid on for five years. Not that they needed it, with all the money they made on America's two biggest excesses, oil and drugs.

"I need no assistance," he added, staring out the window. His course was set. Buchannan's death was also his destiny; no one else would take credit.

The passing scenery held his silent interest for the rest of the drive into San Francisco.

The car stopped in front of a nondescript house in a middle class neighborhood.

"Key's under the mat. Everything you need for the job is in the house, including surveillance CDs, maps, and addresses. Transportation's in the garage." His contact nodded and handed him a cell phone, adding, "I'm just a call away once we're ready to go."

"Sure. I'll let you know when." Rodriguez took the phone from him and stepped out of the car. "Don't worry. I know what I'm doing."

He slammed the door and watched the car speed off.

He went inside to prepare for the job of stalking John Murphy, wondering how long it would take his ex-wife and Buchannan to make their way here. Based on the flight plan Joel Smith filed, he knew when he'd be arriving with the other two agents. It'd be best if he could get them all together, but he wasn't sure he'd have the chance. What he was sure of—it would be a long wait, requiring all of his patience—patience now at an all-time low, increasing an already humongous need to see Buchannan, the sudden bane of his existence, dead. If only Buchannan had died when he was supposed to. Then Rodriguez would be heralded as a hero instead of a failure.

Within the hour, he loitered, dressed as a street person, outside the garage of the Federal building where John Murphy worked.

When he spotted the car he'd been waiting for, he stepped from the curb into its path when it stopped at the four-way stop. He began to clean the car's windows, placing a small tracking device with a magnet below the wipers. He stepped back, smiling and nodding, when Murphy waved him off. He then turned, walking briskly toward his car, parked a few blocks away.

⋘

When Josh closed the bathroom door, Cat went back to her meal, wondering why thoughts of the man weighed so heavily on her mind. Even disguised to be as ordinary as possible, Josh Buchannan could never be ordinary. And he definitely confused her. He could be such a jerk one minute and the next doing something so sweet like bringing her food.

Once done with the soup and sandwich, she sat back in the chair in a much better frame of mind. Now that Josh had returned, the little bit of trepidation she'd felt earlier had dissipated. She felt safe and alive. Safe and alive. There are those two words again, she thought, scanning the now dark parking lot, lit sporadically with streetlights.

Even when she was as irritated as she could be with him, she still felt those things. She sighed, observing an obviously married couple get out of a car. She wished for one brief second, as they walked toward the entrance hand in hand, that she could be one of them.

For the entire time Josh was in the shower, she sat motionless.

Her gaze stayed on the parking lot, people-watching, until the bathroom door opened. When she looked over, he strode out barefoot, wearing shorts and a T-shirt.

"You look refreshed," she commented. The lines of stress on his face were gone, and while watching him, she glimpsed a smile form at the edges of his mouth.

"I feel refreshed," he replied, placing his folded clothes on the dresser. He took a few minutes to shave and brush his teeth. With those chores out of the way, he grabbed his laptop. "I have a lot to read, so I'd better get started." He then plopped onto the bed, sticking an extra pillow behind him before plugging in the computer and turning it on.

His attention remained glued to the screen while he worked.

"Are you hungry?" Cat asked, after secretly observing him for quite a while. "Soup's cooled a bit, but it's still good, even cold."

He glanced at her as if he just realized she was there and nodded distractedly. "Yeah, I guess I should eat."

She rose with his dinner and moved to set it on the nightstand next to the bed.

"You're the one who said you should take advantage of the opportunity to survive."

Josh grunted, placing his laptop aside before he began eating. She made her way to the other side of the bed, plumped two pillows, and grabbed the remote, clicking on the TV before climbing on top of the spread.

"So, what're you working on?" Cat asked, attempting to draw him into a conversation.

"Just an old case Murphy thinks may be tied to this," he answered evasively, lifting his shoulders in a half shrug.

"Really?"

"Yeah." His focus remained on his food and he ate without adding any more to his explanation.

"Can't you fill me in or is it a secret?"

He glanced over at her, holding a spoonful of soup at his mouth. "There's not much to tell that would interest you," he murmured, before he stuck another bite into his mouth.

"There has to be. I thought you could talk to me while you ate. Maybe I can help?" she offered, flashing him a warm smile.

"I don't see how." He wiped his face and let out an impatient sigh. "I've already been over it once, several years ago, since I helped write it. Now I'm looking at it from a different perspective."

When he continued eating, ignoring her again, her spirits sank. His shuttered demeanor seemed locked tighter than ever.

"What're you looking for?" she tried once more, keeping the disappointment out of her voice over his lack of cooperation.

"I don't know. Anything that jumps out at me, I guess." He bit into his sandwich and began chewing, adding when he swallowed, "I'll recognize it when I see it."

"Oh?"

"Yeah." He glanced at her, scrutinizing her face for a lengthy minute. Then, as if it just occurred to him that she expected him to say more, he added, "I know it doesn't sound very glamorous, but that's the nature of the business. If I can find something, it may hold the key as to why someone wants both of us dead."

Silence filled the room again. The minutes ticked by as he ate.

Okay. He doesn't want to talk, she thought. But she couldn't let it drop and gave it one more try.

"And you think it has to do with the case you're reading about?"

"Could be. It's a long shot, but it's all I have right now." He finished his soup, placed the Styrofoam bowl aside, and picked up his sandwich.

Cat studied him, feeling totally discouraged because he was so closed.

When he didn't say any more, just wolfed down his sandwich, she asked, "Will the TV bother you?"

He shook his head.

She sighed and hit the remote. "I guess you were hungrier than you thought, huh?"

"Yeah." He glanced at the little bit of bread between his fingers and nodded. "It did hit the spot."

He finished off the last bite and wiped his hands together over the side of the bed, brushing the crumbs away. Then he grabbed his laptop, setting it back on his lap and getting comfortable. His eyes moved to the small screen in front of him and he ignored her once again.

For the next hour, Cat's gaze surreptitiously followed what he was doing while she pretended interest in a boring movie on HBO. The whole time Josh worked, he never once glanced at her. Why did he have to be so closed? What would he do if she smothered him with kisses? Respond or push her away?

Several times her focus strayed to his fingers moving over the keys, and all she could think of when she spied them was how it felt to have those fingers roaming over her body.

After one such covert look, she sighed. She was missing an opportunity. Josh was right. Now that they had crossed the line, it did seem harder to resist.

More than anything, she wanted to make love with him again. Just one more time. Yet she knew without a doubt if anything was going to happen between them, she'd have to be the aggressor. And therein lay the problem. If only she could be bolder and put the moves on him like she had last night. She just couldn't be aggressive tonight.

She sighed again as the thoughts slid away. Maybe it was for the better because she also knew Josh was right about something else. More sex would only complicate things.

Easy excuse to use, Cat. Face it. You can't make the decision— take the responsibility for what you want, she reminded herself. It seems she hadn't really changed at all. She let out another long, slow breath and turned her attention back to the television.

When the next movie ended, Cat switched off the TV and glanced over at Josh for the first time in almost two hours. A smile touched her face when she noticed his eyes were closed, with his head back against the pillows. The computer sat on his lap, the screen saver in place.

For the longest time, she stared at his peaceful countenance and let her eyes roam the entire length of his body, enjoying the view. In sleep, he looked so relaxed. Ordinary doesn't describe him, she mused. Josh Buchannan was no ordinary man. He had a sleek, powerful body, topped off with a very handsome face...one with symmetry...a strong jaw, full lips, and those long eyelashes that seemed to graze his high cheekbones in slumber. His midnight black hair and eyebrows contrasted sharply with his skin, highlighting his features even more.

While eyeing him, a moment of clarity struck and a feeling of warm emotion swamped her. She loved him. How could she not, she wondered. He was magnificent, even when he was being a jerk.

Once she'd had her fill, she looked over at the clock. It was a few minutes after nine.

She rose and cleaned up their dinner mess before brushing her teeth. When she was ready for bed, she went around the room turning off lights, leaving the one next to her side of the bed lit. She bent over to take the computer off Josh's lap, shutting it down and closing it. She gave him another cursory glance, spying the black lock of hair falling over his face. Without thinking, she bent over to brush it off his forehead, luxuriating in the soft feel of his hair flowing through her fingers.

Groggily, he opened his eyes and for one drawn-out moment their gazes met. Cat stared at him, mesmerized while nervously drawing her bottom lip between her teeth, feeling suddenly tongue-tied. Finding her voice, she said softly, "Sorry. I didn't mean to wake you."

"That's okay. I should be working." When she started to rise, he shook his head. "No. Don't go. Come 'ere," he murmured, patting the spot next to him as he moved over just a bit.

"I don't—" she objected, but was cut off when he grabbed her arm and tugged her off balance. She toppled onto the bed. Then he wrapped his arms around her, pulling her next to him, nuzzling her neck and whispering, "Shush. Let me hold you. I promise to behave. I've been lying here all night with only one thought going through my mind. How it would feel to hold you one more time."

Rigid as a board, Cat lay next to him, wondering why all of a sudden she couldn't move. Couldn't think. Couldn't breathe.

"Relax, would you?" He sighed, rubbing his hand up and down her arm in a soothing manner. "I'm not going to jump your bones, as you so eloquently put it."

Cat complied, relaxing against him. Until she felt what could only be his erection through his shorts after he pulled her closer, spooning with her. When she stiffened again, he chuckled, nipping her neck with kisses. "Ignore it," he teased. "I can't help it. I can't be this close to you and not think about being inside you."

The edges of Cat's lip curled into a smile despite the heat she felt creeping up her face. She nodded and let out a long breath, allowing her muscles to go limp. She leaned into him, enjoying the feeling of warmth now spreading through her at his touch and words, and wishing she had the guts to take charge of her life.

After minutes of being wrapped in his warmth, she was comfortable to the point of falling asleep. Sporting a silly smile, she said, "Light's still on."

"It's your turn to get it tonight," he grunted, not budging.

"I'm too relaxed to move," she answered, feeling his grin on her neck.

He nuzzled her neck again, whispering in between kisses, "Leave it, then."

Chapter 24

Josh came awake to a ray of bright sunshine, peeking in from the window and landing on his face. His first thought was they'd forgotten to close the draperies the night before.

Next thing he noticed was Cat's cute little rear end nestled right over his groin.

"Christ," he muttered under his breath, when his erection grew. Why had he left himself open to such torture? But instead of moving away from her, he pulled her closer, not understanding his urge to keep her near. He'd never felt such a compelling need to simply hold someone before now.

He hadn't lied when he told Cat that he was a flop in the relationship department. Those few he did have while he was a field op all ended poorly because his job took so much of his life. Finally, he gave up trying. He'd simply done without the luxury of a human body next to him, mainly because nights spent with women usually led to expectations he couldn't follow through on. Over time he'd gotten used to his solitary life, even thrived on it after his grandmother's death, so he couldn't figure out why the idea of having Cat next to him felt so natural. Unwilling to dwell on uncomfortable thoughts, he pushed them to the back of his mind and tightened his grip. He was only enjoying her nearness.

Josh held Cat close until she stirred. He knew the exact moment she felt what he couldn't hide.

"It's still there," he whispered, nuzzling her neck and then moving his lips to her ear where he nibbled for a bit before adding, "And if you keep moving like that I'm not going to be able to keep my promise of not jumping your bones."

"Sorry." She stopped in mid-movement, giggling. "What time is it?"

He leaned away from her, releasing one hand to reach for the clock on the nightstand, holding it up so he could read the digital numbers.

"Seven thirty." He dropped the clock and put his head back down, lying flat on his back. "I guess we were tired."

"Yeah." She stretched and rolled so she was now facing him.

He placed a hand behind his head, then situated her so that her head lay in the crook of his arm and shoulder with her hand resting on his T-shirt-covered chest.

"I realize it's easier to sleep in when someone's not trying to kill me," she said, now drawing figure eights with her finger.

He chuckled and closed his eyes, enjoying her soothing, light touch. "It does help, doesn't it?" When her hand moved further south, he stiffened. And when fingers wrapped around his erection through his boxer shorts, his eyes snapped open.

"Cat?" he warned, closing his eyes and working hard to keep the thoughts of finishing what she was starting from infiltrating his brain.

"What?"

He winced at the definite challenge in the one word.

"You know *what*," he ground out. "This is not a good idea. You promised you wouldn't jump my bones if we shared a room," he reminded, reaching for the feeble excuse and placing his hand over hers, stilling it. Damn, the woman was so good at testing his restraint. Why had he taken off his shorts last night? He should have known he'd need the extra layer of protection. She was too hard to resist as it was. Though prudish in her thinking, she definitely had a way with her hand that was now turning his mind to mush.

"I lied," she said, chuckling, clearly amused. "And you can't deny what's so undeniable in my hand." Her fingers grew bolder, accentuating her claim with a squeeze. "Don't tell me you don't want me, because I won't believe you."

"You know I can't, but that's not the point," he hissed. God! What a nightmare. Making love with her wasn't a good idea, but he was slowly losing what little resolve he had to hold her back. He *so* wanted to make love with her.

"That's right." She continued stroking and squeezing. He groaned as those hot fingers of hers sent his need shooting off the chart. When she added, "This is the point and I'm dying to have it inside of me," he almost exploded in her hand. "Come on, Buc-man. We have to celebrate life."

Josh was quickly moving past the point of no return. Do

something, he told himself, anything…and do it fast.

"Please, Cat." He grabbed her arm to stop the sensations of pleasure coursing through him. "You mean something to me and I don't want to hurt you." He spoke his labored words softly while snaring her gaze with his. "You know this is the worst thing we can do."

"This isn't your call." Holding her chin high, she eyed him with purpose. "I decide what's best for me. You got that?"

He groaned, unable to articulate anything else.

She smiled. "Right now, I want to make love with you. I'm done having other people make choices for me. And that includes you." She bent to kiss him, taking his mouth as unwaveringly as her hand that moved over him.

Oh God. If she kept doing that, he would be history in mere moments.

When she lifted her head, she declared even more boldly, "If it's a mistake, then it'll be mine to make and I can live with it."

"I don't want to be a mistake," he got out, breathing heavily. "Don't you understand?"

"Are you so sure it would be a mistake?" she asked, as something like sadness crept into her eyes.

"Yes…no…hell, I don't know," he replied, not knowing what he felt anymore. His whole system had gone wacko and he couldn't think clearly, not when she looked at him like that and touched him as she did. His head fell back on the pillow. He released her hand. Just allowed the sensation of what Cat's fingers were doing roll over him, weakening his willpower further.

As if she knew his surrender was at hand, she became more daring. Pushed his shirt out of the way. Kissed his bare stomach. Slowly worked a path from his chest to his neck, adding her mouth and tongue. When her mouth neared his, he groaned and crushed her to him, meeting her lips head-on in a grinding kiss.

Cat broke the connection and gazed at him with eyes flashing triumph. She knew she'd won…knew she'd worn him down…he could see it in her expression. But he no longer cared because from then on, his sole mission became one of finishing what she'd started.

In seconds flat, he had them both naked and he was pushing into her, feeling her warmth surround him and wondering how he was ever going to live without wanting this—without having her.

Her hands possessively caressed his body.

"Let me set the pace," he warned, before he lost total restraint and all coherent thought dissipated into a burst of pleasure. Everywhere she touched he burned, which along with what her mouth was doing to him, only added to his incineration.

He smiled inwardly at her ready compliance, and held on for as long as possible using slow, thorough strokes before he became more frantic with desire, unable to resist her heat, unable to stop his body from pumping fully, unable to stop himself from giving in to the need she so easily elicited from his soul. In the next instant, he erupted into hot flames as her release lit the fuse and they both came simultaneously.

☙

"What am I going to do with you, Cat?" Josh muttered under his breath.

Lying in the crook of his arm while he gazed at the ceiling, Cat sighed at his question that came in the aftermath of their spent passion.

"Nothing. Simply enjoy." She ran her fingers through his thick mat of hair, luxuriating in the feel of strength underneath. His muscles flinched under her touch and she smiled. The man really was magnificent, she thought, lifting up on one elbow and staring at his splendid, naked chest and well-proportioned, muscular limbs.

"We're living in the present and right now I love you. So just accept it." She felt him stiffen at her declaration and her grin expanded. He may not want her love, but somehow, she sensed it was something he needed. She also wasn't sure he'd ever take it, but that didn't mean she couldn't give it to him.

"It's not real." He sighed. "It's only heightened emotion caused by circumstances."

"Sure, Buc-man. Whatever you say," she murmured, kissing his chest. Though his statement saddened her and wasn't the declaration of love she'd rather hear, a surge of power washed over her. She gave something without expecting anything in return. It dawned on her just then that her power came from taking charge of her feelings. She couldn't stop herself from loving him any more than she could force him to love her, but she also couldn't let him walk away without telling him how she felt. "Go ahead and use the excuse, if it'll make you feel better."

"You don't know what you're saying," he whispered a few

minutes later. "You don't even know me."

"That's not true." Cat's hands moved through his hair as if to gain courage before she added in a soft voice, "I'd say we've both gotten to know each other pretty well over the past four days."

He blew out his favorite expletive and rubbed his closed eyes with his thumb and forefinger. "I knew you were trouble from the first moment I met you."

"Me?" Her hand stopped in midstroke and her attention flew to his face.

"Yeah, you." He chuckled, meeting her gaze with eyebrows raised. "You're a walking contradiction. Nothing like I thought."

"Oh, I get it," she snorted out. "Not comfortable with me spouting my feelings so you divert my attention with a teasing joke."

"See what I mean?"

She ignored his gibe and shook her head. "Yeah. Nice try, but it won't work." Then, maintaining eye contact, she added, "I love you. And nothing you say or do will change the fact."

"Cat, let's not go there." His tone held warning.

"Why can't you just accept my words?"

"Because when a woman says those three words, she has expectations of them being returned," he said gruffly, pulling away from her. He moved to sit over the edge of the bed, planting his feet on the floor while he shoved a hand through his hair and rubbed his neck. "I've yet to meet those expectations."

Staring at his back, she blinked back tears and tried to pretend the hole in her heart wasn't there, getting bigger. Watching him now, she saw his mental shutters slamming closed. He'd locked himself off from her, and that's what hurt the most.

"I'm not asking for anything in return," she said softly. "Why can't you see that?"

"I don't believe that. What's more, I believe all I can do at this point is hurt you."

"So, I should stop loving just to avoid being hurt? Stop feeling because there's risk?" Heat stole up her face. Darn it all, she thought, as tears trickled out. How could he be such a jerk about this? "You know, Josh, I used to think I was the one who was afraid of life." She sat up, wiping her tears away. "But looking at you right now, I have only pity, because you're much more afraid of it than I ever was." She spied her T-shirt on the floor and bent to pick it up, quickly throwing it over her head. She rushed toward the bathroom before she burst into tears in front of him. She would not let him see her cry.

☙

"Shit," Josh ground out, pushing off the bed and slamming his fist against the wall. "You knew better," he muttered, looking for his clothes. He found his T-shirt, boxers, and shorts, and quickly shoved into them, thinking all the while what a bastard he was.

Rule number one had always been never have sex with a woman like Cat. And he broke the rule. Not once, but twice. Could he be any more of an asshole?

He grabbed his laptop from the nightstand and moved over to the table, pushing Cat and his sick need away.

But he couldn't do it. He found himself looking out the window, his mind drifting to her words. Not just her declaration of love, but her parting shot. He didn't like thinking they held a ring of truth. He was afraid. But not of her loving him. That actually gave him some ray of hope deep inside his gut and it shouldn't be there. He'd just do something to screw it up and hurt her in the process.

No, it was better not to wish for it because what scared him the most was losing her love once she learned he didn't deserve it. Hell—he'd been the one responsible for her parents' deaths. That was going to go over really well if and when she ever found out. How do you tell someone something so despicable? Reading about it last night brought it all home again and he almost choked when he heard her asking her questions, telling him she wanted to talk about what he was working on.

Once he heard the shower running, he stood up and went over to their bags, searching for a cell phone.

After pulling one out, Josh quickly placed the call to Murphy, waiting until he heard the familiar, "Murph here," before he let out a long breath and started pacing.

"Yeah, Murph, it's me."

"Buc? It's good to hear you survived the night," he joked.

"What?" Josh snorted into the phone. "You had no faith in my ability to stay alive?"

"I figured you would," Murphy shot back. "Have you gone through those files yet?"

"Most of them. Last night. I'll go through the rest this morning."

"What do you think?"

"I don't see anything, at least nothing that jumps out at me." He stopped his pacing and sat on the edge of the bed while rubbing his forehead with thumb and forefingers. "I still think revenge of some sort is involved, but there's no one other than Cat and her ex that fits the scenario. And I gotta be honest. It doesn't fit with Cat. The ex maybe, but not her. She's a target just as I am and even if she wasn't, I've gotten to know her in the past four days. My gut tells me no."

"Well, I believe in your gut." Murphy sighed audibly into Josh's ear, producing a rueful smile. "It has to be there somewhere."

"What about the fanatic who committed suicide?" Josh asked, voicing something niggling in his mind after assessing all the information he'd read so far. He got up to pace again, ending up at the window.

"What about her?"

"I can't help feeling this is somehow tied to her."

"You really think so?"

"It's the only unknown in the operation."

"With no trail, it seemed an impossible task to unravel, so we just assumed she was some crazy religious zealot." Murphy's voice faded. A moment later he added, "You were there. You saw her. I'd hoped reviewing it again might spark something in your memory. Did you recognize her?"

"No. Her face was partially covered by a burka. But I'll never forget the look in her eyes. It spoke volumes right before she blew herself up." Sighing heavily, Josh's thumb and forefinger moved to the bridge of his nose and he rubbed, striving to forget the look. How he wished he could when it still haunted him. How in the hell did someone give themselves permission to do something so senseless? Cat was right. Could people really believe that anyone's God would condone such a waste of life, for any reason? "It wasn't the best time in my life," he said honestly, pushing the memory from his mind. "I'm sure you realize that by now."

"Yeah. I do. I know this operation was the main impetus for your resignation. Something's going on and my gut tells me it's big. If anyone can figure it out, it'll be you."

"I hate having to look at it all again."

"I know, Buc, and I'm sorry to have to ask you to do it, but I trust you. I don't know who else I can trust anymore. How stupid is that? With the new policies since 9/11, things should've gotten better, but somehow they're worse. It's become a political nightmare."

"There's still nothing to indicate who she was." Josh leaned against the wall as his gaze moved to the view outside the window. He watched several people get into their cars and drive away before adding, "What was her motivation for dying? Who was she working for?"

"We never found out. It's all speculation since there's no mention of her before this incident."

"Yeah." Josh sighed. "I read the file, but now I'm questioning it. It's the only loose end—with no connection to anything. I can't stop thinking about her or the look of horror filling her eyes right before she died. Why would a woman try and kill innocent children?"

"Who knows what motivates others?"

Murphy's question hung in his ears. Still, something about the woman bothered Josh and he couldn't let it go. The memory of her eyes wouldn't leave his brain.

"Why did we never try to figure out who she was? I can't help feeling we should've tried harder to find out who and why."

"There was nothing to go on. It's all in the report. With no body as evidence after it was blown to smithereens, where would we begin, especially given no one claimed the honor?"

"I guess we'll never know." Josh sighed. Then changing the subject, because he didn't want to think of the woman's expression any longer, he asked, "What about the guy in Winnemucca?"

"Bad character. An assassin who's wanted in five countries for killing enemies of Islam. His specialty is strategy. I'm thinking he's the ringleader. He's still being followed in hopes that maybe he can lead us to what's going on."

"Do you have any more on Mark Zinger, AKA Anthony Rodriquez?"

"Still digging. He seemed to come outta nowhere. Homeland Security was only interested in him because of his relationship with the Tylers and their work over in Afghanistan. He had an Israeli passport when he traveled in this country. Marriage to Candace Tyler allowed him to obtain a green card. There's nothing to show he tried to attain citizenship. We now believe the passport was forged."

"What if he took over some Israeli's identity, just like he did

Rodriquez?"

"It's a scary thought but I don't think it's a consideration, especially since there's no reason to go to the trouble. The fake passport got him here without a lot of scrutiny. Still, I'll see what I can find out. Both agencies are keeping this under wraps. No one outside of those directly involved will be brought in until we can contain him."

"Seems logical," Josh murmured distractedly. He turned to pull out a chair and sat at the table, keeping his eyes on a couple in the parking lot below. "Has there been any sign of him?"

"Yeah. I stopped to get gas and noticed a transmitter hidden behind the wipers. Only person who could've put it there was a street bum who tried to wash my windows last night when I left the office, so I figured it was our man. I didn't drive home afterward. The agency has a place to use as a diversion for such purposes. An old warehouse I've converted south of Market. Has all the comforts of home, but is much easier to monitor what's going on outside."

"What's the address? I take it you'll be there tonight and you'll be waiting for me."

"Among others." He rattled off the address, as well as a cell phone number. "What time should I be expecting you?"

"Let me think." Josh sighed. He broke off and counted the hours mentally in his head. "Let's shoot for sometime after four. That'll give me a chance to spend a few hours here going over the files one more time with a fresh eye."

"Okay."

"Have you heard from Smitty?" Josh asked as the bathroom door opened. He turned at a noise to see Cat walk out of the bathroom with one towel wrapped around her head and another wrapped around her body.

Pointedly ignoring Josh, she strode to her things on the dresser, dug for a moment, pulling out clothes and underwear, then turned and marched purposefully back into the bathroom. Once inside, she shut the door with a final click.

"Yeah," Murphy said, answering his question about Smitty. "He flew here in one of your planes with his sidekicks, Laurel and Hardy. They're all staying at the warehouse."

"Good," Josh said. "I hope the business isn't falling apart."

"He says we need to figure this out so you can get back to work." Murphy snorted. "Says he's getting tired of the responsibility.

He told me to tell you everything's fine. Well, as fine as it can be with both the office manager and an instructor dead, and the principal owner on the run."

"Sounds like Smitty," Josh said distractedly, leaning back, forcing out a grin.

"Yeah, his humor is almost as sick as yours. I wonder how he's handling those two agents this morning. He had a brief reprieve last night. They went out and didn't come back until late, much to Smitty's delight."

Josh chuckled. "You know he's having a blast. Hey, if we didn't have Feds to pick on, life would really be dull."

Murphy's bark of laughter burst into his ear. "You know, Buc, someday they just might retaliate."

"Nah! I'll never give 'em the chance."

"Humph," was all Murphy said, before saying, "I gotta go. I'll see you later. Drive carefully."

"I will," Josh replied, a semblance of his grin still lurking when he snapped the phone closed.

Things were looking up, he mused, eyeing the street below while waiting for Cat to finish dressing. He could handle this. All he had to do was try and smooth things over with her, and the rest of the day would be easier to bear. Once they made it to San Francisco and they nabbed Zinger/Rodriquez, they'd find out why. Then it would be over and life would go on.

Yeah! Life would go on without Cat.

A minute later, she emerged from the bathroom, dressed much like the day before only she didn't have the wig on yet. Josh watched as she stood at the sink and brushed her teeth. Next, she grabbed the wig and bent over, letting all of her hair fall forward. When she scooped long strands and formed them into a knot, Josh's hands flexed open and closed, stilling the urge to run his fingers through the lustrous blonde locks.

He exhaled a breath he didn't know he was holding when she tugged the wig in place and headed for the door, saying over her shoulder, "I'm going to get something to eat in the buffet downstairs. It says on the little card that breakfast is served from six till ten a.m."

The second the door closed behind her, all tension drained from his body. Shaking his head at how crazy things had gotten, he stood. Then he padded toward the bathroom for a shower.

Half an hour later, he walked into the lounge area of the lobby doubling as a morning breakfast bar, complete with a wide range of food. He grabbed a cup of coffee along with a bagel and a banana, and moved to the table where Cat was just finishing.

When he sat, putting his food in front of him, she rose. He placed his hand on her arm and met her gaze.

"I'm sorry," he whispered, allowing the sincerity of his words to show in his eyes.

"I know." She held his gaze without flinching. Josh could see the hurt inside, lurking, and he felt like a monster for putting it there.

"Why don't you stay and keep me company?" he cajoled, letting the edges of his lips curl into a smile. "Please?"

"I don't think so," she said softly, shaking her head and looking down at the floor.

"Come on, Cat!" he hissed, gripping his cup too hard until the urge to hit something died. She was the one who had started it all. And now she was the one running. "I said I was sorry. What more do you want?"

"Nothing. I already told you. I want nothing from you that you can't give. Don't you understand?" She pulled her arm out of his grasp and turned to go. "I'm going for a walk. I'll be back soon."

"Shit," Josh muttered under his breath. It was already starting. He'd hurt her, and he couldn't quite figure out how he'd gotten into this position. He tore into his bagel and began chewing, not tasting it as he washed it down with coffee.

Chapter 25

Cat walked out of the breakfast bar without looking back, knowing that if she did, Josh would be watching her departure. Darn it all, she thought. Exiting in a huff wasn't a great way to handle things, but when he sat down expecting her to accept his apology, as if he expected his words to solve everything, something inside her snapped. She pushed one of the glass doors open and stepped outside to a bright day that was a stark contrast to her dark mood.

She had to squint to see. The sun, now warming the brisk air, was making an appearance in the cloudless bright blue sky. She ignored the sun's warmth and the beauty of the perfect October morning because sadness permeated her soul.

Josh was right. She should never have forced the issue. But somehow she couldn't quite regret making love with him. Not when the whole incident made her feel so powerful and so alive. She'd hold on to her memories forever. Of course, it hurt to realize her feelings weren't reciprocated. Oh well, she sighed. She'd get over it. Once she was away from this entire mess, she could go back to her life.

And do what? Go home and wish for things that would never happen? Yeah. What a laugh. That's exactly what she'd do. Why oh why did I ever fall in love with him?

She wound her way through the parking lot aiming for the sidewalk, having no real destination in mind. She realized when looking around after hitting the concrete walkway, this wasn't the best place for a stroll. Like most interstate exits, it was geared toward cars, not pedestrians. Still, she continued her trek, not wanting to be stuck in the room with Josh just yet. Her feelings were still raw and she needed time to get herself back under control.

After walking for twenty minutes, she turned around, dragging her feet the entire way back to the hotel. When she couldn't procrastinate any longer, she let herself into the hotel room.

Josh gave her a cursory glance and grunted a greeting when she entered. He sat at the table with his laptop open. She nodded a reply, even as the small screen absorbed his attention, and just like the night before, he ignored her.

Okay. If he could pretend nothing happened, then so could she. So much easier said than done, she thought, as she sat on the edge of the bed. Josh Buchannan simply wasn't a man she could ignore for long because his presence filled the room. Trying harder, she grabbed the remote, clicking to one of the morning shows.

During the program, her attention kept wandering to Josh. He'd taken off his disguise and had changed into his shorts and T-shirt. Barefoot, his long, muscular legs were stretched out. While watching him, her heart twisted.

Surviving the day might be more arduous than she first thought.

"What're you working on?" she asked, throwing out one more try to loosen his tongue.

"Same thing as last night," he answered evasively, brushing her question aside without glancing at her.

She got up from her perch and moved to stand behind him, looking over his shoulder.

"Maybe I can help?"

"I doubt it." He hit the minimize button on the screen and the file disappeared. "Just going over it one more time to see if I've missed anything."

"I don't understand why you're being so evasive. You seem like you don't want to tell me," she said, after he remained stonily silent for too many minutes. "I thought you trusted me."

Josh sighed and rubbed the bridge of his nose with his thumb and forefinger. His gaze went to the window where it stayed, while he seemed lost in thought.

Her stare followed his to the parking lot below, where guests packed up cars and exited. She didn't think he would say anything more until the sound of his voice interrupted her thoughts.

"It's a case from the past that ties you and me together."

She glanced at his handsome features, but he wouldn't meet her gaze and his expression yielded nothing of his thoughts. Icy fingers of dread streaked across her back. Why was he being so weird? Brushing an errant strand of wig hair out of her eyes, she cleared her throat and licked both lips nervously. Then she knelt in front of him, placing her hand on his leg. The subtle movement drew his attention and finally he looked down at her.

"What case from the past could possibly tie us together?" She searched his chocolate-brown eyes for some clue, and noting the worry etched in their midst, more alarm streaked through her system.

Josh took a deep breath and let it out slowly. He wiped his face. "What were you told about your parents' deaths?"

"Why?"

"In a minute. First answer my question."

"I read a report. I know it was a senseless act of violence." She offered a half shrug. "I wasn't there, so the rest of the information came secondhand, mostly from my ex."

"What was his reaction?"

"Mark was incensed. Blamed the American government. So did several others who were involved with my parents."

"What about you? What did you think?"

"As to responsibility?" When he nodded, she said in all honesty, "I wasn't as convinced as he was, which caused several heated arguments. The way I saw it, it was a series of events. If the woman hadn't threatened the school, my mother wouldn't have done what she did, and the whole incident wouldn't have happened."

"That's a noble way of looking at it." He smiled wistfully and expelled a steady breath, moving his attention out the window for a long moment while rubbing the back of his neck. He then turned back to her. "Now that I've gotten to know you, I realize I should've expected you to think that way."

"It's not noble. What good would blame do? It won't bring them back." She eyed him intently. "Why? What do my parents' deaths have to do with you?"

"Because I was in charge of the mission, Cat. My man shot your mother."

"I don't understand." Her gaze narrowed, searching his eyes as if they would yield some clue. But instantly, his expression closed, becoming as shuttered as it had ever been, revealing nothing of what she was trying to find there. "How? What're you saying?"

"I'm ultimately responsible for your loss."

She gaped at him for the longest time, meeting his blank stare as the meaning of his confession sank in. When full realization hit, pain ripped her heart in two. It was hard to stay kneeling and remain calm when the urge to bolt from the room screaming seemed overwhelming.

"And you've known about this connection all along and kept it from me?" How could he do that? How could he expect her to follow him blindly and not trust her? How could he make love to her and not tell her of the connection?

"I didn't learn of it until after the crash, and by then I felt I had no choice. I didn't know if you were involved and I didn't trust you."

"Of course not," she sneered. "You thought the worst of me. You always have, right from the beginning. I'm surprised you trust me enough to tell me now."

If his earlier actions hadn't completely hurt her to her core, this nailed it. How could she ever forgive him?

"It's why I am telling you now. Because I do trust you."

Oh Lord. He was telling her now because he trusted her? What a load of garbage. She wouldn't let his admission or his intense, too expressive gaze affect her now. "Screw your trust, Buc-man." Her voice sliced through the air as sharp as a razor splitting hairs. "You have the nerve to tell me you trust me when you purposely kept something so important from me?"

Josh visibly flinched and averted his eyes. "I've never lied to you and nothing was covered up in the operation." He still wouldn't meet her gaze, but his voice was steady. "You were given a full declassified report on what happened."

"Oh my God. Now I remember. You must have been the field commander on the knoll who gave the order to kill the woman," she whispered, sitting back on her ankles while her attention moved to the floor. Her chest tightened, as if the world was crashing down on her. She stood, pulled out the chair next to Josh, and sank slowly into it. "It *was* all there in the report."

"Yeah. That was me. Josh Buchannan, known to you only as the field commander." He nodded, indicating the computer, and added, "The more comprehensive classified information is in here. I've been going over it all again, trying to find something I missed."

Cat closed her eyes, trying to remember all she'd read in the thick folder—words describing what had happened in succinct detail. Then it hit her. "Smitty. He told me you two have worked together for years. Was he part of this too?" She glanced at Josh for verification. When he nodded, she shook her head and a sad smile formed.

He cleared his throat. "Joel Smith was the sharpshooter," he said softly, still studying the designs in the carpet.

Blinking back tears, she swallowed the lump of pain lodged in the back of her throat and forced herself to breathe. First one breath, then another, and over and over again, as she absorbed this news.

"So, you were in charge of the mission and Smitty pulled the trigger?" she finally asked. Her focus landed outside the window. Now more than ever she wanted to be one of those carefree people down in the parking lot, laughing and joking without a care in the world, but she wasn't.

And suddenly it hit her. She had to know more. "What happened that day? What went wrong?"

"Everything." The whispered, tortured sound drew her gaze and she tried to find understanding in his pained expression. "You read what happened. It was all there."

"Words in a report. I want to hear what really happened. You were there. You owe it to me to tell me why a sharpshooter missed his target and hit my mother instead. And why did my father have to blow up because that same sharpshooter couldn't take a second shot. Tell me!" Tears streaked down the sides of her face, and she didn't bother brushing them away. "Why?"

"I don't know why."

"How could you let it happen?"

"I've asked myself that same question at least a million times in the past four years. It was the worst day of my life. I take full responsibility for their deaths. I couldn't save her or your father. It was a tragic accident, Cat. In seconds, life changed…everything changed. They were talking. I don't know what they were discussing, only that the wired woman was very upset. The next instant, your mother jumped in front of her. My guess is she was trying to reason with her just as Smitty took his shot. I'd given him direct orders to kill his target. His mistake gave her the needed seconds to detonate. No one foresaw this outcome. I live with the knowledge. The senseless killing of two innocents is a steep price to pay for saving a hundred and fifty children."

"Why would *she* do such a thing?" Cat took in his revelation, assimilating it into some kind of order in her mind. It was so much to absorb at once.

"We never knew and probably never will." He expelled a long

breath, shaking his head, as more torment spilled out of his expression. But she wouldn't let him affect her and steeled herself against his tortured words. "So senseless. The look in her eyes right before she self-detonated haunted me, haunts me still. I've been struggling with the memory and question of why since that day. Trust me. You can't hate me any worse than I hate myself for allowing it to happen."

The tortured sound of his voice floated past her ears and more tears streaked down her face. She couldn't move, just silently sat there and let them fall. Finally, she took a deep breath, wiped her face, and reached for control. She'd get through this. What other choice did she have?

"Such a small world we live in. Here you are running a flight school out in the middle of nowhere, and Smitty's dating my best friend." She waited until he met her tear-filled gaze, and added, "Does he know about the link?"

"I never connected Candace Zinger with Cat Tyler. I had no clue you were related to the Tylers in this report, so I don't think he did either, but I'm sure he does now. Some coincidence, isn't it? How we all ended up in Bozeman together? I was looking for somewhere to hide—somewhere as far away from my mother's death and that day as possible. I learned to fly early in my career and trained others. I'd already planned on opening a flight school after I retired."

He inhaled deeply and blew the breath out in a long sigh. "Since I resigned a good ten years earlier than planned, I used family money I swore I'd never touch to escape. I told you a little about my father. I didn't like depending on money he provided, but need took precedence over ego. My dad and I have never seen eye to eye."

"Your dad?" she asked, wondering why he was telling her all of this.

He snorted and his tone changed to one of derision. "My grandmother was always the buffer between us. Joshua Harrison Buchannan, Jr. is a hard, unbending man who's always felt I should've taken the helm at the family business. When I joined the CIA right out of college, he couldn't handle my decision. Once my grandmother died, our relationship deteriorated even further. I haven't seen him since Grandmother's funeral."

Cat listened to him talk, blocking out the pain of him being so open now. Why now, when it was too late? "So, how did you and

Smitty end up together?"

"Smitty and I are partners in the school." He raked a hand through his hair, then continued speaking. "He joined me within six months. I know why I quit. I assume his reasons were similar, but I've never asked him directly. Some things you just don't get into."

When she kept her gaze on him, he sighed. "Murph, my former boss, found out about my plans. It was his idea to open the school in Bozeman because of its proximity to the Canadian border, and he pulled strings to help me get settled. He asked me to be an extra pair of eyes and ears once I got everything up and running. At the time, Murphy had taken over in a new position for Homeland Security on the West Coast."

He put his elbows on the table and rubbed his face, appearing distraught, taking several deep breaths.

"I'm listening," she prodded, when it seemed he needed encouragement from her to continue.

"My work for Murphy entails connecting with others who operate flight schools within the region. I look for anything out of the ordinary, something that comes easily to me. I also monitor pilot applications from suspicious applicants for the FAA. After 9/11, small airports and flying schools all over the US came under Homeland Security's scrutiny. Along with being my partner, owning ten percent, Smitty works for Murphy, using his job as a flight instructor as a cover." He wiped his face again.

"I'm sorry I didn't tell you, but I can't talk about my past, Cat," Josh said. He sat motionless for an endless moment before adding, "This case is classified. I shouldn't even have it, but everything points to it, so Murphy's using me as a pair of eyes. The work I do for him now is routine and not worth anyone's scrutiny."

So much to take in, Cat thought, as she leaned back into the chair and let her gaze roam to the parking lot below. "It seems like a lot of coincidence to me," she said, voicing her thoughts out loud.

"Yeah. And it's starting to make some kind of sense. The incident involving your parents' deaths is the only thing tying us all together. Since I now know about Mark Zinger's ties with terrorists, I've got to assume it's somehow related. Once I find out his motivation, I can solve the puzzle."

Cat let out a deep breath, thinking about all Josh had relayed while her eyes focused on two birds chasing each other outside. She'd always tried to block off the memories, memories of everything falling apart. She didn't want to think about how everything felt so familiar right now—like having a rug of her life pulled out from underneath her. Her parents' deaths severed all hope of ever gaining their acceptance. Then the man she'd married and thought she knew, one she'd promised a lifetime to, turned out to be a false impression. Her life had spiraled out of control and she'd been running in fear ever since.

And now this. Not only is Josh responsible for my upheaval, he didn't trust me enough to tell me, she thought. He'll never trust me enough to love me.

And those unbearable truths hurt, so much that she didn't know if she could endure the pain. But she couldn't ignore the one other truth she'd come to understand about herself in the past four days. She needed to have someone believe in her enough to trust her completely. Sadness engulfed her, wrapping around the pain. Along the fringes, she felt another emotion—anger. She'd use that anger to get past this. And with that thought, her resolve strengthened. Once this was over, she'd get as far away from Josh Buchannan as she could and stay far away from him.

"What do we do now?" She got up from the chair and moved to sit on the edge of the bed again.

"As soon as I finish here, we're driving to San Francisco. Rodriguez/Zinger's already there. I expect this to come to a head fairly quickly because he'll finally make his move."

Nodding, she grabbed the remote, punched the button bringing the television to life, and pushed the pain away as best she could. "I'll be ready to go whenever you are."

Chapter 26

Motionless, Josh sat and observed Cat watch television while ignoring him the entire time. Sighing, he grabbed the mouse and focused on his computer screen once again. He'd screwed up royally and he had no clue how to fix it. The best thing he could do at this point was to figure out what was happening so he could get the hell out of her life. The sooner he did, the better off she'd be.

He spent another two hours scouring the files. When satisfied he'd done all he could, he glanced at his watch and noticed it was well after eleven a.m. Checkout time was noon.

"I'm done here." Stretching, he rose from the chair. He glanced at Cat with eyebrows quirked. "Can you be ready to leave in ten minutes?"

Cat hit the remote and nodded. She stood and began gathering all her things together.

Twenty minutes later, Josh was talking to Henry and getting back his eighty dollars. In another two, he and Cat were both in the car, heading out of the parking lot and onto the main road leading to the interstate.

"So, are you going to sit there for the next three hours and not say anything?" Josh asked, glancing over at Cat after they'd been driving for over an hour in complete silence. Her demeanor was depressing as hell. In all the time he'd known her, he'd never seen her so down. He didn't like the knot of dread twisting in the pit of his stomach her stony silence produced. Knowing he was the cause only tightened the knot.

"What's there to say?" She didn't bother glancing at him. Her head rested against her hand with her elbow perched on the door, while her attention stayed focused on the passing terrain out the window.

"I thought we were friends."

"I did too. But friends trust each other. Face it, Josh. You don't trust me."

"I do."

"No, you don't."

"Of course I do." He struggled to keep his irritation at her remark from rising in his voice.

She turned to face him and waited until he glanced at her, before asking without flinching, "Enough to trust me with your heart?"

He blew out one long exhale and refocused on the road ahead. Keeping his hands on the steering wheel, he remained silent and drove.

"I warned you not to get involved with me," he finally said, ten miles down the road. "I told you from the beginning this was a bad idea."

"I know." She sighed. Josh couldn't miss the note of sadness, the sound gripping his insides tighter. "And you can keep on saying that because if you do, you can keep on believing it."

"This whole thing is an illusion," he ground out. "What you feel isn't real."

"You really believe that, don't you?"

"I believe it because it's true," he said in a low voice without looking at her, but feeling her eyes on him again. "When things die down and we're both back to our normal lives, you'll see me as I really am. You pegged me right, Cat. I'm a selfish jerk."

"And by using that excuse, it absolves you of all responsibility. Doesn't it?"

"Shit," he muttered under his breath. He wasn't about to dwell on her accusation. He couldn't. But what if it held truth? Rolling his eyes, he swore under his breath again. He never should have challenged her the first day they went flying together. Hell, he couldn't deny he'd been fighting his attraction for her from the moment she flashed that icy blue glare at him. Only he'd been too afraid to admit it. Damn, he groaned silently. Could things get any worse?

He'd done everything in his power to keep their animosity alive for that very reason—so he'd not have to face it. And here it was hitting him like a battering ram. The more he got to know her, the more he wanted to know her. And now she was talking about letting him trust her with his heart. Problem was, he had no heart. He'd lost it a long time ago. The sooner she realized that, the sooner she could get over him.

When he braked at the tollbooth for the Bay Bridge leading into San Francisco, Josh heaved a sigh of relief. Their ride was finally coming to an end. Neither had spoken a word in almost three hours, and by this point, he couldn't take any more blaring silence.

Twenty minutes later Josh turned onto a side street, quickly finding the address of the warehouse Murphy had given him. He pulled the car into a driveway and stopped, keeping the motor running. Then he grabbed a phone from the backseat, punching in Murphy's cell number.

The words "Murph here," shot through the small device.

"We made it. We're sitting in the driveway right now."

"See anything suspicious outside?" Murphy asked.

Josh smiled. Taking a long look around, he shook his head while saying at the same time, "No one's parked on the street. No one's walking either, but there's a bunch of garbage right next to me. What's up with that?"

"Bad neighborhood." Murphy sighed. "It's impossible to keep up with the dumping. I called the garbage company for a pickup, but nobody's responded yet."

"Everything looks calm."

"I'll open the door." The garage door slowly opened. "Our guy's out there somewhere, lurking. There's an all points bulletin out for him, but he's not going to be easy to catch. He's too cagey. A few agents from the office are on guard outside. Things are calm for the time being. Come on up," Murphy added. "You'll see the elevator. It'll bring you right to me."

"Sure." Josh shifted gears, hit the gas, then drove inside the underground garage and parked close to the elevator Murphy mentioned. "Who all is with you?"

"Miller from my office. And Smitty. His cohorts went to check in with the San Francisco bureau office, then they were going to stop for a bite to eat."

"Good. I have no desire to see those two anytime soon. Cat and I'll be up in a minute."

Murphy grunted an assent and Josh disconnected, sparing a glance at Cat. "You ready? The sooner we get this over with, the sooner you can get back to your life with your aunt."

Cat nodded and together they climbed out of the car. Josh walked around to her side. He grabbed her hand and pulled her along so she had no choice but to follow him. "I expect this to all be over within twenty-four hours."

She stayed a meek few feet behind. When he got to the elevator with an obvious camera above it, he gave a brief nod to indicate the machine. "That's for show. There are probably three or four we can't see."

Josh pushed the call button. Once the doors opened, he stood to the side, waiting until Cat stepped in before following.

☙

On a rooftop a couple of buildings away, Anthony Rodriquez looked through a telephoto lens, watching the garage door go down and timing how long it took. He turned to another machine and flipped the switch, rewinding the recording of Buchannan's intercepted phone call. He smiled after listening to the conversation. When the two agents returned from dinner, he'd be waiting.

Then he glanced through the lens one more time, spying several boxes piled near the curb close to the driveway and his smile dimmed. One particular box stood out among the others. His comrade's work. He wished he hadn't needed the bastard's help to make things right.

On his way to the curb, he made sure he remained outside the range of the cameras. Slowly, his gaze did a one-eighty, taking in the quiet street. After receiving the "all clear" from his unwanted partner, he lifted the planted box, knelt on the his small prayer rug after removing his shoes, bent over his bag and secured the box around him. He made sure he faced toward Mecca and began to recite his daily prayers, begging Allah for the courage to complete his mission.

☙

The first thing Cat noticed when she stepped off the elevator and walked into the large warehouse was an older man with striking good looks coming toward them. John Murphy appeared to be in his late forties or early fifties—the same height and build as Josh. Intelligent green eyes captured her gaze and held it for a moment. She noted those eyes were the focal point of his handsome features—aquiline nose, firm chin, and a head full of dark auburn hair, accentuating them like an exclamation point.

Then she did a three-sixty, letting her gaze roam around the room—one with high ceilings, looking as if it had been totally refurbished with top-grade materials. Lots of tile, granite, glass, and wood. Half the first floor had partitions blocking it off below the second and third floors. Those floors overlooking the open area had walls of glass windows.

"Buc. No wonder the Feds couldn't spot you," John Murphy said, stopping right in front of Josh with his hand out in greeting and a ready smile covering his face. "If I didn't know you were coming, I'd have never known it was you. It's good to see you!" The two shook hands and before Josh could pull away, Murphy had him in a bear hug.

"Hey, Murph. Good to see you too," Josh replied, grinning when it became obvious he couldn't avoid the hug. When Murphy released him, he stepped back and indicated her with a nod. "This is Candace Angela Tyler, or Cat, as her friends call her."

"Nice to meet you, young lady." He took her hand in a strong grip and pumped. Cat couldn't miss the warmth in both men's voices. It matched the pleasure written across their faces. It was clear their association was more than mere employee and employer. Almost like father and son. "You don't mind if I call you Cat, do you?"

"No, sir," she murmured, giving in to the urge to smile.

"What's this 'sir' shit? Call me Murph," he insisted. His smile reached his eyes, which had taken on a mischievous glint. "Otherwise I'll feel old."

"Quit flirting," Josh practically snarled, and she almost laughed, but didn't as he added, "You are old." He looked around the room and gave a slow, low whistle. "Pretty nice digs. What'd you do? Get promoted?"

"No. When this was built, there was all kinds of money in Homeland Security's budget." Murphy chuckled, popping a couple of antacids into his mouth. He turned to the luxurious seating area and pointed. "Make yourselves comfortable. Smitty's upstairs manning the monitors with one of the guys from the office, on the lookout for our suspect." Both Cat and Josh moved further into the huge room while he continued talking. "This building is a state-of-the-art safe house. Of course, now the enemy knows of it, I'll have to sell it and start all over. But hey, I started a craze of renovation in the neighborhood and prices have skyrocketed. Now my department will reap enough profit to aid in the next building. Plus I won't make the same mistakes I made with this one."

"Mistakes?" Josh asked, his voice booming behind her.

"Yeah. The area's too commercial and I only need about half the space. Plus, you saw the dumping. Happens every now and then, off and on since we've been here, and usually up the street a ways. This time, he dumped right at the edge of the camera's line of vision. Too bad the cameras didn't capture the bastard on film."

As the two men talked, Cat sat down in one of the plush chairs. She pulled the wig off and tossed it on the floor, shaking out her full head of blonde hair and running her fingers through it, luxuriating in the feel of having the wig gone.

"I stocked the place yesterday with food. No sense starving while we're here."

"Leave it to you to think of eating," Josh said.

"Don't start." Murphy groaned, placing a hand on his stomach, while pushing in on it and grimacing. "It's my only vice since I gave up smoking and had to cut down on alcohol. I'm dying for a cigarette and I'll be damned if I can give up everything I enjoy just because my stomach hurts a little afterward."

Josh grunted while doing what looked to be a slow walking tour of the first floor. Murphy followed until he got to the kitchen area in the corner, which sported high-end, restaurant grade appliances.

"I got marinated chicken baking for an early dinner. Should be ready in less than an hour."

"New recipe?" Josh asked, peeking around a partition.

"Nah, it's nothing special."

"The man's a gourmet cook," Josh explained, turning back to Cat and nodding at Murphy. "He can make a feast out of ordinary hot dogs."

"Would you like anything to drink before we get down to business?" Murphy asked, ignoring the praise and opening the refrigerator. "I could use a beer, but I'm on duty. I have soft drinks, tea, or coffee, if you'd rather."

"I'll have a soft drink," Josh said. He'd finished his tour and came up behind Murphy, waiting while Murphy looked at Cat with his eyebrows slanted.

When she nodded and said, "That's fine," Murphy grabbed two cans and one bottle of water. After pulling them out, he handed a can to Josh and took one to Cat, before sitting across from her with his water.

"Your pictures don't do you justice." He uncapped his bottle and took a hefty swig.

"I told you to quit flirting," Josh said in an annoyed voice, following him and sitting on the same sofa.

"How is stating a fact flirting?" Murphy shot back after gulping another long drink. He looked over at Josh, and the smile he flashed was all-knowing. "Don't tell me you're jealous?"

"Of you?" Josh snorted. "Dream on, old man." He chugged a deep swallow of Pepsi before giving Cat a wink and adding in a teasing voice, "Besides, I should warn you. She thinks I'm a hunk in this outfit."

"You dream on," Cat shot back, hiding her amusement at their bantering behind lifting her can and drinking. The man exuded cockiness. Why add more fuel to feed his vanity? She forced herself to focus on the beautiful hardwood floor in front of her because she knew if she glanced back at Josh right then, she'd end up forgiving him for being so stupid. Heck, he couldn't help being who he was, but that didn't mean he deserved forgiveness. Plus, she wanted to wallow in her misery for just a bit longer. Too much had happened in the past four days. Everything culminated this morning with Josh's admission for her to so readily dismiss her feelings.

She gave herself a mental shake and the absurdity of her situation hit her. She couldn't stop the grin from moving over her face, even as annoyance set in. She surreptitiously shifted her attention to Josh for one brief glimpse.

Why couldn't she hate him? Or at the least, find fault with him?

But Josh Buchannan had a way about him that just wouldn't let her be. Even his disguise, which hid the best of his features, did nothing to stop her attraction for him.

Still, the fact that I find him attractive changes nothing, she thought miserably. He'll never love me.

Silently, Cat returned her focus to the floor, ignoring the heat now spreading through her because she sensed Josh watching her.

The two men talked amicably for a few more minutes while they all finished their drinks. Cat was relieved when Smitty hurried down the stairs and entered the room, giving her something other than Josh to think about.

While observing the reunion between the two friends, Cat felt her lips settle into a full smile. It warmed her to see the camaraderie between all three men as Smitty joked about something the two agents he nicknamed Laurel and Hardy had done on the flight down.

She wanted to hate Smitty for his part in her parents' deaths. But she couldn't. She chose not to. Hate only produced more hate. The four-hour drive had given her time for reflection. She had to remember both he and Josh were victims of circumstance. Her parents always espoused love and understanding. Even though she didn't want to devote her life to their causes, more hate would make their deaths meaningless. She fully understood that now.

"Do you have a spot in mind for me tonight?" she asked Murphy, rising from her perch and glancing at him a moment later. "I'd like to get out of these clothes while you guys talk." Risking another quick peek at Josh, she could see by his expression he knew exactly what she was doing. Okay, so she was running away. But all of a sudden the room closed in on her—the events of the day becoming too overwhelming. Right now she needed space, and she needed to get away from the man who sat too close—one whose presence she couldn't ignore any longer.

"Sure. Let me show you where you can bunk." Murphy turned to Josh and Smitty and added, "I'll be right back."

"Cat?" When his question floated past her ears, she stopped and glanced at Josh.

He stood and walked toward the elevator. "I'll get your things from the car."

She nodded, then followed Murphy up the staircase.

"All the bedrooms are soundproof, built with security in mind. Plus, they're in the same area. I put you and Buc away from Laurel and Hardy." He glanced back at Cat and smiled sheepishly. "They got me calling 'em that now. I've got to quit. I'm supposed to be a professional. God forbid I should slip and call them that to their faces."

"I don't know them, but I think Smitty may have pegged them right," Cat said, grinning.

"Oh?"

Cat couldn't miss the speculation in his voice, speculation also present in his expression. Not wanting to address his subtle inquisition, she skirted it. "Let's just say I've spent too much time with Josh to believe he'd be involved in drugs or murder."

"Seems you've gotten to know him pretty well in the past few days."

"We're friends," she answered evasively.

Murphy grunted and didn't add anything more. After walking in silence, they came to a hallway with several doors. He stopped outside one and nodded toward it. "You're in here. Buc'll be right next door. The door locks from the inside and the room is virtually impenetrable. Once inside and locked in, you'll be safe. Take your time. Dinner should be ready in less than an hour, but it's flexible."

"Thanks," Cat murmured and scooted past him. Once the door was shut, she closed her eyes, leaning against it. Slowly, her body went limp as the tension she'd been holding on to slipped out. One more night, she thought, sighing. If she could make it one more night without losing it, she'd be okay. While standing there with her head against the door for support, a discreet knock sounded. She let out another long sigh and turned to open the door.

"Thanks. I can take those." She reached for her things.

"No problem." Josh ignored the outstretched hand and stepped into the room, pushing past her. He placed the packages along with her bag on the bed and faced her.

"So, are we still not talking?" he finally asked after staring at her for several minutes. His hand moved over his face, rubbing it, before he pulled it through his hair in agitation. "'Cause I've got to tell you, it's going to be a really uncomfortable evening if you're going to continue to pout."

"I am not pouting," Cat ground out, not appreciating the note of irritation she caught in his voice. His impatient stance telegraphed confrontation, and she'd be damned before he'd rile her further. There was no way she'd let him get away with twisting this. This was *not* her fault. "I've done nothing wrong and I'm not going to apologize for my feelings. If you can't handle them, then go to hell." She grabbed hold of the handle and opened the door wider. "Now please leave so I can get out of these ugly clothes."

"Still pouting. Got it," he taunted, keeping his hot gaze on her as he moved deftly around her. "I only hope Zinger strikes tonight so life can get back to normal."

She slammed the door behind him, kicking it as hard as she could once it was shut.

Limping, she marched as best she could to the bed and threw herself on it, erupting into tears.

Chapter 27

Cat's door crashed shut behind him with finality. Josh aimed for his own room, as edgy as a caged tiger. He shoved inside and slammed the door with force, making twice the noise as Cat's door. Annoyed as hell, he paced, then yanked his flight bag open and unbuttoned his shirt before slipping it off. Why he let the woman get under his skin, he didn't know, but she was there, embedded deeper than any infection. He slipped out of the rest of his disguise and reached for his own clothes, wondering what to do about Cat Tyler the entire time.

With his shirt open, he stepped into his jeans. After zipping them up, he headed to the sink in the bathroom and began washing his face, ridding it of makeup. When the last remnants disappeared, spinning in the water running down the drain, Josh found his spirits rising. He'd survive this, and in the meantime he'd figure out how to deal with Cat.

Whistling, he headed back downstairs with a light step. Spying Smitty and Murphy seated at the dining room table when he got to the bottom of the staircase, his mood improved even more. Between the three of them, they'd solve this mess and once that happened, he could get far away from Cat.

"You should see these pictures, Buc. We're going down memory lane," Murphy said, glancing up as Josh neared them. He placed two snapshots on the table, and nodded. "I can't believe how young you two look."

Josh pulled out a chair next to Murphy as the older man said, "There's more Pepsi in the fridge," Murphy said.

"I'll pass," he grunted, plopping down beside him.

"You act as if we're the only ones who've aged," Smitty said, chuckling.

"Yeah, but I haven't changed much in ten years outside of a few wrinkles. You guys, on the other hand, went from boys to men right in front of my eyes." Murphy handed Josh a picture taken right after he'd finished his flight training, and added, "You were so full of promise and had such high expectations."

After glancing at the picture, the memory of that day flashed through his mind. He'd been with the CIA for less than six months, right out of college. Christ, had he really been that young and idealistic? In the picture, Murphy—a stand-in for his father who wasn't there—was shaking his hand and congratulating him. His grandmother had taken the picture for Murphy.

Josh picked up the other two pictures the older man indicated, both showing him with his grandmother. He eyed them for several minutes. Nostalgia streaked through him while he looked at more photos Murphy kept handing him—pictures not only documenting his past, but substantiating it as well. He started his ten-year career in the CIA with John Murphy always in the background. He ended it after spending seven of those years with Smitty, their relationship as close as brothers. Murphy and Smitty had become his family, Josh realized, and the last four years had done nothing to erase the feelings.

"Where'd you get these?" Josh asked a few moments later after going through too many. The pictures made him feel old—made him feel as if life was speeding by and he wasn't a part of it anymore. "I don't remember half of these being taken."

"How can you forget that during every celebration we ever held, Murphy was there with his camera," Smitty teased.

"We were a team," Murphy grunted. "It's always good to have something solid to help us remember the good times and judging by these, there were some wild times. I've been meaning to send them to you for a while. I dug them out when I realized you were headed here."

Josh tossed the photo he was perusing on a pile of pictures in front of him, shoved away from the table, and aimed for the kitchen. He needed a beer. Just one.

While walking, his thoughts stayed on the pictures. They brought back to memory a life he'd walked—no run—away from years ago. He didn't like admitting that maybe he'd run too far, for too long. Seeing it all in vivid color made him realize they'd had so many more successes than the one failure.

Cat's words came rushing back as he opened the door and rooted through the fridge. Had he used the incident and his grandmother's death as excuses to retreat from life? Both had weighed heavily on his decision to quit. At the time, he thought he'd been using his exile to heal, but he knew now he'd simply closed himself off from everything, including Murphy and Smitty, so he wouldn't have to feel pain any longer.

Problem was, he'd cut out all the good with the bad. How had his life gotten so screwed up?

Spying the beer in the back, he pulled one out. He uncapped it and brought it to his lips for a long, deep swallow and returned to the table, pushing his melancholy thoughts to the back of his mind. Later...he'd think of this later.

He stood behind Murphy's chair and glanced at the shoebox of pictures. One caught his attention. After reaching for it, he held it up for a closer inspection. He studied the people posing, recognizing a much younger Murphy. But his focus kept returning to one of the women in the old photograph. She had beautiful eyes. He recognized their haunting quality.

"What're you looking at?" Smitty asked, studying Josh with a curious expression.

"I don't know. Looks like friends of Murph's," Josh replied, looking up and flashing him a quick smile before nonchalantly tossing the picture back into the box.

Murphy glanced at the discarded photo and picked it up. "Now here's a picture worth a thousand words." He offered a reflective smile toward Smitty and sighed. "Your parents, Smitty. Grace and Tom Smith with me and my Vickie. Shit, that was a long time ago."

"Really?" Smitty asked, taking the picture and looking at it. "I barely remember my dad. I was so young when he died." His eyes remained on the photo for several minutes. "Everyone looks so happy here."

"Yeah, we were. I don't remember what we were celebrating. This picture was taken right after you were born, so it has to be at least thirty years old," Murphy replied, his voice taking on a wistful tone. His stare became more distant, as if he'd retreated into the past for a bit before he shook it off. "Seeing Vickie so young and alive brings back that time like it was yesterday. You remember her, Smitty?" he asked, looking expectantly at him. When Smitty nodded, Murphy turned to Josh and added, "You never got a chance to meet her. It's been almost fifteen years since she died, but I still miss her. And I miss your parents. We thought we were invincible back then.

Thought we'd live forever. Now I'm the only one left."

Josh nodded toward Smitty and said, "Let me see it again. I don't think I've ever seen a picture of your parents. You've never talked about them."

"Everyone said they were a good-looking couple. I'm told I'm the spitting image of my father," Smitty said, flashing a brilliant smile while handing the picture to Josh. "Whaddaya think? Am I?"

"Yeah, you are. I see the resemblance now. You're definitely not the mailman's kid," Josh teased, glancing first at the picture and then at Smitty. "Although I see a little of your mother in you too."

Josh took his time with the picture again, focusing on the woman's haunting eyes. When he looked up to see both Smitty and Murphy looking at him with interest, he shook his head. "Sorry. It's just that you and Vickie look so young."

"I wasn't born with an ulcer, and everyone is young once." Murphy snorted. "Besides, it's true what they say."

"What's that?" Josh asked, grinning because he knew what Murphy was going to say. He'd said it too many times in the past few years.

"Youth is wasted on the young. You don't appreciate it until you're pushing fifty and realize you're on the downhill slide. We all do stupid and crazy things when we're young."

"Speak for yourself." Josh grunted and threw the picture into the box and took another hefty swig of beer. "I think I've had enough nostalgia to last for a while. This shit's making me feel old, so let's quit looking down memory lane. I'm ready for dinner."

"So am I. Then we'll have nothing to do but wait for our guy to make his move." Murphy stood and tossed the rest of the pictures into the box. "You guys can take whatever pictures you want before you leave," he said, setting the box on the counter behind the table. "Anyone wanna keep me company while I finish dinner?"

"I told Miller I'd relieve him for a bit. Call me when it's ready," Smitty answered, rising and racing for the stairs.

Once Smitty left, Murphy turned expectantly to Josh with slanted eyebrows.

"Why not?" He stood. "Cat's pouting, so I got nothing better to do."

Murphy grunted and followed him into the kitchen, stopping at the oven. He opened it. "So, what's up with you two?" After seeming pleased with what he saw, he closed the door. Then pivoting back around, he crossed his legs and arms, leaning against the counter with his attention on him.

"What do you mean?" Josh met his inquisitive stare without blinking.

"I mean you two seem to be skirting around each other as if something's happened, so I'm asking what happened."

"Such a nosy question. So unlike you, Murph."

"Intrigued is a better word," Murphy grumbled, before moving to the fridge. After rooting through it, he brought out fresh asparagus, butter, and a lemon, saying on his way to the sink, "I've never seen you react in such a way toward one of the opposite sex, so I'm intrigued."

Josh didn't answer, remaining silent while he watched the older man work. Murphy grabbed a pan and filled it with enough water before placing a steamer inside. Next, he began washing the vegetables and snapping off the ends, placing the spears in the pan that was now on the stovetop. Once that task was completed, he turned back to Josh. He quirked his eyebrows, leaned against the counter again, looking very relaxed. "Well? What's up? Did she slip past your guard?"

"Maybe I'm still trying to figure out what's up with her," Josh replied honestly when it was obvious Murphy wasn't going to drop it. He took another hefty drink, finishing it off before he added, "I'll keep you posted."

"Good. You do that," Murphy murmured, returning to his cooking.

"Vickie was a beautiful woman," Josh said softly after minutes of comfortable silence. He knew Murphy had been a widower—knew his wife had died a year or so before they'd met, but John Murphy had never mentioned her and Josh, not wanting to pry, had never asked about her. Until now.

"Yes. She was."

"How long were you married? And how did you keep it all from ruining things?"

"We met my last year of college. From the first moment I saw Vickie, I knew she was special. She handled me and she handled the job. How she did it and made it look so easy, I never knew. I just accepted," Murphy answered without having to explain what "it" was. The long absences and the secrecy of their jobs made relationships hard to manage. Very few actually succeeded at it long term.

"We dated for three years before we were married," he went on. "You know me. I was worried about everything. But Vickie laughed my concerns away, until I finally gave in. After that, I always loved coming home to her—couldn't believe how I'd lived so long without her." Murphy stirred the melted butter in the saucepan on the stove and nodded at the pan. "You'll like this. I found this recipe for hollandaise over the Internet." He was then silent for several moments, seeming lost in thought before he continued speaking. "She'd been my wife for a little over twelve years when she died. For fifteen years, she was the best part of my life and then she was gone. She went so fast. People aren't supposed to die of cancer in their thirties."

"Sounds rough," Josh said, hearing the sadness, the sound drawing his attention to Murphy's face. What he saw in his expression gave him another glimpse of his mentor, a facet he'd never seen before. He'd always known about his sentimental side, especially given his penchant for taking pictures all the time. He'd just never thought of him having such strong feelings about a woman. Though they'd been in life and death situations together too many times to count, there were some things men simply didn't discuss.

"It was," Murphy agreed. "But you survive and move on." He pulled out a blender, set it on the counter, and then turned toward the refrigerator. He grabbed a bottled water, let the door close on his way to the sink, where he stood, crossing his legs while uncapping the water before swigging half the contents. "I'll deny this if you repeat it, but I've actually gotten used to this shit." He took another sip and grinned. "Once you do, nothing ever quenches thirst quite the same way—nothing except beer, that is. And I am trying to watch my beer intake these days."

"I knew you were friends with Smitty's dad, but I didn't realize how close you must've been," Josh said, changing the subject after picking up on Murphy's cue. John Murphy was clearly uncomfortable talking about his dead wife.

"We came from the same neighborhood. Even though he was a couple of years older than me, we were good friends. Tom Smith recruited me for the CIA."

"Smitty's never mentioned him." It seemed there were a lot of things he didn't know about the two men who were the closest thing to family Josh had left. "I know his mom's death hit him hard, but I was busy with my grandmother, so I wasn't much help."

"Yeah. I feel real bad about not seeing Grace during those last couple of years. Things were exploding everywhere in the years following 9/11, and I was pulled in too many directions." The older man shook his head, and his expression turned thoughtful. "But hell. I realize now, it was only an excuse. Grace took Vickie's death hard and was never the same afterward. I couldn't face her—couldn't deal with my own pain, let alone hers, so I stayed away."

"What happened? Smitty never talks of it. Just told me she died tragically."

"It was a tragedy. Grace was so delicate. Barely survived Tom's death. I wasn't close with her after that but she and Vickie were still tight. When Vickie died, she went into a major depression. Eventually, she'd signed herself into a French sanitarium. Killed herself a few years later." Murphy shook his head, sighing. "So sad." By this point, he had everything for his hollandaise sauce in the blender. The next moment, he turned it on and waited until he was done blending. "She spent a lot of time in Paris after Vickie died, so I only saw her a handful of times in between her death and Vickie's."

"Why Paris?"

"To be close to her father, since Smitty was off doing his thing by then. As I recall, her dad was attached to an embassy there. Had been for over twenty years. She was the product of a divorce. He wasn't an American citizen and once the divorce was final, she split her time between both parents. She lived with her mother in Chicago and visited him in Paris during the summer months, long before it became fashionable for kids to have two homes."

"Funny what you pick up about friends you've known for years during innocent conversations," Josh said after listening to Murphy's explanation. "I guess everybody has things they keep inside."

"Painful memories are hard to talk about. Sometimes they're better off left unsaid. You're no different. You rarely talk about that day, nor do you talk about your grandmother's death."

Josh only grunted and nodded his head slowly, asking a moment later, "What's talking going to do?"

"I don't know. Vickie used to make me talk—not about specifics. You know we could never discuss such things. But about feelings. She was pretty good at drawing me out and getting me to release some of the stress in my words. Probably why we lasted so long. I don't think I could be that open with anyone else. Guy or girl."

Josh watched him reach for a hot pad, then bent to open the oven door and pulled the dish of chicken breasts out. After setting it on the counter, he opened a drawer.

"Here. Do something useful," he grunted, handing Josh silverware.

Josh followed his command and began setting the table. When his task was done, Murphy nodded toward a dish he'd prepared. "Take this to Miller, and let Smitty and your young lady know dinner is served."

"She's not my young lady." Josh grabbed the plate and hurried toward the stairs, ignoring Murphy's mocking chuckle and parting shot.

☙

Cat entered the room minutes later. "You guys all seem pleased," she said, sitting down and looking around the dinner table. She noted the easy atmosphere between the three men, and all seemed in good spirits. Her brief reprieve had worked wonders for her own mood, and remembering Josh's comment about pouting, she smiled, working extra hard not to appear sullen. "Has anything happened?"

Murphy shook his head. "Just old friends reminiscing."

She ate amid the three recounting the past. Soon they were bantering back and forth about one particular incident, including a bar fight in some unsavory place a world away. Their obvious enjoyment from those times spent together in the past was evident.

In minutes, the discussion turned to embarrassing moments, and before long they were trying to outdo each other with the most uncomfortable tale. Smitty pulled her into the conversation when he asked, "What about you, Cat? What's your most embarrassing moment?"

"Oh no, you don't. I don't know any of you well enough to tell you anything so personal," she teased, laughing and feeling the red steal up her face because all three of them were looking at her expectantly.

"She has this thing about upsetting balances," Josh said with his eyes on hers, not letting her look away.

When he finally released her gaze, she cleared her throat and bit the inside of her cheek, pushing away the memories his statement brought forth—memories of that night and the events following it. Too much had happened between them for her to feel comfortable with Josh's teasing. She certainly didn't feel like sharing anything right now. "I think I'd rather listen," she said softly a moment later. "You guys are much more entertaining."

An awkward silence ensued as she broke off and looked at her plate, stirring her food. She felt Josh's gaze, but refrained from meeting it. She heaved a sigh of relief when she heard Murphy's voice, but almost groaned aloud when she realized what he was saying.

"Yep, something happened and I see you're still skirting around it. You should just admit the inevitable, Buc. And accept it." He gave an amused chuckle and added, "Won't do you any good to fight it."

After his comment, the atmosphere crackled with tension. Josh appeared annoyed and Murphy's oblivious attitude seemed to grate on him as the dinner progressed, despite Smitty's attempt to pick up the slack of Josh's silence, keeping up a lively conversation with Murphy.

During the rest of the meal, Cat remained quiet, eating a little faster. Escape became her main goal.

"I hate to leave, especially after such a nice meal," she said, scooting back and rising when she finally finished. "But it's been a long day and I'm really tired." She nodded at Smitty and Murphy, offering both a warm smile. Then glancing at Josh, her smile fled. She couldn't conceal the hurt she'd worked to hide from spilling into her eyes. She turned, rushed out of the room, praying he hadn't seen it, and ran up the stairs as quickly as her legs would carry her.

Once away from prying eyes, Cat slowed until she was outside her room, then stopped, her gaze on the floor, her hand on the knob, and inhaled a calming breath. Without turning around, she felt him behind her. One thing about Josh, she thought, as a wistful smile appeared. She could always feel his looming presence whenever he was near.

She jumped slightly when warm hands on her shoulders turned her toward him. In the next moment, his arms wrapped around her, drawing her closer.

"I'm sorry, Cat. I never meant to hurt you. Please don't hate me," he whispered, kissing the top of her head. "I couldn't bear it if you hated me."

She closed her eyes and breathed in his scent. How she loved being embraced in his warmth. Heaven couldn't be this appealing.

"I could never hate you." Her smile widened into his shoulder before she pressed her lips against his soft shirt, feeling his muscles bunch under her mouth. The task to pull away was impossible, so she buried her face deeper, permitting his soothing touch, forgetting for the moment how wretched she'd felt only seconds ago.

"Do you think we can ever be friends?"

Cat tried to ignore the yearning in his voice. She leaned back and met his sincere gaze without flinching, not bothering to hide what was pouring out of her heart. "You really think we can?"

Genuine hopefulness was apparent in his eyes, and his earnest, lost expression yanked on Cat's heartstrings. Of their own volition, her hands reached up and wrapped around his neck. Then, lifting up on tiptoe, she tugged his head lower and brushed her mouth across his with the lightest touch. She meant to pull away quickly but Josh stopped her, dragged her closer, and deepened the kiss, which began as a brief sizzle of heat that soon flashed out of control. His mouth ground into hers, his lips and tongue demanding, extracting her response and not letting her back away. His groan a moment later surged through her bloodstream via her ears. Her heartbeat quickened, shooting flashes of desire straight to her core.

"Damn you taste so good," he said softly after breaking the connection, his breathing labored.

"Now you see why it may not be such a good idea to be friends," Cat said, breathing just as heavily and gently disentangling from him.

"We're doomed," he teased, tightening his grip, not allowing her to escape so easily.

"This is not a joke." She froze. Feeling his eyes on her face, she glanced up and with a stiff back, met his gaze, jutting out her chin. "I won't have you joking about something that means so much."

"You're damned right, this isn't funny," Josh shot back, his eyes now flashing anger. "And you know what else? I don't give a shit if I hurt you or not, because you win. Murph's right. I can't fight it anymore. Why should I when I can't be near you and not want you." He released her and stormed down the hallway, saying over his shoulder, "Leave your door unlocked. You'll find out soon enough what you've gotten yourself into. Don't say you haven't been warned."

As Cat watched him go, hope burst up from her soul and touched her heart. A rueful smile flitted across her face when she realized what his actions and words meant. Could he actually believe he didn't deserve her love? In her mind, no one deserved it more. And did he actually believe he didn't love her? She saw it in his gaze, felt it in his kiss. Somehow, someway, things would work out. For the first time since this whole nightmare began, she allowed herself to think they had some kind of future.

☘

Josh thundered down the stairs, his thoughts on Cat. As usual.

"Shit," he said under his breath, wishing he could shut off that portion of his brain. He shouldn't be letting the woman distract him from his job. Yet the feat was impossible to implement as thoughts of the night to come infiltrated his mind and wouldn't budge. Once he decided to forge ahead and see what would develop from a relationship with her, he realized he was eager to get started.

His ear-splitting grin died as he rounded the corner and caught Murphy watching his approach with interest.

"She okay?" His concern was evident in both his face and voice.

Josh nodded and drifted to the spot he'd vacated.

"She seems like a nice lady. Don't screw up."

His back went ramrod and he struggled to keep irritation out of his tone. "I can handle it."

"See, that's where you're wrong," Murphy countered, sending him a chiding look before he added, "She has pluck. She'll handle you, if only you let her."

"Drop it," Josh warned, wiping his face. "We've got more important things to worry about with Zinger out there than for you to be dissecting my love life."

"Yeah." Murphy chuckled. "You're right, but you can't say your love life isn't more interesting than some crazy terrorist double agent coming to kill you."

"You do have a point. So, let's talk about something else entirely."

"I got a better idea." Murphy moved to clear the table. "After cleaning up, why don't we play cards?"

Chapter 28

Outside on the street, Rodriquez peeked out from a small hole in his box. Darkness had set in. His cover was now up against the building, flush with the garage door. He filled his lungs with air. Let it out slowly in prayer recitation, silently begging for the opportunity to make amends, for his long wait to end, for the chance to finish his job, so that he could make the ultimate sacrifice. If Allah permitted.

Within minutes, a car pulled into the driveway.

Hank McMann was driving. His partner, Frank Adams, pushed the automatic garage door opener. McMann hit the gas pedal once the space opened enough to drive through.

"What?" Smitty asked Miller, looking away from the monitor as McMann and Adams' car entered the garage.

"I can't believe these pictures of you guys," Miller said, handing him one of the pictures. "I didn't know you and Buchannan worked together with Murphy. Man, I wish I'd been there. Looks like you guys kicked some butt."

"Yeah, I guess." Smitty gazed at a photo as Miller made another similar comment.

Agents McMann and Adams opened their doors together and climbed out at the same time.

Neither agent, nor the men in the room with eight monitors, noticed the box. One that had stealthily moved. A shadow emerged. Slid along the wall. Blended with other shadows, nearly invisible in the dark recesses of the garage.

One moment the FBI agents laughed at some jest. The next, a shadow took aim and fired.

By the time the garage door had finished its descent, both agents lay on the ground, blood oozing from their wounds.

He felt his way further along the wall, keeping his face from the hidden cameras. He swiftly pulled the lifeless bodies out of their view, then crept toward the elevator. He had seconds at best, so didn't bother to check to see if they were dead. Given the severity of their wounds, if they weren't dead yet, they would be shortly.

He wore similar clothing as the agents, hoping that they'd think he was one of them, if anyone was watching on the security camera. The elevator doors opened. He stepped inside, and once they closed, he stood, patiently waiting. In moments, he felt movement. Someone had finally called the car.

When the doors opened, a bullet to the chest surprised Miller just as he was about to step forward. Rodriquez moved to grab the lifeless form. Pulled him into the elevator car. Then he punched the button to return it to the parking garage, where he dumped Miller's body in a spot out of the cameras' eyes.

Back in the elevator, he pushed the button for the main floor.

 C8

"It's about time you guys got back," Murphy joked, as the elevator doors opened. But his face registered shock when instead of the two agents he'd been expecting, Rodriquez stepped out, waving a gun with a silencer at him. The doors closed behind him as he asked, "Where's Buchannan?"

Still too stunned to speak, Murphy didn't respond.

"Tell me now," he barked. "You know I won't hesitate to kill you."

"Go ahead."

"You think I won't?" Rodriquez aimed straight at his heart. "Now, where is he? And where's Candace Tyler?"

"Very clever, you infiltrating the CIA like you did." Murphy smiled. "I'm impressed."

"Your admiration hardly matters. Where are they?"

"Since you're here to kill us, why not tell me why?" He slowly started walking toward the tiled seating area. "Appease my curiosity and I'll appease yours."

"I have my orders." With the gun trained on Murphy, he followed. "You're not the target. Buchannan has a Muslim death warrant on his head."

"Why?"

"Revenge for working against us. Anyone who fights against Islam must die."

"But he's no longer an agent. Hasn't been for years."

"There is no statute of limitations on his crimes."

"And the girl?"

"She's a personal enemy, as well as an enemy of Islam."

In the next instant, the elevator opened, distracting Rodriquez. At the same time, Josh burst out of the bathroom. As if in fast-forward, McMann appeared, leaning against the elevator door, injured and bleeding. He fired at the terrorist, hitting him in the shoulder before collapsing.

Smitty took the stairs two at a time with his weapon drawn.

Rodriquez fired in quick succession, first at Josh and then at Murphy. Both men dove for cover while grabbing their own weapons. At Smitty's approach, Rodriquez turned and yelled, "I'll not die in vain," taking careful aim at Smitty. But Smitty beat him to the trigger by seconds.

Rodriquez's body jerked as several bullets ripped into him.

No one spoke in the ensuing silence, one so loud it was earth-shattering.

"Shit," Josh let out on a breath. He sprang into action along with Murphy and Smitty and ran to McMann. "What else can go wrong?"

"He's lost a lot of blood."

"I'm okay," McMann whispered. "Get Frank. He's worse off, down by the car."

While Murphy pulled out his cell phone and began punching buttons, Smitty and Josh were descending in the elevator. At the garage level, they spotted Miller, taking only a brief moment to confirm he was dead, before finding Adams barely hanging on to life. Their expressions said it all. Having seen these near-death situations too many times together, both men worked as a team, doing everything in their power to keep the agent alive till help arrived.

03

"You look like shit," Smitty grunted to Josh, as the three of them climbed out of Murphy's car several hours later. The investigators had finally released them, convinced there was nothing more they could learn from the crime scene.

"I feel like shit," Josh answered truthfully, nearing the elevator. He hit the button. "I'm really ready for this to be over."

Murphy had pulled rank and procured another safe house with an underground garage and elevator, much like the place they'd vacated, also making sure Cat had been moved safely while they were answering questions.

"Yeah, well, once the reports are filed, it should be." Murphy sighed and rubbed the back of his neck. His haggard face mirrored Josh's exhaustion. "Course even though Zinger, AKA Rodriquez, is dead, both of you probably still have Muslim death warrants hanging over your heads. He had help, but his help has disappeared into the woodwork. We'll catch him when he surfaces." He broke off as the elevator doors opened. The three stepped inside, and Murphy added, "Langley thinks Zinger and company were working for the terrorist the FBI picked up outside Winnemucca. Figured he knew you were on your way to see me, Josh. He's a well-known assassin whose family has strong ties to Afghanistan. He's thought to be the mastermind in several other deaths. He isn't cooperating, and because we don't have enough evidence against him, he'll probably only be deported once we can't hold him any longer. He isn't speaking without his lawyer present. Funny how terrorists berate our ways, yet use them for their own convenience when it suits them."

Josh nodded solemnly. "I'm still not sure why they went to the trouble of implicating me with the drug operation, though."

"To discredit you. Your reputation in the Arab world is larger than life. If they can impugn it, showing you as a drug dealer, it solidifies their position against the capitalists they're trying to stop."

When would it all end, Josh wondered. But at least Zinger/Rodriquez and his accomplice weren't a threat any longer.

The elevator stopped on the third floor and as they all exited, Smitty said, "I'm glad Laurel and Hardy'll make it." Adams' condition was still critical. He was fighting to stay alive in intensive care, but everyone was hopeful. McMann had been luckier. His injuries weren't as extensive and his prognosis was a full recovery. "Who'd a thought a Fed would've saved the day?"

"Hell of a thought, isn't it. From now on, we'll have to be nicer to them." Josh sighed. "This whole ordeal's topped off a hell of a night, capping off a hell of a week."

"We should try and get some sleep," Murphy said. "I'll have to deal with Miller's family tomorrow, and I want to make sure I'm at the hospital to thank McMann personally."

Nodding his good-nights, Josh stopped at Cat's door and waited until both men made their way down the hallway. He grabbed for the doorknob. Then placing his forehead against the door, he hesitated for a heartbeat and closed his eyes.

What the hell was he doing? Could he really involve Cat in all of the shit he was feeling right now?

At that moment, he knew the truth.

No! She didn't need Josh and was better off without him.

He turned to leave, had taken only two steps, when the door opened.

"Josh?"

Her quiet voice filled the air around him and drew his attention, forcing him to face her. His eyes locked with hers before roving over the length of her.

"So beautiful," he whispered, still staring. Cat, hair flowing freely, was dressed in nothing but an oversized T-shirt and looked like a vision with the soft light behind her, silhouetting her shapely body, making him realize he could no more leave than he could stop breathing.

He needed her tonight.

"Is everything okay?" She grabbed his hand, pulling him into the room before closing the door.

"Thank God you're okay."

Josh meekly followed her to the bed, letting the concern in her voice flow over him. He sat on the edge of the bed and grabbed her to him, clutching tightly while squeezing his eyes shut, trying to blink back the tears lurking at the thought of something happening to her.

"I told you to keep your door unlocked. That was stupid of me. Can you imagine what would've happened if we hadn't stopped him? He'd have killed you too."

"Shush," she soothed. She brushed back his hair, her cool hand acting like a balm against his forehead. The next moment he felt her lips kissing where her hand had been. "It's okay. We're safe and alive. I'll always be safe and alive when I'm with you."

"I don't want to need you. I don't want to feel what you make me feel," Josh admitted. He hated the fact that he needed her. Needed her touch…needed her warmth…needed her love. Only God knew how much he needed her. And when her lips roved gently over his face, he couldn't deny it any longer.

"Shut up, Buc-man. We'll deal with it." She snuggled closer and began undoing the buttons on his shirt.

He groaned and pulled her with him. He scooted across the bed and got into a more comfortable position, after kicking off his shoes.

Seconds later, her cool hands slid under his shirt. She pushed it off his shoulders. Her hands wandered, her cool touch sending heat directly to his groin. His erection grew, straining to break free from the tight denim of his jeans. Next thing Josh knew, soft lips covered his. If he thought his need was great before, he was shocked at how, in seconds flat, it exploded inside of him. He surrendered to need, even as desire engulfed him. He wanted her, and he would have her for as long as he could.

After unsnapping his jeans, she peeled them back while her fingers continued the journey up and down his body, searing him with heat. When he could take no more of her gentle torment, he pushed her back on the bed. He followed her actions, his hands doing some of their own roaming over her body. In three swift strokes, he'd relieved her of both T-shirt and underwear. In another, he rid himself of the cumbersome denim, then shrugged out of his shirt. With both of them now naked, he slid inside her, feeling as if he'd found something he never knew was missing.

☐

"So, I gather it's over?" Cat asked Josh once she could think again. His gentle hands continued caressing, touching, stroking up and down her arms, making her feel cherished. "The agent who drove me here told me the suspect was killed. I figured that meant Mark's dead."

"Yeah, he's dead." He stared off into space. His mind had clearly drifted miles.

"I know I shouldn't be glad, but I am." Seeking more warmth, she curled into him. "Now I don't have to be afraid of him. Do you know why he came after you?"

"We were on some hit list. Most likely tied to Afghanistan and your parents' deaths. The guy in Winnemucca was part of this, a known assassin, but proving it's another matter. He's being deported."

"Are we still in danger?"

"No. We stopped them." He continued stroking. "There are some twisted people in this world. Makes me wonder when it'll stop."

"Mark wasn't sane. He let his crazy beliefs rule his life."

"He did seem a little unhinged, considering he didn't give up when he knew he was beat. God save us from zealots who're willing to die for their cause. Makes fighting the war on terrorism so much tougher. They're determined. Will stop at nothing, much like the Confederacy when they were outmanned and outgunned. Sherman had to march to the sea, totally decimating them, leaving nothing in his path before they would admit defeat. Their cause was that powerful. These people see their cause in the same way. Something they believe so fiercely in, they'll fight to the death over it." He broke off and his breath came out in a long sigh. "Maybe that's the problem with us Americans. We have it so easy, we've lost our cause." She looked up when he stopped speaking again. He bent his head to give her a soft kiss. "Is there any cause you feel strongly enough to die over?"

"I would die if anything happened to you." She touched his face, reassuring herself he was there. "I was so worried tonight. I love you."

"I love you, too. I fought falling, but I realize it does no good to deny my feelings."

"Sometimes you just have to accept what's there. You and I were meant to be."

He chuckled and brushed her shoulder. Kissed the spot, brushed it again. "I knew I was in trouble on your first flight."

"You were such a jerk."

"Self-preservation."

"Self-preservation?"

"Yeah." He swept hair off her neck and kissed her there. "No one's put me in my place quite as eloquently as you did when I tried to trip you up with my question about the working engine. From that point on, I only sank deeper." He worked his way lower.

"Really?" She grinned. "That feels good." Leave it to Josh to tease her about her first lesson, all while making her feel alive. "And as I recall, you deserved everything I threw at you. I can't believe I actually had the guts to say all those things. It was so unlike me."

"No." He tugged on her nipple. "I disagree. It was exactly like you."

Sensation built. She smiled, nipped his shoulder. "I've never in my life done or said such things."

"The real you emerged. I saw it in your eyes. Though cold in color, they flashed pure fire."

"You pushed me to the brink of reacting." Just like he always did.

"Maybe. But you were the one who reacted and there was nothing timid in your reaction. God, by the end of the lesson, I was dying to learn more about you. I hated Maxwell and hated you even more for daring to attract me." He bit her nipple. Smoothed it. Bit it again. She shuddered. "But the fact didn't stop me from setting it up so you'd be forced to take all those lessons with me."

"What?" Not sure she'd heard him correctly, she flashed him a disbelieving look, one mixed with contented pleasure. "Stop distracting me."

He just laughed, kissed her breast, and lay his head back. "Hey, what's the purpose of owning a business if you can't manipulate it at times. Maxwell did work for me. And no way I was going to let him take you up if I could. I got a little creative."

"But you were always so mean to me." She nestled her head on his chest, while he stroked her arm. His touch was soothing, as was the steady thump of his heartbeat.

"Like I said, self-preservation. I had to do something to keep you at arm's length, though it did little to stop me from saying things to spark the fire in your eyes."

"I shouldn't love you. Not when you were such a jerk." She worked her hand through the thick mat of hair on his chest, playing with it a bit before asking distractedly, "So, when can we go home?"

"I'll make the arrangements with Smitty tomorrow. I want to finish a few things and make a visit to the hospital. After that, I see no reason not to fly back to Bozeman."

"What about us?"

"Let's take it a day at a time. Okay?"

"As long as the day includes you, I don't mind."

"Good. Come here." He pulled her closer and kissed her for what seemed like forever. "I don't think I'll ever get enough of you." The next thing Cat knew, he filled her. Everything but the sensation of him moving inside of her slid from her mind.

Chapter 29

After a refreshing shower, Josh dressed in record time. When he let himself out of the room, Cat was still sleeping peacefully. His smile, compliments of their night of lovemaking, wouldn't budge. He took the stairs two at a time, realizing he didn't care what anyone else thought. He loved Cat Tyler, and somehow, he'd find some way to make her happy. He needed her…couldn't live without her.

How had his life changed so drastically in less than one week?

Murphy grunted. "You look well rested." The long, uncomfortable moment Josh strode in his direction, Murphy's focus never faltered. "You finally figure it out?"

"Maybe." Josh broke eye contact and poured a cup of coffee.

"Well, at least something good's come out of this mess."

He only nodded. Movement out of the corner of his eye caught his attention. He glanced over as Smitty sauntered into the room, barefoot, looking like he'd just climbed out of bed.

"What's up for today?" he asked, grabbing a mug and taking the coffeepot from Josh.

"I'm leaving in a few minutes for the office." Murphy sighed. He ate a few bites of cold cereal before adding, "Once I file the report and check with some sources, I'll stop at the hospital. I called earlier. The nurse I talked to said McMann's doing better and should be able to have one visitor at a time. Adams is still critical, but he made it through the night."

"Hopefully he'll live. I'm glad McMann's doing better." Josh took a much-needed sip of coffee and moved to sit next to Murphy, reaching for a section of the newspaper. "I plan to drop by before I leave to thank him. Even if he did think I was a drug-dealing murderer for a while, he redeemed himself with his well-timed diversion."

"You may want to get out of town before the six o'clock news hits. My office sent out a press release clearing up the misunderstanding that you were involved in any illegal activity." Murphy frowned. "Reporters will be hounding both of you if you don't.

"I flew the Beechcraft here with Laurel and Hardy, so we can all fly back whenever you're ready to go once we get the reports filed." Smitty grabbed the Honey Nut Cheerios and filled a bowl.

"Sounds like a plan," Josh said. "I'm just glad I'm not public enemy number one any longer."

Smitty opened the fridge and pulled out a gallon of milk, poured some on his cereal, then replaced it. With both coffee and cereal, he sat next to Josh.

No one spoke while they ate until Murphy got up, rinsed his bowl, and placed it in the dishwasher.

"I'm leaving as soon as I shave and shower. I shouldn't be gone for more than a couple of hours," he said on his way out of the room.

Josh watched him go before going back to the paper and finishing his coffee. In minutes, Smitty rose. "I got a few errands to take care of. Let me know when you want to leave and I'll have the plane ready."

"Sure," Josh grunted to his back.

Later that morning, Josh sat on the sofa with his laptop open, going through the file one more time, looking for something he'd missed, and wondering why he was torturing himself.

There had to be something in the file. Why else would Murphy give it to him?

The picture from yesterday flashed in his mind and he didn't like the doubts now roaming there. They fed the suspicion that there might have been another reason Murphy had given him the files. He prayed he'd find something else, as the alternative was too hard to believe.

He was still working when he looked up as the elevator doors opened. The movement sent a feeling of dread throughout his system. Nerves, he thought, snorting. But erring on the cautious side, he pulled his gun from behind his waistband and stuck it in between the cushions for easier access.

"Just in case," he muttered softly, shaking his head at his reaction.

He relaxed, slumping slightly into the cushions. Out of the corner of his eye, he saw Smitty step out. As he headed with purpose toward the living area, Josh's back tensed.

Something in his friend's demeanor alerted him.

"Shit," he muttered, not liking where his thoughts were going as the fleeting idea of his friend's involvement solidified inside his brain. He concentrated on his computer screen until Smitty was within ten feet, then glanced up.

"What's up?" He forced a nonchalant half smile.

"There's no more reason for pretense. I know you figured it out," Smitty said as he closed the distance, raising his arm and pointing a weapon at him.

"Figure what out?" Josh shot back. He flashed another ready grin, hoping to stall. He swallowed hard when he caught a glimpse of two men sporting automatic weapons, getting off the elevator and coming to stand behind Smitty. One of them he recognized as Steve Johnson, one of Murphy's agents. That didn't bode well.

Smitty turned to the other man, a definite terrorist henchman, standing next to Johnson. "Go and man the cameras. John Murphy shouldn't be back for hours, but no sense trusting fate or making assumptions. Doing that has already compromised this mission." When the man departed, he turned back to Josh, shaking his head slowly and sighing heavily. "It won't work, Buc."

"What won't work? What's going on?"

Smitty chuckled. The sound sent a chill of terror up Josh's spine.

"You forget. I know you too well. I caught the recognition in your eyes when you saw the picture of my mother. Damn Murphy's sentimental side for keeping it."

"Yeah. Imagine an innocent picture from the past adding a piece to this puzzle," Josh answered honestly. The feeling of doom settled in the pit of his stomach over the confirmation of his suspicions ever since seeing the picture. He kept his attention on Johnson, who walked to a spot in the room and leaned against the wall, aiming an automatic rifle directly at him.

Schooling his face to show none of his rising anxiety, Josh's gaze resettled on Smitty. "I've never seen a picture of your mother before. If I had, I'd have remembered her eyes. Now I know what was bothering me. Her eyes were the same shape as yours. Different color, though."

"I thought as much. You were the only one in Afghanistan besides me who got a good look. I should've shot you then, and made it look as if one of the others had done it. I let sentiment get in the way. Sorry, old friend, I can no longer do so." He offered Josh a sad smile, then heaved another audible sigh. "I didn't know Murphy had any pictures of my parents. It was so long ago since my father died. I was just a boy. Why would he keep it?"

"Memories? You know Murphy. He's into that," Josh said. He broke off for several moments, eyeing Smitty critically, looking for some clue as to why. Finally, he couldn't contain his curiosity any longer and had to ask. "How could you kill your own mother?"

Smitty appeared to be taken aback by the question and it took him a moment to respond.

"It was my holy duty. I had no choice." Josh's eyebrows slanted up. Smitty complied with his silent request but his answer didn't make sense. "I don't expect a Westerner like you to understand."

"Duty? Westerner?" Josh laughed. "You can't expect me to buy that. You're an American. What'd they do? Buy you off?"

"Don't mock me or my cause." Smitty's face tightened with disgust. "We're fighting a Jihad, a holy war, and we're committed to using any means."

"Wait a minute. You're telling me you believe all that shit?" He stared, totally dumbfounded. "But you fought right along with me. You've killed just as many terrorists, and you and Murph go way back."

"All part of the role I was meant to play." Smitty chuckled. The sinister sound sent a chill up Josh's spine. The chill got colder as he listened when Smitty added, "My mother had her role and she failed her duty. We had her under control in a sanitarium in Paris. When her loyalty shifted, we had to be creative to gain her cooperation. Grace Smith thought extremists had me and we used her fear. Did you know she was trying to save me?" he asked, chuckling again. "I always thought her so fragile, only she surprised me. I think she would've gladly died for me, but Sister Tyler had to step in and reason with my mother."

"Is that why you killed Cat's mother? Because she tried to talk your mother out of blowing herself up?"

"The Tyler woman had no business interfering. I watched them talk through the scope and knew she was trying to convince my mother to surrender. I had no choice but to silence her or risk failure. Maybe Grace thought she could get out of her duty…that she could escape it somehow. But she couldn't. It was her destiny to die a holy death in the explosion and I had to be the detonator. Her death would take away the sins of the father. When Grace's gaze swept the area and spotted me I could tell she realized her mistake. Imagine her horror at seeing her son safe and sound with a weapon pointed at her." If Josh's blood hadn't been chilled, the cold, impersonal way in which Smitty imparted this would have done the job. Smitty was truly convinced his purpose had been holy. Josh could see it in his eyes.

Smitty walked over to the bar. Aiming his weapon at Josh, he picked up a bottle with his other and looked at Josh holding it up. "I don't partake of your western crutch, but would you like one before I have to kill you?"

Josh nodded and Smitty poured a drink before adding, "I had no choice but to kill the Tyler woman first—to make it look like some kind of accident because my mother panicked, causing me to detonate her early." He shook his head and sighed. "If only the plan had been carried out."

"But innocent children, Muslim children, I might add, would have died."

"All part of the casualties of war. Missionaries spouting love and understanding are our biggest enemies. We can't allow their influence over our young any longer and we have to do something drastic to drive them out of the country."

"That's quite a sacrifice."

"Not really. This is a holy war and the sins of the parents are revisited on the children." Smitty put the decanter down and left the drink on the bar. Then he nodded toward it, indicating for him to retrieve the glass. He waited until Josh got close. "Hold on. You don't mind if I check for a weapon, do you?"

Josh stopped, held out his arms, and let Smitty pat away.

When he was satisfied, he nodded. "Okay, go ahead. You're clean."

Josh moved to take his drink, ignoring Johnson in the corner and concentrating on Smitty as he sat back down. He sipped the liquid slowly, letting the warmth of the alcohol warm his cold insides while Smitty continued his tirade.

"My mother was making up for a mistake her father had made. He fell in love with a Westerner and Grace, her name had hidden meaning, was the product of that mistake. To try and make amends, her father used her Caucasian looks while also making sure she was raised in the Muslim tradition to know her place and to know her role."

"You mean she had another role besides dying?"

Smitty went on speaking as if he hadn't heard the sarcasm in Josh's question. "To all outward signs, she was a Westerner thanks to her mother, my grandmother, who had no idea of Grace's importance. Every detail was attended to, so it would appear she would be an asset to the CIA when her time came. America was more concerned with threats from Russia back then, so her connection to her father wasn't given more than a cursory glance. She always spent the summers with him in Paris, where he secretly began indoctrinating her for her greater role. She understood she was chosen. She knew her role. To become our secret weapon—a Trojan horse."

Josh didn't say a word or move an inch as Smitty broke off for a moment, seeming to be lost in thought. He watched Smitty's face, too astonished to say anything, could only wait for him to continue talking.

"She did her duty and married Tom Smith, the man my grandfather picked for her. I have my father's coloring. Blond hair and blue eyes. Very American and apple pie, wouldn't you say? But Grace failed her father and dishonored him by falling in love, refusing to honor the rest of her duty. And for that, her punishment was her husband's death."

To hear Smitty talk about his father's death as if he was reciting something he'd memorized, totally without feeling, sent more chills down Josh's spine. The feeling intensified as he listened further. In his worst imaginings, he couldn't fathom such horrendous deeds. That his best friend, a man he thought he knew, was espousing them, chilled him to the bone.

"The threat of losing me kept her in line after that. My grandfather was ecstatic because he could see how I could be used to aid him in our holy war. Every summer, my mother visited Paris and I went with her. By the time I was ten, I knew my life held a holy purpose. I learned the Muslim truths, but was told to keep my beliefs secret. I'm a Trojan horse too. I understood my role. From the moment I met my grandfather, I knew I'd achieve greatness." He snorted, his expression turning smug. "People in this country are so naïve. Can't see past their own noses. Terrified by anything different, but look how terrifying I am, though I'm no different than they are on the outside." He laughed. "A blond-haired, blue-eyed terrorist. What's even more terrifying—I'm not the only one."

"Not the only one?" Josh asked, hoping to keep him talking.

"Stalling?"

"No, I'm curious." He threw out a forced laugh. "Since it's obvious I'm going to die, why not enlighten me."

"The CIA thinks to stop us. Nothing can stop what my grandfather has started because he's begun using American tactics. He understands his enemies."

"American tactics? Come on, Smitty. We're peace-keeping by nature. America gets caught up in world politics."

"You condone America when her politics are greedy?"

"Most Americans aren't. You know that."

"Do I? Annihilation and brute force are the only things Westerners understand. And over the last two thousand years, we've learned to retaliate."

"My God, Smitty, you're one of us. Why would you retaliate?"

"We're infiltrating as we speak. This plan has been in the works for over fifty years. Look at what's going on in rural areas. Unrest and drug abuse like there's never been. Who do you think is funding so many of those meth labs? We are. Or you are, according to records I planted. Actually, the drug endeavor's been so lucrative and easy to implement." He chuckled, the sound becoming more menacing. "We're manipulating America's excesses to our advantage. You'll eventually destroy yourselves. We're simply giving you a nudge. Your society chides us for our ways, then fails to look at its own stupidity."

"But it's your society too. You were born here."

"No. I chose not to be an American. My loyalties have been with my grandfather since my first visit."

Josh met Smitty's fervent stare, and the hatred he saw reflected in his eyes stunned him into silence. How had he hid it so effectively all those years? When he could speak, he asked, in another attempt to keep him talking, "So, why the elaborate plan to kill me? I'd have never figured it out because I pushed that time out of my mind."

"You'd have remembered eventually. I left that loose end for too long." He sighed. "You've really made my life a misery. Such a perfect plan, only you just wouldn't die."

"Sorry to be so unaccommodating, but you haven't answered my question. You already had access as a double agent. Why kill me?"

"You're mocking me."

"No. I really want to know. What have you got to lose by telling me?"

Smitty leaned against the bar, eyeing Josh intently. Josh could see Smitty's mental struggle. His face lit with a fierce pride. He was dying to talk...dying to boast of his plans. He hoped to feed on this need for a few minutes to gain some time, but glancing at Johnson with the Uzi, he didn't see how the extra time would yield him a ready solution.

"We started killing off the field ops we knew about," Smitty offered, once the battle was won as his need to boast overcame his need for discretion. "You were the perfect diversion—the perfect scapegoat. Knowing the agency wouldn't stop till they got answers as to why, everything had to lead to you, the perfect traitor, giving me more hidden access. With you dead and discredited with ties to drugs, and things in chaos, it would take years to unravel the truth, if ever. I'd take over your role in Montana and the region reporting to Murphy. We had to abort the original plan once Maxwell died with Bin Al Kashid, but I can still salvage something...still have things point to you. And we have similar operations in the works. This is a holy war and we will win. America will be brought to her knees. And once she falls, the rest of Western civilization will tumble behind her."

"Why Cat? Where does she fit in?"

"Mark Zinger. She was his lure. He'd been easy, followed his calling well, but it never hurts to have an extra incentive. Such a waste I had to kill him, but he did disappoint me. He was recruited early on because of his deep hatred of the US, and it was his job to get close to the Tylers. He derived profound joy out of letting them think they'd converted him. I used his anger with the US government and his anger with Cat to the cause's advantage. His manipulation was effortless. No different than it is with so many who are searching. We've learned from our adversaries. Give them a cause and they'll become fervent, believing enough to pass lie detector tests and other fail-safes the CIA has in place."

"Really?"

"Yes. Mind control. Look at what the SLA did with Patty Hearst. We've tweaked the process a bit." He flashed a sinister grin. "Let's just say we've learned how to fool our enemies by running extensive experiments frowned upon in this country. That's the problem with Americans, who want everything without any sacrifice. We're willing to die for our cause."

"'A mouth that praises and a hand that kills?'"

"I'm familiar with the Arabic quote. And I must say, it's fitting in this instance."

Josh stared at Smitty, absorbing it all. Amazing what goes on in the minds of those we think we know. Does anyone really know another person, he wondered.

His friend was always so controlled and calculating and Josh never once suspected Smitty of having such crazy ideas. Looking at him now, there was an excitement in his demeanor…fervency in his words, so different from the man Josh thought he knew.

"Then why'd Zinger try to kill you?" Josh now fully understood that whatever they'd had together had been skewed with hate. Had anything been real between them?

"Zinger was a sacrifice to lure both you and Murphy into security so that I could finish what I started. He sealed his fate when he tried to kill Cheryl Green and let you and Cat escape. He knew the consequences for his failures. It was his job to keep my cover."

Listening to him, Josh cringed inwardly. The man is certifiable, he realized. How could he have worked with him for so many years and not notice? He shook his head, sadly realizing he hadn't been paying attention and even if he had, Smitty had been too good at hiding his true self. "Why'd you kill Gloria?"

Smitty shook his head. "Too bad about Gloria. She was a victim of circumstance. She knew too much about the books I had doctored to point to you. Plus, I couldn't let it be known that you hadn't died in the plane crash, for all the good it did. You should be dead right now."

"And Brad Maxwell?" Josh asked, noting his annoyance and hoping to keep him talking for a bit longer. "How does he fit into all this?"

"Maxwell was a stupid pawn. Let his habits and greed get the best of him. His death was too easy. You Americans are so weak, your habits so destructive. You'll destroy yourselves with your own excesses eventually."

"Josh?"

Josh's heart stopped at the sound. When he glanced up, Cat stood at the bottom of the staircase.

He swore under his breath. He'd prayed somehow she'd be spared, but now she was right smack in the middle of things. Could things get any worse?

"Come on in and join us, Cat." Smitty waved the gun in Josh's direction. "I was wondering if and when you'd get here." He waited till she treaded hesitantly into the room to sit next to Josh, before asking, "Would you care for a drink before you die?"

Cat grabbed Josh's leg in a tight hold. He moved his gaze to hers, urging her with his eyes to hang in there. He could see her fear. See her confusion. At that moment, the urge to protect her—to keep her from harm—flowed through his body. Somehow, someway, he'd found his heart and lost it to the woman sitting next to him, clinging to him as if she knew he'd keep her safe, and he damn well wouldn't let her down. Not this time.

When she shook her head, Smitty continued talking as if nothing had interrupted him. "Maxwell worked into my plans, bringing Cat to you. You were always the main target. But I still wanted her, not just for Zinger. 'An eye for an eye,' as your bible says." He turned to Cat. His eyes glazed with hatred. "Your mother destroyed my mother's honor, so I have no choice but to destroy you. And you, Buc. With your death, I take out one of my grandfather's biggest enemies at the same time."

As Smitty ranted, Josh watched him closely, leaning into Cat, saying softly so that only she could hear, "When I give you a nudge, jump as fast as you can behind the sofa. Got it?" Her fingernails dug into his thigh. He placed his hand over hers and squeezed. "Remember, I love you, okay?"

He gave a slight nod at her whispered, "I love you too. Please don't die, Josh." He squeezed her hand again and winked at her, flashing an encouraging smile, and turned his attention to Smitty, who now paced back and forth.

"The fact that you both care for each other makes it sweeter. I'll derive much pleasure in seeing you watch each other die. If only you two had died in the plane," he said, sighing.

Just then, the elevator opened, diverting both Smitty's and Johnson's attention.

Josh made use of the distraction, grabbing his gun and pushing Cat, who reacted instantly. He rolled and fired at Johnson, hitting him. When his right arm exploded in pain, he realized Smitty had shot him.

After that, everything happened in slow motion, though only seconds elapsed.

He glanced up and caught Smitty's goading smile. "'At the narrow passage, there is no brother and no friend,'" he quoted, his eyes narrowing for a more accurate shot.

Josh's arm hurt like hell. He wasn't sure he could hold his weapon steady enough to actually hit anything. Still, he took aim, knowing he stared death in the face.

Several gunshots rang out. He could only gape. The man he'd loved more than a brother jerked with the impact of each bullet before falling to the ground. Looking beyond Smitty's lifeless body, he spied Murphy, holding his weapon and walking toward him. A horrified expression filled his mentor's face as tears streamed down his cheeks. Murphy wiped his eyes, then bent over Smitty's body and inspected it for signs of life.

"Shit, Murphy," Josh grunted, holding his arm in an attempt to stop the bleeding. "It took you long enough."

"Sorry," Murphy whispered. He cleared his throat and went on speaking in a stronger voice. "I wanted to hear what he had to say, since I didn't think he'd let us take him alive after that bit about Grace." He broke off. "He's dead. You okay?" Murphy asked seconds later.

When Josh nodded, he rose from Smitty's body, going over to check on Johnson. He felt his pulse and turned to Josh, shaking his head. "He's dead, too."

"What about the guy upstairs?"

"Dead, but not by my hand. I guess he didn't like the idea of being captured." Murphy reached into his pocket for a cell phone and began making a call.

Chapter 30

"Oh my God. You're hurt," Cat shrieked from behind him.

Josh turned. "I'm fine. It's only a flesh wound."

Despite his denials, she rushed up to him, gently pushing him back, so that he fell into the sofa.

"Careful. That hurts," he growled when she began tugging his hand away to check out his wound. When he glanced at her, she appeared to be coming apart at the seams. "You okay, Cat?" he asked in a concerned voice.

"Shush," he soothed, when her tears started flowing. He pulled her to him with his one good arm, wrapped it around her, and kissed the top of her head. "I'm fine. We're fine. It's all over and we're safe and alive. Just like you said."

"It was Smitty all along? He killed my parents on purpose? He wanted us dead? How? Why?"

"He was obviously twisted in his thinking. That's the only way I have of explaining it." He nodded to the drink Smitty had poured. "Here, drink that. It will help take the edge off."

Cat reached for the bourbon and sipped, holding the glass in a firm grip while tears tracked down her face.

"And remember one thing." Josh hugged her tighter, kissed her tear-streaked face, and whispered, "I love you. We're alive and I love you. You got that?"

Smiling wanly, she nodded.

"Investigators should be here in minutes." Murphy snapped his cell phone closed.

"Are you okay?" Josh asked, as the older man dropped into the chair across from him, his expression etched in pain. As Murphy wiped more tears away, a sense of sadness engulfed Josh. He'd never seen such sorrow in his mentor's face. "I'm so sorry, Murph."

"I feel like I've just killed my own son. Hardest thing I've ever had to do. I didn't want to believe it, but I couldn't overlook the possibility. Too many coincidences for me to do that." He broke off for several moments, lost in thought. "Such a senseless loss. When will it ever stop?" he asked, sighing and staring into space.

"I didn't want to believe it either," Josh said softly. Eyeing Murphy, his concern grew. He prayed his friend would get over this. "Tragic is the only word I can find to describe all this. How is it that children can be used in such a way? How can so much hatred pass from generation to generation? It's tragic how people spend so much energy hating and killing, even their own blood, all in the name of a religious cause."

"It was my fault. I should've been there for him when Tom died. He needed me and I let him down."

"No. You can't blame yourself."

"And I didn't do a thorough job when Grace died. Just relied on what Smitty told me. I trusted him." He sighed and looked at his hands before shaking his head. "It was my job to investigate the incident. I screwed up and cost lives."

"You had every reason to trust him. Hell, you can't beat yourself up for trusting someone you love. I always thought he was too good of a shot to have missed that day, but I trusted him too, so I never questioned it."

"But I allowed it to happen."

"You didn't. You thought he was with the people he needed most and they misled him," Josh said firmly. "Family affects us all. Smitty believed in what he was doing. His grandfather dominated him. I don't think you could've stopped it. I've ignored my domineering father for years and done what I felt was right. I also mourned the loss of my mother and grandmother. I couldn't ever hurt either one. Smitty's grandfather killed his grandson's father and then allowed his own flesh and blood to kill his mother. Grace Smith was the man's daughter, for Christ's sake. How could you have prevented something so twisted?"

"I don't know. It was his suggestion to operate out of Bozeman. I should've seen through it."

"You did and you stopped him. I knew you were there somewhere and I knew you planted the picture. I was meant to see it, wasn't I?"

"Yes. I wanted you to see it after you read through the case file again, when your memory would be fresh."

"If you suspected, why didn't you just tell me?"

"I needed an unbiased opinion based on what you remembered, not my suggestion, because I wasn't sure, though I became more convinced when Smitty followed you…wouldn't go into hiding. Then I had to be careful so I wouldn't tip him off. After looking at the security tapes and noticing how Zinger stayed out of the camera's eye, I realized he had inside help, inside information. No one's that good."

Murphy's cell phone went off. "Yes?" he said, answering it. "Okay." He closed the phone, looked at Josh, and sighed. "Time to get to work. Investigators are here along with the coroner."

"I'll deal with them, Murph."

"No. This is my responsibility and I'll finish my job. Besides, you need to get that wound checked out."

"It's just a flesh wound," Josh scoffed.

But Murphy wouldn't hear any more about it, and soon he was swept into an ambulance with Cat sitting by his side.

He realized at that moment that as long as Cat was by his side, he'd be okay. Even better, he trusted her completely and finally understood that she could trust him. He would never let her down.

Epilogue

The shakeup that Smitty's admission caused over the next few months within the CIA could only be described as all-encompassing, hitting at a time when the CIA was already under attack. Secret investigations led by Murphy's division of Homeland Security unearthed several double agents, who were left in place so that even more information could be learned. Once identified, the terrorists were kept under close scrutiny from that point on.

Smitty's grandfather, the diplomat in Paris, had retired and returned to his homeland after his grandson died. He became the target of a covert operation handled by the CIA's most trusted field ops. But the investigation yielded little useful information. The man appeared to be grieving and had all but stopped functioning, according to sources close to him. To all involved, it seemed as if the loss of his grandson had broken him.

The press had fully exonerated Josh, even heralding him and John Murphy as heroes for stopping Smitty and his co-conspirators. Yet no amount of accolades would erase the hurt both men felt over Smitty's betrayal. Murphy might never get over it, Josh thought, but he was tired of hiding from pain, deciding to face it head on, rather than let it spoil his future with Cat.

Cat's friend, Cheryl Green, had healed from her bullet wound, but her heart was another casualty of Smitty's betrayal. According to Cat, Cheryl was dealing with the loss as best she could.

Josh pulled a small box from its hiding place, opening it and peering inside. The solitaire, a brilliant cut stone of perfect clarity and color, sparkled back at him. He snapped the lid closed and stuck it in his pocket, whistling as he headed out the door to meet Cat. Today he planned to pop the question, and though he was pretty confident of her answer, a streak of uncertainty still unsettled him at times. But the sensation always dissipated the moment he was with Cat, so he no longer gave it any credence.

They'd been living together for the past two months. May as

well make it official.

When he spied her sitting so serenely on a park bench with her pale face lifted toward the warm sun on this cold December day, a burst of love swelled inside of him.

He sat beside her. Then, placing a finger over her lips, he said, "No! Wait. Don't tell me. Let me do this first, so you'll know I'm not doing this for any other reason except that I want you to be with me for the rest of my life. Child or no child."

He held out the open ring box and looked into her eyes.

"Will you be my wife?" The heat he saw reflected in Cat's expression warmed him. "I realize I'm asking a lot. I'm a bear to live with and I have a cynical side that can be tough to take at times, but I'm willing to try to keep it under control if only you give me the chance."

"Oh, Josh. I should have known you'd guess my secret." Her grin stretched even as tears streamed down the sides of her face. "How perfect. How can I refuse?"

"I'm only glad you trusted your instincts and didn't give up on me."

"I love you. I would've never given up. I always had hope that you'd come to trust me and trust yourself."

"Thank God I figured it out before it was too late." He pulled her close and kissed her tears, tasting their saltiness. Next, he took the ring out of the box and placed it on her finger.

"It's never too late. We should never give up. As long as there's love there's always hope."

Smiling, because no words rang truer, he looked down at her and realized he'd found what he'd never known he'd lost—his soul.

~~~The End~~~

Thank you for reading *A Matter Of Trust*. If you enjoyed this story, please help others find it by posting a review on Amazon – http://amzn.to/XWJsZ1 or Goodreads—share a link, tweet about it, Facebook it... Everything helps in this new internet world.

About The Author

Sandy Loyd is a Western girl through and through. Born and raised in Salt Lake City, she's worked and lived in some fabulous places in the US, including South Florida. She now resides in Kentucky and writes full time. As much as she loves her current hometown, she misses the mountains and has to go back to her roots to get her mountain fix at least once a year.

She spent her single years in San Francisco and considers that city one of America's treasures, comparable to no other city in the world. Her California Series, starting out with Winter Interlude, are all set in the Bay Area.

All of her series, including her romantic suspenses consist of interesting, heartwarming, as well as thrilling, stories about crazy friends who, like single people everywhere, are seeking that someone special to share their lives with among thousands of eligible candidates.

Email her at sandyloyd@sandyloyd.com
or visit her website at www.sandyloyd.com.